JOHN F. DEANE was born on Achill Island in 1943 and now lives in Dublin where he runs the Dedalus Press. In 1979 he founded Poetry Ireland, the national poetry society, and its journal, *Poetry Ireland Review*. His first collection of short stories was published in 1994 and his fiction has since been published both by Wolfhound Press (*One Man's Place, Flightlines*) and Blackstaff Press (*In the Name of the Wolf, The Coffin Master*).

undertow

JOHN F. DEANE

THE
BLACKSTAFF
PRESS

BELFAST

First published in 2002 by Blackstaff Press Limited
Wildflower Way, Apollo Road
Belfast BT12 6TA, Northern Ireland
with the assistance of
The Arts Council of Northern Ireland

Typeset by Techniset Typesetters, Newton-le-Willows, Merseyside

Printed in Ireland by ColourBooks Ltd

A CIP catalogue record for this book
is available from the British Library

ISBN 0-85640-728-3

www.blackstaffpress.com

For Jack Harte
and Padraig J. Daly,
in companionship
and with admiration

July 1996

There, and not there . . .

He was leaning out over a rock pool, absorbed. He had a piece of water-coloured gut wound round the spool of his thumb, a pin bent into hook-shape, the mucous-soft flesh of a periwinkle wound onto the pin. His shadow darkened the pool like a thundercloud. He unwound the gut; pin and bait dropped, twirling through the pure water. He let the hook dangle a few inches from the bottom.

The sea dominated his life. The restless Atlantic Ocean. It was as if he had been born out of it, as from a womb. He found calm beside its wildness. He knew a wildering passion at the edge of its lulling calmness. His body moved with a sense of the sea's movements. When he lay down to find sleep he lay down in its great comforting arms, sometimes on its shifting, disturbing motion.

But that first day, when the sea actually set his wits astray, he began to hurt as if the beginning of some new life in him was also the ending of that same life. The water was still and pure, silver-blue as the sky must be over some South Sea island of dreams. The rocks were greywashed with millions of tiny limpets, miniature Chinese rice-hats with the crown awry. He was there, and not there. Out over the stilled turbulence of the rocks the ocean moved, tranquil that day as if it, too, was absorbed in present contemplation. A crab, its body of so light a green it could have been mercury, moved slowly across the floor of the pool as if it had a purpose. In the dark and cool underwater crevices other creatures would be waiting, at rest, or lurking, that tiny world no less electric with predator and victim than the great world of humankind.

He loved to contemplate the dark-blood humps of the anemones, all the varied foliage of that underwater universe – sea-lettuces, cucumbers, sea-snails – a cosmopolitan world concentrating on itself, ignorant of the immeasurable ocean only metres away. Suddenly a fish no bigger than his thumb darted from a crevice towards the bait. It was beautiful, plumped, dark-green with a patterning of gold along the side, its fins so small they were invisible. Its pinpoint eyes were focused on their purpose. He became a rock, watching, a tensed shadow, urgent with a small excitement. The fish nibbled at the bait with such delicacy his finger on the gut sensed nothing, no echo of that tiny life reaching him. A small gobbet of flesh broke from the bait and the fish swallowed it, hovered mid-water as if surprised at its luck and then darted back into the shadow of its crevice. He waited a little while before his patience broke and he let pin, bait and gut fall from his hand to the bottom of the pool. Then he jumped in after them.

The sides of the pool were uneven, he slipped, fell backwards and the base of his spine thumped against the rocks. He slithered down into the water, it was deeper than he had thought and the water reached almost to his chest. He stood up quickly, flailing his arms. He was angry. In that little world he stomped about, kicking the rocks, scraping his shoes against all that admirable growth in a frenzy of destruction. Like God, perhaps, in one of his angers, wreaking havoc in a moment of frustration or out of a dulling tedium. Or like one of the old gods, petulant, in an orgy of defiance.

Soon he grew still. Quickly the pool seemed to clarify again though fragments of anemones and sea-flowers floated about. He could hear the slow patience of the waves beyond. He was drenched and the coldness of the water began to make him shiver. He climbed out and moved over the rocks towards the sea. He found the top of Tinkers' Cove and slipped down onto a ledge of rock. The water was heaving far below. He took off his shoes and his clothes and spread them out in the sunshine. He stood a long time, like an alien creature newly risen from the sea. Then he began to climb down into the cove.

To be seventeen. And to be so angry.

The sides of Tinkers' Cove were deep and shelved. The sea reached in under the shoreline to form a cave where the waters slapped and echoed out of a deepening darkness. On wild days the ocean rushed in there in fury, waves reaching high along the walls, clawing at the earth as if some day it must swallow up the world. But today the sea was calm and beautiful. He could climb carefully in along a narrow ledge towards the end of the cove, towards the looming darkness of the cave beyond. The water below was clear and a blue light shimmered from a visible part of the cave floor. Drops of moisture fell one by one from the black roof, plopping loudly into the gently heaving water. He made his way along the ledge into the cave. All before him was black. It was cold. Naked but exhilarated he kept his hands stretched out in front of him, his feet reaching cautiously along the ledge. He called: '*Woooooo*' and the sound reverberated all about him with a deep and thrilling power which seemed to tremble through the very underbelly of the earth. He was already far too cold. He stood another short while, certain he would come back some day and make his way as far as possible in under the earth, to the limits of the cave, certain, too, that here was a hiding place, provided the sea was calm and the tide would not rise too high.

Back in the sunlight he felt exultant. He leaned against the wall of rock and absorbed its warmth. Small things floated and bobbed on the water in Tinkers' Cove – flotillas of froth, sea-weeds, sticks. In the clefts were other things flung up by higher tides and rougher seas – a blue and battered buoy wedged tightly between the rocks, dried-out wrack, a tail of thin red rope frayed at the ends. He watched the lift and fall of the waves, fascinated and lulled as he had always been. He basked in the rhythm, the warmth. He let his body cream itself along the face of the rock until he was sitting, knees drawn-up, eyelids heavy with pleasurable ease. He was at peace.

Until the white hand lifted out of the heaving froth below him, lifted, smooth and buttermilk white, rising almost to the shoulder, the hand moving gently, as if beckoning. His body chilled at the sight and a deadly silence seemed to settle all about him – the sea had gone mute along with the gulls and breezes and his very breathing.

He thought a voice had suddenly called out his name, *Marty, Marty*; a calm, woman's voice, high-pitched though sweet, the call echoing round the cove as if it, too, had risen out of the water. He could see no one. He stood then, shivering, and when he looked back into the waters of the cove he could see nothing, no body floating, no arm rising, no hand beckoning. Tensed and upset he moved slowly to the rim of the ledge and looked down into the water; there was nothing, only the fronds of seaweeds trailing in the underflow, swaying to the pull of the tide, and they were green and brown and obvious.

He looked for the tiny fish that move in shoals, shifting ghosts through the corridors of the sea; but there was nothing. He searched for the shape of a seal that might have slipped into the cove and turned gracefully over before moving back out into the sea; there was nothing. Everything was still. He stood a long time, waiting. Anger, emptiness, frustration had grown in him again, that familiar debilitating clenching about his stomach. He screamed; a scream that mocked itself as it fell back about his shivering nakedness. For he knew nothing, nothing of the great world, nothing of love, nothing of his own past, nothing of the future. He knew only longing, deep and terrible and wholly unfocused.

September 1951

There, and not there . . .

Big Bucko pushed open the bog-brown, crumbling, stable door. It stood heavy under layers of paint though rot was spreading upwards inside the wood from its shattered base where a hobnailed boot had kicked it open years ago. The hinges gave a low whine as the light from another morning moved reluctantly ahead of Big Bucko into the foul-smelling cave within. A donkey stood still as a boulder against the far wall. The two cows in their stalls each turned an indifferent eye towards the intruding world. Big Bucko slapped the rump of the first cow with his big, open, palm. 'How's she cuttin', cow?' he bellowed.

The cow's jaws worked on relentlessly.

Big Bucko kicked a small wooden stool into position by the cow's flank. He squatted heavily onto the stool and shoved a battered enamel bucket under the full udders. He snorted loudly, settled himself more securely on the small surface of the stool, his big knees lifted out to each side, his head pressing against the great belly, his large, hard hands expertly testing and teasing. Then he stopped.

'Come here, luscious,' he whispered, lowering himself until he was on his hands and knees on the dung-and-straw-soiled floor under the beast. He twisted his head up and put his mouth to a swollen, fleshy teat, sucking and grunting with satisfaction, his mouth dribbling warm milk. Then he sat back onto the stool. He worked, and the milk pinged and splashed into the bucket, gradually subsiding into a satisfying, bubbling fullness.

'Ah you lovely fuckin' baste!' muttered Big Bucko, slapping the great rumbling flank with affection. He began on the second cow, first lifting her tail high and looking in at her soiled hindquarters. 'Filthy cow!' he roared. 'What are you? A filthy cow sir!' Then he laughed loudly and slapped the cow hard on the rump. The dull thud echoed like the sound of a wet cloth flapping in the wind.

Big Bucko lifted his head towards the roof of the stable and shouted at the rafters, 'Filthy cow! What are you? Filthy cow sir!' He went down on the cement floor underneath the second cow and rubbed his face against each of her teats, mumbling softly to himself, his hands moving gently up and down, feeling, soothing, tickling. He put his tongue out and licked the warm tip of each teat in turn. Then he shoved the stool in under her and began to milk.

At length, satisfied, he sat back. He placed his hands on his knees and stared at the shifting bubbles in the can. For a long moment he stared, without seeing, his eyes glazed over, his breathing slowed, the leaden pendulum of his thinking stilled. Suddenly, the ass heaved its brown body in a paroxysm of breathing and began its awesome, unstoppable braying song, the foolishness of it rising to a pitch of cacophony that echoed almost unbearably in the confines of the stable, then falling rapidly away, spent, back into the matter of its being.

'You fuckin' eejit of a fuckin' ass!' Big Bucko shouted as he jumped to his feet, kicking the stool back into a corner. He bent and lifted the can of milk. He moved over to the wall where the ass was standing. The big eyes watched him, the big ears twitched. Big Bucko stood strategically back from the donkey's flank then brought his big fist down on the donkey's rump. It thudded. The donkey did not flinch.

'If you work, you eat,' he told the ass. 'If you don't work, you lazy bugger, you don't eat.' He laughed, a short, thumbtack laugh. 'What more is there to it, Ned, oul' stock! And sure aren't you allowed your groan at the misery of this fuckin' world, too!' His great hand came down again with an almost affectionate thump on the hirsute hide of the ass. Soon he would drive the animal out onto the bogs, a thick rhododendron branch thudding against the flank of the reluctant animal, driving him to labour. Big Bucko plodding after, driven by the hard stick of time into the dull arena of another day.

He took a dirty mug from a shelf at the back of the stable and dipped it into the bucket of milk. Then he began to climb the rough-hewn, planked stairway that leaned into the loft above. There was a faint scuffling noise from within. He drew back the long iron bolt that held the trapdoor shut. He put down the mug on the top step of the stairway and, with great caution, pushed the trapdoor upwards with both hands. His head emerged slowly into the airless gloom. There were thick wooden rafters under the slated roof. Tiny holes in the slates were stars glimmering in a dim night. Plaster under the slates was loose and cracked. There was a small window no bigger than a tea tray at the apex of the roof; it was olive-green with grime. At the near end of the loft hay was piled high against the gable wall, masking the lime-whitened, hay-darkened roughness. There was a crude wooden table against the slope of the rafters and a crude wooden chair. Straw was strewn thickly over the floor. Carefully, Big Bucko held the trapdoor raised and looked about the loft.

'Christ but you stink!' he hissed, 'you fuckin', fuckin' stink!' In the deep gloom of the furthest corner he could see a shape squatting low into the darkness, motionless. He lifted the mug from the step and placed it on the wooden floor of the loft. Quickly he lowered himself, letting the trapdoor bang down heavily after him. He shot the bolt into place and backed down the stairway. The stable waited, without poetry in its flaking white-washed walls, its splintering unpainted timbers, its floor thick with animal shit and urine, slippery with rotted straw.

Big Bucko whistled tunelessly through his teeth. The first chores seen to. The first shove given to another day. He banged the stable door shut behind him.

July 1997

Walking on water . . .

When he saw the girl for the first time she was sitting on the edge of the pier, legs dangling over the water, hands under her buttocks. The lovely sheen of her black hair astonished him and the way she had tied it into a knot so tightly he could imagine at once a great anger in her, too. There was something about the hang of her body that made him feel she wanted to let herself drop off the pier down into the shifting sea and set off walking on the water, out and out towards the horizon until she walked herself into salt. He watched her from a corner of the stone shed. There were several curraghs upside down on the starved grass above the pier, held down by ropes tied to heavy stones lest they lift like great rooks into a night of storm. In the lee of the pier were the rocks of the shore and the sea's detritus – kelp and wrack, flotsam, jetsam, shredded sea-ropes. She seemed to him to be a magical presence on the dunted grey pier.

When he moved from the corner of the shed and came down a little along the pier he knew she was aware of his presence. She did not look up. She shrugged her body more snugly into her anorak. He hesitated. Beyond the high wall of the pier he could hear the Atlantic surge and break. She seemed distressed. He gathered courage and squatted down on the pier not far away from her and let his legs dangle, like hers, over the water. She didn't stir. They sat quietly for a time, apart.

'The sea is beautiful,' she said then, without looking up. A city accent, he thought. Soft.

He looked at her. She was lovely, with fine, perfect features. He looked back at the sea. The water, shifting with the tide, was very clear. Rocks shimmered on the bottom. Bits of weed, like tissue paper, shifted in and out with the rise and fall of the water.

'Yeah,' he managed. 'But she can be a right bitch, too.'

She did not respond but he knew she was taking in his words, his voice; she was testing them, to name him, his presence and his purpose.

A large crab, the bright red of old rust, sidled out from somewhere amongst the pier rocks below them and moved lazily out along the seabed. They watched it disappear under a rock. For a moment he almost envied it its life, the simple goals it must have, the lack of complications in its living.

'I wonder why everyone talks about the sea as feminine?'

Her voice was merely ruminative, not argumentative.

'Like cars,' he offered. 'And like boats. I don't know.'

She kicked her heels softly against the pier, a gentle, dunting rhythm. She glanced up at him. Her hands came out from under her buttocks and she thrust them into the pockets of her anorak. She sat hunched up, as if cold.

'Are you from here?' she asked.

'Yeah. I suppose so. If I'm from anywhere, then it's here.'

She chewed on those words, too; with sympathy, he hoped.

He tried to take his words back, then. 'I often watch the sea come right in over the wall of the pier, there behind us, great waves that can cover the whole of the pier. It's massive.'

'I'd like to see that. I'd like to be in a storm on the sea. I'd say it's scary. But you'd really be alive then.'

He put his hands in under his thighs. His body's weight pressed down against the rough stone surface of the pier, hurting his palms a little. He didn't mind. 'You're on holiday?'

'I suppose so. If I'm here, then I'm meant to be on holiday.

We're from Dublin. The parents take a house every year. For two weeks. I hate it. I fucking hate it!'

The anger, the words, quietly spoken, took him aback. He glanced at her again. He found her utterly attractive, Indian almost he thought, with that lovely tan. But he was aggrieved that she should speak like that, as if she must reject him, too, if she rejected his island.

'Well, I hate the tourists,' he found himself saying, not sure if she would take offence, hoping she must know that he didn't include her. 'In the summer. They're like bluebottles about cow shite. They muck up the whole place. Take it over as if they own it. Then disappear. And in winter the place is desolate. And deadly empty. And wild. That's when I really love the island, when it's out of control and strong and free and there's no tourists to whine about it.'

'I'm not a fucking tourist,' she spat. 'My parents are. They do all the tourist things. Hire bikes. Hire fucking fishing rods. Imagine! Hire rowing boats on the lake and make fucking eejits of themselves. Join in the sing-songs. Jesus! Lie on the beach. All of that shitty stuff. I get away from them. Hide. Escape.'

'Yeah,' he said, understanding. 'That must be awful for you.' She looked straight at him for the first time. She smiled a little. Then looked away again, quickly, her gaze following the dull contours of the low hills on the other side of the bay. But he had caught that smile and held it. And he had seen the loveliness of her dark brown eyes and they had pierced down deep inside him.

'What's your name?' he ventured.

'Danni.'

'That's a boy's name,' he blurted.

'Danielle. My fucking name is fucking Danielle. I hate it. It's Dublin posh. It's so pretentious. I call myself Danni. D-A-N-N-I.'

'Danielle,' he said it out lingeringly. Pronounced it slowly, as if licking it all over. 'I think that's a beautiful name. A bit foreign or something, exotic. But it's a lovely name. A real woman's name. Danni is a boy's name and you're no boy, that's for sure!'

He was surprised at himself. He knew so little of life, nothing of girls. Then he was terrified. And she was looking at him, wide-eyed, but pleased.

'What's your name, then?'

'Marty. Short for Martin. M-A-R-T-Y.'

'I like that name, too. Marty is a gentle name. A bit country-ish, like cattle markets, or something sensible and solid. But you don't seem a bit like a bogger.'

'A what?'

'A bogger. An eejit. A fucking culshie.'

'Thanks!'

'That's all right. You're welcome.'

A black-backed gull swooped low over the sea before them, screeching. It tipped the surface of the water before soaring up again and flying determinedly inland. Now there was silence between them, as if something had ended. He knew a sudden and almost overwhelming sense of desolation. He wanted to take her somewhere still and warm and hidden and wrap himself naked inside the safety of her nakedness and he knew how impossible that would be, now, or ever.

He got up quickly, rubbing violently at the seat of his trousers. He stood there, uncertain. She did not even look up. Again he noticed that blue-bright sheen in her black hair, how it seemed to join the blackest depths of the earth with the brightest light of the sky. And he wanted to run his fingers through her hair and bury his face in its wonder. He started back towards the road.

'Did I say something?' She had scarcely raised her voice.

'What?'

'Because you're fucking legging it away so suddenly.'

He turned back. She was looking up at him, her face serious. She looked vulnerable that way – her pretty face suddenly hurt, and those large brown eyes watching him.

'No,' he said.

'No what?'

'No, ma'am!' He laughed and that laugh released something in him. 'No, you said nothing. It's just, I'm useless.' Oh, how he wanted to reach her, to have her understanding so that she could hold him and crush him with comfort. 'I'm just no good at this. And anyway, I'll have to be heading home now.'

She looked back out over the sea.

'I was just beginning to enjoy myself. In this dump, I mean, this fucking island of yours. Is there any action in this fucking place?'

'Action?'

'Yeah. You know, how do you spend your hours? Your days? Your nights?'

'There's the sea, and the mountains. The cliffs. The old villages.'

She looked up at him again, her face hard with disdain.

'Jesus! You sound like my fucking parents. Sea, mountains, villages. I withdraw my statement. You *are* a bogger. Fucking sea! I mean *real* action. Fun. Excitement. Living, for fuck sake!'

'There's not much, I think. I don't bother with that kind of stuff. There's discos, sure, lots of them. For the tourists, mostly. I just love the sea. That's all. There's this cove, Tinkers' Cove it's called, for some reason I could never figure out. But you wouldn't be interested in an old cove.'

'Try me.'

'It's only a cove, really.'

'OK, a fucking cove. Let's see a cove. Will you show me this fucking cove sometime?'

He couldn't help it. He was stung.

'I don't like the way you talk,' he said, and he could feel his voice trembling. 'Danielle,' he added, still savouring the name.

'My accent isn't my fault,' she said, tetchily. 'I was born in Dublin and I speak Dublin and that's it.'

'I don't mean your accent, I mean – the bad language.'

She looked away. She kicked her heels softly against the pier. There was silence. He turned away again, slowly, to head for home. But she looked up at him and she was smiling.

'I'm sorry, Marty. I am sorry. I just do it out of habit, I suppose. So, will you show me your lovely cove?'

He felt exultant.

'I'd love to. I'll meet you here tomorrow. About ten?'

'Ten? In the morning?'

'Sure. Not ten in the night.'

'I don't get up till, like, twelve.'

He was genuinely astonished.

'Alright, alright,' she said. 'Before you start giving out again. 'Cos then you'd sound just like my fucking father. Sorry, my father. OK, I'll meet you here at ten tomorrow morning. Thanks, Marty. I'll see you.'

She turned back towards the sea. He smiled, aiming his joy at the back of her head. He walked on air, slowly, back up towards the road.

October 1951

Mahon & Sons . . .

The words 'Mahon & Sons–General Merchants–Providers' were painted in black on a white board along the front of the store. There were no sons: only the twins, Grace and Alice Mahon. Grace 'n' Alice, Alice 'n' Grace. They were plump and whole-bodied, happy in their lives of commerce. They dressed alike, dark skirts and blouses, indistinguishable blacks and greys, reluctant spatterings of colours – muted and go-between. They wore scarves day and night, in shop and house and out-of-doors, around the yard, perhaps in bed – how could anybody ever know? – scarves wound tighter when in church. Their skin was already patched like fraying cloth, their lives ripening a little too quickly as the years seemed to gather speed. There were hairs that sprouted on the chin, short, grey and intrusive, hairs too, though soft as goose-down, in the small valley between chin and lower lip.

Grace was bent over the dark brown wooden counter. At her right hand a bottle of dark blue ink; between her stumped fingers a narrow wooden pen, its nib bent upwards under the weight of her calculations. She dipped, stroked the nib on the rim of the bottle, and wrote, making her calculations from slips of paper laid out on the counter. She wrote in a small, brown-paper-covered notebook that held the accounts for the McTiernan family, McTiernans-of-the-Cross. Grace's handwriting was neat and not ornate, like that of a young girl grown fluid from headline copying, and her tongue protruded from between her lips, moving as if to shape the letters, to mollify them, to ring them true.

> To: Mrs Sissy McTiernan, McTiernans-of-the-Cross; In a/c with Mahon & Sons–General Merchants–Providers. 1951. Nov.15. To: sugar, tea, biscuits, Ovaltine, sago, large c. flake: 11s.6d. To: sugar, w. meal, pan loaf, cigarettes: 5s. To: tea, sugar, fly-paper, cigarettes, strainer: 5s.6d.

Grace chewed the tip of the pen as she added. Her lips moved soundlessly, as in prayer. She called over her shoulder, 'The McTiernans must be bothered by the flies again. More fly-paper, Alice. Flies and cigarettes. God help us!'

She bent, absorbed, over the desk. Carry forward. She turned the page with a sigh of satisfaction and wrote the total at the top of the next page.

'Someone with a bad turn, Alice! Milk of Magnesia again, God help us all but where would the world be without the Milk of Magnesia?'

There was silence for a while, except for the loud breathing of Grace Mahon and the slow scratching of her nib.

'Sonny McTiernan is smokin' away like a train, Alice,' she shouted again.

Alice came through the passageway from the kitchen. 'Poor man,' she said. 'Like as not it's a wee consolation to him in these dark times.'

'Rinso,' Grace said.

'What?'

'Rinso.'

'What?'

'How much is the Rinso, Alice?'

Alice bustled away behind the long counter.

'One and fourpence,' she called back.

'Bovril.'

'Bovril's eightpence, Grace. Can't you remember? Or is your head full of too much other important stuff?' There was a hard edge to Alice's question. Grace sniffed.

'Suet?'

'How much?'

'Half pound.'

'Fourpence.'

There was silence between them while the pen scratched softly. Another page was turned.

'There'll be a burnin' at the Larkins's any day now,' Alice ruminated, laying her elbows and flour-sack bosom on the countertop.

'Mmmmm. Lard.'

'I've ordered a few sheets an' blankets an' a few sticks of small furnishings an' a mattress, for I expect they'll want to be settin' up the room again as soon as it's safe. Elevenpence the lard. Elevenpence.'

'That's four pounds, fifteen shillings and two pence. I hope to God we'll see that money before the year is out. Sonny McTiernan'll likely forget the account – if he can. Have we whiskey an' stout an' tobacco an' pipes an' all to that, Alice? Against the wake? The likely event, God help us, at the Larkins's.'

'Yes, yes, yes, all to that, done days past. There was a grand burnin' up at Coveney's, Tuesday past, a good burnin' to the world out. I sent young Eddie Dwyer up to watch on the quiet, on our behalf. A good boy that, Wee Eddie. Mrs Coveney's clothes an' all, an' the wardrobe an' tallboy that held 'em . . . '

'Wardrobe and tallboy, too?'

'The lot! An' the pillows were thrown on from a length an' they busted an' there was feathers flyin' all over the yard. Like a flock of birds shot to smithereens by a shotgun. A fair sight it was, too, Wee Eddie said. An' sheets an' blankets an' even the rugs off the floor. A great blaze. An' they disinfected the bed, an' the whole room. An' still poor Jane is splutterin' an' gaspin' an' there'll most likely be another blaze at the Coveney's before long. God help us all.'

'Raisins one and eightpence, half-pound sausages sevenpence ha'penny.'

'It's a right killer, this TB, and no cure. I bet half the world will be dyin' of it. It's a judgement from God, that's what it is, a judgement against the sinfulness of the whole human race. God help us.'

Alice hefted herself righteously from the counter and ran her hand over the new till. It was gleaming: the buttons with all the numbers and symbols clearly marked on them were clean, scarcely touched by coin-blackened, podgy fingers. Alice believed in the future, in spite of the TB and the judgements of God. She believed in the coming times. Hadn't Mahon and Sons been doing wonderfully well? And there was a sense in the air of new things, of speed and movement, of flight and shipping and the miracles of mechanisation. The till now, wasn't it a wonder – adding up all by itself, jerking open with a no-nonsense bell while the precise amount in figures leapt upright in the little panel on top. No embarrassing, unnecessary whispering of costs across the counter, no hesitant and annoying questions from Grace and her lazy memory, no scrabbling for bits of brown paper on which to tot up with the runny nib of a pen, no fumbling in a wooden drawer between the apples and the biscuit tins. Money all ordered within, the notes held firmly by little mousetrap springs, the coins all laid out in their own little beds.

'Ointment. Sixpence. Vaseline. Thruppence. An' a bottle a' sauce's a shillin'. Makes – four pounds, fifteen shillin's an' tuppence. There now!' Grace closed the notebook with satisfaction and placed it on a high shelf with the others. She drew herself to her full height, folded her wrists about each other in a determined manner, faced Alice and said, quietly, but with the quiet of an ocean on the turn of the tide, 'Alice, dear,' – the 'dear' coming as a poignard, touched merely to the nipple of the other – 'Alice, I will not have you casting aspersions on what you seem to consider I have no right to, namely, a little bit of happiness. If it is my will to do a little bit of cooking – a little bit of cooking I shall do. And if I look about the small patch of a world I happen to be living on, for to seek out some happiness for myself, if there's a chance at all, and us both getting on in years, and no longer as young as we were, and then, I mean, what I'm saying is, if there's to be a child in the house . . . I am getting on in years, we, we are getting on in years and we shall not be in this world forever. And Mahon and Sons will not go on forever, either, when you and I are gone, Alice, and God Himself has said . . .'

'Oh porridge, Grace!' Alice said, staking herself upright on the surface of the earth with firmness and certainty. 'We are young yet, we have a great future, a great future. And I simply do not wish to see what we have worked for over such a long period, you and I, dear, together,' – this 'dear' a kid-glove, soft on one side, a rasp on the other – 'I do not wish to see it all going down the drain on food that nobody will eat. Not yourself nor myself nor anybody else. And there isn't a man in the countryside that's worthy of you. There now! That's a compliment to you, dear. That's all. Not any old Ned nor Ted nor Big Bucko, God help the mark! Now, please do not be getting up on any high horse. You cook away to your heart's content, but please do somethin' easy an' normal an' acceptable that we can all get our mouths around.'

'Big Bucko!' Grace responded, as if the words were lemon-bitter on the palate. 'If I may say so, dear, it is you yourself, and not me – oh no no no – that our Big Bucko has the –'

Wee Eddie Dwyer burst in through the door of the stores, a grim, patched satchel hopping on his back. He stopped almost at once, finding himself faced by the twin sisters, both of whom seemed to be bulking larger than usual in the shop, while he stood alone and defenceless, the half-glass door swinging shut behind him. Alice's fingers moved instinctively towards the buttons of the till.

'A penny's worth o'cough lozengers, please,' Wee Eddie managed to announce. 'An' here's th'eggs my mother –'

'Cough lozenges?' Grace said, as if intrigued. 'Someone with a bad throat then up in your house, Eddie?' She had taken down a glass jar from the edenic row of glass sweet-jars on the second shelf.

'No, it's meself. I do like them. They last . . .'

'They do indeed, they do indeed.' Grace picked up one of the square pieces of old newspaper they kept ready-cut for such purchases. 'And how are all up at the Dwyer house, then?'

Grace expertly rolled the square of newspaper into a cone, tucking it in tightly at the bottom. She dipped her plump forearm into the jar and drew out a fistful of the grey-brown, fragrant lozenges. Holding the twist of paper in her left hand she dropped the lozenges in, one by one, the fingers of her left hand deftly squeezing perhaps a little more tightly than generosity ought to allow. She dropped the rest of the sweets back into the jar and folded down the top of the spill of paper. She handed the cone to the boy who advanced cautiously, the penny in his fingers. Alice pressed the button on the till and the machine leapt to life.

'And if,' Grace said, holding the paper just a little longer, 'if you call into me on your way home, I'll fill that up again for nothing since I've a small box of groceries you might deliver to the McTiernan's on your way home, an' a small envelope of accounts you might hand over with it – into Mr McTiernan's hand? You'll be savin' Alice an' myself a great deal of bother. We're busy here, you see, find it hard to get out an' about.'

Wee Eddie nodded, safe at the other side of the counter. He would be happy with a bag of lozenges as a reward for such an easy task. He took the twist of paper carefully, left his coin on the counter, and was gone. Alice dropped the penny loudly into the till and pressed the little drawer shut with emphatic firmness.

'A good lad, Wee Eddie Dwyer,' Grace said. 'And very useful. Betimes.'

The door swung open again after the careless run of the young boy. Alice sighed with infinite patience. She glanced once out the door onto a day of greyness and a landscape that was bleak and damp. She shut the door, quietly, and turned back into the gloom of the stores.

July 1997

An island off an island . . .

For Bendy Finnegan it was all a question of boats. When he stood at the wheel of his half-decker, feeling the sea winds nuzzle like a foal against his body, feeling the controlled bucking and siding of his craft over the hummocks of the sea, Bendy was riding; he was a knight upon his charger, he was Hopalong Cassidy on his white horse, he was Bum the Jockey leading the field and waiting for the cheers and flag-waving of big bank holiday crowds.

That bright summer day it began with a pathetic complaint from the engine, a crude belch of smoke and a quick vomiting of stale water from the bilge out into the quiet, turquoise water of the harbour. A satisfactory thrumming and a pretty shuddering beneath his feet, like the early chariots of the gods the day the Father made up his mind on the creation of the worlds. The great ball of the earth, Bendy knew, plotted by seas and oceans, was meant for the cute and corny craft of the half-decker. Bendy did his morning dance on the boards of the *Saint David*, the seagulls lifting with quick complaints from the shoreline, the early sun cleansing the air to a salt sharpness, the breezes still abed.

'Let her go there, Jackie!' he roared, and his cockerel-faced gangly son untied the heavy ropes from the pier's walls and flung them onto the deck. Jackie Finnegan stepped from the pier out across the already opening gap between land and gunwale, balanced a moment like a circus clown on a high rope, then dropped down onto the deck.

Bendy favoured most of all the manoeuvring of his craft in the tight confines of the island harbour. Sometimes, when the day was still and human beings had not yet encroached upon its loveliness, Bendy would test his skill by swinging the craft rapidly about, splashing into eagerness the other peaceful boats and almost skidding the *Saint David* – the way Jackie would skid his Honda to a halt down along the gravel road to the pier – in a dangerous gambol of sheer exuberance.

'Yer out on the sea an' yer singin',' he called to his son. 'Yer out on the sea an' yer dancin', an' 'tis the golden age of man come surely round again.'

Jackie ignored him. All of that was a lorry-load of ostrich shite. Parents! He gathered the ropes into neat circles against their return.

The *Saint David* rounded the outer pier wall and turned north to face the sea between the islands. At once the boat kicked and snorted against the sudden swelling of the ocean. Bendy was strong, his upper body hard as steel from working the furrows of the sea, his arms sensitive to the trembling flanks and working muscles of the boat, his fingers gentle and responsive to the whims of the wheel. He planted his feet wide apart, gave a jerk to his testicles with his right hand, easing them where he stood, opened the throttle to full and the *Saint David* leaped with ease into the way of the sea.

Soon she was moving swiftly, 'like shite through a goose', Bendy would say. He began to sing in his harsh, loud voice as the land eased away from them on the right; the fields with their fences and gaps, their hedges and barbed wires, their weeds, their whingeing demands for more nourishment, their meagre offerings in return. Jackie, straightening himself like a mast, climbed back along the gunwale, balancing precariously, then jumped down onto the wooden planks of the deck. He called into the small wheelhouse.

'Might as well sling out a line.'

There was an old enamel bucket, half-filled with mackerel heads. He dropped a long line over the stern and watched it churn its way through the boat's wake into the mysteries of the sea.

'Ye could be crossin' a meadow, Jackie,' Bendy called to him through the open door of the wheelhouse. 'The sea's yer grass full an' generous. Them waves are yer hillocks an' humps an' hollas, them splashes an' bubbles an' froth are yer daisies an' yer clover an' yer buttercups. It's a perfect world out here. No woman to annoy yer head. No bells ringin'. No phones hoppin'. No animals bellowin' to be minded. It's a golden age out here I tell ye, a golden age.'

They spent some hours moving slowly in under the great high cliffs of Cruaghan, lifting lobster pots, replacing the baits, lowering the pots again. Bendy had three lobsters and a crayfish in a battered plastic fish-box. Rich-pickings to please him, and the hotels would have their eyes out on poles for them. Jackie hefted a few large colefish on his line and they lay, tarnished and bloody, on the dirtying planks of the deck.

Bendy turned the boat towards the open sea once more, quickly leaving behind the great looming walls of the cliffs. He was silent now, urging his boat to its fullest effort as he headed out into Blacksod Bay and the lonely prairies of the ocean. The sky was still clear; there was a gentle swell but out there it rose high and precarious – the ocean could be treacherous even to its most faithful lover.

He was no mean fisherman, Bendy Finnegan. Out beyond view of the islands were his favourite fishing grounds, where cod, haddock, whiting and an occasional exotic gift offered by the ocean, could be had. 'The Widow's Purse', he called this area. 'Yer fuckin' widow willin' to spend all she has on a wicked handsome man like meself.'

After two hours they had reached the fishing grounds and gratefully Bendy cut the throttle. The boat seemed to sigh with relief and ease herself down into the swell. The silence that was left was beautiful; only the soft, unthreatening slapping of the sea against her flanks, the restful falling of one small wave over another. For a moment Bendy stood, savouring the day as if this were the very first moment of the creation of the world, his hands thrust under the braces that strained over his chest and the dirty woollen vest he wore. He lifted his right arm and sniffed at the stench of his sweat. 'Call on Angie one day soon,' he muttered to Jackie. 'Wash meself first. She'll have me. She'll want me for be Jaysus I'll have her.' He laughed aloud into the silver sky. 'Right Jackie, you young jackass's arse, lets get this fuckin' net into the water.'

Bendy felt, somewhere in his chest, that the fish would be plentiful today. Together father and son prepared the net. Bendy started the engine again and while the trawler purred like a stroked cat they dropped the end of the net into the sea. The high post of his son then eased it out carefully as Bendy took the boat into a long, slow circle. With the most loving of whispers the net slipped gradually overboard. When it was all payed out Bendy took the trawler slowly in a wide curve, allowing the net to open its great mouth and sink down into the rich treasure chest of the sea. Bendy dreamed to himself. He was a god, a lesser god perhaps, but he was presiding. And loving it.

Some time later the *Saint David* slowed. Once again Bendy cut the engine. This was the hard part. Jackie was at the winch, his long thin white arms grasping the handle.

'Right Jackie me lad, let's haul aboard our wealth.'

Bendy stood on the other side of the winch, his powerful hands gripping the second handle. The winch was black and well-greased. The net began to come back in over the side of the boat. The handles strained as they turned. Bendy began to sweat. Jackie's strength was not great, but it sufficed. They laboured on, slowly and with determination.

Suddenly Jackie stopped. Bendy looked up at him. His son was watching far over Bendy's shoulder, out over the sea. A trawler was bearing down on them from the north, coming straight towards them, seeming to have slipped through some tiny crevice in the sky. Father and son stood astonished. Bendy locked the winch in position, rubbed his hands on the dirty front of his vest and went to the side of the boat to look.

'She's a massive thing, by Christ! A hundred feet long if she's an inch.'

'She's smooth,' Jackie called out. 'She's cool, cool, cool!'

'I'll bet she's one of them Spanish cunts!'

Quickly, Bendy moved down into the small wheelhouse and pressed the horn. He let three long loud screams from the *Saint David* shatter the glass of the day. There was one short snigger of a reply from the big boat. Bendy came back out on deck. The great trawler had changed course slightly; it rode high on the waves, its prow a face of pride and aggression. About one hundred metres from the *Saint David* it slowed and turned a little to starboard, moving on a course that would take it close by the half-decker. Bendy could see the great size of the new arrival, its shining up-to-date tackle, the great height of her in the water; there were five or six men on deck, one of them watching with binoculars. Gradually, Bendy grew aware of their intention.

'They're circling us, the whures, they're circling us.'

Jackie was straining to catch a name and port on her stern as she passed, but there was a great tarpaulin hanging low over the boat, and more hanging over the prow so her name was hidden from them. She flew no flag.

'Fuckin' Spanish hammerheads!' Bendy screamed. 'Way inside the limits. Seein' what we've got. Quick, Jackie, lower the net again.'

They dived to the winch and began to lower the net back into the ocean. The great trawler had come round behind them now and was beginning to creep back up on their port side.

'She's a beautiful job of a boat!' Jackie sang out in admiration.

Bendy raised his two fingers in the air. There was a loud jeering from the men on deck as the trawler edged closer to the *Saint David*, coming within forty metres of the half-decker. There was a quiet flurry on the deck of the great boat and then one of the sailors appeared with a rifle in his hands. He raised it and aimed.

There was a long pause in the turning of the world, the sea sounds moved dreamily, the sounds of half-decker and trawler softened like summer humming in a garden, soft and wondering. Bendy heard the dull thuck of the shot over the noise of the trawlers and a small splinter of wood lifted delicate as a butterfly from the stern stanchions of the *Saint David*.

'The fuckin' mad hammerheads of Spanish bastards are shootin' at us!'

'Tryin' to scare us, that's all,' Jackie volunteered. 'Well they'll not win at that game!' Suddenly Jackie was up on the gunwale again, holding on to the side of the wheelhouse, his back turned towards the big trawler. There was another thuck from the rifle and Bendy heard the high whine of the bullet passing somewhere over them. Jackie had lowered his trousers and was bending forward, his small white arse bared to the dark invaders.

There was a long moment when Bendy stood in the Spaniard's shoes, imagining the rifle in his own hands and that irresistible target offered, its dark bull's-eye exposed, and Bendy knew there was no way anyone could resist that temptation. Just then the *Saint David* bucked from the wash of the big trawler and Jackie fell gracefully backwards, overboard, still bent over, his two hands holding tightly to his trousers. Bendy watched him fall; it was such a graceful fall, just like those done in slow motion on the television; the splash into the ocean so quiet that the whole thing seemed little other than a dream. But at once Bendy knew that his son had disappeared under the surface of the Atlantic Ocean while already the half-decker had moved on some distance from where he had fallen.

Bendy ran to the stern of the boat. There was no sign among the waves. Apart from the small wake left by the *Saint David* there was nothing, no hands raised for help, no small, stupid head up and gasping for air, no mouth caterwauling in distress. Bendy knew he was standing useless as a fence post. He could hear laughter from the Spanish trawler. He moved then, cutting the engine dead. Still he could see no sign of his son. He pulled in one of the tyres that hung down the side of the half-decker and untied it. But then, bursting to the surface of the sea, exploding into Bendy's greatly relieved vision, Jackie was on the waves, bobbing peacefully. He waved his hand calmly towards his father and raised two fingers to the already departing Spanish trawler. Bendy was stricken as to how far behind the stern of the boat his son had already travelled. He swung the old black tyre a few times, gathering purchase and collecting force; he flung it high into the air towards his son. Jackie saw it come; it was a great black scavenging bird in the sky above him. He ducked under the water but the tyre splashed well short of him. Jackie swam, slowly but strongly, his long body like a conger eel's in the sea. He ignored the tyre and was soon alongside the *Saint David*. Bendy leaned over the side and grasped him by the wrists. One brave hoist and Jackie was up on the gunwale and hopping down onto the deck, bringing with him a small portion of the Atlantic Ocean.

Bendy stood looking at his long and dripping son. Then he gave him a rough, quick hug. Bendy pressed his lips tight, his big brown face a wild sea of emotions. Then he stepped back quickly, 'I thought ye were gone,' he said. 'Ye were so long under the water I thought ye were gone.'

'I had to pull me trousers up. I didn't want to come up with those bloody Spaniards watchin' me with me trousers half-on-half-off.'

'Ye didn't seem to mind showin' them yer arse but, an' you up on the gunwale.' Bendy laughed with the pleasure of his relief. Then, as it dawned on him, he drew back his arm and slapped his son hard across the cheek. Jackie screeched in pain and staggered back against the boards of the wheelhouse.

'You fuckin' hammerheaded eejit!' Bendy said. 'Don't ye ever pull a stupid fuckin' stunt like that on me again. The act of a hammerheaded madman, that was! Now get ye outa them wet clothes an' hang them up on the cabin an' the sea wind will dry them out quickly. Throw a blanket from the bunk below about ye an' come an' get the bleedin' net on deck before the fish think we're all gone queer up above.'

Jackie's long face was red; he went into the wheelhouse, leaving a trail of sea water behind him as he went. The trawler was a small spot now against the horizon, tail up, its wake proud and certain.

The half-decker headed back towards the island. The late afternoon sun was dim behind grey clouds. Jackie gutted some of the fish; the heads, tails and entrails he flung out into the half-decker's wake. Quickly the boat gathered long streamers of gulls that came dipping, swooping and screaming.

'What was all that about, Daddy, with that big Spanish trawler?'

Bendy spat out over the side of the boat.

'Europe!' he said. ''Twas about fuckin' Europe. They're lettin' all them boyos in on top of us, takin' our stocks an' fishin' our waters. Us little fellas on the arsehole-end of Europe will be done out of our heritage an' our livin' by fuckin' Europe. We're on the very edge an' always have been an' we've always got on well an' happy without Europe, an' now, look! Them Spanish is able to come flyin' in here with their fine ships like a fuckin' Armada all over again an' take our stocks an' fly off out an' not be caught 'cos we're too small to catch them. An' if we do catch one they only laugh at the few pounds we fine them an' they're back again before you can say "shite". That trawler today came lookin' to see how we were doin' an' you can be sure an' certain they've marked the spot an' they'll be back before you can fart an' they'll bleed our fishin' places dry. Them an' their echo sounders an' shoal finders. That's what that was all about. Bullies. That's what they are. An' Europe is the father of bullies!'

Jackie was dressed again when the *Saint David* pulled slowly back into the little harbour. With skill, and no little showmanship, Bendy drew the half-decker across the water and let it glide gently to a halt against its mooring place. There were a few cars parked up on the road above the harbour, parked, too, on the grass verges. Mercedes. Pajeros with their aggressive shapes and their threatening bullbars. BMWs. And here and there the tourists wandered, taken with the romantic foolishness of small trawlers and the wondrous might of the great Atlantic Ocean just off their starboard bows.

Some of them wandered inquisitively towards the docking half-decker. Among them Jackie spotted a very attractive, young girl with long black hair. She stood some distance from two people who must have been her parents; she shrank away from them as if she derided their every move. She was dressed in light blue jeans with the knees ripped open. She wore a white blouse tied provocatively above her navel. Jackie was stunned.

Her parents pushed forward determinedly and asked Bendy if he would sell them some fresh fish. Bendy looked up quickly when he heard the Dublin accents; he saw the young girl draw back in shame at the forwardness of her parents. But Bendy drew out of his chest his most deferential voice and reluctantly sold some of the gutted fish to people who believed in their hearts they were dealing with a simpleton.

'That's a nice-looking fish,' Danni's father said, pointing down into the boat. 'What is it?'

'That's a turbot, mister, a fine fish surely.'

'How would you cook that, now?'

Jackie was watching the girl and he saw how she cringed. Bendy scratched his head with his fingers which were covered in fish scales and fish blood.

'Well now, you'd throw that fella on the pan in a nice little pool of butter, so you would.'

Another tourist bought some plaice from Bendy. They told him to keep the change, and Bendy did. They asked him had he any fresh cod and he sold them some cuts of whiting. They asked for whiting and he sold them a piece of porbeagle shark. They asked for mackerel and Bendy just managed to find the last six under a heap of flatfish. They asked him for turbot and Bendy found it hard to sell his last one; they pleaded, offered him more money. Reluctantly Bendy sold another turbot. And he sold on, finding more mackerel if they were asked for, sending the tourists away happily wrapping the day's edition of the *Irish Times* around their treasures.

Jackie leaped up from the gunwale onto the quay. Bendy was about to roar at him but he hesitated, guessed, and stayed quiet. Jackie walked over to where the girl leaned languidly against the wall.

'Want to see the Honda?' he asked her.

October 1951

There, and not there . . .

Big Bucko lumbered across the rough earth towards his house. The bucket in his hand looked small, a child's toy against his slow bulk. The earth was uneven where he walked. What had once been meadow was trodden, by man, ass, cow, dog and hen, into a bleak, pockmarked fieldscape of labour and exhaustion. The day was a grey one. Clouds moved in slowly and heavily from the sea, carrying the ocean's burden over the land. Across the trodden area of naked daub stood the house, rising from the ground without street or flowerbed or haw to mark it off. A low cottage of whitewashed stone, the timbers of the windows flaking their light blue paint, the rotting timbers of the door showing through the dark blue gloss. The windows had been painted tight shut over the years, the kitchen window open at the top and propped up permanently with a wooden lathe. Net curtains, moth-chewed, gone from white to grey to near-dust, like a long abandoned bridal veil.

Those days Big Bucko never stopped to watch the world that sloped away from him over field and ditch and hedgerow and stone wall, across numerous other small fields of rush and shivering grass, to the muddy foreshore of the sound. Sometimes he tethered the donkey to a post in the middle of his field and let him chomp and worry at the tufts of scutch grass, the thistles and burdocks and cowslips and nettles that struggled under the winds from the sea. Sometimes he let the cows loose in there, when a good summer gave a modicum of sweet grass. He closed off the gaps in the fence and ditch, stuffing them with dried thorn branches or broken planks, and let the animals shift where they would, day and night. Sometimes one of the cows would come to the open door of the kitchen, pressing her head and shoulders in towards the warm and musty gloom as if she were looking for a lover to come out and test the summer evening along with her.

Big Bucko eyed the clouds. It would rain the day. But the day was long that did not allow some space for labour. Some for rest. And there was labour to be done today. As every day. And then, after the labour, there would be the easeful slide into near-oblivion in Donie Halpern's pub just down the way.

He stepped off the daub field into the kitchen.

'Any stir outa' her today?' Florrie muttered from the fireplace.

'No, Mam, not a peep,' Big Bucko said, putting the bucket on the table near the door. 'Quiet as cow shite lying in the hollow of a field.'

She looked at him. Her Big Bucko. Jeremiah James. Wasn't he big, too? Big in bone and big in muscle and big in heart, much bigger than Florrie and she was renowned in the parish – in the island – for her girth and elevation. Jerr. Jerr Dwyer. Jeremiah James Dwyer. A big name for a big bucko. Son. What could she be but proud?

She had sat up in the bed, there in the lower room, twenty and four years ago. She had heisted herself out of her sweats and fluids and agonies to see what had been refusing for so long to come forth into this world, to see what had taken so well to the warmth and darkness of her womb that it did not seem to want to stir itself into motion. She looked to see what it was that had gripped and clutched at the scaffolding of her insides, to see what had knifed hot hands into the yielding softness of her flesh, refusing for hours on end, while the midwife pushed and pulled at the outside walls of her life and scolded and cursed and spat, while she, Florrie Dwyer née Casserly, screamed at the fires this cruel thing was lighting in her womb. She twisted and jerked against it until it came, rending the delicate passageways of her being with the antithesis of loving, pulling her flesh away beyond all possibility of its surviving, and then refusing, falling back into her blood to sharpen once more its scythe and shears towards a further violent punishment of her for ever having loved a man. She had sat up with a mighty groan when he had at last slithered out among the waters and bloods that had nourished him and drained her, and she had said, through her tears and spittle and relief: 'Jesus he's a bucko! A fuckin' awful big bucko entirely!' and had passed away into the relief of exhausted sleep. That was the labour and those were the labours of long ago, she thought; there were other labours now, other labours less sharp and instantly demanding, but harsh and hurtful nevertheless.

Florrie took an enamel basin out of the big sink under the window. She put it on the floor and splashed in cold water from a bucket beneath the sink. She hefted the basin towards the fire and put it down before a wooden chair. She poured scalding water into it from the black kettle hanging over the fire. Her feet were bare. She sat down, hoisting up her skirts, and eased her feet into the basin. She sighed with satisfaction.

Wee Eddie was twelve. He was getting ready to be a man, to finish with teachers and inspectors and scholars in the primary school, and stand up and be nominated a labourer amongst labourers. He was almost as tall as Big Bucko, high and thin as an oar. But, when he was born, compared to Jerr he seemed so small, so little, they had called him Wee. Wee Eddie. He wore brown corduroy trousers that were already too small, hanging at half mast between knee and ankle. Woollen socks. Black boots. Bare feet between April and October. Like Big Bucko, Wee Eddie's skin was dark and his eyes – big and brown – were still pools. Unlike Big Bucko's eyes that darted and swerved with the demands of every spark and sunshaft, Wee Eddie's were as yet shining with wonder and possibilities. Although he would have to labour the bog before the house and the bog behind the house, Florrie wanted a little bit more out of life for Wee Eddie. But he had slipped so easily out of her womb, coming with the speed and ease of an eel, that somehow she could not pay him so much attention, he had left so little memory of his coming even though he was a special child of love, a living testimony to one great act of forgiveness and contrition.

Breakfast – porridge, milk and home-made brown bread – was eaten in silence while Florrie soothed the night out of her feet.

'Right, lads,' she said. 'I'm for the makin' of me flood.'

Big Bucko and Wee Eddie lowered their heads and went on chewing. Their mother stood in the basin, gathering her skirts in both hands. She squatted low over the basin, her knees spread wide. She sniffed loudly. There was a moment's silence. Then the urgent splashing of her urine came loud across the kitchen, the rush of it passing violently into the water of the basin about her feet. Little splashes leaped out from the basin onto the floor. This had been so for years, accepted as naturally as the rain coming in over the darkened bogs. The turf settled loudly on the fire. Wee Eddie sneezed, sighed with the satisfaction of the sneeze. The stream into the basin began to ease. Then stopped. Florrie sat back heavily on the chair and grunted with pleasure. She moved her feet around slowly in the basin. She was a believer in the strengthening power of natural ammonia on the skin of old feet.

At length she lifted her feet out of the basin, shaking them over the stone floor. She moved the basin aside. Then she drew a pair of thick, grey stockings and black, laced boots onto her wet feet. She left the laces undone; she stooped and gathered up the basin. Making a pleased, gasping and rhythmic noise in her throat that could have been an effort at humming, she crossed the kitchen and went out into the hard daub yard. Prince, the black and white mongrel sheepdog, dozed carelessly near the angle of the house. Florrie swung the basin with both hands and the fluid went splashing across the air against the wall, much of it soaking the dog into a startled, unhappy yelp. He leaped back and disappeared around the corner of the house. Florrie chuckled.

'Caught ya nappin', ya useless bugger!'

Then she stopped. She stood facing the wall of the house. There were patches of green mould showing through the flaking paint. Along the gutter a small tuft of grass was growing and streaks of rust and grime snaked down along the wall. The basin, dripping, hung from her right hand. The silence about her was grim with emptiness. She stood, stooped and dark, ageing, worn and bent far beyond her years, a woman dressed in the penitential dark wool and homespun of a miserable widowhood, all her energies drained from her at once into the infertile soil. If her Eddie, if only her own Augustine James Edward Dwyer, were alive . . . Big Bucko, she knew, was too dense and slow to notice the walls, the gutters, the pipes. Wee Eddie, already drawing close to his last months in school, was still too young and she regretted the bright edge to his face and eyes that would inevitably send him from her to find brighter fields in other lands.

She howled, then, a high, quivering howl, like a bitch at night with her head hauled towards the impossible moon. She raised the basin high and flung it with all her strength against the wall of the house. It clattered, dunted, and spun back onto the grass. Inside, her sons heard the howl, they heard the clanging of the basin against the wall. Wee Eddie frowned, glancing anxiously at his big brother. Big Bucko grinned his slow, wet-flour grin, and kept on eating.

'She's exploded again,' he muttered, tiny crumbs of bread coming with the words through his teeth. 'Do her no harm so 'twon't.'

They heard the basin being clanged and banged again and again against the wall. Then there was silence.

'Have to buy another fuckin' basin from Mahon's,' Big Bucko remarked.

Florrie was leaning against the wall of the house, spent. Her face was white now as curdled cream. Her body sagged. Who was there in the world to whom she could speak? And if there were somebody, how could she know the words that would ease her spirit of the great poison spreading slowly inside? Nobody ever had given her the words; books and papers were great vaults locking her out. All her life had been a falling out of grace, caught now and held in the sad dungeon of middle earth where she must labour, labour upon labour, back into the grace that is only beyond decay.

'Fuck you, Eddie!' she shouted into the glowering sky. 'Fuck you to die on me and leave me fastened into woe!'

She lowered her head, her left side leaning for support against the wall. She breathed deeply through her nostrils. She closed her eyes and shivered. She went still then for a long time, allowing the weight of her living to slide slowly and by its own momentum, down into the clay about her feet. Then she had come through again. She stood straight, blinking her eyes rapidly against the day. The ugly skewed form of the stable across the daub, with its loosening slates and its small, blind window, held her for a moment.

'Maybe there's some things is worse than death,' she whispered to herself. Then, fixing her face again into its hardened, well-prepared features, she turned back towards the house.

'Eggs! Wee Eddie,' she called out from the door.

'Aw, Mam!'

Wee Eddie hated hens. Leaving their little grey shits all over the field, setting up a stench on days when the wind came up from the south and left rain behind it, ever so little, and the sun shone down greasily. A stench that was insipid and loose and unsettling. Chicken shit. And then their chuckling together like bands of little old women who had succeeded in changing the world, who had something to cackle about. And their striding, high-stepping, eye-wide continuum; their caution, clucking their way stupidly in through the open door of the kitchen, fussing about, no matter how often they were shooed out. Rhode Island Reds. Oh the bitches!

Wee Eddie had a burning desire to take a long, uncluttered run and boot just one Rhode Island Red high into the air! Just one. Just once. He imagined the feathery thud of the body against his boot, the great arc of the flight, with the feathers falling out of the sky like coloured snow, how the hen-claw and hen-wing and hen-head would swirl in one throughother mess of humiliation and come thumping back, its lesson learnt, onto the earth! To teach it the seriousness of living, the need to strive, to labour, to stretch its being out of the same, single unblossoming field of existence. But the little bitches avoided his coming, their anxious kerfuffle and sidestepping flutters when they would not stand to receive their lesson but rather went scattering away in scolding groups from his dashes, berating him, squawking in high dudgeon.

Wee Eddie travelled the field, for always some of the hens would have escaped their dark and comfortable corner of the hen house. He searched the known roosting places and the likely new ones, the warm rooms under the hedges, the half-hidden hidey-holes in the tufts of grass, the sheltered parishes in the lee of the old green wooden toilet that stood down by the ditch near the house. He clumped about, irritated but well-behaved, the eggs he gathered bringing much-needed shillings into the house. He gathered them, one by one, into an old wicker basket that used to be fixed to his father's bike – a basket Wee Eddie kept lined with straw – and he left it down on the kitchen table before his mother.

She took twelve of the best brown eggs and wiped the little scums of mucus and shit and tiny clinging feathers off with the tea towel. These she put in a brown paper bag. The rest, the white ones, the small pullets' eggs, she left in the basket and put them away under the sink. Two large white eggs she set aside for the small loft outside.

'You'll drop them eggs into Mahon's on yer way to school, Eddie,' she said, indicating the brown paper bag.

There was a pause, a halt for risk, a holding of breath.

'Can't I skip school today, Mam? Just for today? Jerr needs help in the lower field.'

She turned on him at once, with that dark grey overwhelming

suddenness that takes no reply.

'You bloody well will not skip school today Mam nor any other day ye're in the full a' yer health. Haven't I told ye often an' often ye must be able to read an' write, ye must know yer sums, yer addin' an' subtractin' an' dividin' an' ye gotta know all yer holy catechism and yer bible or ye'll become like a big block of the thickest stone that every dog an' fox an' badger'll lift his leg against for to piss on ye all through yer days. An' I'll not have that for you, Wee Eddie. One of us in this house will know what's what. Them's me words, and that's it!'

He was gone from the kitchen at once, the old torn schoolbag flung over his shoulder, the brown bag of eggs held in his left hand, one eye for his mother, the other for the slither-traps too well hidden in the soft muck of the front yard, that would take him and the eggs into one sorry and horrible mess before he could say feck!

October 1951

By name and nature . . .

That afternoon another big man was grunting his way from the hard concrete of a station platform into a carriage. The train would be heading west, out of Dublin, towards the island.

They called him Anus, innocent of the significance of their mispronunciation. He was thickset. A heaviness on the earth. Aenghus. Aenghus Fahey. Brawn and bully of those early years when only happiness ought to have chimed for him and for the other children among the ticks and tocks of time. He had bullied then, and he had bullied since; bullied the earth and the people and the streets, cursing the sea he crossed occasionally to make his living away from his own poor bullied country.

Here he was, bursting out like a boil on talcumed flesh, in a carriage of the train heading from Westland Row to Westport. Heading home. Back to the original landscape of innocence. The sun shining in through the carriage windows. The train on its slow way west, into the past.

There was a young man on the seat beside Aenghus, a fresh young man, clean, eager and polite. He wore a waistcoat of delicate blue, a white shirt, red tie. Beside him a young woman, pretty, hair black as tar with a sheen of plum. She wore a long pleated skirt of grey, a white blouse with golden buttons sparkling on her full bosom. She took the young man's hands furtively in hers and the awareness of happiness shone in her eyes. They sat tinglingly close in the confined space of the carriage, locking out the bully and the movement and the sunshine; the young in one another's arms as if it were possible to live forever inside their allocation of joy.

Aenghus lurked in his corner of the carriage by the window, his feet up on the seat opposite, guarding the carriage from further passengers. He watched the bustle on the platform, hearing the train test its breathing power in sharp hisses of steam and great puffs of smoke. Aenghus was tired after the night crossing from Liverpool and the slow progress across the city of Dublin to the train. He leaned his head back and tried to doze.

Aenghus Fahey's hands and face were pink and marked with angry splotches of red. His hair was grey, standing on his head like tufts of thistledown though he was still only in his thirties, his grey eyes bloodshot from lack of sleep, his jowls touched with the shadow of a black beard. On the rack above his head was all he owned, packed roughly into the same two suitcases he ferried back and forth between the island and his labouring on building sites in Liverpool. Anus. This time, he hoped, this time he would be home for good, escaping the madness of the building sites. He dozed, snorting occasionally, his head lolling.

Just before the train drew into Athlone it began to rain, forcing bursts of water in shivering diagonals across the window of the carriage. Aenghus came awake with a grunt. For a moment, surprised, he watched the journeying of the raindrops, haphazard, yet guided by the forces of the train's impetus and of their own moist existence.

'Fuckin' rain!' Aenghus blurted to the lovers on the seat beside him. The young woman blanched and drew back further into the upholstery. The man clenched his lips and nodded his head, up and down, slowly.

'Comin' home from fuckin' England I am,' Aenghus went on. 'Country's fucked, rightly. Stupid people. Fuckin' eejits. Mark my words. I've been there. I know what I'm talkin' about.'

The young couple drew closer still, a distant and polite smile on the man's lips the only response to Aenghus's words. Aenghus sniffed loudly. He stood up, staggering a little under his tiredness and the uneasy jogging of the train. He lifted down a heavy grey coat from the rack and began to rummage in the pockets.

'Fuckin' ale's all gone, too!' he said, putting the coat back up. The train was slowing gradually and the engine puffed the louder with great, exhaled, blasts.

'Where we comin' to now, then? Belfast? Ha, ha, ha.'

'I believe we're coming in to Athlone,' the young man said. 'A ten minute stop, so far as I know.'

The train shunted slowly across the bridge over the Shannon river. The heartbeats of the wooden beams sounded underneath the heavy wheels. Aenghus's spirits visibly lifted; returning. Playing the role of exile. Emigrant. Small boats rocked complacently on the water below, moored against the currents and the winds. For that long moment the train and its passengers were held, suspended between east and west, between future and past, between times. Aenghus sat down again, heavily.

The train drew in along the platform; it slowed. Stopped. There was a sudden, uneasy silence. Bodies shifted outside the window, faces glancing in. Aenghus got up again, lowered the window by its strap, leaned out and opened the carriage door.

'Don't let any eejit take my place now!' he commanded. 'I'll be back.'

He stepped down onto the platform and disappeared. The young man heaved a great sigh, smiled quickly, got up and glanced up and down the platform. Then he went back and kissed the young woman quickly on the lips. They snuggled closely together for a while.

An old man came into the carriage and gestured towards the seat opposite the couple.

'Excuse me,' he said, 'is that seat free?'

The woman nodded and smiled; she would be happy to welcome someone to take the big man's attention from her. The newcomer took off his coat which was slightly wet from the rain, folded it roughly into a ball and left it on the rack above him. He sat down, smiled genially towards the young couple, sniffed quietly and crossed his legs in satisfaction. There was a moment's quiet in the carriage. The train puffed contentedly. A porter passed in a leisurely manner, his peaked cap askew. The vague sounds of human bustling came muted and soporific from the platform.

Then Aenghus was back, lurching into the carriage with his big navy blue suit out of the labouring yards of Liverpool, his baggy trousers with the sheen of its seat from long shifting on bar stools, the back of the jacket creased and wrinkled from his travelling. He jarred the carriage door closed behind him and stood, bull-like, a rock, looming over the enclosed space that held the others fettered to his presence.

''Nough in now,' he muttered. 'No more room. We need a bit of space to stretch our legs. Wha'?'

There was no response. The young woman let go the hands of her companion, nervously pulled at the hem of her skirt, urging the pleats lower, and folded her arms across her breasts. Aenghus sat down and stared into the face of the man opposite. A western man, old from the fields and the demanding ways of weather. Cleanshaven. Pink-skinned. Fragile as a stem of bog-asphodel, and as strong. He wore thick-rimmed glasses, the right side of the frame held together by a little brown bandage. A grey tweed cap fitted his scalp like a glove. He sat, contained. He glanced quickly at Aenghus, suddenly aware of the big man's stare, smiled a short self-conscious smile and tried to wrap himself quickly in himself.

There was a sharp, high whistle, a great shout from the engine, and the train began to shunt its way out of Athlone, huffing and snorting out through the back yards and indecent hind holdings and in among the small fields and back roads of the west.

Aenghus stood up abruptly and lowered the window, sticking his head out into the air. His bulk darkened the carriage.

'Fuck!' he said, drawing back quickly. 'It's them smuts from the engine – gets in yer eyes.' He drew up the window again and sat down, grinning. 'Home is where the thirst is quenched, wha'?' he laughed, and drew a bottle of Guinness from one jacket pocket, a large bottle of whiskey from another. Big red face, hard exile's features, lined. The young couple whispered something to each other. Some fancy, small and intimate and real. Aenghus glanced at them and the glance quelled them, lest they draw his unwelcome attentions back to their world. He drew the cork from the Guinness bottle with his teeth and spat it onto the carriage floor. It hopped and bobbled in under the old man's seat. Aenghus put the bottle to his face.

The fields were changing slowly, from lush to rush, from fresh to rust, losing that brash and hurried impulse towards commerce that is the argument of the east and of the future. Fencing changed from concrete post to wooden stake and rickety barbed wire. In the carriage Aenghus was growing bigger.

'Who might you be then, old fella?' he asked.

'Mike Joe Canning is my name,' was the reply, pitched in a gentle, self-conscious voice. The old man leaned forward courteously.

'I'm Aenghus Fahey. Call me Anus. Anus by name, Anus by nature. You've of course heard of the Irish god of love? Well, that's me. Anus. You'll have a little drink with me now. To celebrate. A whiskey?'

'No thanks, ah no, I shouldn't.'

But Aenghus was insisting, pushing the bottle into the old man's hand. The old hand trembled as he raised the bottle and took a little sip. The train was gathering speed, wiping water from the window while a wet sun shone feebly over the western world, turning it fabulous beyond the dirty glass. Aenghus took two more bottles of Guinness out of each pocket and placed them ostentatiously on the carriage floor. He stood the large bottle of whiskey beside them. Then he sank back into his seat as if he had performed wonders.

'Now Mike Joe, we're goin' to celebrate my return. A party for the homecomin' wha'? I'm home from England. From Liverpool. What do you think of that?'

'It's very kind of you but . . .'

'Drink up man. Put your mouth round that hole there in the top of the bottle, tip your arse back and let the good spirits in. Stuff the pig with shite and you get a sick stomach, but stuff the pig with whiskey and she's flyin'. Are you goin' the whole way to Westport, Mike Joe?'

'No actually, I'm –'

'I am, then. And after that it's the bus across Mayo. West. Can't beat the headin' west. Here's to the greatest county of them all!'

The old man took another small sip from the bottle of whiskey.

'I knew Cannings once,' Aenghus blundered on, 'in Claremorris. Right fools they were. Thick as a ditch of scraws. Money-grabbers. Cattle-jobbers. That sort. Would you be related to them now, by any chance?'

'No, we're from Ballina originally, near –'

'An' what were you doin' in Athlone, now? A big day out in the city, wha'? Chasin' a bit of leg, I'll bet! That's the man!'

Aenghus turned the bottle on his face and drained the Guinness. In one quick movement he lowered the carriage window and flicked the bottle out into the air. The young woman was smiling indulgently. She and her man were embraced by the loud breathing of the homing exile though she felt safe enough to assume he had found his prey and would ignore them. There was a long way to go yet. The marching line of trees beside the track leaned in towards the train for shelter from the prevailing winds.

'I'm married, as a matter of fact,' the old man said. His face was red.

'Of course you are. And no great harm in that either. But sure that wouldn't stop a man with rage in his blood from chasin' a leg here an' a leg there now, would it? I'm partial myself to the female arse, don't you know. Mind you, I never found a woman myself to suit my needs. I'm a free bird yet, Mike Joe, and happy to be so.'

'Birds marry too, you know, in a manner of speaking,' the old man hazarded.

'In a manner of having it off, Mike Joe. God bless your innocence. Are you good in the bed, Mike Joe?'

The old man lifted his head, like a feeding duck suddenly pierced by gunshot. He shifted in his seat, then raised the bottle of whiskey to his lips and took a gulp.

'Ah don't mind me,' Aenghus went on. 'Sure from the look of you I'd say you've been ridin' over several counties. Worn out by sex. Like meself, Mike Joe, a fine horseman. Anus, the god of love, that's me. Never let the women take over your life, wouldn't you agree Mike Joe? They'll sit on you and shit on you and make you pay for it, that's what I've learned.'

There was silence. The old man again took refuge in the bottle. The young couple sat still as tree stumps. They had long ago stopped holding hands and the woman was slowly searching through her handbag. There was a plopping sound and Aenghus spat another cork onto the floor. The train was passing across a dull landscape; flat, ochre, brown.

'And what are you doing beyond in England, if it's no harm to ask?' The old man was trying to reorganise his afternoon.

'No harm at all, Mike Joe. Sure the cat can piss on the flowerbed and the king can piss on the queen. I'm what's known in the streets of Liverpool as a communications engineer.'

'That sounds impressive.'

'I'm an impressive man, Mike Joe. Welcomed and famous all over Liverpool. Sure they all watch out for my comin' – the women I mean.'

'I don't quite follow you.'

'I'm a postman you old eejit – a postman! And don't all the young women stand inside their doors waiting for me to drop something into them while himself is away at the office? Shaggin' exhaustin' work it is, too! Have another little drop with me now!'

The young woman winced. She took out a small magazine from her bag and hid her face behind it. Aenghus smiled with satisfaction.

'My wife is meeting me at Castlebar,' the old man offered. 'I don't want to be staggering about.'

'Bugger that for a life, Mike Joe, sure isn't the woman's place in the sink? This is no country for growin' old in, right? Sure there isn't a young fella left in the country now, haven't we all to go migratin' to keep body an' soul together? Anyway, you must be able to have your glass of pleasure, the woman's place bein' at the sink, when she's not in the bed. Don't you think?'

Aenghus took the half-empty bottle of whiskey from the old man, drank some of it and shoved the bottle back into the old shaking hand. Mike Joe looked at the bottle in dismay. Outside the fields were thistle-crowded peat oceans; tufts of wool on barbed wire swayed like white horses on the tips of breaking waves; a world of distances, of silences, of a slowly building lonesomeness.

'To hell with the missus and let's you and me head off tonight to a dance in Castlebar, Mike Joe. Pick up a nice young woman for yourself with big breasts and a welcoming arse and take her out into the nearest ditch behind the parochial house. Corsets and bras and knickers will come off for you like the rain in Mayo coming down onto the bog. Sure don't the young ones go mad for mature men like you and me? Then you'll go home and tell herself to give you a feed of rashers and eggs and blood puddings. That's what life is all about, Mike Joe.'

Mike Joe giggled a small, embarrassed giggle and took a big gulp from the bottle. The young man had hidden himself behind a newspaper.

'What kind of a man are you at all, at all?' Mike Joe ventured, his words beginning to run into one another like ink on a copy under a fall of rain.

'Have you a litter then, Mike Joe? Are you a man or a duck? Have you pups? Sucklings? Runts?'

'My oldest son is in Cleveland, in the United States of America, and I have a daughter married beyond in London. My wife'll be waitin' for me in Claremorrish sht – at the shtashin,' the old man managed.

'Shtashin? Shtashin? The word is stay-sion, Mike Joe. You'll have to mind that tongue of yours. Tell me now, would there be any sexy women singin' concerts in Castlebar tonight? Ginger Rogers maybe, or Vera Lynn? An' maybe Anita Ekberg might be in town. There's a fine woman now, Mike Joe, 'd put it up to any man in bed. You an' me could have a great night.'

There was no response from Mike Joe. His head was drooping forward onto his chest, the cap had come askew and was balancing on one ear, the peak had come down over his forehead. He began to snore softly. Aenghus pushed him roughly back onto the seat so that he would not fall forward and the old man half opened his eyes, muttered 'Shtashin, shtashin', smiled, and slept. The carriage filled up again with silence, Aenghus sitting supreme, drinking steadily.

At Claremorris the old man was wakened by the young couple and helped onto the platform, Aenghus laughing quietly. At Castlebar the young couple got off, silence between them, and distance. They moved away into the gloom. Aenghus Fahey was on his own again as the train moved on towards Westport.

The day darkened. The rain brought a pall of grey over the countryside. The fields looked nude and barren, plaques of mud and villages of flourishing rushes. A dim light came on in the carriage and Aenghus watched his own big face in the window. His eyes were narrowed. His lips clenched. He rose suddenly, holding his balance in the swaying train, then flung the whiskey bottle hard against the carriage door. It shattered and the rest of the golden liquid blackened quickly on the floor.

'Fuck you, Aenghus Fahey for a fuckin' bastard!' the big man said out loud. His eyes were bloodshot, watering, and he brushed his hands roughly against them. Anus was coming home.

July 1997

Our Mother, who art . . .

Angie found it hard to pray. But she kept trying. Our Father, she began, who art in heaven. But the God who had been familiar to her once and for so long had gone bad in her life, like a fruit fallen rotten in a favourite bag. Every plea she had offered up over the years seemed to have fallen back on her own head in a shower of cold spittle from the skies. Our Father, she began again, forcing her eyes shut, forcing her knees harder into the wooden floor of the bedroom, forcing her elbows down onto the bed, forcing her two hands together pleadingly, who art in heaven. She'd be distracted at once, because heaven seemed so utterly far from her life, so wholly beyond all she now knew about the world that she could form no concept of it any more. There was only blankness, and endless vistas stretching like a silver-blue desert under a silver-blue sky. Still and blank and silent. And even the word Father sent vague shudderings of distress through her soul and body for what did she know of Father? She sighed, straightened her body and heard the sudden excited barking of dogs from out beyond the back of the house.

The sea heaved below the furthest field. Angie often went down along the ditches by the fields, climbed the crude barbed wire fence that dipped and sagged, and moved on to the rocks of the shore. She could sit there and find some calm, watching the movement of the waves, hearing the soothing murmur of the sea. Our mother, she would sometimes pray, who art the sea.

She would take some of the smaller stones from the fields and fling them out across the rocks of the foreshore to watch them crash and burst into pieces or plop softly into the water. Sometimes she made her way out carefully onto the rocks, out closer to the sea that rose and fell beneath her, sometimes enjoying the quick caresses of sea spray. She searched for loose rocks here, too, to drop them softly into a rock pool, filling the pool over the years, as if she would fill the ocean itself in order to win back the dead; for the stones and rocks were the bones of the earth, which, washed by the living sea might be urged to form life again, to gather back onto the earth the souls of those who were young and lost.

Angie was still a handsome woman, though she took little care of her looks any more. She did not shirk the tasks of the house, or the tasks of motherhood. She would bend over the potato ridges in the near field, her back sore, her hands hardening. She would weed the rhubarb patch and hack the rough growth back into the wind-beaten hedge of fuchsia bushes and furze. She cultivated a small patch of peas and one of onions, but her greatest joy was in the hens, the creatures that gossiped and chuckled under her care and provided a steady stream of eggs she could deliver to the store, into the hands of the general manager there.

The second field was a meadow that she had set to Bendy Finnegan; he took five cocks of hay from it at the end of summer and kept it clean and tidy for her. And for the few bags of turf he delivered to her in exchange, she was grateful, and for the occasional gift of a salmon, or even a lobster that he offered her, with something more than a sense of justice urging him. She smiled a little at the thought of Bendy, of his unspoken messages, of his hesitant, obvious intent.

The quarry field was the most barren field, next to the rocks of the shore. It was salt and wet. It produced the wild iris, nettles and a crop of rushes. It was rough with deeply embedded rocks and boulders as if it had once been the very shore of the Atlantic Ocean itself. Decades before men had quarried here, leaving a sunken field, rough and tumbledown at the edges where it seemed to merge into the foreshore rocks and boulders. A few times she, or Marty, had looked out in the early morning and had noticed a seal resting on the lip of grass before the movements of humankind forced it to heave itself back into the sea. Now Angie kept a donkey in the field, and an old enamel bath she tried to keep filled with water in under the solitary whitethorn bush; she left handshakings of hay from Bendy's work, a few mangles, anything to give back to the creature some measure of peace for all the centuries of slavery to which it had been subjected.

Sometimes the quarry field became another world. Late summer, slipping in almost unnoticed among the luxury caravans of the city folk, among the caravels of the German tourists, the house-vans of the French, the travellers came; two or three families of them, with their own bright vans and caravans. Carpets, brasses and appliances they would offer for sale, and Angie would waken to find they had come back again after their wanderings, back for a while to work among the settled folk and the unsettling holiday visitors. They would open the makeshift gate of fencing-posts and wire and drive their vans and caravans up on the ground of that lower field. Angie would be thrilled, as if a grey and louring sky had suddenly opened and a warm sun had shone through. And she would tether the donkey on a long and easing rope that allowed her as much scope as she needed.

That morning, when she tried to pray, Angie found a small surge of hope lifting her words. She knelt a while, settling her body back into a once familiar shape of pleading and of waiting. She closed her eyes. Outside, the day was a warm one, sunlight softening the curtains, sending a gentle honey light into her room. Her sense of contentment that morning seemed to be a prayer she could offer to whatever infinity there was, whatever presence survived the ravages of the past and stood unfretful before the days to come. She savoured a long, sweet moment of peace.

She opened the curtains and saw the caravans in the quarry field. They were back! The morning sun seemed to gleam off the chrome and the windows. Their presence between her and the ocean comforted her and offered her the promise of company and talk for weeks to come. Their arrival she saw as an answer to her unworded prayers. When she came into the kitchen she was surprised to see Marty at the table. She was even more surprised at his cheery greeting.

'Good morning, mum!'

'Good morning, Marty. We're bright and breezy today.'

Marty wasn't often bright and breezy with her and he could see she was relieved that he wasn't scowling. 'I'll put the kettle on,' he said.

She stood a while at the kitchen window, watching down towards the caravans while he fumbled about behind her.

'I wonder if they've got any fresh water yet,' she murmured.

'I filled the bucket from the tap and took it down to them,' Marty announced.

'Oh, but I thought you hated . . . Who did you meet below?'

'I was talking to Nora Connors, and to Jim and Eileen. Then there's Jack and Mary Ellen. The three families. And their lorry loads of children.'

She was watching him. It must have been a year since he had shown her any affection or offered any information. Now he was moving about eager to help, tidying away the things, making a pot of tea for her.

'I suppose they're alright,' he offered. 'I mean, they don't seem to do any damage or anything. But they don't pay you for the use of the field.'

'You couldn't ask anyone to pay for the use of that old blanket of scutch,' she said. 'Anyway, they're company. I can pass the time of day with them. Nora and Eileen come and help me with the garden, and I help them with their washing. They tell yarns. I like them. They're good people.'

But he had already forgotten about the travellers. He put the big teapot on the table before her and stood back, leaning on a chair, watching. She smiled, gently lifted the pot onto a mat and began to butter some bread.

'I was wondering –' he began.

'Don't, Marty,' she pleaded at once. 'Don't ask me any questions this morning.'

'No, no, no, I wasn't going to ask questions. It's just that I want to meet some of the lads today, back along the coast, maybe get some work in Darby's Hotel, loads of tourists in, you know. I mightn't be back . . .'

She looked up at him. 'That'd be great, Marty. I'd love you to get some work, even a little bit. Make some money for yourself. You know. Have a bit of a time with the other boys. That's great. I'll be fine. Just take care, love, won't you. Sure it would be just wonderful if you found a few weeks' work.'

He hesitated. He knew he had hurt her so much and she was so alone now, and looked so vulnerable, there at the table in her cotton dress with the tiny pink flowers, looking up at him and believing what he said. He turned at once and went out the front door.

When Angie went down to the quarry field she found the caravans looked already as if they had always been there. A clothes line had been stretched between an iron pole and the highest branch of the whitethorn tree. Clothes were hanging out, lying idle in the warm breeze of the morning. Beyond them the ocean sparkled. She could hear skylarks filling the air with their insistent melodies. The underbass tones of the sea were reassuring. And out on the horizon a trawler was passing towards the fishing grounds.

'Who art in Heaven . . .' she murmured aloud and smiled ruefully to herself. She paused beyond the old tumbling gate into the quarry field. Small children were playing in a sandy hollow of the field, the naked bottom of a little girl so vulnerable and yet so safe in the lee of the caravans. She saw Nora Connors moving behind one of the windows and her heart lifted again in anticipation. She closed the old gate noisily behind her.

*

Marty and Danni were moving together down towards Tinkers' Cove. Marty felt stiff and awkward. He knew there was a strange, invisible dance beginning between them but he had no idea at all how she viewed him, or the dance. He caught her hand to help her down onto a ledge at the south side of the cove and his whole body tingled from the touch. She was wearing jeans, stonewashed, her sweet body was plump and firm. She wore a white blouse tucked and tied under her breasts, leaving her midriff naked, her white stomach stretched to the sun. As he helped her down he glimpsed the wonderful plunge of darkness between her breasts and for a moment he felt choked with something both terrifying and inexpressibly exciting. They sat for a while on the rocky ledge overlooking the waters of Tinkers' Cove. Below them, the sea slurped lazily along the rocks and slabbered softly in and out of the cove it was hollowing in under the earth. She strained forward and looked down at the sea. Then she shivered and folded her arms against her breasts.

'Are you cold?' he asked.

'No, no, I just got a strange feeling. About how awful it would be to fall in there. Just a strange, shivering feeling.'

'The water is very deep,' he said. 'But this cliff isn't much higher than a diving board. You'd be OK even if you fell in.'

'Thanks!' she said. 'I'll stick to the swimming pool in Dublin. It's safer. And I bet it's a lot warmer, too.'

He persuaded her to climb down with him to a lower ledge. She was awkward and he had to hold her hand tightly. Then she asked him to stand on the ledge below and hold her as she came down. He held her cautiously about the midriff and almost wept with a fierce longing as his hands touched her warm, firm flesh.

'I bet you're having a good look at my arse!' she laughed, grinning down at him.

He couldn't respond to that, his mouth had gone dry again.

Soon they were standing on the ledge that stuck out about a metre above the water in the cove. The sea was easy below them.

'This is my favourite spot in all the world,' he told her. 'I come here and I can be alone. The sun is on this ledge most of the day and nobody ever comes by. I have sometimes spent the whole day here. Skipping school.'

She looked at him.

'That's cool,' she said. 'But don't your parents find out?'

He hesitated. But she was so beautiful and somehow vulnerable, there, on his ledge.

'They don't know,' he said. 'I don't do it too often, so as not to arouse suspicion.'

'What do you do here all day?'

He let his body slide down the wall of rock until he was sitting at its base. The soft cloth of her jeans stirred him. He looked away, across at the dark wall on the other side of the cove.

'I read. I might swim a few times. I lie on the rock and doze. I even sleep. I just watch the sea.'

'Do you swim in there?' she asked doubtfully, eyeing the power of the swell in the cove even though the day was calm.

'Oh yes. It's cold, and safe, the rocks on each side are close and easy to get a hold of. Rough days it's wild exciting!'

'Do you swim ball-bare?'

'What?'

'In the nip. Naked. Nothing on. Ball-bare!'

He laughed at the immediacy of her imagination.

'Yes. Always. It's special to be naked in the open air. More special still to be naked in the sea. It's a great feeling. The water everywhere on you, as if you were part of it, a part of the sea or of the universe. Of something bigger than your own small self. Makes you feel you belong. In a way.'

She was standing above him, leaning against the warm rock face.

'You're a spanner,' she said, but he grinned at the sense of admiration he detected in her voice. 'So this is how you get your kicks.'

She lowered her body until she was squatting at the base of the rock beside him. He grinned. There, in his own place, he felt more secure, more in charge of the day and more in charge of himself. Her eyes were alight with merriment, her face bright and peaceful. She was smiling at him and for a moment his impulse was to reach over and take her hand. But he was afraid. He was awkward. He looked back at the water. At the rock-end of the cove a small red buoy bobbed contentedly.

'There's a big cave in there,' he said, pointing. 'You can get in when the tide is out. It's high enough to stand up in and sometimes I go in there and see how long I can stay before the rising tide locks me in. You're in there, far in under the earth. It's dark and echoing. It's a challenge. And I've never gone as far as the very end. Too dark. Deep and dark.'

'I was right,' she said. 'You're a bogger and a spanner. Must have the blood of a fucking fish in you.'

He looked up at her quickly.

'Sorry,' she said. She reached her hand and touched him softly on the shoulder. 'Write out the first verse of "Easter 1916" twenty times.'

'Did you ever think how we are all made of water?'

'Jee...ee...sus!'

'No, I mean, really. In science they say most of the surface of the earth is water. And we're so much water, too. I feel sometimes that I'm really a part of the sea, that I'll go back into the sea some day and stay a part of it for ever.'

She stood up, stretching herself, and he knew she was suddenly surprised to be there with him, listening to the things he said. But he felt, too, that she was content. She stepped forward to the ledge, close to the sea. They could hear the screaming of kittiwakes somewhere over the sea.

'I'm out on a date with a fish!' she said, glancing back at him over her shoulder, and smiling.

'Is that what this is?' he asked quietly. 'A date?'

She looked away again. She shrugged.

'I was down at the harbour last evening,' she said. 'My fucking father was buying these fish from a weird guy in a boat. Jee...sus! More fucking fish. Mackerel or something. Yuck! And there was this tall skinny guy on the boat, tall as a street lamp like, and he really looked like a fish. An eel maybe. Anyway, he came up to me bold as shite and said there was a disco on tonight in Darby's hotel. He asked me if I'd come. He'd pick me up. He has this motorbike he's full of, thinks it's a fucking Mercedes or something. A fucking eel on a fucking motorbike! That's a date? Anyway, I said I'd go with him. I said yes because I know my fucking father would say no if I asked him, so I said yes, there before everybody. He couldn't say no after that. And I need something better than playing cards in the evening with a load of fucking wankers from Dublin 4. Anyway, Dad was being all friendly with this boatman, swanning it, pretending he knew everything about everything. My father. Fucking Aristotle. As if he knew where a fish's arsehole was. I needed to embarrass him. So I said yes, like. Anyway, I need a bit of excitement and I guessed you wouldn't be asking me.'

She had turned back towards him. He sat, dribbling tiny pieces of shale through his fingers, looking down at his feet.

She waited.

'So. Do you think, like, you'll go to the disco, too?' she asked again.

He shrugged his shoulders, sullenly.

'That's Jackie Finnegan,' he said, 'and Bendy. Bendy sometimes brings fish to my mother. And I think you're very lucky to have a father at all!'

He was going to say more. He felt hurt, somehow, and lost. She just stood there, looking down at him.

'Jee...sus!' she said at last. 'Aren't we having a fucking wonderful time!'

How could he respond? He felt guilty, and hopeless. And he knew she was right. How could he ever hold her? So all he could do was pretend not to care any more.

A great black-back gull swooped in from the ocean and flew low over the sea inside the cove, its screams echoing loudly from the cliff walls. It dropped onto the water at the end of the cove, floating among the seaweed near the red buoy. Marty stood up slowly and moved out to where she was standing.

'I'm sorry,' he said. 'It's just . . . there never seems to be excitement here. Life is dull, boring, monotonous. There's no light in it. But I live here. It's my place and it's my life. I love it down here. Sometimes you can see a seal swimming in along here. Right near you. Shoals of sprat, too, and mackerel following them and then the sea comes alive, like it's electric, its whole surface boiling with their tiny lives. And the sound of the sea, if you let it, soothes you. And there are the birds, and the sky that seems so huge from here, then suddenly there are clouds, huge and grey and black, and the world changes colours and then the sun comes through and again everything is different. And you can jump into the ocean, naked, and be part of something for a while and forget about all the annoying things. Forget all the rubbish. Parents. School. Jackie Finnegan. All that rubbish.'

He stopped. She was looking at him, astonished.

'Did you ever,' he went on, 'did you ever feel your whole body wanted to stop living in this world? That you wanted to let your mind go still, the way you let the air out of a balloon, and just be there, part of something so much greater than you are. Not God, not that kind of crap, just your whole self wanting to soar high into that great sky, float and float away out into space, out into darkness, and just forget?'

'You are a fucking corkscrew,' was her reply, though she said it gently. She reached then and took his hand for a moment and she could see that he was stunned by that tiny gesture of affection, or caring, or whatever it was. 'Maybe you're right,' she said. 'The world is beautiful down here and maybe it makes you look beyond yourself. In the suburbs it's not like that. Ecstasy gives me the kind of feeling you're talking about. Music, and rhythms, and the swirling of strobe lights, the little tablet, and your head becomes light and your body thrums like a violin and you're not there anymore. You're everywhere, you're in control, like. And that's what I need, I need to be in control.'

She was still holding his hand. He was looking at her and he knew the sadness he felt must have come across to her and that she felt somehow ashamed. She looked down.

'And then you want to die,' he said. 'The longing in you is so great you can't get hold of the ordinary dull world of muck and stone and you know that the crap is going to win and you have to go back to all the crap and all that longing that's so hopeless you just want to give up, go away, die.'

She laughed nervously, for release.

'You're talking about a hangover,' she said and at once she knew that was just silly. 'I'm sorry,' she went on. 'It's me is the fucking corkscrew. I do know what you mean. I think.'

Her brown eyes were soft now and he was smitten by the perfect whiteness of her teeth. He noticed how her breasts heaved gently under the white cotton of her blouse.

'You're very beautiful,' he said. He felt his face burning. He let go of her hand at once and turned away towards the wall of the cove. He put his hands firmly into his pockets and felt his body stoop with sadness.

'Thanks, Marty,' she said. 'You're pretty neat yourself – for a bogger, and for a spanner. So,' and she began to move towards him, 'will you take me to the disco tonight, instead of that Jackie longbeam?'

'No!' he said. 'I'll leave the disco to him. And to you.'

He knew his words sounded petulant and he knew she would resist him.

'It's your choice,' she said, dismissively. 'So where's the action at right now?'

'It was you asked me to show you the cove,' he answered sullenly. 'I didn't promise anything. It's just a cove, that's all.'

He was aware he had angered her. She moved away to the rock of the cliff wall and began to try and climb back up. She reached and found a grip. She began to draw herself up but her shoes kept slithering off the rocks and she let go again.

'Fucking island spanner!' she hissed. He was taking his shoes off, pulling off his socks. Ignoring her. He left them neatly beside the shoes at the base of the cliff. Then he began to undo the buttons of his shirt, slowly, as if he was totally unaware that she was there. He took the shirt off, folded it carefully and left it beside his shoes. He glanced at her quickly and began to open the belt of his trousers.

'Not a single hair on your mighty chest,' she commented. There was a smile on her lips.

He wore light blue underpants. He folded the trousers carefully and left them on top of the shirt. Then he hesitated.

'Go on,' she said. 'D'you think you've got anything I haven't seen a hundred times before?'

He turned and moved at a half-run to the rock's edge and dived over into the waters of the cove. He went under the surface, relishing the sudden cold and excitement of it, relishing too the hold he had over her now. He came up quickly, close to the opposite wall of the cove. He shook his head and grinned over at her. Then he raised his hand above his head and waved the light blue underpants in the air. She laughed.

'Fucking island spanner!' she called. 'You're a nutter! A fucking bagging nutter!'

He grinned again and went back under. He stayed down a while and surfaced again, close in to the end wall of the cove. She had approached the edge and was watching him. He swam as if oblivious to her presence and to anything but the pleasure of his body moving in the ocean. He touched the end wall of the cove, tumbled over and dived. He went down deep and swam underwater into the cave, leaving her, and surfaced in the darkness within. He abandoned her a while, hoping she'd feel lonely and inadequate and then he dived in again, swam as deep as he could and surfaced, treading water, just under where she was standing.

'Come on in!' he called. 'It's cold but it's delicious.'

She folded her arms across her breasts and shook her head.

'It's perfectly safe,' he called. 'You get carried along on the movement of the swell. You'll love it.'

'I've no suit!' she said.

'That's OK, I won't mind.' He laughed up at her.

'I'm sure you won't,' she said, 'but I'm not getting into the water with a fucking spanner and me in my fucking nip!'

'You're scared!'

'I'm not scared! And I'm not going nude in front of you.'

'I'll turn my back.' He dived. When he surfaced further out he waved the underpants in the air again, like a flag. He was laughing, at ease and in control. He swam to the far side of the cove and left the underpants on a rock near the water's edge. As he swam she could glimpse the white outline of his buttocks under the water. Her stomach began to ache. She shivered. He swam powerfully towards the open sea at the mouth of the cove. He seemed to have forgotten her again. At times he dived under the water, staying down for longer and longer periods. She felt bested.

Then he was back again, treading water just beneath her.

'Come on,' he urged. 'You're wearing a bra and pants, aren't you?'

'I can't swim!' she admitted quietly down to him and at once she regretted the hours she had wasted fooling about in the pool in Dublin, refusing to take the lessons because she knew that was what her parents wanted her to do. 'I never learned to swim,' she went on. 'I can paddle a bit in the shallow end of a swimming pool but I'm fucking scared stiff of the Atlantic Ocean!'

She was humiliated and angry. She turned away and went back to the base of the rock and sat down. He retrieved his underwear and was soon climbing out of the water and onto the ledge before her. His body was fine, well-built, strong and lithe. He stood a long time on the ledge, shaking the water from his hands and hair, watching back into the waters of the cove. The sun glistened off the salt water on his skin. She could see fine golden hairs on his legs and arms. He turned and walked slowly along the ledge, letting the warmth of the sun embrace his body. His underpants clung wetly to him. He left a small trail of sea water on the ledge.

'Wild days,' he said quietly. 'The sea brings in all sorts of strange things and throws them up at the end of this cove. All kinds of strange and wonderful things.'

She was grateful he had not mocked her. Over the winter, she promised herself, over the winter she'd learn.

'You're an island spanner,' she murmured lazily.

He grinned. He stretched out on a level piece of rock beside her, put his hands back under his neck and gave his body to the sun's warmth. He closed his eyes. For a short while she watched the gentle heaving of his body. Here and there salt water lay on his flesh in small drops. She got up and stood above him a moment; she laughed as her body blocked out the sunlight. He opened his eyes and looked up at her. Then she stepped over him, her legs on either side of his white belly. She lowered herself slowly and knelt over him. She touched her finger on a water-drop on his belly and put her finger to her lips.

'Ugh!' she exclaimed. 'It's salty!'

He laughed up at her and she lowered her body quickly onto his stomach, allowing the full weight of her buttocks to rest on him a while. She wiggled her bottom on him and then sat quietly, relishing her sense of regained power, knowing he was glad to feel her weight on top of him. Her fingers moved gently on his chest, touched his nipples; she could see the rippling of his skin in response. He had closed his eyes again, savouring the moment and the feel of her buttocks on him. For a time they were silent, lounging in the warmth, basking in each others presence.

Then, without opening his eyes, he said, very quietly, 'You know, you're really beautiful.'

She hoisted herself a little, then allowed her body to drop down again on his stomach. She laughed when he gasped loudly, the breath knocked out of him for a moment. She rocked her body on him. He was delirious with joy beneath her, gazing up at the brightness of her face, seeing her breasts gently rise and fall under the blouse, and the great blue of the sky above her.

'Have you ever made love?' he asked her suddenly.

'Of course,' she replied at once. 'Millions of times. Well . . .'

He was quiet for a while.

'Have you a boyfriend?'

'Yeah. Sure, lots of them.'

'I mean someone steady? Regular?'

She laughed.

'Not really. You don't do it like that any more, not in Dublin anyway. I mean, when you go to a disco, or when you go faffing around the streets with the gang, I mean, there's always a bit of that going on.'

'But . . .' He was hesitant. 'I mean, the whole thing? Sex, like?'

She laughed again, relishing his uncertainty.

'Well, you'd hardly avoid it, would you? I mean, it's so easy now, everyone's doing it – French kissing, petting, close dancing – your body's free. Then there's the grounds behind the hall, or your friends' places when the parents are away, you know . . .'

But it was evident he did not know. He was silent. Looking up at her. Then he said, 'Tonight, for instance?'

'How do you mean, tonight?'

'At the disco?'

'What? At the disco, what?'

'With Jackie. Will you . . .?'

She laughed again.

'I don't know, do I? We'll have to see how things go, won't we?'

He was very still now and she knew she had lost him. She sat, scarcely feeling the soothing rhythm of his breathing under her.

'Why don't you come to the disco?' she said.

He puckered his lips and made a gesture of disgust.

'I'd better be getting dressed,' he said, petulantly.

Slowly she lifted herself off him. He dressed quickly, then turned and smiled at her.

'I've got a few quid,' he announced. 'Fancy some chips?'

She laughed again and they began to scramble up the rocks together, away from Tinkers' Cove.

October 1951

Smoke . . .

Aenghus was sitting at the kitchen table, the greasy remains of a fry congealing on the plate in front of him. He was sitting back in his chair, smoking a cigarette, and blowing slow lazy ropes of smoke into the air. There was a timid knock on the back door of Fahey's house.

'Will you answer the feckin' door, Anus, for Christ's sake!'

Mrs Ellen Fahey, small and thin, hard-looking as an old rasp, hair grey and wispy but held in a thin brown net, body wrapped tightly in a black apron with a field full of tiny white stars on it, was fussing about the range, cleaning out the ashes onto a piece of newspaper.

With grunts and exaggerated labour Aenghus made his way to the door. There was a tall and dignified-looking old man outside, dressed in a clean brown waistcoat and an open-necked shirt. He was old, his face was lined and furrowed. He was turning and turning an old grey tweed cap in his fists.

'God bless you, sir, and all in this house but would you have any tin cans, tin mugs or saucepans needs fixin'?'

Aenghus stood back, stretched his satisfied stomach under his braces and coughed loudly.

'You're one of the tinkers?'

'Yes, sir, beggin' yer pardon, sir, but if you have any –'

'Yes yes yes, tin cans tin mugs or saucepans. Where are ye camped this time?'

'Back in the old quarry field, sir, as usual.'

'In the quarry field. Ye should be feelin' a mite unhappy in there, sittin' off doin' nothin', where many a good man used to get good work in the old times. An' you lot now lazin' about down there an' doin' sweet fuck all but destroyin' the place with yer thievin' an' fightin' an' dirtyin' the place up.'

The tall man looked down intently at his cap.

'Times is hard sir, an' we've had a run of bad luck . . .'

'Times is hard indeed, then, times is hard. Don't ye know we can't just be handin' out money for any old tin mug or tin can or bucket that's lyin' around? What's yer name anyway?'

'Connors, sir, Connors.'

'Aye, an' I bet ye have fine caravans an' tents an' loads a childer whingein' and shittin' all over the place an' us poor men who has to work hard to earn our keep ye do be expectin' to dig our hands into our pockets an' hand over our hard-earned and harder-kept money to the likes of ye?'

The man began to back away slowly from the door.

'God bless you sir, anyway, I'm sorry to have thrubbled ye.'

'Connors, is it? Wasn't it the Connorses had that poor young girl an' her child drownded back at Tinkers' Cove some years gone?'

The tinker lifted his head and looked sharply at Aenghus. He stood tall and firm and proud and his hands stopped worrying his cap.

'Yes, sir, God help us, 'twas my own daughter an' my first grandchild; there do be a lot of hardship in the world sir, an' it's not rightly shared out as far as I can tell, but you have to keep on an' put up with what you get.'

'Well now, I'm sorry for you an' all but ye ought not to be campin' over in that quarry an' th'Atlantic Ocean so near by if ye can't keep some sort of control over yer own flesh an' blood. What kind of people are ye at all at all won't settle down like decent folk an' earn a proper livin'? Tell me that now.'

'Sir,' said the tinker. 'I'll bid you a good day now an' I'll promise to say a prayer for you.'

Aenghus watched as the man put his cap back on, carefully fitting it to his head; the tinker's eyes were on fire and Aenghus felt cheered that he had risen the man so far. He grinned.

'For feck sake, Anus!' called his mother. 'Will you give over yer blatherin' an' go an' get the milkin' can is out in the shed has a great hole in the arse of it where it fell outa me hands last Sunday an' give it to the man to get it fixed. Ye're not home here to live off the fat of this house, I'm tellin' you, an' it's out that door you'll go to get yerself a feckin' job on this island if it's in this house you'll be wantin' to stop! Now go an' get the feckin' bucket an' give it to the tinker an' tell him he's to have it back to me by this evenin' an' he's to get no more than one and six-pence for it if the job's done aright!'

The tinker smiled as Aenghus sniffed loudly.

'Ah sure wasn't I only jokin' the poor man an' havin' a bit of a leg-pull with him? I'll get the bucket for him now.'

Aenghus rubbed his right hand across his nose and headed slowly and reluctantly across the yard towards the shed. A small black cat moved slowly out from the shadows, miaowing softly, and made to rub itself against Aenghus's trouser leg. The big man kicked out at it angrily and the cat leaped from him back into the shadows. The tinker doffed his cap again, let the smile fall from his face and moved back into the doorway. Ellen Fahey was wrapping the newspaper into a parcel-shape to keep the ashes safe inside. Small wisps of hair fell out from under the net onto her grey-lined face. She came towards the door and the tinker backed slowly out of her way.

'I'm grateful to you ma'am,' he muttered as she stepped out into the yard. She looked at him and sniffed wetly. 'What's the cat's name, missus?' he asked.

'The cat? It's a feckin' cat, not a child. It hasn't got a name, just a mouth, that's all. It's only a feckin' animal, demandin' to be fed, same as everyone else around here – lazy an' demandin' an' hungry an' no good at all at findin' its own food. Good for nothin', that's his name.' The last words she spoke more loudly, her head turned towards Aenghus who was coming back slowly across the yard.

'Animals is creatures too, ma'am,' the tinker said quietly, and he bowed his head humbly before the return of the great man and the damaged bucket.

'Feckin' smart, aren't we now?' Ellen Fahey said, but she grinned at him as she moved off towards the hedge with her burden of ashes.

'I'll have the bucket back this evenin' sir,' the tinker offered, 'right as rain.'

'If I see you back here again after this, mister,' Aenghus spat at him in a whisper, 'I'll strip the skin off yer back an' give it to the pigs for dinner. Fuck off outa here now an' don't let me find you annoyin' me mother's head again.'

Aenghus drew himself up to his full height.

'I'm off up the bog now, mother,' he called out, 'to see what the turf situation is. I'll be back for me lunch later on.'

The tinker took the bucket, bowed his head slightly, and turned to walk back down the yard towards the gate. He whistled softly to himself as he went out onto the sand-track road that led back to his camp. Already he could see the smoke from the fires curling slowly into the sharp, still air of the morning.

October 1951

An island off an island . . .

The Mulligans were the only family left on Innishbeg. Madge and Malachy, and Eoin Mulligan, their son. They were hanging on like barnacles. There were only six houses on the island now, five of them husks, roofless, doorless, windowless, the Mulligan household still huddling low and sheltering, and the only one containing life. The ruins housed families of wandering squalls, ocean winds that were taking them over, nibbling at the drystone walls. There were sheep everywhere; curled up where the kitchen used to be or chewing on grass in fertile corners; sheep dozing where marriage beds had been; sheep with their attendant skalds – hooded crows, ravens, rooks – waiting and watching for the treats of lambs' eyes, or the gristle and marrow of skull meat.

Innishbeg, Eoin liked to say, is an island off the coast of Achill, which is an island off the coast of Ireland, which is an island off the coast of England, which is an island off the coast of Europe. And a man is an island on an island off an island, which is off an island off an island off Europe. Eoin, the last, the son, the only young man. Innishbeg heavy on his shoulders.

He shoved the curragh out from its nest of sheltering rocks onto the water. He clambered aboard, his waders awkward, carrying some of the sea with him. He was a rugged man, tall, built to withstand the gales round Innishbeg, his eyes light blue as if the winds had fretted them, his skin a gentle tan from the same labouring winds, his hair a drift of light brown curls. The day was a grey day and cold, a breeze riffling up along the sound. Between Innishbeg and Achill was a stretch of sea and all the oceans of the world came pouring into its narrow neck, now flowing south with the incoming tide, now north, filling the mighty bottle that was Westport Bay, emptying it again into Blacksod.

'God forbid you'll have to leave us, Eoin,' Madge would say as she heard the storms invade again and clash roughly against the stones of the house, her son pacing the floor of the kitchen, up and down, down and up, hands fastened grimly behind his back. 'For you'll be the last on the island and it'll surely fall into the sea if you go and leave us.'

Malachy sat silent, as usual. He had spent his years in Birmingham, Coventry and Glasgow, labouring. He knew the worth of the big world, its noise and its hard edges, how quickly the vast spaces are fenced about to become slums and prisons and dark, anger-filled pubs. He could not speak of it to his son, for sons will go against the expressed wishes of their fathers until they find out for themselves that the harsh winds of self-reliance are worth more to a man's soul than fat packets of English notes. The world called, the world always called, and what was there to point out to Eoin Mulligan that would hold him firmly on the barren rack of this island?

Eoin grasped the oars and pulled strongly on one side. The curragh moved out towards the sound. He watched the clutching edges of the rushing current, he glanced across at the opposite shore, he calculated, rowed, and yet all his mind was given over to the beautiful woman he had seen. Swiftly and powerfully then he rowed northwards, pulling hard against the insistence of the edges of the current, angling slowly into it, transversing it at a sharp line away from the opposite shore. He rowed north as far as he could, against the current, his body bending into every stroke of the oars, the wood of oar and gunwale groaning and creaking, the water slapping the lifted bows with every thrust, the noise of the current fabulous and threatening just beyond. He cut through the outer edges, then suddenly urged the boat into the heart of the current. He was taken at once, the water greeting its prey with a throaty growl of satisfaction and the curragh was turned sharply south. By now he was a half mile north of the small pier on the other side, in less than two minutes he would be a half mile south; he must row with all his strength, angling now with the current, pushing the boat across and with the flow.

He would have wished to live his life in eremitical silence. There was that call in his soul to distance, to dryness, to the only truth he felt would last; that of the soul in direct communion, day and night, with the fluid source of all creation. He had, before the eyes of his mind, a desert place, sand and rock and scrub, bare of greenery, bare of living things, here and there the ochre land lifting itself in angry rocks that would hide cave and cavern where the soul could lurk, like a scorpion, devoting itself to God. Above all it would be a place without narrowing wall or fence, without bounding sea or limiting horizon. He would build himself a cell, like the upturned hull of a small boat. He would forage for insects and wild honey, trap the desert birds, root like an animal for water.

And then he had seen her, seen and been shaken and had learned how the world can be suddenly cleft apart; nor did he know himself any more nor his own, once familiar, places.

The curragh edged out of the current, close to the shore of Achill. He had to row again, northwards, up the gentle wash, angling always in towards the small, stone pier. An angry snaggle of rain struck, coming down along the water towards him with a small rattling sound, passing him with a swift embrace. But it was easy work now, the great rapids safely crossed, the curragh responding with ease to his touch.

Sometimes, on rare warm days of summer, it was a joy to float with the current on that wide stretch of sea between the islands.

Sometimes he would row directly into the grip of that force and ship the oars. The curragh would be swirled away and he would feel himself so small, there in the great and overwhelming grip of creation, being carried down towards Westport Bay, the water deep and treacherous. Then he would row back slowly, taking over an hour to get home when he would idle in the shallows. Often, on quiet evenings, he would see the shoals of tiny sprat, millions of them, moving and swirling with one movement as if they were great gouts of smoke moving with the will of the wind. Then they would break the surface in a furious dance of death, and he would see the backs of the mackerel, weaving and slicing among the shoals, gorging themselves, the shallows alive with their hunger. Later, perhaps, he would see the head of a seal peering at him from the rim of the current; they would watch one another a moment, eye to eye, man to seal, before the creature dived in among the shoal of mackerel, scattering them in their turn.

He rowed the boat in alongside the pier, stood up and held the pier wall. There was always a moment of sadness when his hand touched the rough stone, a moment of ill ease and disappointment. He would shrug it off quickly and step out into the water. Then he dragged the curragh along the shingle, out of the swing of the sea, and fastened it to a large boulder up on the grass. The spirit, he often thought, fettered to its weight, the body. He took off his waders and threw them into the curragh. He wore his shoes underneath. He straightened his clothes, took one look back at the sea, then turned up the sandy road to the village.

For years, every Sunday evening, Madge and Malachy Mulligan had rowed across the channel, braving currents, tides, storms, rains, to make evening benediction in the small chapel. Eoin with them. They walked slowly, the last, already becoming curiosities to people who had known them for ever. They came, like boats themselves, their frames covered in skin caulked firm by the winds and rains. But they came with a faith that was part of the winds they knew, part of the currents of the sound, part of the harsh clinging on that they knew on Innishbeg. The last.

In the little chapel the people knelt, men on one side, women on the other. There was shuffling from the schoolgirls' choir up on the gallery to the right of the altar. On the other side, above the aisle on the left, some of the better-off people came to kneel. From the men's side, down in the body of the chapel, Eoin could watch up onto that other gallery that was lit from behind by a small and beautiful rose window of coloured glass. It was there he had seen Ruth McTiernan for the very first time.

He had knelt, wet and cold from the crossing and the long walk. Around him there was a restless shuffling noise broken often by the sound of coughing and sneezing. Miss Tighe, on the old breathless harmonium, was playing some soft music. Eoin raised his head and saw the young woman move down the steps towards the front bench of the high gallery. She was dressed in a black coat and black hat with a small white feather and he could see at once that she was elegant, tall and beautiful. She knelt and blessed herself. She lowered her head into her joined hands.

O salutaris hostia . . . She had lifted her face and was looking across, over the priest and altar, towards the facing gallery and the choir. Her eyes were bright, her lips full. The priest put incense onto the charcoal in the burner, the ritual so well known it passed before Eoin's attention the way a cabbage butterfly passes over the hungry grass of Innishbeg. The scent of the incense rose about the small chapel and he inhaled it with pleasure. He could see her hands, long and fine and delicate, the nails perfectly formed. She was so still, so intent, she could have been a statue up there and behind her the evening light shone softly through the coloured shapes of glass – triangles, stars, diamonds, squares.

Eoin had suddenly felt a great pain of loneliness. His father, kneeling beside him, was breathing heavily; he was old, older than his sixty years. On the other side of the chapel Madge would be among the women, her shawls and scarves covering her head and much of her face, her skin already shrivelling from so many years of wind and rain and hardship. Eoin, imagining the island, the tiny flowers that survived clinging low to the little patches of soil that they could find, wondered if his life must be like theirs, insignificant, hard and lonely. His father's skin, on the back of his hands, was brown and flecked with the marks of age; his fingernails were black beyond the possibility of cleansing. Eoin looked at his own hands, strong, used to spade and oars, firm and brown and well developed for labour.

The Mulligans trailed slowly out of the chapel, letting all the others go before them. At the doors Eoin turned and looked back along the centre aisle towards the altar; there was a haze of incense floating on the air; he imagined he could hear the benches creaking their relief; rays of gently-coloured light still fell across the chapel from the rose window. The acolytes had quenched the flames from the six high candles and had carried away the two candelabras. The altar stood white and pure, like a field of untrodden snow. The candle smoke eased slowly into the air, up towards the rafters of the chapel. Again Eoin felt his own loneliness strike him like a blow.

The woman had disappeared. He tipped his fingers in the stoup and flicked the sacred water against his person. Madge and Malachy trudged on ahead, gathering themselves back into the evening, leaning forward into the long haul to the pier and then, on that darkening evening, they faced the crossing over the treacherous waters home.

How a young man can fall silent suddenly, as if the world, familiar and dun and named in all its parts, can slip and reveal another side, untravelled, exotic, challenging and delightful. And how an ageing woman, simple and ignorant and un-lovely now, can instantly divine the source of that sudden silence and smile to herself, as if the future were assured.

July 1997

The quarry field . . .

In the quarry field the travellers had drawn their caravans into a small semicircle, like the great migrants of ancient times who had crossed the prairies, allowing shelter for the small space within from the wild Atlantic winds. Knowing the vagaries and whims of those same winds they had thrown ropes over the caravans and tied them to boulders on either side. Holding them down in case they should take to the air like old biplanes. The sun was shining.

Nora Connors was sitting on the step of her open caravan door. Angie sat on a rock beside her.

'Nora,' she said. 'You make the finest cup of tea.'

'If you'd fancy a wee sup a whiskey now or brandy in it, it'd do your spirits good, girl.'

'No, thanks Nora, I'm in good spirits today.' Angie laughed. There were three children playing in a small puddle of sunshine near the hedge. She watched them, envying their innocence and ignorance.

'That's Jack, an' Jim,' Nora announced. 'My two fuckers. The girl's Jennifer, she's Larry an' Susan's little wan. Sean an' Bridgie hasn't got a chile yet, they're free as mountain goats.' She paused. 'How's your Marty gettin' along?'

Angie sighed.

'He's none too easy, Nora. Resents me for being his mother. Resents me for not having a father around. And for not telling him all about his father.'

'You'll have to tell him some day, girl. He'll have to know or 'twill kill him.'

The donkey in the next field began to bray suddenly, a slow, gut-wrenching voluminous and long-drawn-out bray that was filled with the pleasures of sunshine and ease, filled too with the whole weight of a cumbersome body and a skull too heavy.

When he ended they could speak again. Nora laughed. 'That's the way to be, just sittin' off in the soft grass, content with the thistles and buttercups that be about you, content even with the flies botherin' your arse. Not like us, restless creatures, never content with what we have, always itchin' to move on, to be somewheres else. We shift too fast through the world, Angie, too fast to touch and fondle it, we do be racin' an' chasin' our tails instead a sittin' an' fondlin' the beautiful things about us. I'm tryin' hard to get my Jim an' my Jack to even see things. Some day, an' soon I'd say, they'll be settin' themselves up in a small house somewhere in a small estate an' they'll live the rest a their days lookin' at cement an' the same walls till they die, just like settled folks. It's a hard livin' Angie – pushin' an' grindin' an' worryin' about next week's bit a mutton. We all have a burden on our backs, love, all of us, an' we spend our lives shiftin' that burden from one hump to the next till we lay it down at last an' lie on top of it forever!'

She stopped.

'Jaysus Puddin'!' she gasped. 'There I go again, mouthin' an' mouthin' as if I was Aristotle himself!'

Angie held her two knees in her arms.

'I love to listen to you, Nora,' she said. 'You have wisdom in you. How's Old Ted doing?'

Nora swirled the dregs of her tea in the cup, then swooshed them out into the grass.

'Ah sure Old Ted's OK love. It's Young Ted, me own fella, that's the worry. He's not all that bad of a man, though, is Young

Ted. Off somewhere now with this stuff we do pick up in Armagh. He's a cute whure, is my Ted. He should set up in business somewheres, Ted Connors and Sons Limited, General Merchants. He'll make five pounds into ten pounds if only he can get the five pounds in the first place. An' he's good to me. An' to the kids. An' to his father. An' his latest trick is a good one. He's got this old cart we used to use in the old days, you know, the horse an' cart kind a cart, all painted nice fresh an' gleamin' colours, red and blue and green, for the tourists like. An' on it he's got a whole lorry load a tin mugs, they gets them in cheap in this place in Armagh, a dozen for a quid or somethin' like that, an' they're made over in Tibet or China or somewheres, made all new an' shiny. Young Ted takes them an' batters them up just a little bit, rubs them with wet sand, takes the sheen off them like, scrapes off the Tibet name, then puts a bit of solder on here or there till they looks like the real old tin mugs we used to take our cocoa from when we were knee-high to our own knickers. An' sells them off as genuine antique tinkers' mugs, at two pounds a shot. An' do you know? Half the world seems to want them an' Ted's goods will be endin' up as antique curiosities all over the world – on mantelpieces an' dressers in America and Germany an' God only knows where else. So 'tis workin' well. But he still has the old affliction, God help him – the drink. He drinks as if he has a desert to get across within the next few hours. But he won't come home then, he'll wander away till it wears off him an' I like it that way, love, 'cos there's so many of them gets violent with the drink and there do be rows. But not Young Ted. An' I always have Old Ted to call on, there in his own wee caravan. My Ted just clears out. Carryin' his burden. We're a fallen world, Angie, all of us. Born with a great twist in us takes a lifetime to get out of us. Before we can stand up true and straight before the Lord God.'

They sat together quietly for a while. Cloud shadows raced over the fields, along the shoreline and disappeared. The skylarks were rich through the air. In the distance the cries of gulls, an occasional bark from a dog and the background soothing crowing of a cock. Mid-morning contentment. The women, for the moment, were at peace, and happy to attend.

A tall thin man was coming down from the house, keeping close to the hedgerow at the side of the field, gesticulating, but with obvious hesitancy. The donkey watched him pass, its head a stone sculpture of indifference. The man stopped at the gate into the quarry field and called.

'It's Edward!' Angie said softly.

The man was tall as a poplar tree, thin as an oar, his hair already whitening, his complexion pale. He was wearing shop-soiled light brown dungarees with a brightly-coloured checked shirt underneath.

'He's a very good-natured chap,' Angie whispered. 'Works with Mahon and Sons in the yard and about the shop – where I worked a while myself when I was younger. You remember? The Mahon sisters were so good to me. We've always known each other, Edward and me; it's a small country, Nora, a smaller island and an even smaller shop. But he's a well-meaning and genuine sort of a man, God bless him. Wee Eddie they call him and will you look at the height of him?'

Angie rose and walked slowly to meet him, waving her hand gently back to Nora as she left.

'Come back down as often as you can, Angie,' Nora called after her. She sat on, wondering. She watched as Angie closed the gate of the quarry field behind her, watched as the tall man stooped familiarly over her, watched as they walked slowly together up along by the hedgerow towards the house. 'So that's the way it is, then, is it?' Nora murmured to herself, the words hanging on the morning air.

'When did the Connorses arrive?' Edward was asking as he walked with Angie through the field. There was a pleasing buzzing and humming from the bees in the fuchsia hedges. Edward walked awkwardly, his hands in the pockets of his dungarees, his body stooped and bobbing to avoid branches, and to listen to Angie. He went out to the delivery van parked outside the front of the house and Angie opened the door for him. He carried in a small box of groceries and left them on the kitchen table. Then he stood, awkward and ill at ease, waiting.

Angie moved to the sideboard and fumbled around in her handbag. She rummaged more quickly, then frantically. Her face went pale and she glanced up at him, standing as if paralysed.

'Edward, I'm sorry. I was sure –'

She sat down heavily on the couch.

'What's wrong. Angie? Can I help?'

She looked helplessly at him. She seemed suddenly old, and very weary.

'I had a twenty pound note in here,' she said.

'Marty!' Edward said the name with emphasis. Then he moved forward spasmically, his hands clenched. 'Let me help you, love,' he urged, his tall body bending eagerly towards her. 'It's too much for you on your own. Let me have a part of it. I've always been a part of it. He's a young man now. He'll be going through difficult times. Why don't we get married, why don't we, and let me look after the both of you. You know I'll be good to the both of you. And it will regularise things in the sight of everybody. He'll have a father. You'll have some peace. Please, Angie, love . . .'

She had buried her head in her hands and was sobbing again. She shook her head slowly. She murmured, then, and she was barely audible, 'Edward, we've been over and over this, time and time again. You know we can't get married. I can't. You know it's not possible. Not with the way our lives have been. You're so kind, you've always been so good, so true . . .'

'We'll talk again,' he said decisively. 'We'll talk again. And I'll pay Mahon and Sons for this lot now. I'll sort out this bill.'

She looked up at him angrily.

'You will not, then! You will not. I must face up to this myself. And I must make Marty face up to it. It's the only way. God knows I deserve punishment for my sins. But Marty, and you! God knows you deserve only the best, and I'm not the best, Edward. Not the best. I bring only pain and misery with me.'

She dropped her head again and he lurched towards her, standing over her helplessly. Then he stepped back from her, lost, uncertain.

'I'm truly sorry for everything, Angie,' he whispered. 'Sorry for everything that has happened. Everything. Everything. Everything.'

October 1951

There and not there . . .

She heard the wooden groan of the stable door below her. Instantly she became all-listening, her breathing held lest it impair her understanding of every sound. She was crouched against the wall, her fingers spread against the rough stone. She heard him shuffling about below. He was mumbling and she heard his hand slap heavily against the rump of a cow. Through a narrow slit between the planks of the floor she could see the yellow light of his lamp. There was silence. She knew he was standing in the open doorway, watching out, gathering the soft mash of his will into some shape. She blinked inside her own darkness. The dusty skylight above her offered only the blank greyness of a clouded night sky. There was no comfort from up there. She waited. She was empty of everything except attention.

Her right hand rested on the timbers of the floor. Her left hand was splayed against the wall. Her back barely touching the stone behind her. Her legs knotted under her. She attended. She could sense him thinking about her, there, alone and vulnerable just above him. She could sense his thoughts rising like fumes through the air of the stable, over the animals, up through the floor, to float in a hot miasma about her. His thoughts, the images in that awful brain, rising out of the confusion of his drunkenness.

She hadn't moved. It felt as if she hadn't breathed. If a cockroach, or a beetle, or a mouse had stirred across the wooden floor, or even if an old and experienced long-eared owl had flown a few feet over the roof of the shed, she would have heard the sound and been startled. Because when he came upon her, if he came, she would force herself to be an empty vessel, emptying herself so thoroughly that all the pressures of the universe about her would impel themselves in upon her; then she was no longer there, no longer herself, she became the universe, she was everything there and everything not there, her emptiness could no longer be filled by his big and fumbling body; she would be all darkness, all night, all absence. And so she would survive.

He moved. He coughed. She could picture him flinging the last of his cigarette out onto the earth. He would shrug his shoulders under the weight of his old grey coat. She knew he would turn then, run his fingers over the flank of the cow, pick up the lantern from the stable floor. She had watched him, often, through the cracks in the wooden floor. Now she heard him begin to climb the ladder to the trapdoor. He was muttering something, some wordless incantation sprung from the blackness of his heart that was sodden with drink and barrenness. She heard his big hands fumbling at the bolt. Violently, he flung back the trapdoor, it thudded down against the floor, raising a small storm of dust into the light that the lantern brought with it. His shadow leaped up before him into her space. Big Bucko.

He left the lantern on the wide step below the trapdoor and his face appeared out of the yellow light. His eyes searched for her. She could see his tongue move slowly over his lips. His face looked black from where she was crouched – black and big and ugly. She had her legs drawn tightly under her. She had the edge of her skirt pulled down as far as she could over her knees. His shadow bulked over the wall and across the rafters above her. She was as far from him as she could be, pressed low against the gable wall, already fading out of existence into the cold air of the sky above the stable. He could scarcely make her out in the gloom his shadow cast before him.

He stopped, hesitating. This, too, had happened before. At once her emptiness began to fill with hope and this was what she dreaded most. Should hope come flooding back into her and should he then continue with his intent, then she was uncertain how she would deal with him and with herself. She would fight him, and he would hurt her; he would take delight in her resistance, he would hold her wrists in one great hand and with the other he would grope and fumble all over her body. He would set his big body over her and straddle her, sitting astride her belly uncaring how his heaviness crushed the breath out of her; he would sit heavily while she gasped and heaved and then he would open his trousers over her and force her into subservience. Afterwards, in his anger at the world, he might strike her on the face; she would try to bite him, she would reach her black fingers to scrape at his face, his eyes; her mouth would be open in an animal snarl, her brain would be a flame of anger and despair. She depended so on his every whim; she was a small creature strung on a thread, time shuddering by as she hung subject to the arbitrary swinging of his cramped imagination.

She had not stirred. Not a nerve twitched in the darkness, not a muscle tightened. Only in her own mind had the breathing grown more frantic, the agony more desperate, the anger more intense. She heard his loud breathing, almost a snorting in his nostrils. They watched each other across great and barren distances. And then his shoulders slumped a little. Perhaps, she found herself admitting the hope, perhaps he had not taken so much drink tonight. Perhaps. He breathed in heavily, once, breathed out, then he was gone, his shadow disappearing with him through the trapdoor. She heard him muttering again. She heard the trapdoor thud back into place, the heavy bolt slide over. A welcome darkness filled her space again. She heard him shuffle his way across the stable. She heard the heavy door bang shut behind him. He was gone. He was walking across the hard earth of the yard into the house. For the moment she was spared.

She squatted silently for a long time, her body slumped after the tension, her head raised to the darkness of the night above her. She listened to her own hurried breathing. She slowed it, consciously, calming herself. As always there was an overwhelming urge in her to cry, to let all the bitterness drip out of her eyes onto the floor of the loft. And as always there was the small and bitter mouthful of regret. She pictured him, his great penis out in the dim light above her, she imagined his weight on her stomach and how, sometimes, he would move up to plant his weight on her breasts where he would ride up and down on her, his penis stretching thick and taut above her face until suddenly he would cry out, heave himself back down over her, lay his body down on hers and force himself into her and she would resist the unutterable moment that had become almost pleasurable to her over the months.

She would not sleep now for a long time. As if, in spite of herself, she missed him, his violence, his impersonal sex, the real hurt and the unreal pleasure that he gave her. Slowly, sadly, she moved her hand down to touch the violated secrets of her body.

October 1951

Best for the west . . .

Aenghus Fahey stood a long while on the road, taking in the frontage of Mahon's General Stores. The window to the right of the door contained cans of paint, neatly stacked into three small pyramids. Strategically placed. There was a shovel, its blade only slightly touched by rust, leaning back against the dark green hoarding, to one side. A scythe, its blade stretching like a canopy over the paint, leaned against the other side.

'Hardware,' Aenghus said aloud.

The big window to the left of the door displayed jars of jam, packets of custard, jellies, bottles of lemonade, a jar of sweets. Much of the packaging was blanched by light and looked ill.

'Groceries!' he said aloud with emphasis, with satisfaction.

On the wooden partition that backed the window a white blouse was stretched and the sleeves pinned wide apart, pink roses growing delicately across its snow-pure lawn. To the right and left of it, neatly fastened, a Christmas stocking of red wool bulged with imaginable delights. On the floor, among the jams and jellies and nearer the window pane for the admiration of little eyes, some toy cars, a doll, a neatly wrapped cowboy suit, a nurse's outfit and a small tin gun in a studded holster.

'Impressive!' Aenghus whispered to his reflection in the

window. He stood back to gaze up at the sign over windows and door. Mahon & Sons–General Merchants–Providers.

'Merchants,' he said. 'I thought it was Merch*ents*.' He shrugged his shoulders. 'And they're a bit ahead of themselves for Christmas!'

When he opened the door a bell tinkled sharply above his head. As he closed the door behind him he knew at once what was wrong. It was mid-morning; granted the day was a grey one, dismal and heavy, clouds louring, but the interior was far too dark for comfort and visibility. There was one lamp burning in the middle of the store; smoke had blackened the timbers of the ceiling and the lamp's light was sucked up into that blackness. On a counter to the right stood another lamp, a third on a counter to the left. All the wood in the shop – the shelving, the counters, the shutters – was a dark brown colour. The boards backing the windows let in only the minimum of light. Like a cupboard under the stairs, Aenghus thought.

There were two women standing at their stations in the shop, one behind the counter to his right, the other to the left. They looked pleasantly plump though they, too, in the blackness of their dress, contributed to the sense of gloom and dimness. The woman to his left stood by a till, proprietorially; her features seemed to have a more pronounced bone structure than the other one's, contributing a modicum of hardness to a face that watched him over round, rimless glasses. The spectacles travelled down the bridge of her nose. She crinkled her nose and eyes and the spectacles leapt back into place. The other woman, to his right, sat on a high stool and seemed uniformly rounded and generous-fleshed. Soft. She, too, wore round and rimless glasses and was peering at the knitting in her pudgy hands. Grace 'n' Alice, Alice 'n' Grace, must be, Aenghus thought. The fabulous Mahon twins. Silly old bats!

'Mornin' ladies,' he greeted the air, the years of exile having made him brash and confident before the island simpletons. In his bearing were the great stores of Liverpool with their high bright windows and their aggressive displays of goods. In

Mahon & Sons there was little visible – apart from the chests of tea and sacks of flour and sugar, tools that stood like loafers about the thin, supporting pillars and jars of sweets on the higher shelves. There were drawers everywhere, with little black wooden knobs, neatly labelled, as if they announced their goods then hid them away incase anyone should be tempted to purchase them.

The twin to his right smiled out at him.

'Good morning to you, sir, though it's a bit dark outside.'

''Tis so. 'Tis so. But 'tis the time of year. Can't suck whiskey out of a sheep's tit!'

The words fell on the floor at his feet and their stench wafted instantly all about the shop. Aenghus's hands shot out in front of him in an effort to call the words back, to catch them before they could reach the ears of these gentleladies. There was a hard, sharp-edged silence. 'Bad fuckin' cess to it for a start!' he said to himself and sniffed loudly.

Twin on the right buried her head in her wool. But there was a half-snigger, he imagined, from twin on the left – of disgust, contempt, amusement? He had to go on. He had to.

'Fine premises you have to be sure. Proud of it you are, ought to be too. I haven't seen the likes of it anyplace in England. Bates any premises anywhere about that benighted land, that's for sure.'

The rich music of a cello had replaced the clang of his words and the warmth of the sound spread about the darkness. Twin on the left seemed to stand up taller to her task. The smile on the face of twin on the right was a Christmas smile in the winter landscape he had brought in with him.

'It's not too bad, thank you,' said Alice. There was still a small breathing of frost in the air he had brought in with him.

'And I hear that Mahon's leads the field in business here, in the western world. Sure didn't I hear you spoken of beyond in Cuthbertsons of Coventry itself?'

'You did?' cooed Grace, and the warmth of a dim winter sun had come back into the stones of the earth. 'Cuthbertsons of

Coventry?' She pronounced it slowly, as if it were a conundrum. 'There now, Alice, isn't that something wonderful?'

Now he had them! Alice by the till. Grace at the wool. Alice 'n' Grace, Grace 'n' Alice.

'That's nice to know, indeed it is. We do our best for the west.'

'An excellent phrase, ma'am,' Aenghus offered. 'An excellent phrase. I congratulate you on it. Mahon and Sons. Best for the west. Well said. Well said indeed. A true businesswoman. Best for the west, surely!' Laying it on heavily, perhaps, but he had won back all lost territory, for he could see the sunshine in Alice Mahon's smile.

'Can we help you at all, sir?' she asked.

'Well yes, indeed. I hope so. You help me, and perhaps I can help you. I was just wondering – I wanted to ask –. But now. There, I wonder if I could speak first off to Mr Mahon himself? Mr Christopher Mahon?'

'Father died some years ago, I'm afraid,' Grace murmured.

'Well now, I'm right sorry to hear that, ma'am, sorry to hear it indeed. He was a fine man surely, I was very fond of Christopher Mahon.'

'You knew him well then, did you?' from Alice.

'Oh yes, ma'am, yes. Knew him? We were buddies you might say, though there were some years in age between us. Then I had to go abroad, right after the war don't you know, and our paths, as they say, diversed. Now, would there be one of the Mahon sons about?'

'I'm afraid not!' Alice's voice was beginning to freeze again.

'Just . . .' Aenghus paused. 'You mean to say that you two ladies have developed all this so wonderfully on your own?'

The wind was right; the day might yet be fair.

'We're not helpless, you know,' Alice said testily, but there was a note of pleasure in her voice. 'We're not afraid of work.'

'No indeed, no indeed. But the sign outside. It says. Anyway. You see, it was the war. It was the war done it.'

Now he was standing midway between them, his hands resting on the dark surface of a counter, his head turning slowly from one sister to the other, deferring, uncertain which one of them to address. His voice dropped until he was offering them an opportunity for pity, the compliment of his confidence, the humility of his hope.

'I seen where the bombs fell, over in England. I seen them bursting their lives into bits, destroying their houses, their businesses, their life's work, the work of generations gone in a bang! Bang! Just like that. It was heartbreaking.'

'I thought you said you didn't go until *after* the war,' Alice asked.

'Oh yes, indeed. But I had been there before, early on like, and had to come home to look after the mother. And then I went back, after the war. Like.'

Grace left the wool in her lap. He glanced at her hands. There was no ring.

'It's a terrible thing, war, that's for sure,' Grace offered.

Aenghus shifted his weight a little towards her. She was an open door into a hayloft.

'It is that, ma'am. 'Twould break a heart to have heard them sirens scream an' to have seen the women with their childer running to escape the bombs comin' down with a heartless sort of a whinin' whistle, leavin' all they had won over the years burnin' up in flames and rubble.'

Grace was nodding her head, up and down, a look of misery on her gentle face.

'And what might your name be now?' Alice asked suddenly.

He moved back a little towards her, but not too much, not too far from Grace. Alice had her hands resting on an open ledger before her, two fine plump hands. There was no ring. He was on fertile ground and he knew it; he hoisted his body to its full height.

'Anus, ma'am,' he announced. 'They call me Anus. Anus by name and Anus by nature. God of love, you know, ma'am. That's me. I'm Thady's son, Thady Fahey – lived and died back in forty-five and I've had to emigrate from this island since then, to support the mother, Mrs Ellen Fahey as lives down the road by the chapel.'

'Indeed, indeed,' Alice said. 'A good customer, poor Mrs Fahey.'

'So you're Anus,' Grace said, a light having come on at last. 'Anus, Anus Fahey.'

He turned grandly towards her. 'That's me, ma'am, that's me.' He bent conspiratorially towards her. 'Anus, you know, was the old Irish god of love.'

Grace blushed and lowered her eyes onto her wool. First nail home, thought Aenghus, driven home and riveted.

'And what may we do for you, Anus?' Alice asked.

'Well, ma'am, seein' as how I left Coventry I thought I'd try and find myself a job back home, if at all possible you know. I've been comin' an' goin' to England this many a year an' I think now it's time I settled down at home. Mother's not gotten any younger, you know. She's a bit weak now, can't go about as much as she used to. Needs someone at home'll look after her. So I come home. To help out like. In her latter years. An' I was wonderin' if Mr Mahon would have anythin' for me to put my hand to these times?'

There was a long, strained silence. He watched cautiously from one to the other.

'I was workin' at Cuthbertsons of Coventry you know, big international general merchents over there.'

'Merchants?'

'Builders' providers. General merchents. Like yourselves here. Only a bit bigger, seein' as 'tis in a city.'

'And what aspect of the business did you know, Mr Fahey?' Grace asked.

'Anus, ma'am. Please call me Anus, By name and nature. I was manager of the stores there.' He paused a moment, calculating. 'Timbers, you know. Planks. Wood. Carpentry. I'm a carpenter by trade. A plane man, if you'll pardon me. Chiselled face, too, you know. Ha, ha, ha.'

He looked from one to the other. They watched him. Blankly.

'We've no call for a carpenter, I'm afraid,' Alice said, and she turned deliberately towards her ledger.

'Coffins!' Aenghus said abruptly.

'I beg your pardon?' Grace said, startled.

'Don't people die any more?' he asked.

'Half the country's dying of TB,' Alice snorted.

'And where do they get the coffins for them?' Aenghus asked.

'Westport!' Grace breathed.

'Thirty miles away! You see. People dyin' all round us from that bloody tumberculosis an' they have to get the coffins out of Westport, seems a shame to me,' Aenghus went on, hitching his braces higher on his great chest. 'Seems to be an opportunity lost.'

Grace looked across at Alice.

'Everybody dies sometime,' Grace agreed. 'And they do all need their coffins.'

Alice looked nonplussed.

'Have ye a spare shed, or an outhouse, or a loft even?' Aenghus pursued.

'There's the garage at the side of the yard,' Grace was getting excited. 'We keep the van in there. Petrol's still hard enough to get. And we can't drive it. We could sell it off but it was the pride and joy of father.'

Aenghus took a high, spinning dive.

'I'll tell you what! You take out the van. We'll put a new battery in her. Get her on the road. Do deliveries. I'll drive. Drove a truck for Davenports of Coventry. I'll load and unload. Do deliveries. A travellin' shop even. Mahon's ought to have a travellin' shop. Reach the whole island, and beyond. We'll get the petrol. Th'only travellin' shop is away th'other side of the island, Dineen's isn't it? Dineen's deliveries. We'll throw a tarpaulin over the engine. She won't need a garage. We'll do timber. Planed. Tongued and grooved. An' I'll make the coffins. Deliver them, too. An' I'll re-do the store for you. New timbers everywhere. Make the place big an' bright. Like Davenports. International like. An emporium. An' we'll set up a little office at the top of the shop. Like the captain's cabin, on a ship you know, where somebody in charge of the money can sit, and that's their job, an' there's a system of canisters and springs and you can send the bill and the money up to the little office, to the captain, an' the change comes back down in the canister. So that one person can keep on sellin' and one person keeps charge of the money. An' I can set all that up for you and set up the carpentry an' coffin business an' brighten up the store an' set it all up as the very best in the whole of the west an' 'twould be a shop that'd be known all over Ireland, the most important, even in America, an' people'd come from all over the world to buy there. Here, on the island. At Mahon and Sons, General Merchents. The best in the west. Providers!'

While he was speaking Alice saw herself perched high in an office, looking down on the deck of her ship while the money came flying to her across the sky, like seabirds.

'The till,' she said. 'Where would the till be?'

'In the office. In the crow's nest. Up with the money manageress.'

Alice held her lips tightly shut.

Grace saw herself moving proudly down long rows of shelves stacked with the most modern and the widest range of goods. Aenghus, big and manly, was by her side, assisting, fetching, and they would brush against each other gently, accidentally, and smile and flush and be contented.

'Wages?' It was Alice again.

'What?'

'We couldn't offer much in the way of wages!' She spoke with a tone of finality in her voice.

Aenghus was ready.

'I'll tell you what ma'am. You put a battery and a start of petrol in that van an' I'll do the deliveries for you, an' you give me the run of the garage and a first load of timber an' sure I'll set to and build up the coffin business and pay myself out of the coffins an' you won't have to give me a shillin'! How about that? An' when the coffin business is goin' good an' the shop is set up neat and new and all to that, then you can take me on full-time an' we'll strike a mutually beneficent bargain then on wages. Now. Can I do better? Can any man offer better?'

Alice hoisted her heavy bosom and glanced quickly towards Grace who was watching her anxiously. Alice felt she was doing a good morning's business. She curled the side of her lip.

'We'll have to ring Cavendish's of Davenport for a reference,' she said. 'If you have no objection?'

'Coventry,' Grace interjected. 'Cavendish's of Coventry.'

'Dagenham,' Aenghus corrected. 'It was Cavendish's of Dagenham an' I was with them only for a while, helpin' them get set up. I was with Davenports of Coventry as a carpenter, master carpenter. An' of course you could telephone them. Or write. It's a Mr Biggleforth, he's your man there.'

'Davenports of Coventry?' Alice asked, uncertainly. 'I thought Davenport was a town.'

'No, no, no, that's Dagenham. You're thinkin' of Cavendish's of Coventry. No, I mean, Cavendish's of Dagenham. Mine is Coventry. I was in Coventry. All those years. With, em, Cuthbertsons. And Sons. Limited.'

'Davenports?' Grace prompted.

'What?'

'You said Davenports of Coventry. You were with.'

'Oh, yes, but that was first. They got blew up. Never got back in business. I went to Cuthbertsons after.'

Alice chuckled.

'I hope you won't get us blew up, Mr Fahey!' she said.

'Ma'am,' Aenghus said. 'Mahon and Sons, General Merchents. Providers. Best in the west. You'll see. Best for the west. You'll see. Cradle to grave ma'am. Providers. Cloth nappies, ma'am, the whole way through to the best shrouds a body could want to be wrapped in to take his, or her, place in the best of coffins. No need to look further than Mahon and Sons. No need to cross the bridge. Best for the west, ma'am, best in the west.'

When Aenghus left the shop he emerged into the damp air in a mood of triumph. For a while he stood in the centre of the road, looking up at the sign over the door. Mahon & Sons–General Merchants–Providers. 'We'll start by getting that right, change that *a* to an *e*.'

The sign shimmered before his eyes, then reformed.

'Fahey & Sons – General Merchents – Providers – Prop. Aenghus Fahey.'

He hitched up his trousers, drew his jacket more tightly about him and set out for Donie Halpern's pub.

'And that's another thing,' he decided. 'Licensed to sell beers and wines and whiskeys. A wee snug at the back of the store. My store!'

Inside the shop Grace had taken up her wool again. Alice was gazing dreamingly into her ledger.

'You know what, Grace,' she said. 'That might be a fine man and a fine job of work we've done today. There now!'

Grace giggled. 'You can't suck whiskey out of a sheep's tit. Imagine!'

October 1951

There, and not there . . .

The evening sun bathed Blacksod Bay. The sand was almost golden. It was soft and very fine. At one end of the bay large boulders stood broad-shouldered out into the sea when the tide was full; they rested, dry and individual, when the tide was out. On grey evenings Eoin Mulligan liked to fish here where a fresh-water stream flowed down into the sea at the end of the cove and the sea trout came feeding. A salmon, too, if he was lucky. When the sun shone over the bay and the water was calm in its desultory moving, he would sit on the rocks and gaze out on the beautiful indifference of the world, listening to the breaking waves as they offered a soothing background to his thoughts.

Outside the shelter of the bay the ocean was dark and wild as always. But here, Eoin felt, was the place where God first made the world, where He stopped to take a few grains of sand, breathed gently on them till they grew bones and brain and a sort of soul; here, where the first men stood upright, saw the green growth across the earth and turned away from the teeming offerings of the sea. The fragility of that coupling of sandgrains was still to be felt today along the bones and among the fractious inklings of the soul, and the dream and longing for the embrace of the ever-shifting sea surged and sank like the waves themselves.

In the stillness of dusk a sea trout rose out of the water and dropped back in, so swiftly arching its body that the eye caught only its disappearance and the ripples it left upon the surface of the water, while the ear delighted in the gentle plop of its body touching home. Eoin thrilled at it, feeling in his stillness part of a world that did not trouble itself with thought or will, past or future, that laid itself out under the sky the way a starfish lays itself down on the currents of the underwater and sways east or west, south or north, as the movements of the universe dictate.

He was sitting, idly tossing pebbles at the waves, when he looked up suddenly as if someone had said his name, softly, at a distance. He was looking at a dark head peering at him from inside the wide mouth of the bay. Like a dog's head, he thought, round, a puppy's head, without hair or fur or ears. He laughed as the bald round head of the seal stared at him with its big eyes. How he would love to have mastery of the water-element like that. The seal seemed to have paused in the currents of its own days to view the creature on the shore. Gradually, the grey-black head drifted closer to the land. The spilling in of the tide around the base of the rocks was a soothing sound, a subtle and heaving movement. The creature was some thirty yards out into the bay and Eoin could see the round black eyes fixed in curiosity on him. Around them the evening was at peace, a curlew calling in the distance, the occasional sharp cry of a gull echoing from above the shoreline. For minutes they faced each other until at last the wet round head lifted slowly into the air then slid under the surface without a ripple.

Eoin was back at the cove the following evening. He stood on rocks far out in the water and cast his line towards the currents moving outside the bay. Soon he had several small pollack, their gleaming shapes tarnishing quickly on the rocks beside him. And then the seal was there again, the dark head watching. He knew it was the same creature, something in the hold of the head, its size, its quizzical and knowing features. There was, too, a tiny rip visible, like a scar, above and between its round, staring eyes.

'Hello, Scylla,' Eoin called out. He looked around quickly to see if he had been caught in his foolishness. The creature drifted slowly closer out of its own immense universe. Carefully Eoin drew in his line, his movements deliberate and cautious, and laid the rod at his feet. He squatted on the rock, reaching one hand out as to a dog, calling, softly.

'Come,' he called. 'Come, come, come.'

The creature paused where it was, at a careful distance, to measure its response. When Eoin stood again it raised its head as if to submerge. The man remained very still and then, slowly, he raised his arms above his head, moving them in a slow dance of greeting, rhythmic as the fronds of seaweed on the surface of the tide, his voice still calling, softly.

The seal watched as if bemused. It did not submerge and seemed to have drifted even closer. Eoin felt this was already a victory. He stopped, the seal some twenty yards from him; he lowered his hands, then his body, easing himself down until he could take one of the fish from the rock near his feet. He held the fish out in his right hand, calling, 'Here, Scylla, come, come . . .' The seal did not move and Eoin, with as smooth a movement as he could execute, swung the fish out towards the other life. Instantly the head disappeared under the surface, before the fish had splashed into the water nearby.

The demands of the old-fashioned God of days dominated his. On Saturday he brought his parents across the sound and they trudged through a cold afternoon to the church. On both sides of the building there were small, dark, confessional boxes. Father Dermot Wall, on the right, elderly, a block on the path to pleasure, hissing and whispering like a shower of rain over a hot tarred road. Father Donal Crowe on the left, young and enthusiastic, silent, deadly as a snake with his condemnations and his penances. Madge and Malachy joined the benches for Father Wall. Eoin, thinking more of the evening sand on Blacksod Bay, more of the seal and the sacramental flow of the tides, thinking, too, of the woman he had watched among the golden moments of benediction, joined the few penitents to the left. He confessed to distractions during Mass and benediction.

'Is it a woman distracts you?'

'Yes, Father.'

'Does she place herself in a deliberate way to call attention to herself?'

'No, Father, indeed she does not!'

'If you choose a woman before your God at the great mysteries, how do you expect God to choose you from among the millions of the damned?'

'That I surely don't know, Father.'

'You must keep your head down, you must not let this woman's presence squeeze out your Eternal Father's love. On pain of mortal sin, for it is a great insult to the Lord your God not to pay attention at His court.'

The young woman with her dark curls took greater possession of the young man's thoughts as he willed himself to forget her, as he urged his mind towards the suffering flesh of the Christ. He murmured the Act of Contrition, 'O my God I am heartily sorry . . .' as the priest on the distant shore of the confessional murmured his Latin words: *ego te absolvo* . . . He would have to stay back after Mass on Sunday and recite fifteen decades of the rosary before the statue of the Virgin, his eyes turned to her eyes, his saddened heart pleading to her virginal heart. He hurried through his final prayers, remembering the fingering that the small waves make along the sides of the rocks where barnacles cling, where green necklaces of weed lift and fall with delicacy and grace. 'And I firmly resolve by Thy holy grace . . .'

July 1997

Generations late . . .

There were three old men sitting at the fire in The Village Inn. The evening was calm and warm but they huddled around it, pints on the floor at their feet. A fairground paraded its wares in flashing lights and jangling noises in a field just outside and youths came, hung about, braved the satellite, the bumper cars, became innocent again for a short while and then went back to lounging, smoking, drinking from long-necked bottles, eyeing one another and building up to a night of disco and opportunity. The Village Inn was full.

'Funniest crack of people ever I seen!' commented one old man, taking a deep swig from his pint.

'Aye,' agreed the second.

'Aren't they from the continent an' every place now?' said the third. 'Know no better, God help them, in their shorts an' braces an' sand-shoes an' their hairy legs an' the big women only dyin' to show their tits an' arses to anyone interested in havin' a peep.'

The three men looked deliberately towards a woman who was bending over one of the low tables in the bar, displaying dark cleavage between wonderfully browned breasts, the tantalising purity of white lace at the edges of her bra.

'Aye!' reiterated the second man.

'We were born two generations too late, that's what I think,' the third man decided. 'Gave our all to Holy Catholic Ireland to keep her clean an' pure under the squintin' eyes of the Pope of Rome an' took our pleasure only when he said so, an' then under the guardian care of sheets an' quilts an' blankets when the full of yer eye on a woman's tits was enough to send you down into the gutters of hell for all eternity, an' a couple of years on top of that.'

'Aye, aye, aye. Sure enough.'

There was no bitterness in the voices, merely a lazy nostalgia, a gentle mockery, a great deal of wonder at the vicious speed of the world about them.

Outside the window where the old men sat, a young woman and a young man came by, holding each other, moving in a slow tango of taking and yielding. She was plump and wore the skimpiest of dresses and as she lifted herself to sit on the window ledge her buttocks appeared for a moment with a small blue thong separating them. She settled herself on the ledge and the young man pushed up against her. The first old man put his tongue out and ran it slowly around the top of his pint glass.

'An' her young enough to be my great-granddaughter,' he mumbled. 'An' here I am, me tongue hanging out over her lovely flesh. God forgive me.'

The old men were silent a long time. Their dark suits were shiny from use. Their off-white, open-necked collarless shirts were not quite clean, not quite dirty. Their hats, softened by the years, were on the floor beside them.

'Tourists,' the first man said, meditatively. 'From all over. I suppose they do leave a lot of money after them.'

'Devil's the coin of it will the likes of you an' me ever see then, Mick,' said the third man.

'I doubt so, I doubt so,' muttered the second.

The bar was loud with voices, with the clattering of glasses and a wholly ignored television set worked away high up in one corner of the bar. The door opened and Bendy Finnegan, with his gangly son Jackie, elbowed their way in towards the bar.

'How're the min?' Bendy shouted at the three old ones.

'How's she cuttin', Bendy?'

'Jesus Jackie but you'll want to keep your head down or you'll be buttin' holes in the roof, wha'?'

A well-built man, middle-aged, wearing shorts and a garish tee shirt jumped up from his stool near the window and called to Bendy. 'Here, sir!' He had his hand raised like a pupil in class. 'Let me buy you a drink?'

Bendy turned with suspicion. He recognised the man who had bought fish from him earlier on.

'Begod then an' I'll be grateful to you, sir,' Bendy said. 'I'll have a pint an' a chaser if that's OK and me lad here'll have a bottle of Millers please.'

The first old man at the fireplace was amused.

'Once the womin used to be showin' off their legs,' he commented. 'An' glad enough we were to admire them. Now 'tis the min, showin' us their hairy legs an' knobbledy knees an' it'd turn your pint to vinegar to see the balls of them held tight inside their hot pants!'

'Sure there's Germans an' Dutchmen an' Frenchmen an' Italians an' everythin' now an' the only bit of privacy you get in your own pub is with a few words in the Gaelic.'

Mr Mortimer Lohan was waving a ten pound note in the air, trying to get his order in at the bar. Jackie Finnegan stood amused. He was wearing navy-blue tracksuit bottoms and a delicate lemon shirt, open at the collar. His hair had been carefully brushed and looked as if it were held in place with oil. Mr Lohan handed over the drinks and Bendy thanked him profusely.

'We had your fish for supper, you know,' Mortimer said. Bendy nodded doubtfully. 'It was quite delicious.'

'I'm delighted to hear that, now,' Bendy replied.

'Come and say hello to my wife,' Mortimer prodded. 'Mr?'

'Finnegan's the name, sir, Bendy Finnegan. An' this here's me windy son, Jackie.'

'How do you do?' They were shouting all the time to be heard above the racket of the pub. 'My name's Lohan, Mortimer, and this is my wife, Sue.'

'Mr Mortimer, Mrs Mortimer, I'm honoured to meet you,' Bendy said, stretching out his great fisherman's hand.

'No, no, no – Mortimer and Sue Lohan!'

'Oh sorry, sorry. There you are now. Mortimer and Sue Lohan.'

Sue was the woman sitting on a low stool against the wall; she was tanned, wore earrings, necklaces, bangles and rings. She was big, her full breasts obvious under the low-necked blouse. She was blonde, real or unreal, but effective. Jackie eyed her with great interest, hoisting his bottle to his mouth and peering round it and down at her cleavage. He was trying to guess the daughter from the mother, trying, too, to assess the daughter from the father.

'We're in Europe, you know,' Mortimer shouted, beaming familiarly towards the fisherman.

'We are indeed,' Bendy answered. 'A big bloody place, Europe!'

'No, I mean, I work in Luxembourg,' Mortimer nodded. 'For the Community, you know. We have a little house in Mondorf, outside Luxembourg. It's a spa town, you know.'

Jackie guffawed suddenly. 'A spa town,' he repeated, laughing. Mortimer looked at him expectantly but Jackie did not continue.

'But we have kept our house in Dublin, naturally.'

'Naturally,' Bendy nodded.

'Our daughter, Danielle, goes to school in Dublin – still the best education system in the whole of Europe. Ireland, I mean.'

'Oh I'd well believe it,' Bendy agreed, hurrying to finish his beer.

'And we come to Achill every year, great you know, for the air, the light, the activities.'

'The light is quite wonderful,' Sue added. 'Paul Henry, you know. And the painters. Great.'

'The sea winds do work shite on the walls of the houses, but,' Bendy said. 'Needs repaintin' every two years, or so.'

Jackie nodded enthusiastically and turned the bottle high over his mouth to hide his face and to stop his eyes from growing permanently stuck between the breasts of the big blonde woman.

'A spa town, a spa town!' he repeated, chuckling to himself.

'You're not in the fishin' by any chance now?' Bendy asked.

'Fishing?'

'I mean in Europe, like. Fishin'. All them trawlers from foreign countries comin' in an' takin' our fish. An' takin' our fishin' areas. Europe needs to do somethin' about that. They'll fish us dry you see, then move on someplace else an' leave us to starve. That's Europe for you.'

'I see what you mean,' Mortimer replied. 'Fishing. No, no, I'm not in the area of fishing. I'm in the banking area myself. Financial matters.'

'Is there no way you can speak to someone in your office in Luxembourg about the fishin'? An' about them fuckin' trawlers?'

'Me? Anyone? No, no. I'm afraid not. That's a different area altogether.'

'Fuckin' Europe,' Bendy complained. 'That's it you see, too fuckin' big, you can't find anyone to speak to. Nobody seems to be makin' the rules but the rules gets made all the same. An' they don't suit the fishermen. Not the local fisherman anyways. Maybe they suit some fat man livin' in Luxembourg or Belgium or Spain or somewhere who wouldn't know the arse of a fish from the elbow of a fish but he's the man makes the rules all the same. When do they ever come to Achill an' go out on the ocean to see what's happenin'? If they do that then they can make their fuckin' rules. This feckin' Europe will have me ruined in no time.'

'Oh dear me, no,' Mortimer began, squaring himself for a debate. 'It's opening up to Europe that will ensure . . .'

Bendy and Jackie stood a while, patiently, pretending to listen. Sue sat demurely, listening and admiring. Often she leant far forward to take her glass of gin and tonic and sip from it; then she leant far forward again to leave it back on the table. Around them the surging of people to and from the bar continued, the bedlam of voices growing ever louder. Someone sat in a corner of the bar ready to devour a plate of chips; there was vinegar liberally spilled and a hot and acrid smell floated through the smoke and fumes. Near the fire three old men talked loudly in Gaelic and laughed uproariously to each other.

'Right!' Bendy announced suddenly. 'I thank you sir for the drinks for meself and me son here. But we must be off now. There's the disco for the young lad an' there's a visit I have to make. Deliverin' fish don't you know. But you'll come down to the pier tomorrow an' I might be able to offer you a fish or two, maybe a crab, or somethin', if them feckin' hammerheaded Spaniards don't have them all took off me.'

'You're very kind, very kind indeed,' Mortimer beamed, happy to have struck up acquaintance with a local.

'Spa!' Jackie smiled, directing a bright and friendly face towards Sue. Then they were gone, out into the relief of a darkening evening, the air still clear and pure, only the noise from the fair jangling across the calm.

'Fuckin' Europe!' Bendy spat on the ground. 'Fuck all Europe'll do for the likes of us. Have to do what's needed ourselves, that's all, that's all!'

'Fuckin' spa!' Jackie added, and laughed aloud.

October 1951

The dumb bitch . . .

Wee Eddie Maguire had never understood what was going on. For him, still, there was no need to understand; the world existed, men, women, children existed, the way dogs existed, the way posts existed. He had grown up with her in the dark and smoke-thickened warmth of the house, his bigger, slower and dimwitted sister, Angelica. He had not wondered why she didn't ever seem to leave the house. He did not wonder why she never went to school. It seemed natural to him that she should be forever thumping clumsily about the house, her arms red from washing, her fingers sore from potatoes and the cold water in the bucket. She was his sister, and therefore different. It was her task to care for him, for Wee Eddie, and for his mother, and for Big Bucko. And it was natural, because she was different, that she had to sleep in the settle bed over the fireplace. Big Bucko had to have a room for himself, that was clear, and it was good for Wee Eddie to be tucked into a cosy, safe space behind the tallboy in his mother's room.

It seemed natural, too, that Angelica never spoke, her communications coming only in grunts and spittle, in smiles and tears and nasal mucus, in clenching fists and bare feet pounded on the cement floor. When Wee Eddie grew too big to share even a corner of his mother's room, what could be more normal than to shift Angelica outside into the shed and let Wee Eddie take over the space above the fireplace. For it was a man's world and Big Bucko and Wee Eddie were the men. Mothers were different, closer to men somehow, in their size and wisdom and authority; but Angelica, a girl, and dumb, she had nowhere else to go but the shed.

In the evenings, when Wee Eddie came home from school, he saw her for a short while. She mumbled at times, sounds that approached words, but were not words. But she always smiled at him and he did not know any other world or any other way but this. She ate before the rest of them, or after them, taking what she was offered, or what was left over, as she stood by the sink. When Wee Eddie sat to his homework at the table under the window she had already been sent back out to her own place, to the loft over the stables in the big shed outside.

Once, when he was alone in the house, working at sums, she crept back in like a wary animal and stood watching him. He grinned at her.

'You're lucky,' he said.

She pursed her lips, watching him, listening for sounds from outside.

'You have no homework to do,' he said. 'No sums. No spellings.' He was writing, filling the empty spaces between the thin blue and red lines of a copybook, copying the headline written out above. For a while only the thin sound, like reeds scraping at the shore of a lake, could be heard as his nib moved in a slow, ungainly limp across the page. His tongue worked hard against the inside of his cheek, bulging his face with the effort.

She picked up his reader and lifted it to her face. She opened it, her eyes following the small pictures, seascapes, country scenes, a city street. He watched her now as her eyes squinted hopelessly over the pages.

'G-A-T-E,' he spelled. 'That spells gate.' He laughed, pointing to the picture, pointing to the letters. Her mouth moved soundlessly. Then she held the book tightly against her breast and her whole being pleaded to him.

'You can have it,' he said, waving his pen grandly. 'You can keep it. I'm finished with that one. I know all them words and all them letters and we've got a harder book now. Keep it.'

A fire burned in her dark-brown eyes and she smiled at him, a smile that gave her face a softness and beauty that moved quickly over him like a shaft of warm sunshine. Then she was gone, and he went back to his headlines.

Her schooling had begun. Because it was longed for with a special intensity and because it was carried forward only in the secret place of isolation and longing, every breath of it was eagerly taken and returned. In the dim prison of her loft, under the cobwebbed skylight, Angelica tried to read; her mouth shaping the letters and the words, her eyes relishing the contours of the alphabet like the contours of a new and exciting landscape, her finger following the simplicity of the drawings that went with every word.

Once Big Bucko caught her as she reached and held a book out of Wee Eddie's bag, the bag thrown carelessly on the floor at the corner of the kitchen table.

'What the fuck do you think you're doin'?'

He stood at the door, blotting out the light of day behind him. She sat down on the floor in her fright and clutched the brown paper-covered book to her breast. She looked up at him. Her mouth moved but no sound came out.

'You dumb bitch!'

He sneered. He was lord. He saw her fingernails, how they were jagged and broken, edged with a thin line of dirt.

'A dumb, thievin' bitch!'

He was crossing the kitchen then in his big boots. She watched him come. She clutched her treasure tightly to her body. He reached down and tried to pull the book from her grasp. She held it. She snarled at him like a she-wolf guarding her whelps. Her lips parted and he imagined he saw her slavering. For a moment he hesitated, aware of her teeth, fine and white. He withdrew his hand quickly and stood back from her. Then he kicked her, his boot landing heavily on the side of her thigh. She groaned with the pain of it and fell over on her side, still clutching the book.

'Fuckin' dumb bitch!' he snarled again. Then he turned and was gone from the kitchen, letting the sunlight fall back in upon the floor.

She lay on the cement for a long time, the book clasped against her. The dust particles, light with their own silence, settled about her. Somewhere outside she heard a dog bark in the distance. There was a gentle breathing from the wind in the black fire-place. The floor was hard against her shoulder and flank. There was a dull pain in her thigh where he had kicked her. She lay, huddled away from the world and a few tears fell onto the floor. She closed her eyes against the tears and the hurt. She slept.

When she woke again Wee Eddie was standing over her, snig-gering, his schoolbag hanging from his hand. She tried to smile up at him but her body was stiff and sore. She began to rise. The small brown paper-covered book was still in her hands. She rose to a kneeling position. Her thigh felt numb but there was a strange, hot moisture between her legs. She put a hand under her dress to feel herself. She was wet. When she took her hand away it was stained with a dark coin of blood. She yelped with fright, got up quickly and almost fell against the table. Wee Eddie was watching her. She stumbled out of the kitchen into the afternoon sunshine, ignorant, terrified and vulnerable. Quickly she reached the shed, climbed the stairs into the loft and lay back on the cot of straw and old clothes she had built for herself. The book fell from her hands into the hay. She leaned her back against the wall and tried to breathe more slowly, to calm herself.

In the evening they sat about the table, Wee Eddie, Big Bucko and Florrie Maguire. Angelica had prepared a potato soup. In the big, black pot she had melted a great knob of butter over the fire. She had gathered leeks from the garden, washed them, chopped them, added them to the pot. The white flesh of the leeks was like snow; the green folds held still their little caches of rich, black earth. The leeks sizzled in the hot butter and the kitchen filled with a strong, pleasing scent. Out of a basket under the sink she took potatoes, peeled them, washed them, sliced them and added them to the pot. Then she took the big jug with the blue bands around it that Big Bucko had filled with milk that morning, and she poured it into the pot. She added water, a few rough knobs of fatty bacon. Salt. She stirred it with a wooden spoon. She put the lid on and left it.

Now the pot stood in the centre of the table. Big Bucko dipped the ladle in and piled up his bowl. Florrie did the same. Then Wee Eddie. They began to eat.

'Where's herself?' Florrie asked.

Wee Eddie looked over at Big Bucko.

'I don't know the fuck!' Big Bucko said without looking up.

'She's in the loft,' Wee Eddie said.

They ate on. There was a fine richness of steam over the table.

'Soiled the floor an' all,' Wee Eddie added.

'Soiled the floor?' Florrie was anxious.

'Aye. Lookit. There. That's blood. Her blood.'

'Was she cut or somethin'?' Florrie asked.

'Nothin',' Big Bucko insisted. 'Nothin' at all. She just lay on the floor there an' when she got up, Wee Eddie says, she shouts an' her hand has blood on it.'

'Jesus preserve us!' Florrie said. 'She's goin' to be a womin. Never thought it'd come to that!'

She got up and went to the spot where Angelica had been lying. She saw the small stain of blood on the floor. She poured boiling water over the stain from the big black kettle. Then she took an old rag from beside the sink and mopped the floor with it.

'Psaw!' she hissed, and 'Psaw!' again and again.

She squeezed out the water and blood from the rag, rubbed her hands dry against her old apron and went back to the table.

'Stole one of Wee Eddie's books an' all, the bitch!' Big Bucko added.

'I'm finished with it,' Wee Eddie said. 'She can have it.'

Florrie reached and took the ladle, emptying a generous

helping into the fourth dish on the table.

'Best take it out to her, Wee Eddie,' she said. 'She'll be feelin' a bit queer, I'd say, her time comin' at last.'

'Her time?' Wee Eddie asked.

'She's fit for childbearin' now an' like as not'll bring a heap more trouble into this house. You mark my words now, she's fit for bearin' a child.'

Big Bucko ate on. Wee Eddie kept his eyes down on the table. How could he understand? The world was a strange place. Only weak shafts of light fell occasionally across the darkness.

'Might as well keep her hid out there in the loft till she grows to a womin can take care of herself on the roads,' Florrie said, quietly.

Big Bucko sneered into his soup.

'Or maybe gets a place to do a bit of work,' Florrie added. 'Be a maid in a house or somthin'. We'll have done our piece by her then, done, an' more than ought to be asked of us either. Best keep her in. Best lock the loft.'

They finished the meal in silence. Big Bucko belched loudly and smiled over at Wee Eddie. When they were finished Florrie pushed the fourth dish towards Wee Eddie.

'Just leave it with her,' she said. 'Don't say nothin', leave it an' she'll take it when she has to. Come away from her at once. An' you can shove the bolt on the trapdoor, too!'

Up in the evening dimness of the loft, Angelica had started to puzzle over the first page of the brown paper-covered book. It began: Who made the world? God made the world. Who is God? God is the Creator and Sovereign Lord of heaven and earth and of all things . . . But as yet the words were little more than small black marks to her, meaningless and intriguing.

October 1951

Scylla and Charybdis . . .

Sunday evening, at Benediction, Eoin kept his head lowered over his hands. He whispered the words of the hymns to himself. He darkened his mind to all thoughts other than the pure white Host in the monstrance, yet the dark head of a seal came bobbing inquisitively and the lovely face of the woman he had seen was clearer than ever to his mind. When the bell rang at the blessing he raised his eyes; the sharp sun of a cold evening came slanting low through the rose window and he gasped at the sudden beauty of the coloured glass, how all the colours seemed to blend to a gold that was filled with the warmth and texture of honey. And there she was, her features lit by that fine light, her eyes fixed on the monstrance below her, her long fingers joined and resting on the dark wooden ledge.

Eoin was aware that there was an abyss between him and that dark-haired woman. When he went back to Blacksod Bay he knew there was a different kind of abyss between him and the seal. He clambered down into the bay and there, lazing on a rock far out in the water, was the seal, its dark coat gleaming, its body resting on its small grey flippers, its great head lifted towards the sky, as if dreaming. Eoin paused on the shore, then called out softly, his voice echoing in the small theatre of the bay: 'Scylla!

Scylla!' The repeated name sounding like a slow music over the water. The creature turned its whiskered head towards him. Eoin put down the fishing bag on the sand and took out a small pollack. Moving as slowly as he could he advanced, holding the fish out towards the seal, stepping cautiously towards the rock on which the seal, like an indignant queen, lay resting.

The tide was out, there were only small salt pools among the inshore rocks. Eoin paused often, to ease the animal's nervousness. Then, within fifteen yards of the creature he was forced to stop. The rest of the rocks were in deeper water and he would have to jump from one to the other. As he tried to climb onto the first rock the body of the seal seemed to quiver like a wet sheet in a breeze. Soundlessly it slid from the rock, barely disturbing the water as it entered, and disappeared.

Eoin leaped the last two rocks and stood a while where the seal had been. The water was clear; he could see the sand, a few shells and small stones shimmering like pearls under the light movement of the water. He squatted and held the fish out over the water. And then he could see that dark shape gliding silently towards him under the water, its progress swift and certain. It paused a few yards from the dangling fish and he could see that head looking towards him. He hardly dared breathe as he held the fish, excitement making his whole body tingle. The seal flexed its body suddenly and darted away but Eoin was content. He flung the fish far out into the water. There was silence for a while and an unbroken surface, then the seal raised its head once, slowly, far out, and disappeared again.

Eoin felt elated. He felt he had been made an honorary citizen of that great world about which he knew so little. He stood a long while. Beyond the bay the waves broke and the white of their crests appeared beautiful against the blue of the horizon. The water was rising about him and for a moment he wondered if he could make the leap back to the next rock. He jumped and grabbed the rock and soon was back safely on the strand. And then he noticed a figure standing at the base of the low cliffs behind the strand, watching him.

She was tall, a dark shape against the light of evening but he could never mistake those curls, that head, and his body thrilled again. For a while he stood, wondering if he should climb the beach towards where she stood or whether he should turn away, feigning indifference. She moved then, along the foot of the cliff towards the path and he began to hurry along the beach towards her. There was a great singing in his ears, as if the sky itself was emitting a high-pitched, excited hum. He stumbled foolishly at the beginning of the path, looked up quickly, and she was there, waiting, expecting him. The glow behind her reminded him of the light through the rose window where it had made of her one of the choirs of angels high above and beyond him.

May 1951

Ruth . . .

Ruth McTiernan believed in the perfectibility of humankind. Why should God create beings incapable of reaching the high glory He had intended them for? Why should God have loved His creatures and implanted in them the longings they carry with them, if those longings could never be fulfilled? Why should people embrace sorrow? Could they not avoid all hurt to one another? Could they not stand back from situations as they arose, meditate on them, then take their decisions in the knowledge that good is good and evil is evil? That life, good and evil, must eventually find its balance in this world and in the next – like a great lake that falls to perfect stillness on a bright summer day, the waters lying level and perfectly reflecting the purity of the sky.

Ruth, submissive to a loving God, would choose joy in her life. She was born into a family that lived comfortably, she was an only child, and she was cherished. She had her pleasurable occupation in Cassidy's Beauty Emporium where she presented the latest offerings from Paris, London, New York, and sold over-the-counter the simple things the island people demanded – bandages, lints, headache tablets, Vaseline . . .

She sat at her dressing table, sometimes peering out her great window over the fields, ditches, green-brown humps and hollows, towards the shore. Sometimes she looked into her own eyes and could see the future, gently but determinedly ordered and perfected, and she could see a man, strong and handsome and vigorous – perhaps the sort of man she sometimes watched from the gallery at Mass or at evening devotions, a quietly-moving, self-contained man who walked with his parents, caring for them.

Maud, knocking on her bedroom door, interrupted her reverie.

'Ruth,' she said. 'I was thinkin' of lambs' kidneys for the day?' The plump red face was around the jamb of the door, the soft dough-white fingers clutching the knob.

'Sounds fine, Maud. Fine.'

'An' with potatoes an' spinach an' all?'

'Perfect, Maud. That'll be just perfect.'

The maid grinned a fine turnip grin and withdrew, satisfied. Ruth turned back to the mirror and smiled to her reflection. The day was fair. She would take a walk down by the sea. She would walk the cove where she often walked, to savour the ocean, its rhythms, its silence, and the peace its own movements created in her. To allow the sea to take away her consciousness so she could simply attend, the quality of that attention growing ever purer.

Maud knocked again.

'Sorry, Ruth, but I was thinkin', seein' as I'm for Mahon's stores, an' Mr McTiernan said he'd fancy some herrin's?'

'Yes Maud, do get some. Herrings and potato cakes, with caraway seeds. Wonderful tomorrow?'

'Grand so!'

Ruth watched the man that evening from the small barrier of grass at the back of the cove. She watched his alien bulk suddenly appear in her cove as if he owned the place. For a moment she felt as if he had usurped her kingdom and she resented the fact. But she watched, perplexed, as he leaped on the rocks that stretched out into the sea. Until she saw the seal, how close the man came to it, how it seemed to accept him. She crouched behind the low ditch of grass and sand lest she interrupt the dream. And as she watched him she exulted at last in the evening and in the man's presence in her cove. When he turned from seal and sea and began to make his way across the sand, she moved too, instinctively, intending to encounter him.

Later, much later, she was conscious that to be walking together in the near darkness was an unacceptable thing. They were male and female, far from Eden's garden. Yet they felt themselves to be old and wise beyond the sum of their years. Nor did they need to speak overmuch. The night spoke around them. The day had spoken. Seal and sea and the great dome of the sky had brought them together.

In the hallway, when she had closed the door behind her, she stood a long, long while. The floor tiles shone with a faint reflected light and the mirror in the high hallstand reflected warmth. Softly she reached her hand and drew the bolt on the door behind her. Rather to keep her sense of joy intact about her than with any sense of castellation, for the bolts are never shut on island doors. Mintues passed while the sounds she had heard during that wondrous day faded back into the sound of her own breathing and when, eventually, she sighed, she began to fear lest the beating of her heart disturb the house.

July 1997

The disco; there and not there . . .

Jackie Finnegan came to the foyer of the hotel to collect her. She was ready. She heard the strong purring engine of the motorbike come powerfully into the grounds of the hotel. She looked out of the window. He was sitting on the bike, feet on the ground at either side, sitting proud as a black cock in his leather gear, revving the engine, sure of himself, impatient. He was five minutes early. He must wait. She saw him remove his helmet and place it on the seat behind him. She peered from around the flimsy curtain of the window. His eyes scanned the front of the hotel, the engine still running quietly beneath him. At last he switched it off, pushed down the stand and got off slowly. He moved back a little from the bike and eyed it proudly. It gleamed, its handlebars slightly turned to the right, its chrome sparkling, its purple engine hood cockatoo-wild and proud. She felt a short, strong revulsion as he held himself by the crotch of his black leather biker's suit and hoisted himself, then turned, the helmet still graceful on the back seat, and headed for the door of the hotel. God he was tall, gangly, long and writheful, like a walking tree. She turned back to the mirror. She applied more of this and that to her face. She practiced her smile in the mirror. Now, she was ready.

*

Marty did not come home to his mother's house all that day. After buying her chips and a Coke, he and Danielle had sat a while on the low wall beside the takeaway, chewing and watching the holiday cars pass by, the shapes and sizes and colours of them, the equipment – canoes, surfboards, kayaks – packed carefully on top. There was a sense of frenzy about it all that made Marty shudder and long again for his own cove, and silence. When she left him to go back to her hotel, Marty headed listlessly back towards the shore and to the cliffs, sorry not to have found the courage to offer to go to the disco with her. He couldn't face all that noise, that frantic swirling of lights, the shouting, the desperate attempts to find a girl to dance with him, the constant anguish of wondering whether he should have the courage to edge such contact further.

Danielle Lohan came slowly down the wide stairs of the hotel, conscious of the effect of her young and filled-out body. Jackie watched her, a great grin on his thin face, his hands thrust indolently into the pockets of his leather trousers. Oh he was a confident young man, master and crafty and certain. She smiled at him as she reached the bottom step and he came forward quickly and gave her a kiss on her right cheek. He stepped back, raised his right hand in a quick salute and said, 'Hi!'

She brushed her cheek lightly with her hand, the small black handbag affixed to her wrist catching her momentarily on the neck and nicking her. She grimaced a little angrily and he laughed, catching her quickly by the elbow and propelling her across the small foyer to the door.

'Wait, just wait a moment, will you?' she said. 'I just want to tell my parents . . .'.

She turned towards the lounge where her parents were having their after-dinner brandy. She closed the lounge door and moved a little to the side. She leaned back against the wall, breathing heavily. She saw her parents sitting near one of the windows but she did not approach them. Instead, she went quickly to the bar and ordered a vodka, neat. The barman glanced at her, glanced at her parents, then grinned and poured her the drink. She was ready once again.

Jackie held the hotel door open for her and she smiled up at him and passed through. He watched her, his eyes moving rapidly and in admiration from her heels and ankles, up along the back of her legs, those fine calves, the lovely hocks, the perfect thighs, and the exquisite swell of her buttocks under the short, black skirt. She sensed his eyes. She did not care. She was a little elated by the vodka and the speed with which she had drunk it.

He led her over to the bike. She stood back a moment, admiring it. She waited, but he made no move to mount it.

'You take the helmet,' he said, offering it.

'You must be joking! I'm not going to put that fuckin' thing on my head after all the care I gave to my hair. You must be joking! You wear it.'

He grinned again and slowly fastened on the helmet. She laughed at him; he was encased in black.

'You look like a fuckin' great slug,' she offered, 'or, I'd say, with the sting you've got in your tail, a great black scorpion.'

'The sting,' he responded, 'is not in my tail, darling. It's in front!'

'Ho ho, aren't we the confident boyo now!'

'Hop on,' he grinned.

He waited; he wanted to see her swing her legs over the bike, he wanted to glimpse that fine body hoist itself and straddle his perfect bike.

'You hop on first,' she said, 'then I'll get on behind you.'

When he revved the bike, startling the whole hotel, she sensed at once the power of the machine and she was a little scared. But he took it gently down the slope to the road, then turned right and headed across the island. Now she relished the trip, the breeze in her hair, the freedom of the night ahead of her, the sense of utter superiority she knew before the island youths.

At that moment Marty was standing on the ledge of Tinkers' Cove; he was naked. The dusk surrounded him and away on the horizon the light was a pale grey, the sea lifting and falling softly beneath him. The light was dim over the water in the cove and only where the sea entered in under the land were the waves breaking softly, throwing back a white light. He stood a long while, savouring the breeze that softly touched his body, anticipating the cold shock that would take him, longing for that grip to snatch away from him the sense of heaviness his whole spirit knew. He stood, still as a poised heron, and waited, longing to be no more than a limpid part of the great universe surrounding him, longing to be free of all those disturbing urges and the debilitating ignorance that held him. He felt more alone than ever before, imagining the beautiful girl he had met now moving rapidly away from him into the lively and noisy world which he felt he could never enter. And again a great resentment rose in him against the tall and easy Jackie Finnegan.

At that moment the dark water below seemed to open and once again he was certain that he saw a bare female arm rise from the water and sway, as if beckoning to him. Instantly he was chilled with fear and he moved back quickly from the cliff ledge. He shook his head foolishly and moved forward, cautiously, to look down into the water. What he saw, he knew, could have been merely the breaking swell in Tinkers' Cove, a trick of the dim light and the half-light that tried to force its way into the cove from the open sea. The chill of dread still held him but he forced himself to the very edge and watched carefully down into the depths. Everything was blackness there, save for the tiny ripples on the waves that advanced slowly into the cove, then retreated after breaking without force on the end wall. As he watched he was convinced that a face was peering up at him out of the water; a woman's face, the eyes open, the mouth open too in a silent calling. The sensation vanished almost at once, leaving him again chilled with horror.

Marty had heard of people who had drowned further up or down the coast being washed up miles and miles away from where they were last seen. Perhaps this was someone like that; but he had not heard of any drownings recently. He remembered that he had seen the eyes wide open and if a body had been in the sea for any length of time that could not be possible. Suddenly, as if impelled by the sheer impossibility of his position, he flung himself into the water towards the imagined figure. He dived under the water, expecting at any moment to touch the floating corpse. He surfaced, gasping. There was nothing near him in the sea. He swam, slowly, through the cove; he dived several times but it was so dark that he could see nothing.

Marty remembered that he had seen the same thing some days before. If it had been a body then someone would have found it, or it would have drifted back out to sea and on along the coast to be washed up somewhere else. He scrambled out of the water and back up onto a low ledge; he stood, scanning the water. There was no sign. He was shivering. Impulsively he dived in again and swam towards the end of the cove. Ducking back under the water he entered the cave under the earth. He surfaced inside and could see absolutely nothing, save for the faintest memory of light at the cave-mouth behind him. Cautiously, his hand reaching for the stone roof above him, he moved further in along the cove. Further and further, and deeper into the darkness underneath the earth. As he progressed he found that though the walls were constantly narrowing, the roof of the cave seemed to slope upwards. The waves came fast and dangerous behind him, lifting him and threatening to dash him against wall or roof but he was careful. At last he found himself able to stand on what felt like a shingle beach, several feet wide, before the rough end wall of the cave. The roof was about head height and he could stand almost upright, the waves washing about his knees.

His hands felt about the end wall. He had never been in so far before. The darkness was almost beyond black and he knew a slight thrill of terror at his complete absorption by earth and sea. He could be lost in here for ever. Instantly the thought made him grope about nervously; he was half-expecting to touch that corpse as it could well have been washed in this far. His hands moved slowly about the boulders at the end of the cave and suddenly he touched something, something metallic, round and large and solid. This was no corpse. It felt like a huge ocean buoy, but as his hands moved carefully over it he felt protrusions, like spikes. He gripped two of the spikes and tried to shift the object but it was lodged between boulders. It was only when Marty turned to swim back out of the cave that the thought struck him; it was a mine, like those he had seen washed up years before from the wars within the Atlantic Ocean. He panicked and dived back into the blackness, swimming frantically now towards the faint track of light at the cave's mouth. There he dived underwater and surfaced again, gratefully, in the open cove, under a sky that was suddenly rich with stars. He scrambled quickly up the side of the cliff and onto his ledge, then reproached himself with his own fears. He stood a long time, shivering in the clear air of the night, watching up at the magnificent panoply of stars, knowing again how fragile is the human universe, and how small, too, the human heart that works within it. He would come back with a torch and examine more closely what he had found.

Jackie Finnegan moved on the dance floor like a praying mantis. He swayed in the dark that shivered and shimmied from a thousand reflected prismatic colours darting from the strobe lights in the hall. He danced always, sometimes Danni danced close by, not really with him, but there, and he grew aware of her and grinned; sometimes other girls, other young men, danced close by, in groups, in pairs, and he acknowledged them with his grin and kept on swaying in his own mantis dance. He was a seaweed frond, loose and easy in the tides. He was a limb of the willow tree, stooping and rising in the gentle air. He was Jackie Finnegan, fisherman and fisherman's son, at home on the ever shifting sea. In his hand he held a long-necked bottle of beer and he slugged from it whenever the music stopped or whenever someone came and offered him another. He was an event was Jackie Finnegan, a cause for wonder and a source of merriment.

Danni was amused, bemused, and slightly angry. She felt abandoned on the floor. And then she felt embarrassed that it was she who had come with this long and swavering creature. She thought of the long arms of the great squid that floated through the deepest waters of far-off seas, and she laughed. There were other fish in the sea and all about her there were young men, handsome and merry and easy. She knew she was attractive; she knew she was sexy as she gyrated to the rhythms. She stopped, too, and took her vodkas, making her way slowly to the bar, often accompanied by another hopeful youngster from the island or, and this she preferred, by some Dublin visitor like herself, who knew the world, who knew the story, who could stand upright and not be a fool. She chatted and smiled, and occasionally pointed out the strange creature that floated in his own miasma of music, beer and rhythms, somewhere off the middle of the floor. She was happy, she was gay, she was dizzy, she was young.

At some uncertain hour the music stopped and the white and somewhat sickly lights came on to announce that all this dreaming was now over. Danni could not see her date. The edges of the hall were littered with bottles and cans and the small tables had little pools of spilled liquor. She shielded her eyes from the glare and found one of the Dublin boys watching her. He was good-looking, he seemed reasonably sober and he had chatted well with her earlier on. She walked straight up to him, took him by the arm and began to urge him to the door.

'You can bring me home, can't you?' she suggested.

He smiled happily.

'Sure. And my name is Ronan, in case you've forgotten.

Ronan Brannigan. We danced earlier, you and I. Where are you going to?'

'Ronan. Of course. I remember. I have to go to the Shoreside Hotel.'

'Right. I have the ancient daddy's car. But perhaps we can drive down to the beach first for a while?'

She hesitated. She felt elated after her night's dancing, after the vodka. But she knew she was in control.

'OK,' she said. 'I could do with a short stroll on the beach. Get rid of all the fuckin' fumes that are filling up my head.'

Ronan gloated at his good fortune. She was pretty, very pretty. And sexy. It appeared she might be easy. He gripped her arm tightly and they went out into the night.

There was a swirling, noisy group of young people moving and chatting around the empty barrels outside the end wall of the hotel. Ronan gripped Danni's arm tightly and guided her straight through the group, towards the hotel car park. Danni felt the cold night air touch her and reach quickly the whole way inside her head, making her suddenly dizzy. She stopped, drew her arm from Ronan's and leant for a moment against the wall. She heard her name.

'Danni! Danni! Where the fuck are you?'

It was her beau, the long streel of misery, Jackie Finnegan, coming out from the gang milling about the hotel door, searching for her. He held his biker's helmet in his right hand.

'Are you OK?' he asked her, reaching to hold her.

She jerked away from him and at once regretted it. She felt nauseous and leant back quickly against the wall, her head down between her arms. Jackie started to laugh. In the sickly aura of the car park lights he looked, in his black clothes, like an upright beetle. She watched him out of the corner of her eye. He was ugly, then, she knew, ugly and stupid and nowhere near her league.

'Fuck off!' she hissed at him.

He laughed the louder and caught her gently about the waist.

'You heard the girl, you dirty bastard! Leave her alone!' It was

Ronan's voice, confident and protective. He tried to pull Jackie away from her.

Jackie's grin was dangerous. He stood to his full height, turned from Danni and without warning struck Ronan with all his strength a powerful blow on the shoulder with his biker's helmet. Ronan yelled and staggered away, clutching his shoulder. Jackie followed, laughing loudly. He raised the helmet again and struck Ronan a blow straight into the stomach. The young man groaned and doubled up, gasping. Jackie raised the helmet above his head and brought it down with all the strength of both hands on the back of Ronan's neck. Without another sound Ronan fell flat on his face on the dirty ground of the car park and lay still.

Jackie turned back and took Danni forcefully by the arm.

'Fuckin' tourists!' he said, good-naturedly. 'Don't know how to behave. Come on, girl, you and me's goin' for a little spin.' She went with him, knowing from the grip he had on her arm that she had little choice. Now she was scared – of his violence, his determination and of the darkness of the island beyond the car park. He was humming softly to himself as he sought out his bike at the entrance to the park. Then he turned to her and offered her the helmet.

'Put it on!' he said, softly. 'You'll want it. An' it looks better on you than it does on me. Let's have a bit of fun.'

Without a word Danni fastened the helmet on her head. She looked back into the car park but could not see Ronan in all the movement of the crowds. It would be best to get away from here at once; she did not want trouble with the police or with other guests or the hotel. Jackie was already on the bike and had it purring gently. He waited, glancing at her, grinning. He watched back at her as she hoisted herself onto the saddle behind him and he grinned in delight at the shapely turn of her thighs. He felt her settle herself behind him. Her arms came around him and held tightly. He revved the bike and turned it slowly out onto the island road.

October 1951

A night under the stars...

Emily Vesey became a customer for one of Aenghus Fahey's coffins. She had passed her short life in a dream of ghosts. It was a dream that gradually grew into a faith that would be envied by hermit, saint and presbyter. A faith that enters, like a miasma, into every niche and cranny of a life till each word and gesture is informed by it.

The Veseys lived in a low house surrounded by small fields that were wet and rush-ridden. The fields and yards were below sea level, sinking into earth where generations of creatures had already sunk into watery dust. There was a stream that was formed from the seepages of other fields and drains higher up the slopes of the valley; the stream spread lazily, rather than flowed, through the bottoms that were the Veseys' holdings. And when it rained – and it rained – the stream swelled and spread its flattened limbs out further along the Veseys' meadows until everything was water, water and the leavings of water.

Old JohnJoe Vesey had dreamed the Irish dream and had stuck to the land – because he owned it and it had been bequeathed to him and his, after centuries, by freedom. He had spade, shovel and fork, scythe and rake and slash-hook; these were real and firm to his grasp and he was free to wield them where he chose.

He had the age-old faith of his fathers that kept him easy in his misery, surviving along the callows of his valley. About his home a few tall salleys grew and they hissed and whispered through the long attrition of mists that drew their spectral shapes across the floor of his world. And in her bed, cold and snuffling and uneasy, Emily named those shapes, they were the Father, the Son and the Holy Ghost; they were incomprehensible words like sacrament and transubstantiation, comprehensible words like sin, and mortal and perdition. She watched them form, she felt them pass, they were ghosts that touched her and left her shivering with the delightful chill of obedience.

But the other ghost, the real one, she ignored until it had taken her lungs wholly to itself and hollowed out her breast and painted her flesh to the livid whiteness of lime. The Veseys could not afford hospital nor sanatorium nor night nurse. They could scarcely afford a doctor. And in any case, wasn't this ghost well-known to them all? A ghost that, having begun to haunt the house, could scarcely be persuaded to depart?

'We, the people of Ireland, humbly acknowledging all our obligations to our Divine Lord, Jesus Christ, Who sustained our fathers through centuries of trial . . .'.

JohnJoe Vesey believed that tuberculosis was a punishment sent to mankind for natural leanings towards evil. JohnJoe, with a neighbour helping, carried his daughter – bed and young woman together – out into the good God's open air and had her sleep under the stars where only the angels breathe. The nights were black and silent, save when the salleys sighed and whistled. She looked up to see the moon lying in a deckchair high on the blackness of the sky; she heard a dog barking at some formation of the stars. She could see them, she was sure of it, the angels passing among the constellations with their torches and their great white cans of milk. The night sky echoed again and again to the sound of the dog's barking, as if the world were a hollow drum and the dog's barks were old bones rattled.

Emily's coughing echoed to the coughing of cattle through the night. She retched and bled and offered up her pains for the suffering souls in purgatory. The family heaped cover upon cover over her but she could not get warm. At late dusk and again at early dawn a blackbird sang sweetly in the thin branches of the salley above her and she smiled her weak and grateful smile towards the bird. Between late dusk and early dawn she hardly slept, her body sometimes shivering with a cold that felt it must snap the bones inside her; and sometimes she sweated helplessly, tossing and turning in a fever that left her drenched, as if she had spent hours crossing some great salt sea to be thrown up eventually, spent, on a cold shore.

Morning, when she surfaced from her broken sleep and near-sleep, the darkness stayed in her eyes and she never glimpsed again any of the glories of creation. She lay on through her own darkness, judging dawn and dusk only by the songs of her blackbird, stilled as a stone that has been dropped into the muddy bottom of a stream.

At noon, on a day of frantic winds and slanted rains, JohnJoe Vesey relented, allowing that God seemed to want to take his daughter, and the remedy of the centuries, the pure air, would not cure her. They brought her back indoors, lifting bed and its burden through the gales. They tried to give her mutton broth and she smiled to them out of her darkness. She was a wisp of dried grass. Father Crowe gave her the final sacrament, there was a small white candle lit in the dimness of the room beside her. He touched her senses with the holy oils and she passed without complaint into her own twilight where her breathing was almost impossible to detect. But her pulse still stirred. She lay, unmoving, under the generously bleeding heart of Christ; she lay so quietly that she was like a snowflake lying on snow and they only had to wait until she melted away.

The long, slow day moved into the longer, slower night. JohnJoe sat by the bedside, watching. The candle sank and began to gutter. Noreen brought a new one and JohnJoe was persuaded to try and sleep. In the morning she had not stirred nor changed but her flesh, candle-wax pure and flaccid, was cold to the touch. JohnJoe held her hand a long time, and his eyes were dry and empty.

'She's gone' he said aloud. He blessed himself. He put his fingers on her already darkened eyes and he closed them. He took his bike and cycled away to Mahon & Sons–General Merchants–Providers.

'She's about five feet three or four, Anus,' he said. 'She's light now as a feather, thin as a blade a grass. Make her a box out of the cheapest timber, for she'll not be long in it. She'll fade out of it, before she's rightly settled in. God help her. God help her.'

When he got back JohnJoe found his daughter sitting up in the bed and smiling like the weak winter sunshine. He knew he was looking at a ghost. She had taken a few sips of water. She said she felt well, peaceful and well, but very, very tired. She needed to sleep. She held JohnJoe's hand a while, always smiling. Then JohnJoe and Noreen laid her back on her pillow. She lay a while. There was a distant, small gurgling noise from her throat. She was dead.

The coffin Aenghus Fahey put together was almost good. He had planed and sanded the boards with some success and had doctored faults with putty and a few well-driven nails. The tongued and grooved ends of the boards almost met. They were almost flush. He forced them and screwed them home. The varnish and fittings were exquisite. Aenghus did not charge too heavily but still he came away with a tidy profit.

Three hours after Emily Vesey was laid in the earth, the doors and windows of the Vesey house were opened wide. JohnJoe Vesey built a pyre of branches, broken boxes and dry thorn bushes and, before he threw paraffin over it and set it alight, Alice Mahon had arrived outside the garden fence. She stood there, pen and notebook busy, watching. JohnJoe nodded distantly to her and carried on with his task.

He went back into the house, took a page from an old almanac and folded it. He lit it from the open fire in the kitchen. He went back out into the yard and held the torch to his pyre. It caught with a quick whoop of hunger, then settled quickly into a petulant and irregular quiet crackling. Noreen Vesey brought out sheets and pillowcases and threw them on the fire.

Alice wrote. Sheets. Pillowcases. White.

The sheets caught and grey-blue smoke lifted away among the tips of the salleys. JohnJoe was struggling out of the house, heaving a thin brown mattress that sagged and folded itself about him. He heaved it to the fire and laid it, sideways, against the flames. A dense, sickly brown smoke began to rise.

Alice wrote. Mattress. Single. Brown.

They brought blankets, an eiderdown, a pillow.

Alice wrote.

The pillow burst with a soft sigh and a few feathers floated dreamily upwards on a draft of smoke. It seemed like a distant memory of bird flight. They brought out dresses. Jumpers. Cardigans. Shoes.

Alice wrote.

They brought out an old schoolbag. A dowdy overcoat. A scarf.

Ghostly smoke-figures moved, ragged and lethargic, about the house, the valley, the sheds; reluctant to leave, reluctant to stay. Ugly smells of loss and poverty and ignorance teased Alice Mahon's nostrils. She heard JohnJoe somewhere inside the house working with a hatchet on the furniture. He brought out, in bits, a tallboy, a wardrobe, a chair. They all went on the fire. Alice wrote. Then the bed, an off-green, off-brown iron bedstead that came out in pieces. JohnJoe hauled them down to the bottoms and flung them out into the wetness among the briars and mosses where they would spawn generation upon generation of rust-flakes. The bed springs too. And a cracked china chamber pot. Alice wrote, sucking the lead of the pencil so she could write the clearer. The fire puffed itself up and down importantly. And sparked. And blew.

When Noreen Vesey emerged carrying a picture of the Sacred Heart, when she stood for a moment out of the breathing of the fire, and when at last she threw the picture onto the blaze, Alice knew it was almost over. Noreen stood a while, watching the accumulation of a small life, the ghosts of memories and hopes and dreams, drifting away over the wet meadows. She knew that a small pool of restless ash would be left and even that, over days, would lift and shift and fall until the rains stilled it and the grass would grow back and erase it all. JohnJoe came out with a pitiful dark-green floor mat and a few rolled-up strips of wrecked brown linoleum that smoked a black smoke into the evening sky. Alice wrote once more. She closed the notebook then, folded it and put her pencil away among the mysteries of her person, blessed herself piously, and turned for home. The ghosts would hover sadly round the old house all evening and well into the night. Then they, too, would tire and be gone to join Emily Vesey in the Blessed Kingdom.

July 1997

A night under the stars . . .

With Danni perched lusciously behind him, Jackie Finnegan revved his bike and, instead of turning left and heading back towards the hotel, he turned right and began, at speed, for the further village and the road leading up the mountainside towards Keem. Danni could sense the power of the machine beneath her, she could sense, too, the determination and self-possession of the young man whose waist she was clinging to. The breeze was cool against them as he sped back across the island, down the long hill into Dooagh village, out across the small bridge, past the last houses and up the steep hill towards Captain Boycott's old home and the spectacular high road along the mountainside that swept down towards Keem Bay.

Jackie slowed and stopped at the top of the hill. The night seemed still and empty up here and Danni risked a glimpse out and down, over the high cliffs and out over the sea. The night was bright with stars and the sea shimmered with an uneasy beauty. Here and there sheep were cropping indifferently. Danni felt a small wave of nausea grip her stomach.

'Take me back to the hotel,' she ordered from behind his black-coated back. He chuckled. He turned the bike slowly, facing it back down the long and very steep road towards the village. His headlight shone strongly on the road; the mountain-side to her left lifted steeply into blackness. She shivered, even though the night was a warm one. Then he jerked the bike forward, revving the engine again, and she almost lost hold around his waist. They were speeding at once back down the incline. She could see the lights of the village in the distance, how peaceful they seemed, and how she longed to be part of that peace. She was scared now, his speed was great, the decline rapid.

Then he turned the engine off and let the bike take its own momentum down the hill. He switched off the headlight too and they were humming smoothly and rapidly along the scarcely-visible road. It was exhilarating and very frightening. She buried her head into his back and held on tightly. She closed her eyes firmly against the leather of his jacket. He laughed out loud, like a knight of old charging into the affray. The bike got faster and faster until it whizzed, the wheels now making a loud rubbery sound on the road, over the little bridge, the momentum taking it far in among the houses of the village. He stopped the machine, turned it and faced back up the hill towards Keem. Quickly the engine was on again, he revved it, and shot back the way he had just come, the lights still off, the speed terrifying in the near darkness.

When they reached the top of the hill again, Jackie stopped the bike and switched off the engine. Danni made a quick leap onto the road. She stood a moment on the low bank that verged the road. Far below she could hear the sea pound against the cliffs; the slope began gradually from beyond the bank then fell precipitously to the sea. There was a gleam on the ocean's surface from the shining stars and away on the horizon she could just make out the shape of the mountains of Connemara.

'Is that the way you get your thrills?' she asked him, angrily.

He laughed. 'It's cool, way cool, isn't it? Flyin' through the dark and the silence with the whole of the island asleep around you.'

'It's fuckin' dangerous and stupid, that's what it is.'

'It's no way dangerous, I'm in control the whole time. We

reach speeds of sixty miles an hour without the engine on. It's fabulous.'

'Well,' she said, 'I didn't enjoy it. I was scared shitless.'

He laughed again. 'And you down from Dublin an' you're scared of a bit of darkness and silence? That's stupid!'

'Take me home now. At once, Jackie. Please.'

He was silent for a while. The bike idled powerfully under him where he sat, near her, his hands itching to rev the engine once again.

Then suddenly he was gone, the engine roaring under him, the red tail light quickly moving away, leaving her standing alone and angry on the edge of the cliff. Then, as he sped down the hill, the engine died, the lights went out and she could only imagine him speeding like a ghost through the darkness. She was angry. And frightened. He was foolish enough to leave her here, alone, far from the hotel. She shivered. Away over the sea she saw the sheen of the starry sky, the heavens above her absolutely beautiful in their obedience and their calm. She stood a long while, wondering, lost, and very small.

And then, in the distance, she could hear his engine start again; once more he was on his way back up towards her. He skidded the bike to a halt beside her. His face was bright and laughing in the silver light. She said nothing.

'Hop on then,' he said. 'We'll scoot down the hill one more time an' then I'll take you back to the hotel. OK?'

She climbed onto the bike once more and he turned it slowly so that it faced back down the hill. He revved the engine loudly and then the bike took off again at a great pace, grit flung out behind it. Danni gripped him tightly around the body and closed her eyes, her head pressed in against his spine. The bike gathered speed and Jackie switched off the engine, and then the lights. Once more the bike was speeding in near silence through the darkness and Jackie whooped with delight. She clung on behind him and waited, terrified, expecting at any moment that they would veer onto the bank, down cliffs towards the sea.

At last the bike began to slow. She opened her eyes. They had crossed the little bridge and were moving along the road between the village houses. Jackie switched on the engine and the headlight and they went reasonably slowly back through the village, across the island roads and in a few minutes he drew up outside the hotel.

She got off at once and handed him back his helmet. He stayed on the bike, grinning up at her.

'Don't I even get a kiss?' he asked.

It was her turn to laugh. 'Why don't you give your fuckin' bike a kiss?' she suggested.

He watched her a moment. Then he got off and slowly bent to kiss the seat of the bike where she had been.

'There,' he said. 'Two birds with one stone.'

'You're a right fuckin' weirdo an' no mistake,' she said, turning quickly and heading back into the hotel. It was dark in the foyer but a vague light from the lamp outside shone in onto the carpeted floor. She stood a moment with her back to the door. She heard the bike move off gently down the long slope to the road. Then she heard him rev the engine again and quickly the sound of the bike faded away into the night. She shivered once. Then began to climb the stairs to her room.

October 1951

Who made the world?...

Florrie Dwyer had cautioned Wee Eddie that he must never, ever speak to anyone about his big sister. She was not to be spoken of, ever, outside their own house. He was to live and speak as if he had no sister. Because, Florrie said, she wasn't really his sister anyway, not really. She was, well, different; she was not all there, not a real, full person. Big Bucko too had warned him, holding him by the soiled wool of his pullover and lifting him off the earth, thrusting his foul-breathed face into Wee Eddie's and offering to break all his fingers, one by one, if he as much as mentioned her. She's not worth mentioning, he said; she doesn't really exist. She's wrong. She's not really there at all.

Wee Eddie came to believe it was because she was dumb and stupid. He inquired no further, of them, nor of himself.

But the boys in school were often speaking of girls, of their sisters, of their mothers, of the girls who passed in little giggling groups to and from the girls' school half a mile over the road. The boys had whispering games where they told their own disturbing stories about girls.

'She wears knickers!'

'Yeah. Pink knickers, with elastic. And a little white flower sewed on.'

'How do you know that?'

'I seen her. I seen them. She was climbin' Raftery's high gate an' I was behind her an' I seen them.'

'It must be cruel to wear knickers an' dresses an' have the winds goin' up an' down an' all.'

'And my sister wears bras!'

'Bras?'

'Bras!'

There would be an expectant silence. Unbroken.

'Did you ever see a girl naked?'

Naked. The word stung them into hurt and ignorance and shame.

'A girl's different.'

'Different? Jaysus, aren't you great to have worked that out. Course they're different!'

'They have no pricks, they have cunts!'

This from the brashest of the boys, the one with the greatest hurt. The one for whom words were soft explosions of unharnessed power. Such words were sins. They were wrong in the mouth, like chewed lemons. They would have to be whispered again, in the confessional, to Father Crowe who would scold and whine and accuse. And if you said such words, if you thought such words, and you didn't whisper them in the priest's ear then you were absolutely certain to be pitchforked into the limekiln of hell for all eternity.

In the evening, while Big Bucko was away in Donie Halpern's pub, Wee Eddie made his way cautiously up the wooden steps to the loft. He struggled with the bolt on the trapdoor and at last it shot back with an iron thud that would have alerted the long dead to his coming. He eased up the trapdoor with his hands and raised his head through the opening. He gazed around the loft. The light was already fading from outside and only one last beam fell on a small square of floor from the cobwebbed skylight.

He saw her at once, crouched in the near darkness of the furthest corner, her legs drawn up under her, her hands folded tightly over her breast. He watched her for a while. She was not scared of him. She sat more freely, smiling towards him.

Quickly he climbed up onto the floor of the loft. He strolled nonchalantly to where she was. He scuffed at the wooden floor, at wisps of hay. At the scales of mortar fallen from the ceiling.

'You OK?' he asked her.

She nodded and smiled. She had his book, his brown paper-covered book and she held it firmly against her body. Then she held it up to him, her eyes pleading. She knelt up on the floor and opened the book, her hands running lovingly through the closely-printed pages. She looked up at him again. He had his hands in his pockets. His eyes were like bluebottles, rushing and banging against the glass in a frenzy to be given release. She saw the dirt on his knees, the grey woollen stockings fallen and lolling about his half-laced, black, cracked shoes. His hair was a heather knot. She would gentle him, if she could.

He knew what she was hoping for. And he knew what he needed at that moment, too.

'Can I ask you something?'

She could not catch and hold his eyes. She nodded.

He worked with the words in his mouth.

'Do you, I mean, are you – do you wear, the boys were sayin', you know, in school – knickers?'

She was surprised. Then she was not surprised. She did not smile. She nodded. He scuffed his embarrassment about the wooden floor.

'Can I see?'

She was startled. His voice was so small. His life was so small. She thought of Big Bucko and his violence, his needs, his immediate, unavoidable demands. She was saddened. Were they all . . . ? She was still kneeling but now she sat back on her heels. She shook her head, slowly.

'Please. I'll do anything . . .'

She looked up at him. There were tears somewhere in those young eyes and she could see all the years that lay ahead of him; dark, futile years. He would be another Big Bucko, lost and menacing in his darkness. She could feel tears begin somewhere in her own eyes. She held up the little book before him and looked at him.

'Yes, I'll help you to read it . . . if, just once . . . that's all. Just once. Just quick.'

She smiled. She could bargain. She stood up slowly then and turned away from him. She raised the hem of her dress, rapidly, and let him glimpse the large knickers she was wearing, Florrie's cast-offs, washed to the dullness of old pink. He saw only a pink blur, the flesh shadowed by the dress and the gloom of the loft. He was hurt by the fullness of the flesh he could glimpse, and the way her body seemed warm and soft and welcoming. But he had seen and he was satisfied.

She squatted back down onto the floor, tucking her legs in under her, pulling the hem of her dress out over her knees. She caught his hand and tugged him down onto the floor beside her. Quickly she opened the book. Her fingers followed the first lines in the vague light left from the day. When she reached the place her finger jabbed impatiently at the words. She waited.

'That's easy,' he said, regaining authority. He read for her then, slowly, moving his own fingers along the words. 'Who made the world? God made the world.'

He saw her mouth forming the sounds after him, her fingers working like tiny ploughs over the hardened earth of the letters.

'Who is God? God is the creator and sovereign Lord . . .'

He went over it again.

'Who made the world? God made the world. Who is God? God is the creator and sovereign Lord . . .'

Over and over the questions and answers he went until he was certain she had them in her memory. Gradually the darkness took the words from the page. He was reluctant to go. He felt at peace, there in the loft beside her, the strange words still sounding in the small, vulnerable quietness that had gathered round them both.

October 1951

A candle . . .

Ruth McTiernan came awake in the darkness. For a moment, rising out of a dream, she believed herself to have been underwater. Far down where it was black, where eyeless things were moving, in the salt ocean. Down where there was stillness and such a silence that it pounded along the corridors of the brain and thudded in the engine room of the heart. She felt the impossibility of breathing, something within her lungs was crying out as if there was a living being within her, thumping at the thin wall of her breast and demanding release.

She was wet. She rubbed her hand in the darkness along her forehead and felt the moisture of her sweating. Her nightdress held to her. She breathed heavily in the freedom regained from her dreaming. The darkness of the room was all-pervasive. The house about her was silent. For a moment she touched back into the dream, wondering how she had immersed herself in its salt water. Her fingers touched the sheet. Part of it too, was damp. It felt warm to the touch. Clammy and frightening.

She got out of bed quietly. On the bedside table was a candle standing in a small blue candleholder with the tin ring for her finger to thread through. Her left hand held the candle in the darkness. Her right felt for the matches.

She held the small flame over the bed. The white-yellow glow sent huge shadows wandering over the walls. When she saw the blood, the small island of it printed on the lip of the sheet like the map of a tiny country on the edge of the world, the almost black stain chilled her into terror. She stood, unable to move, watching the stain as if it were a beast that must attack her. She heard the low bass notes of fear come forward along her mind. She knew the wild, uncertain juddering of her heart.

Her legs yielded suddenly and she was kneeling at the side of the bed as if in prayer, the way she knelt almost without thought every morning and evening, pleading with the angel to be with her, lighting her path, guiding her steps. Now her upper body fell forward onto the bed, the candle dripping a small drop of its white arterial blood onto her sheet. She was crying soundlessly, her young face distorted with the injustice of this sentence. And as she cried she coughed, a cough that caught her high in the chest and hurt her. She coughed violently, then caught and held the sheet, pressing it to her mouth. Through her tears she looked at the sheet; there was no blood and a quick surge of hope took hold of her.

She had coughed before, often, but not so badly that she had to pay extra attention to it. Everybody coughs. Everybody. She had colds, she had flu, she had gone through all of those things. Like everybody else. This would be little more than a bad flu. Perhaps some extra little catch in her coughing had damaged her lungs a little. Perhaps.

She knelt a long time, quieting herself, praying to her own special angel. She whispered a few words of prayer to her God, for that is what she had been taught to do, that God who was creator and sovereign Lord of heaven and earth and of all things . . .

July 1997

At sea . . .

When they came down to the harbour early in the morning they found Marty sitting against the pier wall. He looked unkempt and cold. The morning was bright and crisp and clouds hung on the horizon.

Marty called to them, 'Any chance of a day's work out with you today?'

Bendy considered. 'Not much work even for Jackie and me,' he replied dubiously.

'I'm willing to do anything you want me to do. All day. And I'd be happy with twenty pounds for the day, no more.'

Jackie grinned at him. 'Didn't see you at the disco last night?'

'One good reason for that. I wasn't there.'

Jackie grinned again. 'It was a great night. Me an' Danni went, an' she came with me after, on the bike.'

Marty scuffed the ground at his feet and looked down at the tiny pebbles he was loosening. He kicked a few of them off the pier and down into the waters of the harbour. The tide was high, swelling gently under the *Saint David.*

'Were you out all night, by any chance?' Bendy asked.

Marty hesitated.

'Yeah. I spent the night in your boat, under your tarpaulin.'

Bendy was taken aback.

'You've no right to do that, mate. That's trespassin'. An' there's your poor mother to think of. I'll bet she was worried sick. Does she know now where you are?'

'She doesn't give a shit!' Marty exclaimed.

They were silent. Bendy and Jackie busied themselves about the pier and the boat, preparing for the day ahead. Bendy went down and opened the wheelhouse. He disappeared inside.

'Fuckin' cold night to be out, I'd say,' Jackie muttered.

'I was up at the disco late,' Marty said. 'But it was too late to go in. Anyway, I don't give a bollocks about that kind of prancin' around. It's just stupid.'

'That's where the action is, but,' Jackie went on. 'That's where it's at. All the young women out of Dublin an' down from the North. All easy an' willin' an' all.'

Marty looked up at him. Jackie was clearly in great form and Marty imagined the worst.

Bendy's head peered out. 'One or two conditions, son. First, you'll do exactly as you're told all the time. Second, you'll come straight home with me to your mother's when we get back in. Third, you'll not ask to come out with me again. Unless you're a great help an' I come lookin' for you. OK?'

'OK. Thanks.' Marty got up stiffly from the base of the pier wall.

'Get down here then an' get the pot goin' an' we'll have a cup of tea.'

Towards mid-morning they were chugging over a peaceful sea towards Bendy's favourite grounds. At the stern of the boat Jackie had his usual line out and was catching mackerel. Marty joined him. He felt good; the sun was warm, the sea exhilarating and the island seemed a very great way off. He watched a gannet, not far from the half-decker, soar and dive spectacularly into the waves; he watched it surface again, a fish in its great bill.

'You had a good night with Dannielle, then?' he said quietly.

'Who the fuck is Danielle?'

'Danielle. Danni. The girl . . .'

Jackie grinned hugely but kept his eye on the line where it moved with its own small wake through the sea.

'She's a great girl,' he said. 'A beauty, no doubt about it. Fine tits. Big arse. A great lover.'

Marty was silent for a while. He could hear Bendy in the wheelhouse sing a shapeless song.

'Did you . . . you know? Have . . . em . . . sex with her?'

' "Em sex?" What the hell's "em sex?" ' Jackie was master of the moment and relishing it.

'You know. Did you make love with her? Did you have sex?'

Jackie turned his big grin towards him. 'That's none of your business, mate, but I'll let you know anyhow. Yes. An' it was fuckin' wonderful. She's brilliant. Jaysus but she's what you might call experienced, no doubt! Like meself, man, like meself!'

Marty remained perfectly still. After a while he got up and fetched a line like Jackie's for himself. There were some twelve coloured and hooked feathers here and there along the gut. He flung it into the sea and played out the strong, green line. Then he sat back on the stern planks and waited. The half-decker's engine made a pleasing, regular chugging sound that was homely. Almost at once Marty felt an urgent tug on the end of his line that sent a thrill up his arm. He began to pull the line in and brought three mackerel onto the deck of the boat. For a moment he forgot Danni, and his mother, and himself. Jackie was sitting on the boards and seemed taller and straighter than ever before, that huge grin permanently on his face.

Shortly after noon they reached the fishing grounds. The sun was high and the sea sparkled and moved as if it were a child at play in a bright meadow. Together Jackie and Marty played out the great nets while Bendy kept the *Saint David* moving in a slow circle. But Bendy shouted to them that the net was knotted. He stalled the engine and they lowered the rubber dinghy they kept in the stern of the boat. It was attached to the *Saint David* by a long rope.

'Right, Marty,' Bendy said. 'You get in the dinghy and row out to where the tangle is. See if you can't free things up without us havin' to haul the whole feckin' thing back in. Jackie'll keep playin' it out, you make sure she's clear. Right? Row now, don't try the engine, rowin'll keep you in place easier. Anyways, the lock is on th'oul' engine an' the key is here in the wheelhouse.'

Marty was happy in the small dinghy that rode the waves and hollows like a child at play. The long rope played out as he rowed carefully to where the net was disappearing into the sea. As he loosened the mesh from around one of the marker buoys he heard Jackie shouting. He looked up. Jackie was jumping up and down on the stern of the *Saint David* and pointing out to sea. There was a large trawler bearing down on them. It seemed to have appeared out of the very haze of the horizon itself and Marty sat and watched it with admiration.

It was high in the water, the bows reaching towards the sky with a great suggestion of pride and power. The engines were softly powerful, the sound travelling across the sea towards the dinghy.

He grew frightened suddenly. The great ship was coming right towards the stern of the *Saint David* and showed no sign of reducing its speed. Marty could see two sailors standing on the bow. One of them held a rifle. The other was watching out towards the half-decker and Marty could see he was laughing heartily. Bendy and Jackie stood stunned and helpless as the huge boat came looming down at them.

Suddenly it began to turn and was heading now directly for the space between half-decker and dinghy. It missed the stern of the *Saint David* with only a few metres to spare and as it crossed the rope that bound the half-decker to the dinghy, Marty was lifted bodily into the air and flung out into the ocean. He rose quickly and turned to watch as he treaded water. The vessel had sheared right through the rope and the dinghy was floating upside down some distance from where the trawler had passed across. The great wake washed over Marty and pushed the dinghy further and further away. Wave after wave came from the trawler's wake and Marty fought against them, enjoying the struggle, feeling more exhilarated than he had ever felt before.

He could see the trawler moving faster and faster into the distance.

Bendy had brought the half-decker about and was steaming carefully towards the swimmer. Marty swam strongly towards the dinghy and reached it as the boat drew close. He worked it upright with some difficulty, caught the rope and swam to the stern of the *Saint David.* Soon, dinghy and Marty were safely back on board.

'If they think they're goin' to drive me away from me own grounds, them bastards has another huge thing comin' to them,' Bendy said.

'They could a killed us all,' Jackie said, breathless with anger.

'They could easy a killed Marty, him in the dinghy, an' not a chance. Next time he'll have to unlock th'engine. Jaysus! They're wild dangerous whures.'

Marty laughed. 'I enjoyed it,' he said. 'But you'll have to do something about them or they'll destroy you. And I think I have an answer for them. I think I have.'

Marty went into the wheelhouse while Bendy and Jackie wound in the rest of the rope from the dinghy and played out the nets. He dried himself off, laid his wet clothes out on the bow of the *Saint David* and came back on deck wrapped only in a towel he had found in the wheelhouse. The day was warm. Marty was alert with joy and the exhilaration of the encounter.

Towards evening, as the half-decker made its way homeward, Marty's clothes were dry and he joined Bendy in the wheelhouse to dress.

'Was there some special reason you wanted twenty pounds, then?' Bendy asked him. 'You know I'm fond of your mother and I don't want anythin' to go wrong between her and you. Tell me. What's goin' on?'

Marty hesitated. 'I swiped a twenty pound note from her bag yesterday morning, and I know she needed it for groceries. I feel very bad about it and I just wanted to earn it back for her. I'll give it straight into her hand and tell her I'm sorry.'

'Ha! Good man. I thought there was somethin' like that in it.

She's a fine woman, your mother. Has had her share a pain an' bother down the years. You should be good to her. She deserves some kindness for all she's been through.'

'I know, Bendy, I know. But I get upset sometimes. She won't tell me who my father is, and it causes me a lot of worry and bother.'

'Ah, sure maybe it's better that way, that you don't know who the man was. There's none around here as I know that knows who your father was, an' we all stopped explicatin' about it way back.'

Marty laughed. 'It wasn't you then, Bendy?'

Bendy looked at him. His face was rigid with anger. 'You little bollocks,' he hissed. 'I'm fonder than ever of your mother but I have enough respect for her, an' you ought to know that well, not to try an' take advantage of her, an' me a married man already before you were ever thought of. Don't you ever talk like that again!'

Marty grinned. 'You're a good man, Bendy Finnegan. I'm grateful to you for taking me out today. I'm happy too about the Spanish boat, I enjoyed the excitement. And I have an idea I want to tell you about, if you'll give me a chance.'

October 1951

Building . . .

From her small window Florrie watched her son, her Big Bucko. If the agony of his coming had endeared him to her in a special way, the agony of her awareness of Angelica, still in her care, had aged her far too quickly. She knew, of course, the things that were going on up in the loft. But how could she manage her Big Bucko now? How could she manage him when he came home late from Donie Halpern's pub, his eyes blazing and his head a mush of needs and urges? Florrie prayed that no great harm would come of it so long as she lived. That Angelica would not be made with child. That was all. The promise she had made to her husband could extend no further than her own death. Florrie Dwyer would be free then of that promise on the day she knew that Angelica would at last be able to make her own way in the world, in that Ireland where all young women moved warily down a valley of tears, labouring.

If Florrie had known the word *trundled*, she would have articulated it. He moved that way, her Big Bucko. He had harnessed the donkey to the cart, calling out strange cotton wool sounds to the ass every now and then as he worked. Eventually, as if the hours of the day were a great lake and he could wade through them without haste or pressure, Big Bucko was walking slowly, holding the reins about the donkey's mouth, leaning gently against the grey, mid-morning air, leaning forward as if his whole body pushed against a wind, heading out, as if there were no purpose at all in living, no point to it, simply allowing the day, the earth, the animal, to lay whatever urge was in them on his soul. At last he was gone. Florrie looked once at the hull of the shed with its secret burden and again, as so often before, her own being sank under the demands of a sadness she could not control. She turned from the window back into the morning ashes of the room. As soon, oh as soon as ever she knew the girl was ready for service, somewhere, far away, very far away . . .

Big Bucko followed the day back to his own small area of bog. The iron rim of the cartwheels crunched and ground on the road and the hard-toed mincing steps of the donkey offered their plodding counterpoint. Small dustings of turf-mould performed a dervish dance on the old floor of the cart and sometimes Big Bucko shouted at the ass, a lazy, contented sound of pleasure, or perhaps indifference, before the rhythms of the movement.

He left the road, leading the animal down over a stone-strengthened causeway, into the bog. The cart track was soft and deeply rutted and the great, spoked wheels sank into the ruts and went almost silent, except when the axle groaned or the boards of the cart worked lazily against each other. Grinding on. In all directions the moorland stretched to the low hills. There was a fragrance from the heathers, the bog cotton, the secret, hidden plants of the bogways.

Big Bucko guided the donkey and cart off the track, over a rough gangway of old planks he had laid across the deep cutting years ago. He brought them over to the small clamps of turf he had built some months earlier, backing the reluctant animal, pushing him, beginning to curse. Then he stopped and surveyed the work before him.

Six times he journeyed with the ass and cart from house to bog and back, filling the cart with the sods, forking those that were dried ill-shaped creatures with veins of roots and heathers up onto the cart, tipping the load out by the scraggy furze hedge near the house and forking them into the beginnings of a clamp before heading out again. All slowly, deliberately, without waste of effort; with curses sometimes, animal burblings, vacant glances at the world about him, often gobbing loudly into the ditch on either side of the road. Twice he stopped in the bog, opened his fly and urinated out into the bog-holes with a great sigh of pleasure. In the evening Wee Eddie would help with the building of the clamp, the slow, dark and shapely treasure house that would see them warm and would feed the stove through the year.

He stooped and forked, lifted and flung, all with a deliberate slowness that made his body seem a natural part of the bog lands where he laboured. He worked with such strength and rhythm that his body scarcely grew weary, such optimum use did he make of his reserves of energy. When the darkness came, and he and Wee Eddie had to call a halt to their building, there was a fine dusting of turf-mould on his clothes, his face, his hands, and a thicker, blacker line under his nails. He had developed an exacting thirst. He set off, after supper, to walk the long mile to Donie Halpern's pub.

November 1951

At sea . . .

It was morning. Ruth dressed herself in her brightest colours; a purple blouse singing with yellow flowers, her best skirt, purple, too, and her special coat for special days, God-days, Mother-Mary-days. Today was special; Eoin had told her it would be cold where they were going. She left the house walking proudly upright, holding her body as if the world were a place of untainted joy, she walked as if to a festival, her pale face carefully touched into bloom.

He was waiting by the pier. How her heart sprang when she turned the corner of the fuchsia-lined lane and saw, simultaneously, the bright sparkle on the sea and the tall, strong figure of the man she had met. How he turned from ropes and fishing-pots and stood to meet her, moving forward eagerly, his wildered face surprised into beauty by the surging of his joy. She stopped herself from running. She waved. His hand lifted in greeting and at once the knowledge of the illness she was nursing struck her a more deadly blow of loss than she had yet known. She staggered a little at the force of the sorrow that struck her.

'Are you alright?' he called.

She nodded, breathless for a moment. Then he was beside her.

'Out of breath, that's all. Must be the walk, all the excitement.'

He smiled at that. He was unsure, his hands more awkward than he had ever known them. Quickly she raised her face to his and kissed him, softly, on the cheek; she took his big hand in hers and they walked together towards the pier.

As they started out on the sea it was as gentle to her as if they were walking on the water. His slow strokes with the oars were his big, manly strides. She sat in the stern, facing him. She watched his body move, the rhythms elegant; man, oars, boat and ocean like one flesh. They moved northwards, keeping near the rocks along the shore. With each pull on the oars she could feel the thin, frail craft thrust forward, the bow rising over the water, the stern where she sat sinking lower until the level of the sea almost touched the gunwale.

They crossed the mouth of Blacksod Bay. Their eyes met. They smiled. For now they had only to deal with the sea, the small boat that seemed to be part of the sea, growing out of each low wave, growing into the next. He had to deal with the current that moved swiftly and powerfully out to his left, with the gentle push against him of the slip-waves. She had to deal only with her own balancing against the movement of the curragh, to learn the touch of the wood of the gunwale, the occasional spitting of salt water thrown against her hands.

They entered a larger bay that curved away from them under cliffs. The cliffs rose steeply as the land lifted into the slopes of the mountain. Eoin kept the curragh moving with the curve of the landfall, staying some two hundred yards from shore.

They approached the small caves and shelves of rock before the cliffs soared precipitously above them. The basalt pillars, the cathedral reaches of the cliffs, were awe-inspiring. Never had she seen these cliffs before. And then, on the rock shelves, they saw the seals, dozens of them, their dark-grey bodies lurching and slouching on the rocks, their coats shining in the sunlight. Their strange grunting noises carried over the water. They moved about, they lay, gossiping and squabbling, like a crowd of people waiting for the beginning of a football final.

'Oh God,' Ruth whispered. 'What an incredible sight!'

Slowly, Eoin lifted the oars from the water and held them. The boat still moved forward, silent except for the soft slap of the sea against its sides. He grinned, relishing her wonder.

'It's like Mass,' she said. The shifting congregation on the rocks under the high pillars, in worshipful homage to sea and sun and cliffs, their rounded heads intent on the rhythms of their own living, their slow shifting and grunting like the shuffling and coughing of the people, their low sounds like the muffled, half-embarrassed responses to the litanies and blessings of the priest. She saw some of them slip off the rocks, soundlessly, into the sea. Others came clambering suddenly out of the water, flopping back onto the rocks and dragging their suddenly cumbersome flesh across the clefts and edges. They bickered, they scolded, held counsel, they sang, secure and certain in their own aisles, on their own rock pews, under their own steeples.

Gently Eoin rowed the curragh closer. This could have been a congregation aware of an alien presence among them, but as yet they had given no sign. She could see the plumped bodies and rounded heads, the great black watchful eyes, the whiskers. As this visitation from the world of humans came closer, the muttered prayers of all those souls grew hesitant, stammered a while and then fell silent. Eoin lifted the oars just over the water and the boat drifted through an eerie silence in which Ruth felt, not scared or threatened, but embarrassed somehow, an intruder, as if she had been caught in an act of sacrilege. They drifted. All the heads of that stilled congregation turned towards them. And then, with dignity, almost without sound, they slipped back into their other world where the intruders would not, could not, follow.

The boat moved on a quiet ocean. All around them, below them, she knew the seals were moving, in their element, a world peopled by ghosts, or angels. But now they gave no sign at all to the ocean's surface of their presence. A cormorant came flying low towards them, its rapid wing-beats audible, like quick and hurried breathing. It came, swift and directed as an arrow, passing by the curragh with complete indifference, the long neck stretched out, the wing-tips now and then stippling the surface of the sea.

'The black hag,' Eoin said, quietly.

She smiled at him though she felt suddenly uneasy, that silence, that abandoned landfall.

'Shall we go back?'

He dipped the oars and the curragh moved again. He rowed strongly, moving in a wide arc out of the grip of the bay. For a while the curragh headed directly for the open sea. She looked back. Already the seals were re-emerging, back onto their rocks, into the regular patterning of their lives. The curragh moved swiftly, the strokes impelling it towards the current. And then, almost suddenly, they were taken by the rush of water, the curragh's bow gripped, and turned. She could feel the power that had taken them as almost at once the boat was moving at speed, water swirling by. She uttered a quick scream of fright.

'It's OK. The sea is kindly, the current will guide us. It's OK.'

He grinned, his hands reaching towards her. She leaned forward and took both his hands in hers. Swiftly the boat moved, the current taking them out from the bay and past the headland, southward, the ocean narrowing between the islands. She had sensed there was a harmony between craft and man and ocean, a certainty and pleasure in the design and balance. Around them the waters seethed, yet the curragh moved smoothly, as a seal would move. The sound of the water soothed her; she was at peace again.

They had been swept back in a few minutes to the point from which they had set out almost an hour before. He pointed to the small whitewashed house back from the shore.

'My house,' he said, and she thought she had never seen anything so peaceful, where it nestled in the green folds of grass, the sun gleaming on its white walls. They were part of it then and the ocean opened out again before it would close, miles further down, towards the sound. He picked up the oars and began to ease the boat out of the current towards the calmer waters on the shores of the larger island.

'What would happen if you just let the boat go with the current?'

'It would sweep into the sound. There's a fierce whirlpool. If it got free of the whirlpool it would be carried out into the open sea. At the mercy of the Atlantic.'

He was rowing the boat slowly in towards the pier.

'It would be a wondrous thing,' he said, 'to be taken by all the forces of the world. Whipped up and taken, by the tides, the storms. Great, overwhelming waves. A night filled with a wildness of things; to be a tiny, dependent part of all that. To be taken by it. Struggling hopelessly against it. To go out fighting.'

She looked curiously at him.

'Do you believe the hand of God is a kindly one?' she asked.

He turned away from her, looking over his right shoulder for bearings as he rowed.

'We are taught so.'

'Yes, but have you found it so?'

He turned back and looked at her. He was silent a while. He thought of his small island and the crops of stones it produced. He thought of his father's hands. How his mother had lost all semblance of womanhood to labour, how she had come to look brown and dried and failed. He looked into the clear eyes of the girl in the stern of his boat. And he smiled, a bright, open-mouthed smile that made his own eyes brighter still.

'I have found it so,' he said.

She laughed softly at the clear intention of his response, but the laughter shook her chest suddenly and she coughed, a long, painful coughing that turned her face pale as the plumage of a gull and she bent forward in her seat, burying her mouth in the handkerchief he had quickly proffered.

'I've made you catch cold,' he scolded himself, rowing more urgently towards the landing place.

She kept her body bent, her face hidden. When he looked away again, over his shoulder towards the pier, she glanced quickly into the handkerchief. There was a small stain of dark blood. She sat up straight with the shiver of cold that took her and she hid the spoiled linen from him in the sleeve of her dress. He saw the shiver and he blamed himself for bringing this beautiful, delicate young woman into the harsh and demanding environs of the sea. He slewed the curragh round to take the low side of the pier wall.

'I'm sorry,' he said. She seemed small and fragile as she sat shivering in the stern of his boat. He shipped the oars, the drops of sea water falling off the blades onto the timbers of the boat. He stood up expertly and held the wall with both hands, guiding the curragh towards the pier steps. She smiled up at him. He was so certain of his world, so powerful. She suffered then from a sudden, overwhelming awareness of loss so that she could scarcely stand and he lifted her carefully from the boat and held her, cold and shivering, against the protecting warmth of his own body.

July 1997

Questions . . .

It was late evening when Bendy drove his old battered red van up to the front gate of Angie's house. With him, Marty was quite invigorated and excited by his day at sea. He hurried into the house, calling. The woman, visibly shaking, came out into the hallway at once and threw her arms about her prodigal son.

'You're back, love,' was all she said. 'You're back.'

''Course I'm back,' he answered, trying to draw away from her. Bendy stood grinning in the doorway.

'A fine young worker you have there, Angie,' he called, his big frame blocking out the last of the light from the day.

'Where were you?' she asked. 'Since yesterday?'

'I spent the night down by the pier. I wanted to be out today, with Bendy, on the fishing. I wanted to earn the money to pay you back. I took it yesterday.'

And half proudly, half shyly, he handed the twenty pound note to his mother. She took it, hardly remembering, only faintly knowing what he was doing, but in front of Bendy she felt she could say little. Marty lowered his head, but he was smiling quietly. He glanced at Bendy, then moved quickly from them into his own room. Angie hesitated.

'Come on in, Bendy,' she said. 'I'll make a pot of tea. And

thank you for looking after him for me. He has the heart scalded inside me.'

As they sipped tea in the warm dusk of the kitchen, Bendy plucked up a little of the boldness he knew when he was on his boat.

'Angie,' he began. 'You know I think that Marty is a really fine young fella. What's wrong with him is only – he has no father about. A father could help him with his growin' up. Help him with his young man problems. You know. Girls and stuff. I mean, tell him how to carry himself along. Now, Angie, you know, too, I've always been fond of you and my thoughts are always with you, ever since my own poor Maudie died.'

His courage failed him again, he could not see what sort of expression prepared itself in her eyes to answer him. The evening outside was beautiful; they could hear the sounds of a thrush somewhere over the fence. The sea, close by, murmured faintly to them. He gathered his courage again.

'Now, Angie. I've been good to your Marty. I'm fond of him. He's a good lad. I'd make him a good da. And I think, Angie, if only you'd think a little bit about it, I'd make a good husband to you. For what's left of the rest of our days, for each of us, why don't we get together and ease the burdens for one another. I'm offerin' marriage, fuck it! That's what I'm sayin'. An' between the two of us – you with your house here, me with mine, an' the boat, an' the fishin an' all to that – we could combine well, have two sons between us, an' be comfortable an' happy together. Fuck it! I found that fierce hard to get out a me. Think about it, there's a good woman, just think about it.'

There was a long silence. Angie had sat down, slowly, on the other side of the old wooden table from him. She held her cup in both hands, up before her mouth. She could scarcely see him now, just that outline against the dimness of the window. But she felt cold again, and an old dread came over her like a miasma. She knew she could not answer him, not now, not until the shock of his proposal could free her veins and limbs from tension. He sensed it.

'There!' he said. 'I've said it. Now I'll be gone. There's a nice wee salmon in the bag there for you. An' you don't have to answer me until you give it a good long think. Please, Angie.'

He stood up, slowly, and his big shape loomed heavily in the room.

'I have me own sorrows an' loneliness, you know,' he said softly. 'Though maybe you wouldn't think it to look at me, or to listen to me betimes. But I'm a man, an' I get lonesome an' frustrated an' angry with the world. An' I would give all the heart and soul I have to spend my declinin' years with a gentle an' a lovely person like yerself. There now. That's it. I'll away. Thanks for the tea. An' anytime you want me to take wee Marty with me out on the ocean for a day's work, even to give you an ounce of space and freedom, just say it, an' it's done.'

He moved then, slowly, past her towards the door. She still sat, half petrified, the cup to her face. As he passed her he laid his hand so gently on her shoulder that it felt like the merest breath of warm air though she shuddered at the touch. He noticed it, however, and he did not know whether he ought to be hurt at her sensitivity to his touch, or pleased that he had drawn a response. He hesitated again, drew a deep breath, and then he was gone. She heard the front door close gently behind him. Her body sank a little on the chair and she closed her eyes to the dusk about her.

She sat for a long time, lost in herself and in the past. Gradually the darkness settled around her, the birds beyond the house ceased their songs, only the distant sound of the sea persisted. She felt a strange comfort in her silence, in the cocoon of darkness and space in which she sat. She felt no comfort from Bendy's proposal, nor from that of Edward some time before. She knew only a powerful isolation that made her feel as content as she could be, as if, for the moment she could tell herself she had no responsibilities, that everything would be provided for her, that she had no response to make to life but to let it be, let come what may come, let pass what may pass. She sighed.

Suddenly Marty's voice, quietly urgent, broke the spell.

'Are you alright, mother?'

She opened her eyes suddenly; it was almost wholly dark yet she could see him, her son, sitting quietly in a chair just inside the door. She had not heard him come in.

'You gave me a start. How long have you been sitting there?'

'Not long. I'm sorry to startle you. Are you OK?'

'Yes, yes, I'm fine, just enjoying a period of peace and quiet.'

He hesitated.

'I'm sorry if I worried you today. I didn't mean to. It's just, well, things are difficult. I don't feel I fit in anywhere. I have no friends. I don't seem to like what other guys my age like. I seem out of it. And anything that turns up that keeps me busy, that I enjoy. What's wrong with me?'

She moved as if to go to him. But she felt weary, suddenly, terribly weary.

'There's nothing wrong with you, Marty, nothing at all. You're a very fine young lad. You're just growing up, that's all.'

He was quiet again. She could not see his eyes in the darkness.

'Did Bendy ask you to marry him?'

Oh he was cute alright, wise beyond his years. She laughed.

'Poor Bendy, poor lonely soul. Yes, I suppose that's what he asked me. Yes. He's lonesome, alone in the world except for that long son of his, Jackie.'

'And what did you say? Are you going to marry him?' There was merely a quiet seriousness in his voice.

'No, Marty, no. I'm not going to marry anybody. I'm past all of that now. Now that you're almost a man yourself. No, I'll not marry.'

'And is Bendy my father, then?' Again the question was quietly put. But it startled her.

'No,' she said, emphatically. 'He is not.'

There was just a hint of anger, and of pride, in her voice that needled him further.

'I'm glad of that,' he said, still holding his own voice in control. 'I like him, but I don't think he's special enough to be your husband. Or your lover. Or my father. I'm glad.'

Again she felt like going to him, holding him, but she knew he would react against that and pull away from her.

'Who is my father, then? When are you going to tell me? Why don't you tell me now?'

'We've been over this a thousand times, Marty,' she replied, wearily. 'It was something that happened . . . and I don't want to tell you until I think you are ready for it. Or until I'm ready for it. And I'm not ready, not yet.'

'But you know it's causing me all sorts of worries, and making me think all sorts of strange thoughts? That's not good for me.'

'I know it's bothering you, I know that. But I promise I'll tell you just as soon as I think you're settling into your life, that's what I think, that's the way I feel. I want you with your feet firmly on the ground, your heart whole and your soul intact. You're nearly there now, nearly there, and then . . .' She paused. He seemed to be leaning forward towards her out of the darkness. 'Then you'll leave me,' she said, quietly. 'And that will be all for the best.'

'That makes me think you don't love me,' he said, and there was the old peevishness back in his voice, the old anger beginning. But he heard her sob quietly in the darkness and he knew she was crying softly to herself. Once again his young heart was sore for her. He came forward out of the darkness, knelt down on the floor beside her and put his strong arms about her. Then he laid his head down against her shoulder and together, for a while, they were quiet.

November 1951

An island within an island . . .

Aenghus Fahey had grown in stature since he had stepped hesitantly through the door of Mahon & Sons–General Merchants–Providers. He sat now in Donie Halpern's pub, on the low wooden form that ran the length of the wall. The island pub was a fen of smoke and fumes and dimness. The cement floor was uneven. Iron-hooped barrels of dark wood served here and there as stools and more often they were the cause of tumbles and minor accidents.

There were two men standing at the bar when Aenghus came in. They nodded at him.

'Anus!'

'Goin' on, Anus?'

Aenghus stood big inside the door.

'Charlie Pat. Murt. Min.'

'She cuttin', Anus?'

'Aye. Sure enough.' Aenghus was shaking the raindrops off his big coat.

'Wet!'

'By God. Surely.'

'That's what you'd call a fact, now, Anus, that's what you'd call a fact.'

Aenghus moved up to the bar.

'Things, Min?'

'Can't whine, sure, wha'?'

'Grand out, Anus, grand to the world. Yourself, Anus?'

'Ah, heavin' the devil by the hairs of his arse.'

Small men, both, ingrown, home men, scraping a living off the low salt fields of the west of the island, pint bottles of stout in their hands. Aenghus ordered a pint bottle, too, and a glass of whiskey to honour his standing as coffin builder to the island. Donie Halpern was a rotund, bald man, short in stature, crabbed from living in the half-dark and absorbing the fumes and tempers of the island men. He dropped the money into a drawer behind the counter, leaned his hairless, pudgy arms on the bar and relapsed into non-being.

'Weight off th'oul' legs, Min,' Aenghus called, and dropped onto the form. He drank gratefully, sawdust filling his throat and his mind, two buxom women and the wholesome premises of Mahon & Sons filling his dreams.

Charlie Pat and Murt murmured something to the cobwebs. Then a fine silence settled on the dimness of the pub, and occasional slurps and sighs of contentment came from the three men.

'Another stout there, Donie,' Aenghus called, 'and a whiskey to wash it down.'

'You do have a fierce thirst on you, Anus,' Murt commented. 'Me an' Charlie Pat has just the first few hairs of our bottles shaved yet.'

'Must be all that lookin' into the unpapered walls of coffins all day long that does it,' Aenghus sighed. 'Keeps tellin' me I'll be a hell of a long time dead, lyin' there, with only the rain seepin' down through the muck onto my dry lips, an' then I'll be no more than dust. An' dust gives a man a killer of a thirst. Wood dust. Coffin dust. Bone dust.'

He went to the bar to collect his drinks. The door opened behind him and a great cold fist of island air pushed him in the back. Big Bucko came in.

'Min!'

'Jerr!'

'Hello, Jerr.'

'Jerr.'

Big Bucko rubbed his large hands together in delighted anticipation. He stood beside Aenghus at the bar.

'A big friggin' black friggin' stout there Donie like a good man, an' a large friggin' whiskey to kill the germs that's lollopin' about in the stout!'

Aenghus and Big Bucko, standing side by side, between them seemed to dwarf the whole pub. They were broad-shouldered, rock-chested, tree-stump-limbed. They both took up their drinks – bottle of stout in the right hand, glass of whiskey in the left. There was a large, dim mirror on the wall behind the bar. For a moment they stood and eyed each other in the glass, faint as ghosts, threatening as ghouls, looming out of a dark, dross-ridden world. Slowly they turned from the mirror, parallel lives, slowly they plodded to the form, heavily they sat, backs against the wall, cautiously apart. They drank in silence.

'We were sayin', Min,' Aenghus tried to be cheery. 'Somethin' or other. What the fuck were we talkin' about?'

Big Bucko lifted the bottle to his mouth and drank, slugging slowly from the neck while little drops of brown liquid oozed from the sides of his lips and dropped slowly over his chin. He drank until the bottle was empty. Then he lowered it, sighed deeply, closed his eyes and belched, loudly.

'Aaaaagh!' he said to the tainted air of the pub. 'Nothin' like the bogwater landin' in a torrent on a dry stomik.' His eyes still closed, his body relaxed.

Aenghus drank.

Big Bucko opened his eyes again and watched Aenghus in the mirror. He lifted the glass of whiskey and finished it off in one gulp.

'You got big eyes, Anus,' he said, and chuckled.

'Big eyes, Jerr?'

Big Bucko got up slowly, but with obvious contentment, and moved to the bar. Silently he left down the empty stout bottle and the glass on the counter. Softly he slid them both towards the big elbows of Donie Halpern. He waited. No words were spoken. Donie filled a measure into the whiskey glass and opened another bottle of stout. He pushed them slowly back along the counter. Big Bucko left his money down by the elbow and turned, moving slowly back to his place on the form. He drank from his bottle. Drops of porter came out from the side of his mouth and lingered on his chin. He snickered.

'Big eyes. Aye. Two big eyes.' And he laughed.

There was a silence.

'An' big balls! Two big balls!' Big Bucko laughed raucously at the daring of his comment. Charlie Pat and Murt were both silent, leaning on the bar, watching the mirror. Aenghus poured the rest of his stout down the side of the glass and watched the yellow-cream head form and settle. Then, in silence, he emptied the glass in one great draft. He belched.

'Some places, Min, a fella can have an intelligent conversation.' Aenghus was speaking, loudly, to the air. 'An' then there are places where you can't get an intelligent word out of a soul.' He drank his whiskey. He got up and went to the bar. 'Slap me again, Donie,' he said. 'Time passes so quick when you're havin' a party!'

Surreptitiously he was watching Big Bucko in the mirror. Big Bucko was slurping noisily at his bottle.

'Like a sucky pig,' Aenghus muttered, loudly enough.

Big Bucko looked up, lazily.

'Would you like a bottle of stout, Jerr?' Aenghus asked, softly.

'That's good of you, Anus, I'd love another one. The fluid is still only on its way down me throat, lingerin' about me chest, not yet landed on my stomik.'

'Well,' Aenghus said, savouring his moment. 'Donie here might be ready to sell you another one when I'm finished.'

Big Bucko looked at him, uncomprehendingly.

Aenghus lifted his refilled glass of whiskey. 'Let's all drink to distance, Min!' he urged, raising the glass.

'To distance! Surely!' said Charlie Pat. He and Murt lifted

their bottles and drank.

'What the fuck does that mean? Drink to distance?' Big Bucko said.

'It means that Australia is far away, and all stupid fuckers and buggers and bollickses, may they always stay at a great distance too, from decent men.'

There was a heavy silence.

'I hear tell,' Murt offered, 'that once during the war they were plannin' to drop a bum on the Kaiser.'

Aenghus slapped him on the back. 'Sure they were,' he said, 'a great big bum. But it didn't fart for them. It never went off!'

'Fart!' Charlie Pat slapped his knee in delight. 'Fart. Bum. Go off. That's a good one.'

Aenghus carried his supplies back to the bench. There was darkness through the small window of Halpern's pub. Inside the dark brown dimness prevailed. And heavy breathing. And, for a time, silence.

'Those are two fine women, them,' Big Bucko mused aloud.

'Who, now, Jerr?' asked Aenghus. 'I'm not quite followin' the sequential thread of your advanced thinkin'.'

'Your two women, Anus. Grace 'n' Alice, Alice 'n' Grace. The Mahon Sons,' and he laughed aloud again.

'Good souls, good souls,' Aenghus agreed.

'Good bodies, too, an' good money, an' a good business lyin' there for the pickin', like barnacles on a rock, I'd say,' sneered Big Bucko.

There was another silence. They drank. Ordered. Drank. Occasional low murmurs of conversation flowed between Charlie Pat and Murt who were still leaning against the bar. Otherwise the silence grew like a cobweb about them. Donie Halpern leaned on his bar. His body was still as an old fence post and his big dark eyes were filled with the past and the past was nothing to him, as was the future.

'I suppose now,' Big Bucko began again, as if he had worked things out satisfactorily in his mind, 'you, Anus, you'd consider yourself as a class of a migrant, what? A wanderin' bird. Like the goose?'

'Them days are over, Jerr, thanks be to Christ.'

'An exile. A migrant bird. A traveller. A tinker. Like them fuckin' Connors tinkers settin' up their dump back in the quarry field. An' you, landin' among us an' kindly offerin' to put us all into your crooked coffins. An' better than the rest of us, who didn't go crawlin' off the island to take the Saxon shillin'!'

Aenghus was looking warily at him. Big Bucko stared at the floor.

'An' thinks the rest of us are right eejits who don't know our bellies from our arses. Would you say that now, Anus?' Big Bucko looked up, aggressively.

'It's a sorry thing,' Aenghus attempted, 'for a man to have to quit his home and his people and his country and his ways in order to keep body and soul in one piece. And I'll tell you this, Jerr Dwyer, I'll tell you this. What a man learns is that it's a very sorry thing that a man has to leave his own native island. That's what he learns and it's a good lesson, hard learned.'

'An' that the rest of us is eejits an' I suppose he'll think he's got it up on us an' will know all about fast women an' thinks he can have his choosin' just because he's seen the arsehole of the world. Would I be right now, Anus, would I be right?'

Big Bucko staggered to his feet as he slurred out the last words. He held his bottle of stout in the air, pointing it in the vague direction of Aenghus. A small light came on in the dead eyes of Donie Halpern. Aenghus sniggered. Big Bucko swayed on his feet. Aenghus could see a black rim of bog earth clinging to the man's wellingtons.

'An' come back from the arsehole of the world an' take our women an' try to take over all we have, an' try an' put us all into coffins, bullyin' our women . . .'

'You seem to have a right mind on the women, Jerr?'

Big Bucko made a lurch towards Aenghus, the bottle slopping stout onto the floor.

'Are you accusin' me of somethin'?'

Donie raised his elbows off the bar and stood erect, watchful.

''Cos if you are I'll have you know you're not the only man on this island now, an' better men is here an' here before you, to put your big prick in where the poor women, our own poor women, can't defend themselves . . .'

Big Bucko's words slurred hopelessly. The bottle slipped from his grasp and smashed onto the floor at his feet. Aenghus leaped up and his fists were two great stones, ready to be flung. But Big Bucko's eyes were disturbed water and his body was soft as stir-about. He swayed on his feet and Donie was around the bar to catch him before he fell. Donie ushered the big body firmly, and without a word, out into the coldness of the night. Aenghus remained in the pub, silent.

Big Bucko stood in the yard, the door closed behind him. He squeezed his eyes shut and a brown world of brown lights and black mirrors went round and round slowly behind his eyes. He leaned his head back for support but there was nothing there and he sat down heavily on the ground.

He rested there awhile, on the good earth. Aenghus Fahey loomed like a mountain against his own dreams of moving, someday when Grace or Alice, Alice or Grace, came needing him, needing his body, his experience, his strength, his seed. Needing him, Jeremiah James Dwyer, the Big Bucko.

He hoisted himself to his feet, holding the wall of Halpern's pub to gain his balance. He turned for home. His breath came out in a great pillow of air and he grabbed at it, angrily. There was a moon, ringed with mist. He glanced up at it, lost his balance, and fell again. His body reeled to the left and he crumbled silently against the wet cold ditch. He lay awhile, half laughing, half cursing, until the coldness touched through to his flesh the way a memory touches the brain. He crawled onto the road, dragging himself for a short distance, moving on hands and knees and whingeing like a kicked animal. When he could walk again he tried to hold a course where the moonlight cast a cold steel glint on the road before him. At last he was turning in through the old gate. There was a small yellow light showing weakly through a window in the house. Big Bucko clumped heavily over the rough ground towards the door; living things in his vicinity heard his coming and cowered low.

Big Bucko stood at the door of the house. He shook his head, as if to shake raindrops away, although the night was frost-dry. He turned then, and looked towards the shed. It stood, outlined by the weak light from the moon. Big Bucko grunted in anger and moved towards it. Once again he stumbled and fell. He fell on his knees and elbows, his hands scrabbling through hardened mud and hen shit, as if God's long and reaching fingers had taken his legs from under him.

There are moments in a life, Florrie was thinking, when a low point is reached, a point below which it is scarcely possible to go, but a point too from which an ascent may be begun. Perhaps Angelica, in her corner of agony, had cried a prayer that smote through the night's frost and shot across God's vision like a disintegrating star. Perhaps that prayer came from the tense and quivering soul of the mother, aware but not watching from behind her own bedroom window. Perhaps the cry had come from the deepest reaches of Big Bucko's own somnolent spirit.

He lowered his head between his hands and breathed out, heavily. Then he rose, turned, and went back slowly to the house. As soon as she heard the iron rattle of the latch echo in the kitchen, Florrie sighed deeply and lay back on her bed to sleep. Big Bucko's day had ended. Another night. Another day.

November 1951

An island off an island . . .

Malachy Mulligan moved jauntily from the shed into the house. His long arms were thin and hard as sea-kelp, his skin the dark colour and smooth texture of sea-wrack. He was carrying four black sole in his hands. He whistled softly.

In the kitchen Madge too moved about eagerly. At times she hummed, a vague, murmuring non-tune. She glanced up and smiled when he came in.

'Any sign?'

'They're across on the pier. He'll take it handy, bringing her over. Gentle, like.'

'I hope to God she's not too scared of the current. Or of the island, worse still. We're a lonesome place for a grand girl the likes of her.'

Malachy scraped the scales off the fish. He laid the sole on a newspaper and sprinkled them liberally with salt. He rubbed the salt into the skin and left them to one side.

'She mightn't fancy the dulse champ,' Madge said suddenly. 'I'll set aside some of the potatoes and not add the dulse to that. Then she can have her pick of the potatoes or the champ.'

Eoin and Ruth were coming slowly from the landing place. He walked self-consciously, not daring to take her by the hand.

They stood awhile in silence at the gable-wall of the house. The island lay like a lazy animal before them, dun-coloured, wind-levelled. For a moment his heart failed him. How could she possibly consider coming to such a place, labouring across this barren territory peopled by wheatears, gulls, plovers and hares? How could she come to share a small house where his foolish old parents would be a constant press against her, their ways and manners a demand on her patience and her tolerance? A great hole opened inside his stomach and it filled quickly with a sense of hopelessness. He sagged, physically, and when she turned from the landscape to him there was a sadness in her eyes that disturbed him even more.

'It's so beautiful, here,' she said. 'So still, so wild, it's so true to itself, unspoiled. Eoin, it's a special place.'

During the meal Ruth chattered gaily. Father and mother fidgeted and fussed, delight in their faces, a touch of awe before her. They gave her salt dillisk richly veined with red and purple and brown hues, and they chewed it, laughing, and she relished it. They washed the salt away with long draughts of buttermilk.

'You like it?' Madge asked.

'Delicious!'

'I cooked some more of it, in milk, boiled it up with pepper and butter. And I've put more of it in with the mashed potatoes. We call it dulse champ, and it'll be just lovely with the fish. But you must tell me . . .'

Malachy put a large enamel pot on the table.

'Willicks,' he said smartly, and laughed.

'We cook them in sea water first,' Eoin explained. 'They're periwinkles – you can pick them right off the rocks. Then we drain them and boil them up in milk.'

They picked the winkles from their shells with long, silver pins. Malachy went out to the shed and came in with several bottles of stout, chilled from the coldhouse.

'Famine food, 'tis called,' Malachy said. 'The people survived on it. But we find it tasty and true and the stout sends it home.'

Ruth ate enthusiastically. Eoin watched her slender, elegant fingers. He watched the long, thin snail-shape of the winkle that she drew to her lips, taking it delicately. Her eyes sparkled.

Madge brought a bowl of white, home-made butter. She chopped up some parsley and worked it in. Then she produced a lemon and squeezed the juice over the butter, mixing the whole together again.

''Tis known as hotel butter, you know,' she said. 'A lump of it now on the sole and you'll know you're eatin'!'

'The sea,' Malachy said, 'is the real mother. I think we all come from the sea. Look how she provides and we neither sow seeds in her nor feed her. An' perhaps we shall all go back into her when we die. Like sailors buried overboard. To sink down slowly into silence, or be moved about, gently, with the currents. Wandering like spirits, or like pilgrims in a new world. Wouldn't that be grand, instead of the wet earth above in Bunnacurry graveyard?'

He laughed quietly. But Ruth winced and turned pale. Madge noticed it and got up quickly, bustling noisily about the dishes.

'A bit of sea moss jelly, now?' she called out. 'How about that? And to wash it down what better, Dad, than a glass of punch?'

She brought in the carrageen moss, the bleached weed she had simmered with some of the lemon peel she had saved. She had added sugar, the white of eggs, and cream, and had left it all in the coldhouse to chill. Malachy laughed again, adding the boiling water, sugar and lemon to the generous glasses of whiskey. The dark depths of the ocean, or the deep grip of the earth, both receded from Ruth's mind.

'That was a wonderful feast!' she told them. 'Like a banquet to prepare for a journey.'

The old folks were hoping, indeed, that a journey was about to begin. They sat awhile before the fireplace, content and chattering. The afternoon had drawn on and they began to hear the threatening halloos of a rising wind behind the cheer of the fire.

'I'd best be getting you back,' Eoin suggested reluctantly.

Ruth rose and was knocked back down again by a sudden fit of coughing. She doubled up in pain. She had a handkerchief and she tried to hide her face in it but the attack was severe and she coughed and retched dryly. What could they do but give her space and soothe her, offer sips of water. Slowly the attack eased, the coughing died away. Her face was white and she seemed to have become, in those few minutes, almost a ghost. The handkerchief was stained with small gouts of blood.

Eoin knelt at her knees and whispered to her. She was crying. To sound the word in the sacred room where the banquet had been held would have been too great a sacrilege. Father and mother moved quietly about, strained and saddened, gathering towels, fetching water, searching for words of consolation.

'I'll row across and fetch Doctor Weir,' Eoin urged, but she put her hand on his arm and held him.

'It's passed,' she said. 'I'll be alright now. I'll be able to go home.'

She looked at them. They were a gentle group, stunned to sadness and overwhelmed by their lack of words.

'It's not the first attack,' she said to them. 'Up to now I was hoping . . .'

Eoin stood up determinedly. 'Mother,' he said. 'Prepare the bottom room for her. She'll not face the currents this evening. I'll get the doctor over and I'll have him tell Mr McTiernan that she's here.'

'No, no!' Ruth said. 'My parents know; I've been to Doctor Weir. That's all done, I'm afraid, I'm ill . . .'

There was silence. They could hear the wind coming like an angry crowd in the distance.

'I'll be alright now,' she assured them.

Eoin drew her fiercely to him and held her head in against his chest and kissed her hair, wildly, uttering low, unconsoling cries.

The evening was darkening; in the west the sky was layered with anger, dull orange clouds capped by black. A strong wind had already whipped up the water across the causeway and the sea at the shore seethed under the assault. They wrapped her up well and Eoin helped her into the curragh. For a while father and mother stood watching as the curragh faced out onto the sea. They waved then, and went back, silently, into the house.

Eoin rowed strongly. Ruth sat hunched in the stern, watching him, watching the sea and the harshness of the sky. He rowed north, hovering on the current's edge. Then he turned the boat into the rush of water and it was taken, powerfully, and swept back south. He rowed with strength, all his efforts offered to keep the curragh edging across the rush of water. Once his hand slipped and the oar flicked the surface of the sea while the boat bucked like a slapped horse. His eyes met hers and there was a great call in her eyes, a sudden image that momentarily appealed to him, too. That he would let go now, go without hope into that rushing current, go and be swept away without possibility of reprieve, without the slightest chance of rescue, into the gathering power of the elements. But the oars struck with greater energy and determination. The moment passed, faded away to lodge in the dark particles of the air, in the raw, hurt basement of his soul.

July 1997

War . . .

The day dawned bright and still. Marty was up and had left the house before Angie woke. By the time he had reached Tinkers' Cove the sun was already warm although the horizon to the south was a strong and dangerous-looking red. The stillness of the air was ominous.

Quickly Marty undressed on his rock ledge and dived into the water. The swell in the cove was strong and the tide low, but the waves were full and slowly rising against the walls. Marty swam out to the mouth of the cove, then dived under the water. He loved the silence there, the languorous waltz-time movement of the long sea weeds and grasses, the strange shapes and vivid colours of the growths that clung to the rocks. He touched the rock floor of the ocean before rising again and swimming to the other side of the cove.

He climbed out to enjoy the sunshine for a while. There were low rocks here and he sat, naked, on one of them and let his head roll back to absorb the warmth. His fingers touched something among the rocks. There was a long length of blue rope tangled with the sea-growths and the base of the rocks. It was the kind of rope fishermen used to tie their nets to buoys and he gathered it up.

As he stood on the rock for a while, exulting in the fresh vibrancy of the air against his naked flesh, he heard his name called, softly, 'Marty, Marty', as if from a great distance, like the echo of an echo. He looked all about and out onto the water beyond the mouth of the cove. He could see nobody. Cautiously he climbed the low cliff above his ledge and looked out over the fields towards the village. There was nobody in sight. When he turned to climb back down to his own ledge he saw it again, that woman's arm and shoulder, reaching high out of the swell of the cove, the fingers moving as if beckoning him. Again his whole body chilled with the terror of the sight. Again he heard the voice, sounding even more remote than before, calling his name. He stood petrified as the arm seemed to roll slowly over as if there was a body swimming, or being rolled by the movement of the tides, and then it disappeared under the surface. He waited. For several minutes there was nothing, no sound, no sign of anything on the surface of the waves.

Marty shook himself violently, as a dog shakes the water from its back, wishing to shake the illusion from his life. Then, slowly and deliberately, he approached the edge of the ledge and looked down into the water. The sea was perfectly clear in the cove; he could see down to the rocks and the sea-growths at the bottom. Once again he expected to see a drowned body cast into the cove by the actions of the sea, but there was nothing. Gathering all his courage he dived straight into the sea where he had seen the arm rolling. He swam underwater as much as he could, then he surfaced and scoured the rocks at the far side. There was nothing.

He saw the mouth of the cave and he remembered what he had found. Perhaps the body had been swept by a strong wave and had been lodged, like the strange object, in the depths of the cave. He was treading water, trying to build himself up to enter the cave once more, when he heard tiny pebbles falling down the cliff face. He looked up in terror and was relieved and delighted when he saw Danni scrambling slowly down towards him. She had turned and was facing the cliff, moving very cautiously down towards the ledge. Once again he marvelled at the beautiful, full shape of her body, how the jeans outlined her buttocks, how the white blouse she was wearing left a great deal of her back exposed. He watched her skin glisten as she came down, the sun showing the fine texture of her back, the rippling of the muscles about her spine. Then she stepped down onto the ledge and waved to him.

Only then he remembered he was naked. He was still treading water out in the centre of the cove. He waved to her, arched his body and plunged under the water. When he surfaced he was under the ledge, gazing up at her. Lord she was beautiful, tall and strong and dominant where she stood above him.

'Hi!' he managed to say. She squatted on her hunkers and looked down.

'Hi there,' she laughed. 'I can see we're bone naked again. Playing with ourselves in the sea are we?' and she laughed raucously.

Slowly and deliberately he began to heave himself up out of the water.

'Pull-lease!' she said mockingly, dragging out the word. 'Do we have to see sights such as this first thing on a lovely morning?'

She stood up straight, backing away from the edge, watching him. He drew himself out and stood naked and dripping sea water in front of her. He stood without speaking, watching her. She gazed at him and he could see that she was stirred. Then she turned away from him.

'Jee-sus the Lord C Christ!' she said. 'Is this a vision that I see before me? Mr Venus risen from the sea! Make yourself decent before I throw up.' And she laughed, nervously.

Marty scooped up a towel from where he had flung his clothes and wrapped it around himself.

'Danni, did you call me just a while back?'

She turned again to face him. There was a big grin on her pretty face. 'No, I was just sneaking down, wondering if you'd be here. I didn't really expect you to be.'

'Did you see anybody about? Did you hear anybody calling?'

She looked at him. 'No,' she said. 'Sure it's only spas that'd come to a fuckin' place like this.'

Marty pursed his lips and said nothing. Then he dropped the towel, turned from her and dived back into the sea. When he surfaced he smiled up at her.

'I suppose you're too scared to come in?'

She raised her hands and began to unbutton her blouse. She was laughing down at him. Now it was his turn to be embarrassed as she took off her blouse and let it drop beside his clothes. She wore a white bra with a tiny red flower embroidered on it. He was startled and stunned once more at her loveliness.

She laughed again. 'That's as far as I'm prepared to go,' she said. 'And you'll never get me into that water, I promise you. The sea will have to come chasing after me before ever I get myself wet in that fuckin' cold water.'

He was disappointed, and relieved.

'Wait till you see what I found in the cave,' he said, beginning to swim away from her towards the end wall of the cove. She followed him, walking carefully along the ledge, until he disappeared into the black hole of the cave. Then she sat down on the ledge and let her legs dangle out over the water. It was warm, she felt at peace.

Soon she saw him emerging backwards through the water, out of the darkness of the cave. He was struggling with something, trying to get it out under the low, overhanging rock wall. She saw it was a dark, round-looking object, large as an old iron pot. She laughed at his struggles, but then, as the object scraped against the overhanging rock and floated at last into the cove, she saw what it was.

'Jesus, you fuckin' eejit!' she screamed at him. 'It's a fuckin' war mine!' She had leapt to her feet and begun to scramble back up the cliff face as fast as she could. 'Get the hell out of there,' she shouted. 'It might be live. It'll go off.'

Marty had his hand on the metal surface of the object. He looked at it again. It reminded him of a black iron skillet pot, though much larger, and fully rounded. There were several spike-like things protruding from it. Marty could see they were fully welded on and not quite rusted; each of them had something more soft on the tip. Here and there small handles were soldered onto it. The object floated easily, its top half over the water, like a huge football.

'It's a sea mine,' he called up to Danni. 'But it seems pretty safe. I banged it off the rocks and nothing happened. It mustn't be live, or something. I don't know.'

Danni's white face peered down at him from a safe distance.

'Get out!' she screamed at him.

He laughed up at her, then saw the rope he had found. He swam quickly to the ledge, gathered up the rope and threaded it through one of the metal rings. When it was on the middle of the rope he tied a knot around the ring, threw one end of the rope back towards the ledge and swam with the other end to the rocks on the far side of the cove. He climbed out and began to tie that end of the rope firmly around one of the rocks. He glanced up at her again, and suddenly realised that he was naked. She was watching him, and he could see she was still nervous and keeping as close to the ground on top of the cliff as she could. Only her head was peering over into the cove. Marty felt in charge of things again, he felt powerful in his nakedness, in his strength and familiarity with the sea, and he was excited by the danger of the mine in the water close to him. It was bobbing gently in the middle of the cove.

Marty dived into the water again, gathered up the other end of the rope and climbed back out onto the ledge.

'What in Jesus' name are you doing?' Danni shouted down to him. He didn't answer, but drew the rope gently taut so that the mine floated securely in the centre of the cove, safely away from either side and far enough from the end wall not to be driven against it. Then he tied the rope to a rock at the edge of the low cliff he was standing on. When he was happy everything was secure he looked up at her.

'It's safe, you can come down now.'

She laughed. 'It's not safe. It's not the mine I'm scared of. It's the naked man on the ledge that's terrifying me!'

Quickly he bent and gathered up his underpants.

'Now it's safe,' he called to her when he had put them on.

They lay for a time on the rock ledge, enjoying the sunshine.

'What are you going to do with that thing?' Danni asked him.

'I don't know. I have an idea. I'll ask Bendy. He knows everything about the sea. And I'll talk to Jackie about it. Maybe . . .'

He stopped and looked at her. She was lying on her back, her face turned to the sky, her eyes closed. He could see the gentle heave and fall of her breasts.

'Jackie told me you two . . .' he began, then stopped.

'What?'

'He said . . . the other night, at the disco. After the disco. That you two . . .'

'What? What?'

He dived. 'That you two made love. Had sex. Whatever.'

She laughed and then sat upright.

'Well, the little bollix!' she said angrily. 'How dare he say a thing like that. I wouldn't have sex with that miserable string of spaghetti if I was paid a fortune. He's a liar. A fuckin' liar. Kill him for me, if you see him. He'd prefer to make love to that fuckin' bike of his than to a real woman. He loves it, and he loves himself, and he'll never love a fuckin' woman.'

Marty winced and pursed his lips. She was watching him.

'Sorry,' she said. 'I've been trying to be good and not use words like that. But that has really made me angry. And you thought I'd go for sex with a miserable long git like that?'

They looked at each other. And then it came out of him, like a swift released suddenly from a cage, and there was no way he could take it back.

'Would you have sex with me?'

She sat very still. Marty could feel his face hot and red. He turned away, got up awkwardly and began to move away from her.

'I'm sorry,' he said quietly. 'I shouldn't have said that.'

'Why shouldn't you?' Her voice, too, was very quiet.

He turned back to her. She was gazing up at him, and her face was serious and calm, not angry.

'Because . . . because you're so perfect and beautiful and sexy, and you've done it many times before, and I never have, and you couldn't possibly even think of it. I'm sorry. Please forget I said anything. I think I just got so jealous of Jackie –'

'Jackie!' she spat out the word. 'Of course I'll have sex with you. If you want me to. I was wondering if you'd ask me.'

Now she was smiling gently. He was taken aback and a great fear suddenly began to build inside his stomach.

'You're laughing at me,' he said. His whole body was trembling as if, despite the sunshine, he was terribly cold. About them the day was still clear and bright but a slight breeze was starting and on the horzion ominous clouds were beginning to fester.

'I'm not laughing at you,' she said. 'I'm serious. I'm going back to Dublin in two days time and I have to admit that the only thing I have truly enjoyed is being down here with you, in this cove. And you, you're innocent and I think you're kind and thoughtful. And I've seen you naked, don't forget, and you're a much better looking fella than that long stringy motorbike kid. So there. I'm game. Let's give it a go.'

A great happiness flooded through Marty's body and he sat down again beside her to save himself from falling over. As he sat there she took his right hand in hers and brought his palm gently to lay it on her left breast. The gentleness and certainty of the gesture filled him with joy and the touch of her full breast made him weak with longing.

They were quiet for a long time.

'We can't make love here,' she said, looking at the rocks.

'You're serious? You're not just making a fool of me?'

'You must have more faith in yourself,' she told him. 'I wouldn't cod about a thing like this. I mean it. It's important.'

'I think I must be falling in love with you,' he said, slowly, wonderingly.

'Now don't get carried away. You don't have to say things like that. We'll have sex, and it'll be wonderful and we'll both remember it and that's surely enough for the moment?'

He was shivering with pleasure and anticipation. He looked into her bright eyes, brown and ocean-deep.

'Nor can we go to the hotel, they're always just barging in,' she said. 'And the locks on the doors don't work.'

'I'd love to bring you home,' he said. 'Even to meet my mother . . .'

'Oh Jesus!' she blurted. 'No thanks. We're not getting fuckin' married. I don't want to meet your mother. Isn't there some place –'

'Yes!' he said suddenly, with great excitement. 'Bendy has a place. There's a small house right over beside the pier, near the harbour they never use now. There was a landslide years back and the water is too shallow, but they used to spend days and nights in that little house once, waiting for the tides and the weather. Now it's hardly ever used, except if there's a friend of Bendy's here on holidays. He's let me use it several times. There's a kitchen and a bedroom, that's all. I've used it when I didn't want to go home. I know where the key is and all. Could we go there?'

She jiggled his hand against her breast.

'Right! Why don't we meet at the chipper about six o'clock. I'll tell my parents I'm off to the disco again. We'll meet there, have some chips and stuff. How far over is this house of yours?'

'An easy walk,' he said, growing more and more excited. 'I'll meet you at six. I'll tell my mother I'm going to stay the night in Bendy's boat. I did that before, too.'

She looked quietly out to sea. 'You're a good person, Marty, you know. You're a fine, good person.'

He could not speak now with the happiness that was gushing through him. Nor did he know how he would survive the day, the waiting.

November 1951

Mahon & Sons . . .

Aenghus Fahey brought his big body noisily into the stores. He had been brooding all morning, his plane touching the pale skin of the timbers with shaping strokes, his chisel shaping the joints, his naked arms forcing plane and board into place. He had brooded, and his brooding convinced him of rightness and of the justice of his complaint. When he came in there was no customer in the stores. In these days of shortages and want it seemed as if the island was morose, suffering its own isolation, making of darkness and pain what consolations it could. He had worked well. For long enough. For Grace 'n' Alice, for Alice 'n' Grace. And for himself.

He stood a moment inside the door that led from his yard into the stores. He sneezed loudly, coffin dust in his nostrils, and wiped his nose and mouth with the back of his big forearm. He could see Alice Mahon up in the crow's-nest he had built for her, where she sat like a queen, playing her own games with monies, receipts and bills. He knew she often dozed off up there, pleased to allow himself and pear-soft Grace to deal with the buying public: the travellers, the living, the dead, the poor, the rich, the beggars. He could see Grace pretending to be busy behind a counter, taking out safety pins from a cardboard box and putting them back in again. He knew his presence made her shaky and unsure of herself and the knowledge gave him strength. He paused, waiting for another sneeze to come, gathering comfort to himself from the discomfiture of the woman. He sneezed. Loudly.

'Aaagghhh!' he breathed across the shop. 'A good sneeze gives a man a good feeling!' Adding under his breath, 'Like a good fart!'

'God bless us, Anus!' Grace responded.

He moved across the shop towards her.

'Grace,' he began, 'I was wondering if I might ask you . . .' The box of pins leaped from her hands and pinged and twinged across the counter onto the floor.

'Oh my, my, my,' she fussed. 'Such a foolish me, a foolish me!'

Up in her eyrie Alice grinned a nasty grin, sniffled loudly and bent her head over her figures. Aenghus got on his knees and began gathering up the pins. Grace, too, came around the counter, stooped low beside him, clucking away abjectly. Aenghus's big nude arm touched the plump nude arm of Grace Mahon, spinster, and her eyes leaped in alarm towards his. Alice could barely see the animal backs below the level of the counter.

'There you are, Grace,' Aenghus offered.

Grace blushed. Quickly then she gathered her wholesome body into the vertical. Aenghus followed her and they stood by the counter, fixing the pins back into the box.

'Never can get them back the way they were,' she chuckled.

'Do you like it here, Grace?' he asked her, softly.

'Here?'

'I mean, working in the shop, like. Who does the cooking?'

'Oh, that's Mary Alice comes in to do that, and tidy the house. You know.'

'Do you not think it would be nicer for you to be in the home?'

'Home?'

'In the house. At home. A woman's place, after all. Doin' the homely things, like. Family. Children. Cookin' an' darnin' an' such stuff, while the husband is out earnin'.'

'Husband?'

'Aye. Husband.'

'I like it in the store.'

'But do you not think a woman's place is in the home, all the same? Yourself, now, out here, puttin' up with all them snotty-nosed children with their pennies out for sweets, them rough men askin' you for rough items, yourself countin' out nails an' screws an' mixin' paint an' weighin' flour an' you could be within makin' the bed sheets all white and fine and smooth and starched, up in your own sunlit bedroom?'

'Bed sheets?'

'Aye, an' rockin' a smilin' little baby girl in its cradle?'

'Baby?'

There was a pause. Alice was working furiously. Aenghus glanced up towards her. He had closed her in well with glass. He was certain she could not hear.

'There's so much emigration, Anus,' Grace said. 'So many children having to take the train and the boat and sure wouldn't it break a mother's heart to watch them go.'

'Ah, but that's the way to know she has a heart Grace, when it breaks, when it breaks. She'll know what love is then, right enough.'

'Love?'

'Love, Grace, love. And sure emigration is no bad thing. It hardens a man to make his own way in life, lets him see a bit of the big world, Grace, not to spend his whole time on an island, cut off from livin'. For we're on an island here, Grace. Ireland is a little island an' we're in a prison. We think we're free because the sea is all around us like a great wall an' we can't see over it. We're locked into cells, and then when we have to work inside a dark storeroom, all we can do is look out an' see a little bit of sky an' think it's the whole world we're seein'. Don't you think, Grace?'

She was watching him. She was perplexed. He did not seem to be talking to her. She could see the great strength of his chest, the fine dark hairs that were just visible at the top of his collarless shirt.

'Em, you were going to ask me something, Anus?'

'I was?'

'To ask me something . . .'

'I was. Anyway, what I mean is, a woman ought to be in the home, keepin' house for a man, bringin' up his children. And when the children are grown up they must be let fly free. For that's the way life is, Grace, that's the circle of it, the way the world spins.'

'I like it here, Anus, in the stores.'

He looked at her as if only becoming aware of her presence.

'A fine woman like you now, Grace, or like your sister Alice up there on her throne, musn't lack for admirin' men now, what?'

Grace gripped his arm and leant closer, whispering.

'Between me and you now, Anus – and you mustn't breathe a word to a soul, not a soul now – between you and me there has been a gentleman caller,' and she chuckled softly, 'if you could call him a gentleman, and all his attentions fixed on Alice up there!'

'Has there now? I'm not surprised, of course. I mean, the shop an' all . . . I mean but why weren't his attentions fixed on you, Grace?'

'I can't abide the man, simply can't abide him.'

'Now, I wonder who this unfortunate man might be?'

She drew even closer, both hands holding his right arm, her large bosom touching against his wrist, gently. She glanced up at the office.

'You promise me you'll not say a word?'

'I promise, Grace. Cross my heart and hope to die!'

'And I know, Anus, you're a man of your word.'

'Anus by name, Grace, Anus by nature, that's me.'

'Well, he comes in betimes, searching like, pretending to search for something, holds off till he sees I'm busy and then sidles up to Alice and tries his hugger-mugger on her.'

'Hugger-mugger, Grace? Who is this awful devil?'

'So you see, when you fixed Alice up there in the sky, he was a little bit thwarted and I laugh and laugh now when he comes in to see him fidgeting and wondering and plotting and planning.'

'Grace, who the . . . I mean, who is he?'

'Oh he has the honey tongue, you know, when he wants. The walking out bit, the age doesn't matter bit, tells her he's not afraid of work, he's young yet, he's strong and willing, and all to that and then he adds, mind you, the foulest bit of all, adds, now listen to this Anus, he adds –' and she paused, looking around her again, and whispered closer so that he felt the warm breeze of her words in his ear, 'he knows how to make a woman happy! There now. There's for you, Anus, there's a blackguard for you. As if he'd know the first thing about a woman, never mind make her happy. I ask you!'

'For the dear God's sake, Grace, who are we talkin' about?'

'Jeremiah James Dwyer! Big Bucko. Jerr Dwyer. That's who!'

'Holy Jesus Christ!' Aenghus said, too loudly, too angrily, standing upright suddenly as if smitten under the chin. 'Sorry, Grace, sorry. Big Bucko? Well, the cheek of him. And Alice, what about Alice?'

'Oh, she only laughs at him. The cockroach, she calls him. Knows he'd have his eye only on the stores. Drink it up he would, in no time. Drink it dry. The cockroach. Big Bucko. Imagine! Trying to get his hands on the stores by getting his hands on one of us first off! Imagine!'

'Well, can you imagine the cheek of that now? Right enough, the cheek of that!'

Grace was smiling sweetly and innocently at Aenghus.

'But you were going to ask me something, Anus?'

'Oh it'll keep, Grace. It'll keep till another day. It'll keep.'

November 1951

God made the world . . .

'First: I am the Lord thy God, thou shalt not have strange gods before me!'

She followed his words as he sang them out, her finger moving along the page of the catechism, but she grew exasperated at the speed at which he was going. She struck her hand down against the book, then pointed to individual words, one by one, moving her finger along them. He grinned and said it again, slowly, then again. He stopped and she moved her fingers, shaping the words silently to herself. Again. And again.

'Second: Thou shalt not take the name of the Lord thy God in vain.'

They went over and over it, again and yet again. He raised his eyes to the rafters in mock despair, announcing the words, repeating them by heart.

'Third: Remember that thou keep holy the Sabbath Day. Fourth: Honour thy father and thy mother.'

She spent a long time over that one. Reading it to herself. Thinking the words out.

He grew bored with it and began to ramble away from her, leaving her finger to prod, her mouth to move. Leaving her there, squatting on the wooden, dusty loft floor, there, and absent. He moved about, pulling at the bits of furniture she was allowed: her chair, her bedclothes, the few simple books she had garnered. His fingers picked at the dried-out cement, the old whitewash scabs on the walls. She stomped her foot impatiently on the floor, gesturing again towards the book.

'Fifth: Thou shalt not kill.'

He did not even have to look at the book by now, he was beginning to know them all by heart. He was young still, the world forming only very slowly beneath his own fingers, forming and reforming itself, dissolving again, fluid and random. The words had been explained to him, but only in the context of the high brown classroom with the great brown clock, the large maps of the known world, the confinement, the chores, the punishments; explained and reiterated until the words were no different to him from names like Orinoco, or onomatopoeia, or algebra.

He picked at the wall in silence. 'You know what?' he said. 'Sometimes I hate God.'

She looked up at him. He was so frail; she noticed it as if for the first time. Tall and thin, with his brown jacket, the brown corduroys hanging about his body.

'First I am the Lord thy God,' he chanted, intoning the words with mocking emphasis.

She laughed. She noticed a rip in the crotch of his old trousers, she could glimpse the pale ochre hang of his testicles. She was saddened for him then, saddened and hurt. She put down the book and went towards him. He was on his knees in the hay and he laughed, flinging a great handful of it towards her.

'Fifth thou shalt not kill,' he chanted.

She pushed him over into the hay. He clambered up again and climbed the small stack of hay towards the top of the end wall, flailing and falling and tumbling. She caught him and pulled him back towards her, the hay falling about him, the end wall gradually becoming exposed. He lay on his face in the hay and she clambered onto his back, her hands holding him down. He scrabbled under her weight and she sat heavily on him, laughing, keeping him down. Looking up she saw a small square door, the size of the trapdoor, in the wall where he had exposed it, the top of it now clearly visible. She stopped dead, sitting on him still, and her face showed great excitement. He looked up at the wall, too, and then she was scrambling up over the remaining hay, clearing it away from the old brown timbers of the little door. She knelt down before it for a long while, staring at it.

'It's the hay door,' he said.

There was a length of thick twine tying the small door to a large iron hook in the inside wall. It was wound round and round the hook and carefully tied. She looked at him.

'It was used once to fork in the high loads of hay from the top of the cart,' he said. 'Forkin' the hay in through the door from the top saved all the haulin' up the stairs into the loft. They haven't used it in years, now they're keepin' the hay down in the stables.'

She knelt there a long, long time, very still, as if in prayer. He grew fidgety again, watching her, and began to pull at the hay, angrily. She gestured with her hands towards the door and looked at him.

'It's high up,' he said grudgingly. 'From outside, I mean.'

He moved along the hay and began to unfasten the rope from the door. He worked impatiently at it, his small fingers worrying the knot.

'Eighth: Thou shalt not bear false witness . . .'

He got it loose and she leapt forward, pushing at the door. It was stuck as if the timbers had swollen with the dampness of the years. She struck at it with the palm of her hand, then with her shoulder. It did not move.

'Wait,' he said. 'Stand back.'

He clung to one of the rafters, swung himself and shoved hard at the door with both feet. It burst open and she saw the vague greyness of gathering dusk outside. She clapped her hands for him and smiled, then leaned cautiously out into the air. The little opening was quite high above the ground. Underneath was a patch of untended earth, a few clumps of rushes, nettles, scutch grass, and then the ditch with the ragged barbed wire fence on top. Beyond that a field. At the far side of that field another ditch. And then the road, leading away from this shed and away from Big Bucko – the road leading on to the end of the world.

She inhaled deeply, breathing in the clean air. It would be easy to climb out through the door, but the drop below would be too great. She turned back to him. He was sulking now, silent, kicking the hay. She reached and touched him gently on the shoulder. He looked at her. She smiled at him, nodding her head, thanking him. When she smiled it was as if a fine loveliness that lay hidden behind her sorrow took over completely; her eyes bright, her skin like satin, her teeth white and perfect. She held his shoulder for a while, her hand gently stroking his arm.

She looked up then at the rafters, drawing his attention to them, gesturing upwards and then to the open door, shaping a rope of some sort in the air, tying it to the rafter, dropping the end of it out the door. He could see her mime so completely, he could see her clambering down that rope and disappearing into the darkness.

Once before, she remembered, when Big Bucko had gone down the field to empty out the slop bucket she kept in the corner of the loft, she had slipped down the stairs as he had forgotten to bolt the trapdoor behind him. She had hidden for a moment in between the cows, seeing their great eyes watching her with complete indifference, seeing their breath come out of their nostrils in small clouds, the easy switching of their tails. Big Bucko had passed back into the loft, thumping his way up the stairs and she had slipped quickly out the door into the grey of the evening. She had heard him roar from the loft. She had found herself stuck to the ground for a moment, taking in the direction she should run. And he was already pounding down the stairs before she began to run, heading for the fence. She fled over the damp ground, she slipped, she heard him behind her, his weight thudding on the earth, his voice angry, and when she reached the fence she could find no way to climb without catching herself on the rusty barbed wire. It was pathetic. She stood, and he gripped her in a moment, hauling her back roughly, muttering with anger.

He had put her on the steps of the stairs before him and pushed her up and as she climbed he had put his big rough hands up under her skirt, holding her buttocks, pushing her ahead of him. Then he had pushed her down onto the hay and she had fallen on her face. Instantly he was on top of her, his great size and weight sitting high on her back, crushing her. He was heavy, heavy, heavy. Then he had lifted himself, turned her onto her back and sat down heavily again on her stomach. The breath was almost wholly knocked out of her. His big terrible fist was shaped and ready to come down on her face, ready to explode against her, but he hesitated. Instead of hitting her he hoisted himself quickly and moved his body up on her, sitting down heavily again on her breasts, as he liked to do, moving his great weight on her, riding her, laughing down into her face. Then he leaned down and gripped her hair and held her while he brought that great fist close to her cheek and she knew he could smash her face into a mess with one blow. He stayed like that a long time, glaring into her eyes. Then he sat back on her breasts and looked down at her, cursing her, telling her what he would do to her if ever she were to try a trick like that again. Then he turned his great body until his back was towards her face and he sat down again on her breasts and raised his legs onto her so that his entire weight pressed impossibly down on her. She fainted under the pressure. When she came round she was in darkness. He had gone. Now she shuddered at the terrible memory of it.

'He'd kill me,' Wee Eddie was saying to her, knowing what she was thinking.

She shook her head and put one finger to her lips in a shushing gesture.

'He'd find out for sure. He knows everything. He'd kill me.'

She looked at him, then made a move as if to throw herself out of the open doorway. He lunged forward and caught her skirt.

'You'll kill yourself!'

She smiled at him again, that lovely smile. She pointed to the rafters again, shaped the imaginary rope before him. He took his hand away from her skirt and he was sulking again.

'Will you run away for ever?' he asked her.

She had not thought it through. She shook her head, slowly.

'Good,' he said. 'I'd miss you.'

She caught him and drew his small resisting body towards her and kissed him on the lips, pushing her face against his. He squinted his eyes shut and screwed up his face. He drew away roughly.

'Yuk!' he said, rubbing his lips with the back of his wrist, but his eyes were soft, and he was smiling. 'Who made the world? God made the world,' he said, laughing.

July 1997

Troubled waters...

By early afternoon the summer storm had settled in over the island. The day had darkened and great squalls of rain blew in from the ocean. The wind was growing fiercer all the time and the sea was rising. The small boats rocked in the harbours and the few trees on the island groaned.

Marty was cold with excitement. He was nervous. He stood watching out through the window. Angie was down in the quarry field with the Connors making sure that the caravans were firmly tied down against the winds. He knew she would probably stay with them for the afternoon, enjoying their company, chatting with Nora and Jim and Ted. As the afternoon wore slowly on, Marty grew more certain that his nerves would not be able to cope with the wonderful experience he was hoping lay ahead of him. His face pressed against the glass of the window which was growing colder and colder as the rain poured down along it.

He showered carefully, shaved himself with caution – though he did not really need to – applied deodorant and body spray and dressed himself as casually as he could in his best trousers, a shirt, and trainers. He looked at himself in the mirror and decided that perhaps he wasn't such a bad-looking young fellow after all. He consoled himself that Danni would know how to go about doing things; she was experienced and, if he admitted simply and honestly that he did not know how to go about making love, or having sex with her, then she would lead him and show him how. His stomach clenched with a feverish excitement.

Late afternoon and the winds were howling in great gusts about the house. He would be soaked if he tried to go back to the village now. He telephoned Jackie, after much hesitation, told him he desperately needed to get to McHugh's and would be deeply grateful for a lift. Jackie could simply leave him there as he had other things to do. He promised to get his father's old car and would be over later.

When Jackie collected him the rain was coming down in bucketfuls and the winds were as wild as could be. Jackie stopped the old car outside the door and hooted the horn. When he came out Marty was instantly whipped by the wind and had to battle his way to the passenger door.

'Jeez, but you're all dolled up for the fair!' Jackie commented.

Marty grinned, wiping the rain from his face and eyes. He banged the door shut as the gale almost forced it open against him. 'Just felt like looking good, so that I might feel good, too,' Marty said.

As they drove towards the village Marty gloated deep inside his soul. Jackie had to drive slowly. The road was very narrow with deep ditches on either side, and the winds and rain made it difficult to see.

'Getting all dolled up just to go to the chipper?' Jackie said. 'I always knew you were a bit of a weirdo, Marty.'

Marty grinned. 'Ah well,' he said, 'we can't all be as lucky and as confident as you, Jackie, especially with the women.'

Jackie glanced across at him.

'Yes,' he muttered. 'Well, I suppose it's the good looks and the powerful body and the confidence gets you the women alright.'

'So,' Marty said. 'You know, I really envy you with that girl down from Dublin, what's her name again? Oh yes, Danielle.

She's gorgeous. You must be awfully happy to have made it with her?'

'No bother there,' Jackie said, and he seemed to swagger where he sat. 'A fine sexy young thing. I'll probably see her again, too. She kept asking if we could meet again. But of course I can't take the bike out in this weather, so she'll just have to hang on patiently till the weather clears.'

Marty did not laugh. After all, he was getting a lift from this clown.

'Thanks for the lift, Jackie. And you can go off home, and thanks. I'll be staying a while here, have a few chips, then I'll just wander over to The Village Inn. I'll get a lift back with someone in the pub. Thanks.'

Jackie drew the car up as close as he could to the door of the chipper. Marty thanked him, dashed out and banged the door shut behind him.

December 1951

An island within an island...

Ruth came home from the sanatorium, hope lost that the disease could be treated. Her family set up the big bright room at the back of the house to give her some comfort. High windows opened out onto a small stretch of yard, gravel-strewn, then onto the high grey wall that enclosed a grove of pine trees that offered the house shelter from the island winds. Beyond the trees was the road, and she could hear the very few cars that passed and the bus that went by early in the morning and again in mid-afternoon, that returned at noon and again at dusk, letting her know that life still carried on elsewhere with some semblance of normality.

She had become accustomed to the attacks of coughing that hit her, coming in wave after wave of pain and leaving her spent. She had come home to prepare for her part in the dying game, to be near those she knew and loved, who would ease her as gently as they could. They put a bed into her room. They placed vases with flowers. Bright lamps. All comforts.

She was young. She was aware that all she had come to know on earth was as nothing compared to what she did not know. As she lay propped up on pillows, the room as bright and as cheerful as possible, the dusty green of the trees beyond her windows scarcely stirring in the winter morning sunshine, she was aware that what she did not yet know was far more real to her, more important and relevant than all her acquired knowledge. The silence about her, and the quiet echoes she heard from the house moving about its chores, were more full of truth than any words or books could offer.

She was weak. But most of her day she was content. She was trying to reach beyond her living so she would be prepared. But the world about her, its fleshly weight, the heat of its blood, the demands for nourishment, all of these were still obstacles, a great wall to her, a door that would not open for her yet but was, she knew, the way through into reality.

Eoin Mulligan, his hands feeling bigger than ever, his sea-body more awkward and taller than he had known it to be, walked through the long tiled hallway of the McTiernan house and into her room. He sat awkwardly, bemused and hurt, beside her bed and held that small white hand between his own.

'You'll never feel it till your strength gets back . . .'

She smiled at him.

'I'll need a different kind of strength, Eoin.'

'I left some fresh trout outside with Maud. Maybe you'll manage to eat some of it. The flesh is soft and tasty.'

And what else was there to speak about? That he loved her? That she loved him? That their love had no sooner opened into flower than it was blasted? That the future was a jagged and breaking thing, the past was so short, it had vanished so sharply?

'I sometimes feel,' he said, 'that happiness came to nibble at the bait, and I sensed the tug of it and no sooner had I known it than it disappeared.'

She would cough a little, holding a handkerchief to her mouth. When the sun shone outside or when the seaboard winds had eased, they opened the bottom half of the great windows. They sat quietly then, like cut flowers standing in a vase of fresh water.

'If I didn't know this pain,' she said, 'the pain of all this coughing, in my lungs, it would be almost too easy to believe that I had found paradise with you. And that would have been wrong, Eoin, wrong for us both.'

'There's nothing wrong with knowing a little bit of happiness, surely?' He was perplexed.

'We are evil creatures,' she said. 'The wars, the horrors of them. But we believe we will be welcomed into eternal joy. I want you to think of me like that, happy, waiting for you. Heaven cannot just be a gift, if we are so evil, it cannot just be a consolation to our living. We must earn it by suffering, by being purified. We must hurt into the purity of God's presence.'

Even yet he could see her as beautiful. She lay back against the pillows, white against white, and her eyes were rich jewels of clarity. For her sake he would keep his words bright, his news cheery. He could see, almost from one day to the next, how she was being consumed by the illness and how she seemed to shrink perceptibly as if she were being fretted away into the air. And he knew her mind was turning away from the island, from him, as if she had been learning a thirst of another kind.

She held his hand and pressed it.

'I love you, Eoin, you know that. But look at the world. It's winter out there, a cold winter. And we sit in the darkness and call on God and He does not seem to hear. How can we feel at home in a world like this, where so many people, so many creatures, know little more than pain. Only when we are pure as the angels are pure will we be able to dance again, with joy, nimbly, on the great island that is paradise . . .'

'You talk, Ruth, as if you want to die!'

'Eoin, it is easy to die. It is easy to die into God.'

He sat a long time with her. He had not known there could be so much sorrow. In the evening he walked slowly to the pier and sat again, watching out over the sea. It was dismal and grey and a few flakes of snow floated down through the darkening sky. He could see his own small house across the sound, its low length huddling down into the ground for some small shelter. But everywhere was dead for him, dead and grey and shivering. The sun had been taken away by the dying and hung low and useless, misted and grey. It was the Host, held high a moment for veneration. And ignored.

December 1951

By name and nature . . .

The rains were constant, the winds coming in from the Atlantic high-pitched and virulent. Occasional flusters of snowflakes. It was a grey world, heavy with omen. Grace Mahon had spoken, circuitously, to Alice. Alice had agreed, a little testily, that Aenghus Fahey would be their guest on Tuesday evening. Tuesday was an off-day and the stores would be not too busy. But there were orders to be filled. And more expected.

On Monday afternoon Grace undid her apron, settled her ample body into a genteel repose, touched up her hair and went out the side door of the stores, across the yard, and pushed open the door into the workshop.

'Anus,' she called out softly. Her whole body was trembling slightly with anticipation. Naked beams of timber leaned against the walls of the workshop. On the benches lay a coffin, finished, its timbers stained and polished, the brass fittings gleaming. On another bench lay the nude shape of another coffin, the white timbers joined, nailed and glued, here and there still a twisted nail was showing. Waiting.

'Anus?'

There was a deep silence in the workshop. A heady smell of timber-talc and wood-dust, of glues and acrid varnishes.

Shavings were strewn about the floor, dispersed white curlicues of wood. Grace moved cautiously into the workshop, leaving the door ajar behind her. Light came in from two big windows opening onto the yard. She imagined the chisel sounds that would be heard in here, the thud of hammer against chisel, the rhythmic shush-shush of the plane, the whispering wash of the varnish brush across the timbers.

'Anus?'

Grace was almost whispering; she felt it would be sacrilege to raise her voice in here. The coffin lying there so perfect, so definitive. And then the man sat up so suddenly from within the coffin that she screamed, her hands rising to her face in terror, her body falling back against the door, banging it shut, the man, in his vest, sitting up in the coffin, facing her, his two hands holding the coffin sides, his eyes glazed, his hair unkempt.

'Grace, Grace,' he called, clambering awkwardly out of the coffin, climbing like a great ungainly giant off the workbench down onto the floor, turning towards her, the hair of his chest visible through the vest, the hair in his armpits thick and black, the braces of his trousers taut over his belly. As he turned towards her and moved in her direction she cowered back against the door, her hands to her face, whimpering.

Aenghus spoke quietly to her, he touched her shoulder and she shivered from him, her eyes open wide, her fist shoved to her mouth, her lips blubbering.

'It's alright, Grace, it's alright.' His voice was so comforting that she fell forward into his arms. 'I just took a nap, Grace, just finished the coffin for poor Tommy Qualters and wanted to have a rest, it was hot in here, an' I climbed in and lay back an' do you know what? It's lovely and comfy in there, not a bad place to lie for a long, long time! Have a few bottles of whiskey with you, maybe,' (he was holding her to him, prolonging the moment, exulting in the way she lay into the sheltering bay of his chest) 'and I nodded off an' I didn't know from Adam where I was when you called my name. Risin' out of my tomb into Judgment Day, ready to face my God – Anus by name, Anus by nature, praises on my lips. An' there you were, Grace, startled, an' I don't blame you one little bit an' I'm sorry.'

Oh it was a special moment as she inhaled the smell of his sweat, as she felt the great bulk of his maleness supporting her, the big arms about her, her trembling prolonged out of terror into relief so that she sobbed with a whirling of emotions and then, suddenly, there was Alice! Oh the puke! There at the door, smirking, keys in her fist, jangling, and 'I heard a scream,' she was saying, 'and I came running, and there you are, Anus and Grace, there you are, everything well I see.' But Grace did not care and Aenghus said nothing, but released the woman quickly, standing back from her till Grace, drawing herself up tall, wiped tears from her eyes and looked at Alice triumphantly, all woman, all bosom, shaken.

On Tuesday Grace spent the day in preparation. Humming while she bustled about her kitchen. Cocklety pie. Oh how she preened with delight at the thought, donning her special apron, now that she would have someone, for one evening at least, who would appreciate her efforts. Sleeves rolled up. Arms plump and red. Made for action and embraces and lovely feelable rolling pins. She giggled.

Grace scrubbed the cockles thoroughly, the water in the basin gradually thickening with sea grit. She put them on the Rayburn with water and a lot of salt. When the water boiled, the shells opened, slowly, offering their little mounds of flesh. She drained the water, scooped out the flesh and listened for the music of shell on shell in the bucket under the sink. She melted a fistful of best home-made butter in a saucepan, stirred in the flour, the strained cockle water, milk, stirring and stirring while the rich liquid thickened, bubbling, speaking to her, plop, plop, Anus, plop! She added parsley. The flesh of the cockles. Some grated onion. A little pastry for which she knew she ought to be famous, if only – if only there were those who would accept her ministrations.

The cocklety pie was baked and Aenghus whooped with delight as he ate.

'Cocklety pie!' he exclaimed, the gobbets of sea flesh in their rich sea sauce, liquid nourishment in his mouth. 'Grace, you're a wonder! A wonder entirely, God's truth, ma'am, a wonder.'

Grace breathed in with delight. Her face was red with pleasure and only slightly thwarted when Alice suggested that Aenghus might like to wash down the pie with stout. Alice went to the cold store and brought in half a dozen bottles of stout.

'I'll join you, Anus, if you'll let me,' Alice said, pouring the drink carefully down the side of a glass. Aenghus took a bottle and put it to his lips, slugging contentedly. He was sultan, emir, lord of the island and the islanders. Even the loud belch of stout mixed with cocklety pie did not greatly disturb the women, Alice 'n' Grace, Grace 'n' Alice.

Then Alice turned deliberately to Aenghus. 'That bit you told us, Anus, you remember? When you came here first and you were looking to get started with us, about Dagenham and Coventry, and all to that?'

'Yes, I remember.'

'Well, we were wondering if all of that was true?'

Aenghus was swollen with something approaching invincibility. He felt big.

'Well, no,' he chuckled. 'It was not quite true. Not true, I'm afraid. But then a man has to do things, you know, to survive. To help his poor mother.'

'And the carpentry, and all to that?'

'Well, no,' he went on. 'I was a postman, really, but I did do a fair bit of carpenting in my time. About the house, you know.'

Grace was sitting stiffly upright. She was hurt. If there is to be no truth between people then where was trust to reside? She felt cold, lonely, and almost called a halt to the feast. Still, that would solve nothing; she took a deep breath, decided deep down that one must not always rely on one's own judgement. She stood up, took the dishes to the kitchen to put the final touches to the coddle. Alice sipped at her stout. She was smiling contentedly. Aenghus opened another bottle. He looked at Alice. Alice, he thought to himself, is smirking.

'She's a grand soul, is Grace,' he offered. Tempting her.

'She is, Anus, she is. The best.'

The clock ticked on the mantelpiece. Aenghus drank.

'A good soul, God bless her.'

Alice looked straight into his eyes.

'She's a homemaker, Anus, a fine homemaker. She'd love to cook and darn and mend. She'd be a wonderful homemaker, without a doubt, if she had a home to make. This here's not a home, not really. This is a premises.'

Aenghus drank again. He belched, quietly.

'Do you think now, Alice,' he said, leaning conspiratorially towards her. 'Do you think, and you'll pardon me for askin', for I know the two of you are of the one age, and you know I mean only the greatest honour and respect towards you both, don't you, Alice?'

'Of course, Anus. I understand you perfectly.'

'You do, Alice. You understand.'

He drank again, his eyes looking into some vision of the future. Alice was watching him closely. There were comforting sounds from the kitchen.

'What was it, Anus, you were going to ask me?'

'Well, it's a delicate matter, Alice, a sensitive point . . .'

'Anus, Anus, Anus! We're citizens of the great world, you and I, the big world. You've been across the water, you've seen things. You've lived. I've worked this place up to equal anything in the county. Myself. Me. And I've lived too, in my own way. Equal to and better than any man. We know, Anus, you and I. There can be no question held back between two such citizens of the world.'

He grinned at her, leaning closer.

'Do you think, so, Alice . . . do you think she'd be of a child-bearin' age still?'

Alice laughed softly. She reached her plump arm and thudded him playfully on the shoulder.

'Good man, Anus. Well sure, we're of an age, Grace and myself, and I can tell you this. Grace was framed, in body and mind, for the making of babies. Babies. Fit and able. I am certain of it. The Mahon girls, look at us, man, we're fine and fat and busty. Grace would bring babies into this world, all fine and fat and busty, too. You can be sure of it. Babies by the crateful. Busty and gusty. She's a homemaker, is Grace, happy behind her apron, a dusting of flour on her hands, a baby squawking in the pram, another in the cot.'

Alice laughed softly and sipped from her stout.

Aenghus looked at her. 'And you, Alice,' he said, caution softening his voice. 'What about you?'

'Me? I'm fine and fat and busty too. But I'm no homemaker. And I have no ambition to draw more fat and busty creatures into this world where they'll suck all the strength out of you, body and soul, will drag you and weary you till all you're fit for is the grave, till you're long and lean and narrow and ready for one of Anus Fahey's finest coffins. I'm for this world, Anus, for things, the stores and accounts and commercial travellers I can face down and make a fool of while they think they're bettering a poor, soft, stupid woman. I'm for shelves and goods and merchandise. And money, Anus, I'm for money. Commerce! That's my master, my husband, the father of my children!'

She sat back contentedly. Her plot had worked to perfection.

Grace, bustling in her kitchen, had boiled water and dropped in a pound of best pork sausages, a pound of bacon, roughly sliced. She had boiled this earlier for several minutes, then transferring everything to a saucepan she had added onions, potatoes, parsley. She had poured some of the stock into the saucepan, simmered it and served it all up on her best plate just as Alice finished her glass of stout and Aenghus was about to open his fourth.

'Coddle!' Grace announced from behind her apron.

'Cuddle?' Aenghus smirked at her. 'Wouldn't that be just lovely now!'

Grace blushed. A lie or two, she thought, after all what difference does it make? What possible difference could it make to the swing of the world? Give the man another chance, after all isn't his poor old mother ageing and infirm above in her house, and hasn't she got a nice house, too, all neat and warm and tidy, and a pleasant bit of ground to go with it. And so coffinmaster, home-maker and businesswoman settled down to their feast, to a slow, drawn out, delicious time out of war.

December 1951

Augustus James Edward Dwyer . . .

At one ordinary moment, on an ordinary day, Florrie Dwyer stepped from one side of living to the other. She had a tin can of milk in her hand, rim-full, rich bubbles on the top. She was carrying the can from the kitchen door to the dresser, to transfer some to the jug. She found herself sitting on the cold flags of the floor, the can empty, the milk flowing silently into the hollows and cracks between the flags. She was dazed, but without pain. She felt as if she had walked into an invisible wall, a wall more real than stone and cement and whitewash. She shivered, because a voice somewhere within herself told her that a tree had just been felled not that far away; the tree from which the planks that would shape her coffin were to be cut. She heard its fall, the sound of breaking branches as it fell, and when it thumped the earth the world on which she walked had shuddered and knocked her over.

She sat there a long time, a dry, unflickering certainty holding her. She was staring at the can that lay by her side. She was staring at her husband, Augustus James Edward Dwyer who stood, slouched against the bedroom door, lazily lighting a cigarette, grinning down at her. She was thinking of her Big Bucko, of her Wee Eddie, of Angelica. She was thinking, and not thinking, of that fallen tree, of how the long thread of her living had been stretched taut and had snapped. She was cold, very, very cold.

She tried, at last, to get up. But a great part of her body did not respond to her commands. She dragged herself, breathing harshly, dragged and pulled her heavy body across the floor, the milk soaking through her skirts, her left side feeling dead and useless. She reached the bedroom door and, with her hand to the latch, began to cry. Edward stood looking at her, blowing small clouds of smoke into the room. She cried; emptying herself of the tears she had not shed for so many years, of the hatreds and fears and resentments, the bitterness, the despair she had known; emptying herself too of that hard and wilful sense of antagonism she had maintained towards the God of her childhood, many years ago. She felt, in the tingling and dragging sensations in her body, that her tree had been hauled now across the earth, the leaves scattered, and that soon it would become something entirely different. And then she laughed at the idea of it, at the utter foolishness of her life, and of all life.

She sat, planning how she would drag herself over to the bed. How she would climb in among the blankets and stale air and musty scents of her own life. How she would die there, the rosary twined once again about her fingers, someone, Wee Eddie probably – maybe, if God could forgive, maybe even Father Crowe – speaking prayers aloud into the air about her. Her fingers shifted on the latch. The door swung open, slowly. With an ironic grin and a teasing indifference, her husband stepped aside and waved her in.

She would be grateful for space in which she would try to make some peace with God. She could do so now with the authority of the dying, with her knowledge of the bleak unproductive gardens of the world. God the Father. God the Son. God the Holy Ghost. She would make her peace too with those she still cared about on the earth.

July 1997

An island upon an island...

They bought cod and chips at the little takeaway at the edge of the village. The rain was darkening the road outside and the wind was whipping the water as if the road had become a stream in spate. They ate inside the doorway, watching out at the rain, the reek of the vinegar comforting them, the heat in their hands through the soggy paper not an unpleasant heat. They said little. Marty's heart was hammering with anticipation and nervousness and a strange unpleasant buzzing noise seemed to occupy his thoughts. Danni leaned her shoulder affectionately against him and he turned to her, her face was smiling towards him and her eyes were bright and welcoming. Marty tried to slow the afternoon down, to prolong the anticipation and, he knew, to postpone the moment of their final coming together. He would be a fool, he would be a clown, she would be disgusted at him, she would hate him!

But they could not stay in the shop forever. The rain seemed to ease a little and they ran across the road, holding coats over their heads, stepping uneasily into runnels of water at the edge of the road, through the village, and turned left down the sandy track towards the sea. As they rounded the bend and the Atlantic suddenly came into view against them, they laughed aloud into the sudden power of the wind that held them still a moment, threatening even to drive them back into the village. The sea was wild against the rocks; the waves came reaching higher than Marty had ever seen them, pounding and crashing into surf that was quickly caught and blown away into the air over their heads. They held each other close and pushed their way along the edge of the sea towards the small hut close to the top of the pier. The rain came furiously against them again and the afternoon light seemed to fail completely before the onslaught.

Marty found the stone by the corner of the hut; eagerly he struggled with the lock on the door and soon they were inside. He ushered Danni in before him, then he shut the door and leaned back against it in relief. They were both soaked.

'At least it's dry,' Danni said, and the sudden moment of silence after her words startled the boy into a new feeling of terror.

He lay back against the door for a while. The house was small, only one room, the floor concrete and the rafters of the roof wholly bare. There was a small sink, two wooden chairs, and a small table. On the right hand side there were two bunks, built one over the other, with a small fixed wooden ladder leading to the upper bunk. They appeared to have adequate coverings on them. But they were narrow and small and for a while Marty only knew a growing sense of panic.

Danni moved into the centre of the room and began to pull off her coat. She shook it out against the far wall of the house. She wore a white jumper that was tight and emphasised the fullness of her breasts; she wore jeans and Marty could see that they were wet well up on her ankles. She stood, gazing around the room. She shivered.

Marty moved then. There was a gas stove with one yellow cylinder against the far wall. Quickly he crossed the room, found matches, and lit the stove. Then he stood up and smiled nervously at Danni. The window frames shook with the ferocity of the gale outside.

'Are we safe in here?' she asked him.

'Of course. This has been Bendy's fishing place for years. It's a stone house. It's a bit cold, but it's small and the fire'll warm it up quickly enough.'

She moved over and stood close by him. The rain came clamouring against the walls and the roof of the house and completely obscured the small window. They stood a long while together, listening, almost cold, perhaps from the gale, perhaps from nervousness.

He picked courage out of the air. 'I don't know what to do, Danni. Please be patient with me. Help me.'

She turned to him quickly and took his arm. 'I have to admit that I don't know what to do either,' she said, and she smiled at him.

'What? But you said . . . I mean . . . you told me you had done it thousands of times. In Dublin. I mean. You know . . . You must know what to do?'

'I told you lies,' she said quietly. 'I didn't want to admit that I'm as innocent as you, a bogger. After all, I'm from the city and we're supposed to be cool and sophisticated. But with you I want to be honest. I came here with you because it's my last day on the island, because you're a gentle person, and maybe I thought we could both begin together and learn what it's all about.'

He was so relieved he laughed aloud. Astonishing himself then he turned to her and held her face in his two hands and kissed her softly on the mouth. She closed her eyes and he drew back from her.

'Was that alright?' he asked.

She looked at him, and smiled. 'A bit short. More of a peck than a kiss. Here,' she said and she took his face in both her hands and kissed him, a long slow kiss, their lips tightly clenched together.

They drew apart then. At that moment a great roaring sound came from outside and they heard a wave crash over the restraining wall of the pier and come bursting against the road outside. She was startled.

'Don't worry,' he assured her. 'This is wonderful.'

They stood apart for a while, watching each other. Slowly her tongue came out and she licked her lips gently, her eyes fixed on his, a smile playing about her mouth.

'Oh my God!' he said and caught her, reaching both arms strongly about her, drawing her hard into him. They kissed again, long and feverishly. The wind grew ever wilder outside, the sea rose higher, the evening darkened.

December 1951

There and not there . . .

Big Bucko first. Florrie summoned him to her that evening. She was comfortable now, propped up in bed, her talcs beside her, the old prayer book on the sheet by her right hand.

Big Bucko was uncomfortable with the presence in the room. He was big, oh God he was big, filled full, bone and flesh, with the yieldings of time. A grey-brown presence, surly and uncertain.

No, he would not sit on the old green armchair beside her bed. He stood, watching down at her, urgent to leave.

'Jerr. Jerr. Jerr.'

Her voice was filled with a tenderness she had scarcely known for so many years, ever since her own husband, Eddie Dwyer, had stuttered his awful news. In the low music of regret and loss and anxiety behind her voice, Big Bucko had already heard and understood all that she was going to say to him. His eyes narrowed. A quick fear passed through him. His long hand moved, involuntarily, to touch the numb old hand of his mother where it lay useless on the counterpane.

'You must look out for her, Jerr, when I'm gone.'

'She's stupid. She's dumb. She's no good for nothin'!'

'That's as may be, Jerr, who's to know?'

'She's a stupid bitch. She's a thief. And dirty . . .'

'Dirty?'

'She's like a pig in a sty up there!'

'Jerr, when I'm gone, you must promise me now, it's the one thing. The one thing I promised your father. I promised him, at the end of all his arguin', last thing nearly before he went and left us, an' that's a promise must be kept, 'else I'll be certain to go into eternity lame an' broken. You must promise me now, Jerr, promise. Now.'

'What?'

'Get her settled, Jerr, away from yourself and Wee Eddie; get her fixed up somewhere. Maid. Servant. Cleaner. Anythin'. Far away from here. In England maybe. Send her to England. All she'll need, you can tell them, is her keep. For I know she'll break free some day, it's in her blood, it'll always be in her blood, she'll want to go her own way like all her kind. But if she breaks free after you've settled her some place far from here, then we'll have done our piece by her. We'll not be to blame, then. No blame. Promise me, Jerr. Promise me!'

He was sullen still. Angry. Unwilling. He stood, big and dark, a blank wall.

'It's the one thing, Jerr, has kept me from my God all these years. She has come between me and my God because I couldn't care for her, I couldn't accept her, and I have sinned against her and against your father and against my God. And I couldn't confess to Father Crowe because he'd know then, about her, and I couldn't go to Communion because of the black marks against me, and so I couldn't go to Mass, not for years, Jerr, years and years. It has been a torment to me, day and night, night and day. Now I must face my God. And I'm in dread of my immortal soul, that God Himself will reject me for rejecting the girl, the innocent, brought into this world with her own immortal soul, and no fault of hers in the comin' in. I'll need the priest before I go, to make my peace, Jerr. I'll need Father Crowe, to cleanse me of sin. I'll have to tell him all, Jerr, I'll have to tell him all.'

He was growing angrier at her words. 'You mustn't tell him.

It's no business of his,' Big Bucko said. 'He'll have us up before the guards.'

'He won't, Jerr, that he won't. I'll tell him all only under the seal of confession an' then he can do nothin', because he's bound to the silence of the confession box, he's bound by the orders of God.'

'But there's no such thing as God!'

The vehemence and venom of his words startled her, filling the bedroom with a deeper darkness. Her fingers clutched the more tightly on her beads, for comfort. There were tears again in her eyes, although she had thought herself emptied of tears.

'Then I'm worse off than ever I thought,' she said. 'I've failed you too, Jerr. And I've failed my husband. And the poor child out there in the shed, and I've failed Wee Eddie. I'm destroyed, Jerr. I'll go to my grave in a distress, broken and without hope. And I'm sure to be wanderin' forever like a ghost, findin' no peace. And can you let me go like that? My own son, my first-born. Oh Jerr, Jerr, Jerr . . .'

She brought her hand before her face and lay back on her pillow in an agony of distress.

'Don't Mammy, don't,' he pleaded. He went down on one knee by the bed and gently drew her hand from her face. 'Don't. I don't want you to cry. Or be afraid. I promise you. I'll get her fixed up, I promise. I'll get rid of her. I'll find some place. Maybe in England. Or in Scotland. An' I'll look after things. I'll take care of everythin'. Of her. An' Wee Eddie. An' all.'

She looked at him, though the world had become little more than a blur before her eyes.

'I know you will, son, I know you will.'

She drew his big head towards her and kissed his unkempt hair. She held his head between her hands a while, as if she were holding onto life itself. She closed her eyes and for a moment she was back, she was thirty years old again, newly wed and alone with Eddie in their own house. They were a couple islanded together in a young century, where the skies were clear and their God was a simple, island God, a large, bearded, paternal God; the way was bright and straight before them, the dim woods of sin far from their paths. How, when, why – how had it all gone wrong?

Later in the evening she sent for Wee Eddie to come to her. Big Bucko pushed him into the room and shut the door behind him. Wee Eddie stayed at the door, stricken. He had hardly ever come into his mother's room in the last few years. It was dark; there was a disturbing and unpleasant heaviness in the air. His mother, too, looked strange, disturbing and different.

'Father Crowe was in school today,' he blurted out.

Her arm dropped to the counterpane. 'Yes?' she said. 'Come on over here, nearer me.'

He moved, shuffling, reluctant. 'About the confirmations. In the spring.'

'Aren't you in confirmation class?'

He was beside the bed now and she took his two hands in hers. 'Yes, but Father Crowe says I can't do confirmation.'

'Why not?'

'He says I don't come to Mass, or confession, or Communion, or anythin', that you don't go, nor Jerr, that this house doesn't pay its dues nor nothin' . . .'

She did not know there was so much hurt waiting for her, here in her own bedroom, so much more hurt prepared for her, to burden her, at this hour.

'Eddie,' she said softly, allowing the love she owned to flow around the name like warm water. 'Eddie, I won't be with you much longer, and I want you to promise me somethin'. Will you?'

'Jerr says you're dyin'.'

The word struck her a thump low in her belly. She had not formed the word yet in her own mind. She felt cold. She shivered. Wee Eddie felt it and turned to draw his hands from her. She held him.

'Dyin'. I am. I'm dyin'.' She said it. Then her mouth moved softly as if she were testing the word. She sighed deeply. 'And you must promise me several things. You must promise.'

'I promise,' he said. He was frightened and anxious.

'Good boy, good boy. Firstly now, you must start goin' to Mass on Sunday. Go early this Sunday comin'. Go round to the sacristy door, knock, go in, say that you're goin' to Mass now an' you want to go to confession an' Communion every Sunday from now on. You're to do that. You hear? Promise me, Eddie. And Father Crowe will come here, Jerr will fetch him, an' I'll explain all about her outside, about Angelica and then Eddie, I know you've been good to her, she trusts you, I know that, an' you're to take care of her, mind her, until well, until she goes away.'

'Where's she goin'?'

'She's old enough now, she'll be able to go and work for someone, earn her keep, she'll need to do that, she'll need to be free of here, to grow up, to be on her own.'

'Then she'll be gone,' he said. 'An' you'll be gone, an' it'll only be Jerr and me. An' that'll be terrible!'

She had tears again. As if sorrow was an inexhaustible source. She could find no words.

'It'll be lonely,' he said, resignedly.

'You can go and visit Angelica wherever she'll be. And Jerr'll be good to you. You'll see. And I'll be mindin' you out of Heaven. I'm tired now, Eddie. Very tired. Do your homework. I'll see you when you come in to say goodnight to me.'

The night drew in quickly. Big Bucko sat by the dead fire, staring into it. Wee Eddie was at the kitchen table, his sums copy, his readers, open before him. But his fingers stabbed only sporadically at the work, his eyes looked elsewhere, everywhere, beyond the room into his own mind, and sometimes apprehensively towards Big Bucko. They had a perfunctory supper of bread and milk and then Big Bucko went back, without speaking, to the chair and sat again, gazing at the ashes, at the leaves of soot hanging at the back of the fireplace. And all the time there was silence from behind their mother's door.

With the darkness a storm had come in across the island, sounding in the cold chimney, rattling the windows and the door, finally flinging itself, with rain and hissing winds, against the walls of the house.

Then, in a moment's lull in the storm, they heard her calling from the room, her voice weak and distant and high-pitched. It was already like a call from another world. They were startled. Wee Eddie jumped from his seat with fright. Big Bucko looked around from where he was sitting, his face pale and angry. Wee Eddie went into the room.

'She wants to see Angelica,' he said when he came back out. 'I'm to fetch her.'

Big Bucko sat dulled and hooped about himself when Wee Eddie came back in with Angelica. She came cautiously, like a dog anticipating a beating. Big Bucko did not look at her. In the lamplight, there in the kitchen, she was bedraggled and dirty, her legs ugly with a grey dirt, dirt-marks on her face and hands, her dress awry. Wee Eddie led her by the hand to his mother's door. He pushed her inside, closed the door after her and sat down at the table.

Big Bucko and Wee Eddie sat in the silent kitchen. Eddie watched out as the last memories of day faded into blackness. Soon all he could see was the pale reflection of the kitchen in the window, his own face, and the bulked shape of his brother. Big Bucko scarcely stirred, sitting like a boulder set in clay. They heard the wind continue its argumentative romp outside, occasional fistfuls of rain being flung against the window. From their mother's room they could hear nothing, not even the low murmur of their mother's voice. At times the lamp danced and flickered, the wind finding its way through for a moment, scattering ghosts.

Once Big Bucko stood up slowly and made his way to the door, walking softly. He listened. He put his head almost against the door. He could hear nothing. His face was drawn, ready with anger. He shook his head silently and went back to his brooding-place. The darkness settled more deeply.

'She's in there an awful long time,' Wee Eddie said, and the words fell dully into the emptiness.

They were both startled out of half-sleep when the door opened. Angelica came out, closing the door softly behind her. She glanced quickly towards Big Bucko who scarcely lifted his head towards her. She nodded at Wee Eddie who got up and led her back out into the darkness. It seemed, as she passed through the kitchen, that she walked a little taller and with more sureness, with a little more pride in her bearing.

November 1935

Tinkers' Cove . . .

It happens, every so often, that a loss occurs among an island people, a loss that has a wholly unforeseen impact on the whole island. It happens infrequently. The way an unusually violent storm will come and wash away a stretch of shoreline, destroy a trawler, damage a pier, fling heavy curraghs out of the water onto the rocky edges of a village harbour. And it will leave behind it a false quietness, debris, a higher tideline where the flotsam lies. The island people will talk of it in hushed tones, inspecting damage, ready to repair and mend and build all over again.

In those early years Augustus James Edward Dwyer often walked alone up from the rocky shoreline, climbing the old sheep path that led across peat-soft lowlands where mosses and heathers grew and where sleek black slugs came out in the evenings to stretch their glossy ugliness across the path. He would walk quietly, watching out over the sea, his wellington boots leaving their prints deep in the wet ground. Then he would climb the slope along the edge of the lower cliffs, the Atlantic Ocean reaching in and sculpting its hard edges, building its boulder shapes, carving out its coves and caverns that reached imperceptibly further and further in under the earth. Here he would walk over harder ground, the grasses shivering and thin; sometimes he noticed the tiny sea-edge flowers that grew low and lovely in the salted grasses. Bilberry, wild violet, spurge, celandine, sea thrift, vetch.

Cautiously he would approach the lip of the cove where the world ended suddenly and the sea had gouged out a deep and echoing cavern reaching far in, the sides falling precipitously, the water rushing in below in great, angry waves, sweeping along the sides of the cove, crashing into the end wall and sucking at its base. Sometimes he sat on the edge of the cove, watching the angers of the sea, listening to the harsh music the ocean played on the cove walls. Sometimes he smoked a pipe, gathering peace out of the evening, watching the gulls fly across the bay to their night-places on the cliffs.

It was known that he had spent the late afternoon in Donie Halpern's pub. Some say he was sullen and angry that day, but they could not say for certain. Eddie Dwyer drank morosely, quietly, unwilling to be distracted into conversation. So, if he appeared more sullen and distant than usual that may have been the vision of hindsight among those who had been drinking nearby. He left before darkness had fallen although it was hovering at a slight distance. He walked back the mile or so to the bay. Several people greeted him and he offered a polite word or two, or a nod, or a wave of his big hand. Nothing unusual. Nothing strange. Except, perhaps, for the darkness that seemed to be in his face, a darkness mirroring the darkness that grew from the near horizon. That was all they knew. That night the darkness took him. And the sea.

They found his body some days later, lodged in a cleft of rock at the very base of the cove. The body was bruised – consistent with a fall from the top of the cliffs. He had drowned. His face was swollen from the sea. And who could say more? He left only questions hanging on the lip of the cove, and sorrows that went on raging in the waves along the jagged shore of Florrie Dwyer's life.

July 1997

An island upon an island . . .

Marty had at last found courage before her. He knew that her confidence and exuberance was little more than a front, and that she, too, suffered like him from the great uncertainty that is sex. He grinned at her.

'Maybe we should take our clothes off,' he suggested.

She looked at him. She hesitated. How different she looked now, he thought, how vulnerable suddenly, and younger than he had believed. For a moment his sexual urgings seemed to fall away from him and he wanted simply to take care of her, to keep her safe from the wildness of the world outside, to keep her dry and warm and at peace.

'I'm very cold,' she said quietly.

He pulled the blankets and pillow from the lower bed of the two tier bunk and wrapped the blankets around her. He placed the pillow on a chair, drew the chair over beside the heater, and gently urged her down on it.

'It's alright,' he assured her. 'Maybe we don't have to do anything. It's just good enough to be in here with you, nobody around, and nobody likely to be around.' He laughed.

She smiled sheepishly at him. 'I'm a disappointment to you,' she said. 'I'm sorry.'

He took her hand then and kissed it tenderly. He had never felt so happy in his life.

'Maybe,' he offered, 'maybe we could just get into the top bunk together, with our clothes on, and just be together, just be warm together, safe in here out of the storm?'

She looked at him, and at the top bunk. She nodded. 'But I'm not getting in there with all my clothes on,' she said. 'They'd be ruined. You turn away and I'll climb in and leave just my pants and bra on.'

He turned away from her and went to the small window. Peering through the grime he could scarcely make out the wildness of the waves rising over the pier wall in a spectacular display and crashing down onto the little harbour, reaching oftener and oftener onto the small track and touching even the base of the house. He could not see the small group of tourists, in all sorts of raincoats and windcheaters, hats and umbrellas and wellington boots, who had gathered at the turn of the path to watch the great ocean's display of power and magnificence.

He heard her moving behind him. He was so very happy. He was at peace. He heard her giggle softly. He heard her bare feet pitter quietly over the floor. He heard the soft creaking of the small ladder, the louder creaking of the boards of the top bunk. He heard her laughter. She called to him.

'Right, bogger, I'm ready. You can come to bed now.'

December 1951

Angel at the window . . .

Ruth McTiernan was growing weak. Long bouts of coughing took her, leaving her as exhausted as if she had walked a long journey. At times, Maud, rotund and healthy, would encourage her to eat, a little nourishing soup perhaps, mutton broth, a little curds. Ruth would try, sipping at the broth, nibbling at tiny portions of white bread. She looked at herself rarely in the mirror now; there did not appear to be a superfluous ounce of flesh on her body. Soon, she knew, she would be stripped of all that kept her back from God, kept her from passing through the narrow gap into eternity.

Eoin came. She lay, almost fading back into the pillow, her eyes closed, her lips pale, her face taking on the dull glow of glass. He brought with him a faint scent of the sea, of currents and kelp, of shorelines and boat-pitch. When he spoke her name, calling her back out of absence, she heard the sound of waves breaking against a gentle shore. She opened her eyes. It was like coming up out of water into a more familiar medium. He was holding her hand. His hand was big, cool, strong.

'Mother and father are always asking after you,' he told her.

'I'm fine, Eoin, fine. Tired, very tired, that's all.'

Her eyes closed again. He sat with her while the afternoon

moved slowly on. He could hear the soft noises from the branches beyond her window. There was little sound now from the house. He felt he was not in the world, neither he nor the woman he had found and loved. They were together in a vacuum where nothing was real. Nor was he sure that she had not drifted away from him on some current of air, except that now and then he felt a gentle pressure against his hand.

Doctor Weir came with a busyness of doors and a certainty of shoes on the flagged hallway floor. Voices, loud at first in greeting, then a mumbling consultation. What could he do? She would not allow him to hold the pain at any distance from her with his drugs, his tablets, his untruths.

Eoin rose to leave. She looked up at him as he moved away from her bedside. She saw his bulk, the sad stoop of his body, the distress on his face. Suddenly the world shifted from under her and she felt strongly how she wanted to be with him again, out on a boat on the sunlit sea, an unruly congregation of seals about them, the world echoing with the noise and laughter of living, and growing, and loving. Her cry was too late for him to hear, he had left the room and had begun the long walk down the hallway away from her, the trudge back down to the shore, the effortful heaving of the boat across the sound, the drawing up of its heavy body on the shore of the barren island.

When he called again she seemed brighter. There was a sense of warmth in the room, of unusual winter light. She was propped higher on the pillow. On each cheek there was a small pink glow and her eyes were bright, larger than he had remembered, their blue clear again and alert. She was smiling. She wore a pink cardigan.

'I heard the early bus this morning,' she said. 'Very early. It was pitch dark. I don't sleep too well, you know. I heard the family coming, I think it was the Maddens. I heard the sound of the cartwheels on the road. Louder, coming through the darkness. I heard the donkey's hooves on the road. It was only just after five when I heard them coming. Why they came so early I don't know. The waiting out there in the darkness and cold must be the worst. I could hear the voices then, just out there, beyond the trees. They unloaded the cases from the cart and I could hear them talk, quietly, at times only, as if they were working to find things to say. There was someone crying, too, softly. And then, a long hour later, someone cried a quick, high cry of loss, the kind a curlew seems to give from across a shore. And almost at once I could see the lights of the bus, away in the darkness, shining faintly through the trees. Then the sound of the engine. The headlights lit up my room, all the shadows became huge. The engine hummed softly when the bus stopped and I could hear the voices, busy and loud, pretending cheerfulness. A few good-byes. The engine getting loud again, the shadows shifting quickly. There was someone crying, not loud, just low and somehow black and hopeless. How I felt for her, Eoin, how I wanted to go out there and say no, no, no, it'll be all right, every-thing will be alright, but I knew it wouldn't be all right. A son or a daughter heading for America, or Scotland, somewhere far away, and maybe they will never come home. And I heard the wheels of the cart, that slow grinding sound on the road, until it faded slowly and all I could hear was the branches again, shifting in the breeze.'

She was silent then, a long time, and he held her close to his strong body. She whispered to him, very softly, so that he was not sure he heard her.

'They passed by me last night.'

'Who did, darling?'

'The dead.'

He shivered, the back of his neck chilling suddenly. Her hand was cold now in his, and trembling.

'And the angel,' she added. 'Last night, too. I saw her.'

'Who did you see, Ruth?'

'The angel. There. At the window.'

Her fingers were like bird claws against his strong flesh. She was gazing into his face and there was a gentle rapture in her eyes that disturbed him.

''Twas a wild night, love,' he said, reasonably. 'A terrible storm. Kept us half awake all night with the noise of the sea and the winds. Things rattling in the house, out in the sheds.'

'She put her face against the window,' Ruth went on, ignoring him. 'She was young-looking, and her eyes were alight with wisdom. And behind her I knew there were storms and rain because the world had opened up to let the angel through, and her eyes told me so much. Oh, I know how small we are, how we must melt back into the universe, and then Eoin, then we will be one with the world, with the storms, with the sea, I will be one with you, Eoin, with your seals, the trees, the angels, God.'

She was animated. Her hands trembled in his. Her thin, strained body seemed taut with unfocused energy. There was colour in her cheeks, a colour, he knew, that would quickly fade.

'You see a lot in the middle of the night,' he said, half laughing, wholly tender. 'And did you speak to this angel?'

'No, Eoin, she was beyond the glass. She was part of that world out there. But she told me, with her eyes. And I heard her, I heard her the way I hear you, her footsteps, her fingers on the glass, and I see and hear many others, too, many who have gone before . . .'

She lay against him for a while. What could he say to her? That the procession past her of the dead, the visitation to her window by an angel, all of this was no more than the distorted and delusioned dreaminess of physical exhaustion? The way light-headed drunks will hold their visions, the way the frantic eyes of those close to starvation will see bread in the stones, the way those blinded by thirst will see palaces and gardens of the greenest foliage where there is nothing but a waste of sand? He was glad for her relief. He was devastated by his own impending loss.

July 1997

An island upon an island…

Marty laughed softly. All his inhibitions seemed to have fallen away, as if the great blundering ocean, the sky that had opened over them its wildest powers, had whisked away his every hesitation. There was a great racketing sound on the roof of the shed. Danni screamed.

'It's OK, it's OK,' he assured her. 'Sounds like a slate that has come loose and been blown down along the roof. That's all.'

She cowered in under the sheets and blankets of the upper bunk. He laughed again to see her. Then he began to undress. Great reaches of rain came smashing against the house and they could hear the roaring of the Atlantic waves in their wild raging just outside the house. The world beyond was drenched, the rocks of the shore were drowned and even the path from the village down to the pier was being quickly washed away. A great crack in the pier's restraining wall had grown wider and the sea came pouring through it, foaming in its exultation. He took off his clothes, folding them neatly, laying them on the chair before the stove. He hesitated only when he was down to his underpants. He looked towards her. She was watching him, grinning, only her face visible over the bedclothes.

'Go on,' she taunted him. 'Won't see nothing I haven't already seen.'

He laughed again and flung his underpants with abandon onto the chair. Quickly he began to climb the ladder to the bunk.

That was the moment. How carefully chosen, how impossible, how wrong, how right. There was a noise from the world outside as of thunder, or as of a war in progress, with guns firing together. The winds seemed to rise to a fever pitch, the ocean reared higher than it had ever done before and a succession of huge waves came rushing over the pier wall, smashing it as if it were of timber, taking a great chunk out of the road, and washing away the front wall of the fisherman's house. Suddenly the sea was covering the floor of the house, washing over the lower bunk, reaching as high as the knees of the naked boy climbing towards the upper bunk. There was a hissing from the gas heater as it went out, the heater itself taken like a rubber ball and flung against the end wall. As the wash of the waves receded, table and chair and front wall were washed away with it, the timbers of the ceiling creaked and shifted and the slates on the roof came tumbling down onto the earth. But the foundations held, and the cornerstones. The watchers on the road above saw the whole front wall of the house removed, the way a lid would be lifted from a box, and they saw the naked body of a young man stunned into immobility where he stood.

December 1951

There and not there . . .

Florrie Dwyer came awake in a dark cavern. There was a pale line of grey-blue, sickly light, reflected from one wall. The sea was at her feet, placid but deep, heaving softly. As she watched its shifting surface, the water broke and her husband's head pushed through, terrifying her. In the gloom his face, eyes closed, mouth open, assumed the grey-yellow tincture of disease. She could make out the dark shape of his shoulders under the water, the gleam of his white, collarless shirt, as his head bobbed lazily on the water. There was no sound. And then, suddenly, his eyes came open and he was looking up at her, the mouth smiling, mocking her. She closed her eyes. Her hands clutched and held the bedclothes and when she opened her eyes again there was only her bedroom, only the stale air of her own living, the pale light of dawn behind the thin curtains of her window. She was damp with sweat; almost, she thought, as wet as if she had been thrown into the water of the sea. She knew, too, this was more than a dream, more than a nightmare. It was a warning. Even – an invitation.

When Wee Eddie came in to see her before going to Mass she made him promise to tell Father Crowe to come and see her.

'Tell him it's urgent. Tell him I'm goin' and that I must make my peace with God. The sacraments. I need the sacraments. An' you must tell him that you want to be an altar boy. You must be confirmed, Eddie, you must!'

Eddie opened the heavy sacristy door a few minutes before the end of Sunday Mass. He knew fear again, entering the big echoing room with its high ceiling, its narrow windows, the smell of polished wood. He could hear sounds echoing from the church beyond the small door, yet the sacristy seemed so hushed that he scarcely dared move. The door opened, there was a rush of sound from beyond, then four altar boys came in, hands joined, wearing white surplices over black soutanes. Eddie backed into a corner beside a cupboard and tried not to exist. Father Crowe, tall and certain about all the joists and varnishings of the world, came like a storm behind them. He wore bright green vestments, he carried the chalice in his hands, he wore a black biretta on his head.

The acolytes helped him divest. Slowly he folded away the vestments. Nobody spoke. The boys were alert to his every movement, to their own tasks. The priest bent and kissed the bench under the crucifix. It was a signal. The boys rushed to take off their soutanes and surplices and again they were only poor island boys in poor island clothes; jackets with pockets undone, thick woollen socks. Their knees were bare, scarred and scabbed. Cornelius. Thady. Vinsheen. Peter Joe.

Father Crowe attacked them.

'What is the fifth commandment of the Church?' he barked.

His face was pale with weariness, or anger, or authority. His thinning hair was black and Wee Eddie could see the tiny cut on his neck where he had stuck a bit of paper to hold in the bleeding. There was silence. The priest put his hands on his hips and glared at them.

'Come on! Come on! Don't be thick! The fifth commandment.'

They were watching the toes of their boots. Their faces were contorted with effort. Wee Eddie couldn't stop himself.

'The fifth commandment of the church is that we contribute

to the support of our pastors.'

Father Crowe looked at him in astonishment.

'Eddie Dwyer, is that you?'

'Yes, Father.'

'Well, well, well. Wee Eddie. Good man. Good man.'

His face was bright with amusement.

'What are the seven deadly sins?' He was staring at the reduced acolytes.

'Pride. Lost. Angry . . .' one of them began, and faltered.

'Lost indeed!' Father Crowe humphed. 'And damned to hell!'

'Gluttony, Father,' another offered.

'Gluttony, indeed. We're getting there. Another week now and we'll have them all.'

'Counsel,' another blundered.

Father Crowe's right hand shot out and grabbed Vinsheen's ear. He pulled hard and the boy squealed. Wee Eddie intervened.

'The seven deadly sins are pride, covetousness, lust, anger, gluttony, envy and sloth. Father.'

Father Crowe let go of his victim and turned to Wee Eddie.

'Which are the three divine virtues?'

'The three divine virtues are faith, hope, and charity.'

'The seven gifts of the Holy Ghost?'

'The seven gifts of the Holy Ghost are wisdom, understanding, counsel, fortitude, knowledge, piety and the fear of the Lord.'

'The second commandment of the Church?'

'To fast and abstain on the days appointed.'

'Well, well, well.' Father Crowe's face was a garden under sunlight. 'And I thought we had a real pagan here. Wee Eddie Dwyer. I'm delighted. We'll have you up for confirmation straight away. Good man. Good man.'

Wee Eddie beamed. 'Mammie wants me to ask you, Father . . .'

'Yes, child, yes?'

'If I could become an altar boy, Father. Please.'

'Well now, a man with your knowledge of the catechism

would make a fine altar boy. Of course you can. Come back next Sunday before Mass and we'll give you instructions. Get yourself a surplice, a soutane, shoes. You'll get them in Mahon's. Bring them along and we'll get you going.'

He turned away to usher the boys out in their shame. Wee Eddie stood perplexed. Surplice. Soutane. He knew his mother could not afford to buy such things. He looked at his boots, his best boots; there were rips in the leather across the toes and the laces had broken so often they were now too short to thread them through the eyes in the leather. Surplice. Soutane. Shoes. It was impossible.

Father Crowe was putting the vestments away in the cupboards. He had to travel several miles to say another Mass in the convent chapel. The boys had edged quickly out of the sacristy and were running and scuffling down the avenue from the church. Wee Eddie turned away, disconsolate. He heard the heavy thud of the sacristy door as it closed behind him. He was almost home before he remembered his mother's words: 'Tell him it's urgent. Tell him I'm going. Tell him I must make my peace with God.'

December 1951

Scylla and Charybdis . . .

Eoin Mulligan walked slowly down the fuchsia lane. Soon, he was thinking, she would be gone from him, having lifted him for such a short while from his loneliness. He stood at the pier's end, the current rushing by beneath him. He looked across to his island. How drab it was. He would have to leave it, leave his father and mother to suffer their own loneliness in their last years. He turned and walked aimlessly along the path beside the sea. He climbed down the track into Blacksod Bay where the wind scarcely touched. The tide was high, swelling quietly in its own impetus. He walked along the shingle, his body hunched low against sorrow as if against a piercing wind. A few flakes of snow drifted down, as if they did not have the heart to fall with any seriousness.

Slowly then, deliberately, he walked down the rough slope into the water. Here at the shore the water lapped easily, leaving a long and straggling line of white froth along the sand. At times the breeze lifted parts of the froth into the air and mingled it with the falling flakes of snow. Out over the sea there was only emptiness, a cold grey sky. Quickly he took off his warm greatcoat, his thick shoes. He took off his jacket, shirt and vest. The cold hit his chest like a blow from a fist. He took off his socks, his trousers, his underpants and flung them all into a heap on the wet sand. He was standing naked before the sea and sky while the wind came cold off the north. He shivered violently. It was here she had come to him first, here he had moved close to harmony with the universe, close to a friendship with the world.

He shouted aloud his loss and his anger. He bunched his fists against the low, grey clouds. The white sun had vanished from the western rim of the sky and the first, even colder, winds of night had begun to slice along the bay. He walked, slowly, into the sea, out and out, the water rising about his calves, his knees, his thighs, his body shaking violently with the cold, the dreadful chill that took him as a breaking wave struck his chest so that he fell backwards into the water, his hands flailing, his breath filched quickly from him with the coldness of it, his whole body taken by the ocean and flung back towards the shore, as if the world rejected him. He struggled then like a mindless thing, for breath, for life, swinging his arms, kicking his legs until he stood upright once more. Then, shivering through with a coldness he could scarcely bear, he headed out again, bracing himself against the waves until his feet lost purchase on the seabed and his head sank under the water. He closed his eyes, willing himself into another world, but almost at once he was flung back again with the force of an incoming wave. He opened his eyes and found himself half-swimming, half-scrabbling back to the shore, his body shaking with the cold. Another wave took him and pushed him to his knees and he was back again on the shoreline, kneeling and crawling where the froth lay.

At once a great sense of guilt took hold of him. It was here he had met Ruth, it was here he had first seen the great new possibilities life could offer him. It was she who had been stricken by the incomprehensibly cruel hand of God. It was he, Eoin, she now depended on for some sense of hope, for some small awareness of love. He knew death did not want him, not yet. He must be with her for a while longer. He prayed, then, pleading for forgiveness. He was naked, blue and purple with the chill of near-death, begging for strength to live, to struggle still, for her sake, and for his own soul's sake. *Lead us not into temptation but deliver us from evil.*

Then, not far out, he saw the dark head of a seal, motionless in the water, watching him. His heart leaped with extraordinary gratitude and he moved, too suddenly, for the creature bobbed at once out of sight.

'Come back,' the man whispered the words. 'Come back, come back, please!'

The seal surfaced again, further out, and Eoin laughed softly at the roundness of the head, the whiskers, the great round eyes. He stepped forward again, still naked, into the sea. The creature did not move.

'Come.' Eoin said the word shyly, out of his shivering nudity, into the sea that did not seem to want him. A wave broke and the water ran high about his knees and thighs, splashing him with its cold. He did not care. He moved out further. The sky was a heavy grey above him, the sea dark and endless and, to his right, scarcely interrupting the skyline, stretched the grey, sad shape of his island.

'Ruth!' He surprised himself as he spoke her name into the greyness. The sound was soft, like a small wave breaking, a bright summer day about it. 'Ruth. Ruth. Ruth.'

As he said her name he advanced towards the seal. The water swirled about his stomach. The dark head bobbed with the motion of the tide, not far now beyond him. A cold breath of wind came across the bay, its movement visible in the ruffling of the sea's surface as it passed. He raised his arm, carefully. The water washed about his chest and the coldness was hurting him more than ever, numbing his entire body. Then he was breathing hard as the waves reached his neck and washed over the lower half of his face. The seal watched, the blank eyes dull, round and wide and cautious.

'Ruth!' He made a soft caress of the name, but his teeth chattered against the cold. A wave came and raised him off the seabed, lifing him onto its buoyancy, though he felt heavy now as sea-wrack, salt-chased. He was closer to the seal, the creature's head motionless on the water. He moved another step and the wave hoisted him and he fell sideways into the water, his body submerged as the wave passed over him. When he found his feet again and shook the water from his eyes the seal had disappeared and he felt suddenly distraught, betrayed by his own foolishness. He was shivering violently.

He turned and faced the shore. For the first time in weeks he found that he could cry. He stood in the sea, his back to the wide expanse of ocean and he put his hands to his hair and cried aloud, cried and moaned his sorrow and loneliness as a child would, saying her name often through his weeping, shaking his head in a fine abandonment to grief. And if there were tears, salt tears, they fell into the salt ocean about him and added their tiny weight to that wide expanse of water.

The next wave hefted him further in towards the shore. He stood, allowing the waves of sorrow their own force, allowing his body to rise and shift with the sea. And suddenly it was there, the seal, its dark and lissome shape moving like a shadow through the water near him. He stood perfectly still. The seal circled in the shallow water in front of him, went round behind him. He stood, tensed with excitement. He could see its shape move with beautiful swiftness a small distance to his right. Then the head appeared again. They were motionless, watching one another. There was a trembling in his body that seemed to be joy, that took away all sense of chill. The seal did not move; it watched him. He still held his hands to his head. There were no more tears. Cautiously he lowered his arms and stretched his right hand towards the seal. It disappeared at once under the water and he could see it move in a slow balletic half-circle, out from the shore, around behind him. It passed closer to him then, between him and the shore. It paused in front of him, the shadow almost motionless under the surface. He reached his hand under the water, bending towards that dark shape. The beast moved, with slow deliberation, towards his hand and he felt its head nudge gently againt his palm; he knew the cold smoothness of its shape as it touched him and then it moved swiftly away and was gone, its shadow disappearing almost instantly in the great vastness of the sea.

He turned, watching for it, but it was gone. He knew the great privilege he had been given, a grace offered once and for ever. He tingled with the joy of it. The waves seemed to be coming more gently against him and he stood strong and momentarily at peace.

When he turned for shore the day had darkened perceptibly and the coldness had chilled him through. He reached the sand. He was surprised to see how the tide had risen higher up onto the shingles, lapping at the sad pile of his clothes. He shook himself, like an animal, scattering drops of sea water over the sand. He began to run, then, he ran and ran, up and down the sandy shore as the day darkened further. At last, chilled still but exultant, he dressed hurriedly and went to untie the curragh from the rocks.

July 1997

By candlelight . . .

That day's storm had gutted roads and flung great boulders high along the strands of the island. It had swept away a bridge and had brought down sheds and outhouses, had lifted boats out of the water and had left them cracked and ugly on the lips of the harbours. It had torn in two the small house where Danni and Marty had hoped to begin their dreams and it left them both shaken and hurt and exposed to the laughter and reprimands of their elders. The storm, too, had brought down the power lines here and there about the island so that when Danni was brought to the hotel, cowed, distressed, shivering and embarrassed, in Bendy Finnegan's van, the only light in Marty's home was the light of a candle.

Dried, warmed and softly comforted, Marty sat by the open turf fire and told his mother the whole truth of his affair with the pretty Dublin girl. He told her of the great misery of his life that had driven him so often from the house to seek peace and solace somewhere else along the edges of the sea and lately in the arms of a young woman who might love him. He talked on and on while the fire cast its strange shadows on the wall and the small white candlelight sent the shadows of mother and son in uncertain patterns about the room. Angie listened and understood.

When he had finished his tale of sadness Marty was silent a long time, his tears all dried up now and his distress at the inevitable loss of his friend holding him stiff and sore, the disgrace of his position leaving him sorry but indifferent to the notions of the island people. Angie held his shivering body close for a long, long time.

At last, out of the warmth of her presence and her understanding, he heard her tell him what he had so much wanted to hear.

'I will tell you this now,' she said. 'For my own sake as well as yours. It has haunted me and troubled me but I have come to understand it. How I touched on something once that left me changed and lost, yet contented enough with my life. I had been deeply unhappy for many years, deeply unhappy and hurt. But that is a story for another day, when I am stronger still, and you are able to hear it. Another story, a sadder story still.'

She paused. The room was dim and haunted by the slowly dancing candlelight. Marty held his body tighter in the blankets he had wrapped around himself. His mother reached and added sods of turf to the easy fire. At times she leaned in and stirred them with the poker, sighing, lost to everything but her own memories, her story.

'It was September. I had worked for a long time in the stores, and the Mahons had been very kind to me, Eddie Dwyer, too. But I was restless, I wanted something more. I stood at a gate in a high wall, in a town in the east of the country, far from here, far from what I wanted to forget. I remember the wasps, they were everywhere, but I was not afraid of them. It was the harvesters I was scared of, always, the daddy-long-legs, those long, bent and wobbling legs that would catch in my hair. And earwigs! I was always terrified of earwigs, their terrible shapes, like scorpions. Anyway, I pulled the chain outside this gate, outside the huge high wall that was lightly greened with dampness. I had brought with me all that I needed, packed into a small brown paper bag. I had some underthings, a few pounds in notes I had saved from my time working for the Mahons, an old catechism and a crucifix that had been intended for the lid of a coffin out of the stores.

'Before the gate opened I could smell that gatekeeper. It was a smell of sweat and old age, of clay and the carelessness of dress. I had expected a sister to arrive, her sweet smell, soapy and demure, but this was a clumping, muttering coming, the gate's bolts drawn back loudly, almost scolding me for my interruption. "Miss Mahon might you be?" he asked me, for that was the name I had taken to see me through. He was old and grey and gaunt, staring at me with rheumy eyes out of a cadaver face. "Yes," I answered. "Mahon." The name would serve, had served me well till then.

'I got my first glimpse of St Agnes's, the high grey walls with their small windows, the tiny lawn starved for light between house and garden wall, the gravel pathway leading to the house. I picked up my brown package and stepped inside. He closed the gate behind me; there were two bolts, heavy and strong. He shoved them to. I had not thought I'd feel like that, empty, grey, and that the house would be so silent and my arrival so uneventful. I followed him, feeling heavy and lonesome, along that gravel path.'

Angie paused, gazing far into the depths of the fire.

'Were you going to be a nun?' Marty asked, his voice soft and yet startling her out of a reverie.

'Yes, Marty, yes. A nun. A sister in an enclosed order. Away from the world and its horrors. I was running away, I suppose, running from everything. I spent the first morning in a washroom out beyond the kitchens. Two sisters, Raphael and Michael, came and helped me wash and prepare myself. I had wonderful hair in those days and they clipped it right down to my scalp. Then they took away my clothes, my skirt and blouse and cardigan, even my shoes, parcelling them all up in brown paper to give to the gardener for his fire, or to the almshouse for the poor. They sat me down in the postulancy room and dressed me in a coarse shift that pricked and scratched and chafed against my skin. Then they left me alone a while.

'There was a great crucifix dominating that room, Christ suffering, the lover, the alabaster body gone grey with pain and it was Christ I longed for, I wanted to know such love as he had shown. I wanted to find his peace in the midst of all the grief that humanity is capable of, for this was a dream I had, his was an example I would follow, a call. I prayed for peace, for holiness, for love.

'Mother Xavier herself came after a while, tall as a poplar tree, novice-mistress. She instructed me how to put on all the things that those postulant nuns would wear, the long cloth that covered my scalp that she wound slowly around and about my head, the coarse sleeve of her habit brushing against my cheeks. Then she slipped over me the brown habit of the order; it was like diving in dream into the smothering sea, diving so slowly that the dream feels as if it will never end. The cloth was rough and heavy, yet that was the moment I had dreamed about for so many years, that moment of hiding myself away at last from the world that had troubled me. Mother Xavier showed me how to tie the wide black leather belt about my waist, how to gather the folds of the habit within it. She showed me how to hang the big and raw wood rosary from the belt so that I could scoop up the Christ in one hand and kiss that figure. And finally she dropped about my neck the black and stiffened voile that hid all of me away save for a small portion of my face.

'And then she gave me a new name, Gabriella she called me, Sister Gabriella, she said, welcome, welcome little sister of the angels. She left me kneeling a long while and when I looked up there was only the grey light from the window shivering high on the arms of the crucified Christ. I had escaped the world. I looked forward to peace and joy.

'I walked often in the walled garden of the convent. The walls were high, there were moss-green spots of dampness on the walls of the house; there were gravel pathways among the flowers – rose beds, dahlias, late summer plants. Gus was the housekeeper's name and he was everywhere about the grounds although you could scarcely ever see him. I was learning, along with the others, how to despise the world so I could draw ever nearer to the Kingdom of Heaven. I would sit on the stone bench in the garden and pray. There was an old plum tree, I remember, a lot of plums fallen on the ground. Now we did not eat much in the convent, plain food only, plainly served, and I was often hungry. Once I bent to eat one of the fallen plums and saw only the ear-wigs and wasps that were crawling through and over them. And I never tried again to eat when I should not. There were butter-flies, too, dozens of them, savouring the decay, the sweetness. We are born for annihilation, I thought, and I had come to push that annihilation to the forefront of my being.

' "We are angels," Mother Xavier would say, her arms folded, her hands buried in her sleeves. "We are angels, fallen, but gra-ciously held by God from falling the whole distance down to Hell. We are caught in a middle kingdom and we must fall back, labour after labour, into God's grace." I envied her; she seemed to have achieved that late winter bareness that prepares a rowan tree for its fullest beauty. I still sat, fleshed, unsteady, scared but resolute.

'Then there were months while I courted the love of Christ crucified. We rose early to pray, we washed and prepared our-selves, hastening to chapel to sing matins, to hear Mass. It was hard, then, not to fall back into sleep because the body has gar-nered over years so much love of rest and silence. I had not loved my own body; it had been abused down the years, it deserved all the suffering I could give it so it could be cleansed and purified of sin. My cell was small but contained all I needed. There was one small, high window, a plain brown curtain; the walls were painted grey. I had a bed, narrow and hard and adequate. On top of a chest of drawers there was a delft handbasin with a delft jug I kept filled with fresh, cold water. I prayed, let me, too, be crucified, let me un-create myself so I may give myself back to you.

'One day, in the deep cold of that winter, I found in the walled garden just one white rose remaining of that year's growth. I plucked it and brought it with me back into my room. That, I knew, was something sinful and when I bent down to inhale once more its perfume, an earwig came scurrying out from beneath the petals. It fell to the floor and I stomped on it, terrified, hearing its carapace shatter beneath my sole. Oh how I shuddered with the horror of that, trying to clean away the stain from my wooden floor.

'That night my cell was very cold and I found it difficult to sleep. I was having dreams, bad dreams. My body, too, ached for some peace and comfort but I fasted the more and laid myself down on the floor of my cell to offer my pain to God to cleanse me from the blackness of my past life. And when I tried to sleep I heard a frightening scraping noise from somewhere outside my window and I shuddered although I knew that window was several stories high. And then I thought I heard a sound from right within my cell. I know I screamed and leapt up to switch on the light. There was nothing. Nothing at all. And I began to starve myself the more to make up for all my sinfulness.

'In the deep darkness of the following nights the same sounds came to me in my semi-wakefulness; a scraping, scratching sound that seemed to come from outside my window, that seemed at times to be within the room and I would clutch the rough blanket of my bed and close my eyes and mind tightly against whatever it was that was invading me. I spoke to no one of what I was going through, night after night, sleepless, day after day, starving, but growing purer and more transparent to my God. And then one night, utterly exhausted yet unable to sleep, I felt something touch the end of my bed in the deep darkness and I sensed a delicate fragrance that was not wholly unpleasant. I was distraught, so much so that my eyes remained shut, my voice useless. I was not unhappy, I knew, I felt some sort of ease, some release from all my suffering. I had learned to ignore the soft sounds I heard but this time everything seemed so gentle and relaxed that I began to relish them, and to relish the soft weakness of my own body. Memories of that great man's body that had ravished and abused me came slowly back into my mind and I eased myself into the memories, touching my body, touching, touching until a great surge of pleasure took me and I opened my eyes. The room was flooded in moonlight and I saw a gentle fall of white rose petals come down over me as if from the very sky itself. It was then I gave in to the longing for that great naked body to take me physically and roughly to itself and I closed my eyes again, moving with joy and expertise before the imagined body on top of me until when I came I did so with a great sigh of satisfaction and peace that left me exhausted, spent, and immeasurably happy.

'It was easy for me, after that, to see the kind of soul I was, to see the kind of life I would have to lead if I wanted to stay alive. Early next morning, while the sisters were at matins, I shook out my hair which was beginning to grow back to its original innocence. I bathed my face in the cold water of the jug. It was then I felt a strong and sudden prick in the skin of my lower back and when I reached there was a thorn there, a small thorn from a rose bush. I pulled it out and laughed and flung it on the floor where it lay beside that tiny stain from the earwig I had killed. I slipped quietly to the laundry room where I knew some of our worldly clothes were kept and I dressed hurriedly in what I could find. I thought to escape that world without being caught but as I came to the garden gate there he was, Gus, the housekeeper, as if he had been waiting for me. He pulled back the bolts and opened the gate in the high wall; he turned to watch me as I looked back once at the convent walls. "God be with you then," he murmured to me as I passed. "God?" I said, "No sir, no wizened old God, there will be no God for me, malevolent and self-absorbed and filled with bitterness, there will be no God for me but the sweet wilderness of the ocean clamouring against the shores of my small island." And I smiled sweetly at him and turned, feeling light and carefree, back into the world.'

The candle had burned low while she was speaking and now it suddenly went out. There was a great groaning outside from the dying storm and a dull light from a chilling moon just filtered through the clouds into the kitchen. Marty could scarcely make out his mother's face where she sat, absorbed in her memories, wrapped up in that past that seemed ever more alien to him. But he, too, sat silent and absorbed, taken by her tale and somewhat shaken by the intensity of her telling it. And then his mother sighed long and deeply once again and shifted in her chair, breaking the moment's spell.

'But you haven't told me yet,' Marty said, whispering, the sound of his voice coming strange to him in the insulated space of the room. 'You haven't told me who my father is, or was. And now you must tell me, now you must, because I will never know any peace until that's clear to me.'

Angie seemed to grow taller where she sat, as if the darkness gave her a little more courage. Outside still they could hear the winds move roughly about the house and in the distance the sound of the ocean came loud and troubled. She reached a hand towards him and held onto his.

'Many years ago he left the island,' she said, and her voice was soft and cautious. 'And I was very, very glad to see him go. He went to England, or to Scotland or somewhere, I'm not too sure. And I was at peace while he was gone. My life seemed to take on some meaning. I had work to do. I had dreams. But he came one summer, he came back like a thief, slipping onto the island in quietness to discover what had become of his home, his family, his old life. And when I saw him I was suddenly overwhelmed with longing for him in spite of all that he had done to me. In spite of everything. Or perhaps because of everything he had done. For he was the only one I had ever really known.

'And he seemed changed to me, he seemed gentle and loving and full of sorrow and regrets and I gave myself to him again, one more time, for old time's sake, he said, and I gave myself willingly to him for the first and for the only time, and I have never given myself since then to any man. And we made a holy and passionate love in the abandoned house where he had been born and lived and he spoke quietly to me, promising he would come back for me, back from exile to claim me and he swore we would be married, that he would take me away from here, away to his new country and that all would be well and good and true. And I believed him, fool that I was, I believed him.'

Marty could hear the terrible sorrow that lay behind his

mother's voice and for the first time he knew an overwhelming love for her, and a pity he could scarcely contain. He knelt down beside her and put his arms about her. She turned towards him in the darkness and her hand gently moved through his hair.

'He left, of course, he simply left without another word, and I knew for sure that I would never, ever see him again. And it was only after that, only a few days after I had known the full depths of my foolishness, that I decided I would become a nun and give myself wholly up to God. And only after all of that, only after all of that suffering and loss and foolishness, that I knew you were to be born, you, Marty, the only person I have ever truly cared for in my sorry, broken life.'

She was silent again. She fell so still that her son simply watched her, knowing the strain that must have been her life, feeling sorry for her, and for himself, too. And then he asked her once again, 'But you haven't yet told me who he is?'

December 1951

Flight...

The winter wind had risen during the afternoon hours and darkness came down rapidly, hitting the island as the first onslaught of rain came in from the sea. There were slates loose on the roof of the shed and the storm whistled and groaned above and around her where she sat, thrilling with nervous anticipation. Big Bucko would not go to the pub tonight, it was too wild; he would stay at home, he would sleep early. In the morning, long before he came in to see to the cattle, she would be gone.

She got up and went over to the hay. She had built it all up again to form a wall that hid the door from Big Bucko's eyes. It was almost dark now. She squatted, slipped her hand in under the hay near the wall; she fingered the rope Wee Eddie had brought her. She laughed quietly to herself. She would be a bird, free, a wild flower, a cloud, an angel. Tomorrow. Soon. Tomorrow.

She was cold. The nights were so long and bitter. She gathered about her all the old clothes Florrie had sent across to her over the years, cast-offs, cardigans, dresses, stockings. She had already set aside the best clothes she had, a white cardigan, not too shredded, a yellow dress with tiny white flowers, blue woollen stockings.

As soon as dawn light eased into the shed she would wash herself as well as she could in the bucket of cold water Big Bucko allowed her. Then, then she would go.

She settled herself on her cot and tried to calm herself. The winds and rains held her in a wild cocoon of safety. She prayed, deep within herself, to that God she had come to fear and trust through Wee Eddie's catechism. She prayed for courage, guidance, company. She would go as far from the shed, from the island, even, perhaps from the country, as she could. She scarcely understood such things, knowing the world only from the books Wee Eddie had brought her, from the glimpses she had been allowed outside. She shuddered again with anticipation.

Sometime in the darkness she came out of a restless sleep to hear the harsh thumping of his boots on the wooden stairway to the loft. She felt lost suddenly, stunned into terror at his unexpected coming. The night was black, black beyond black. Quickly she groped for the clothes she had put by and pulled them in under the mattress on which she lay. She heard his boots clumping heavily. He was not mumbling and cursing as he usually did. She saw the thin line of light at the edge of the trapdoor. She heard the scraping of the bolt. And then the trapdoor lifted and the yellow light from his storm lantern lit up the walls and rafters of the loft, filling her world with looming shadows.

His head visible in the opening, he watched her for a while. He was strangely quiet. She drew herself back against the wall, pulling her legs in under her, drawing the dress down over her knees. He came up quietly onto the floor and lowered the trapdoor behind him. He held the lamp out and moved across the floor towards her. Oh he was big, bigger than the world, blanking out the rafters, creating a space of chill blackness that loomed its menace behind his bulk. He stood over her. She saw his boots, laces undone, the grey of dirt settled deep through the leather. His trouser ends too, were caked with dirt. He stood motionless awhile and she was surprised. She looked up slowly; he wore a grimey white shirt, most of the buttons, and the collar, undone; his jacket was too small for him, the sleeves high on his wrists, the shoulders crunched.

'She'll be dead soon,' he said. The words were dropped quietly into the emptiness. They seemed meaningless. His boot reached and touched her calf, pushing at her. She drew her body further back from him. 'We're supposed to get rid of you,' he said, and he laughed, an ugly, dried-out laugh.

She did not understand. She shook her head, slowly.

'What good ye'll be to anyone I don't know. Ye're a mistake. A fuckin' mistake an' that's all ye are.'

He left the lamp down on the floor and squatted before her. He reached his hand and touched her on the breast. She knew better than to try and stop him. He fondled her breast.

'Your tits'll get better. They're just tomatoes now. Tomatoes.' He reached his other hand and held both her breasts in his fists. 'I'd miss them tits, though. I would. I'd miss them tits, an' your arse, an' your little cunt, of a night.'

She was wholly passive before him. There was a glazed, distant look in her eyes.

'Can't let you go, though, can I?' he said. 'You'd blab. You'd be tellin' lies an' all. An' you'd get me into trouble. That's the thing.'

She looked into his face, into those dark-grey eyes already flecked with tiny specks of red, that thick and greasy black hair that hung over his forehead, the big jaw, coarsely shaven, the black stubble of the morning beard already roughening his face, the neck thick and powerful, the hairs at the top of his chest visible to her. She felt cold, chilled through with a new fear. She shook her head emphatically. She opened her mouth, moved her lips soundlessly, pointed to her tongue, shook her head vigorously.

'Oh yes, yes, yes,' he said. 'Young women blab. They blab, an' call a fella criminal an' he's sent to prison. Oh yes, oh yes. They can learn to write, you see, write things down. On paper. Yes, yes, yes.'

His hand moved to her knees and she knew again the awesome power of the man. Then he moved his hand in under her dress, moving it slowly up along her thigh. He was leering at her now, his mouth open, saliva visible like a web between his teeth. He moved his hand higher. She could feel her flesh shivering. His palm was hot. His fingers probed.

'Little cunt'll be missed sure enough,' he said. 'An' all that lovely hair that'll be growin'! What'll I do when you're gone? What'll I do at all?'

He was grinning at her. His other hand began to move up along her leg. He was kneeling in front of her now, both hands up about her crotch, feeling her, probing. She closed her eyes, in fear. And yet there were moments when his touch could be gentle, when he was not drunk he could be gentle and she could even know a certain pleasure, an arousal.

Suddenly his right hand was round her throat. His face had gone ugly with anger. He was squeezing her, squeezing. She caught his wrist with both her hands but she knew she could not budge him. He was hurting her, she was choking, she could not breathe.

'No, no, no,' he was mumbling. 'Sure I couldn't ever let you go, I couldn't ever let you go. Never, never, never.'

She felt great pain about her throat, her lungs. Her vision had blurred, there was a haze over his face where he loomed, blurred and distorted, before her. He let her go, just as suddenly, and she fell back onto the floor, gasping, fighting for air. He was kneeling over her, his face suffused with anger.

'One more time,' he mumbled. 'One more, for old time's sake.'

She was still gasping for breath when he straddled her where she lay, her hands raised to her throat. Once again he positioned his great body over her, feeling for her breasts with his hands, then sitting down on her so that his buttocks pressed heavily on her breasts. She gasped under his weight, her breath almost leaving her. He sat a long, long time, growing heavier on her, shifting his weight with a slow, unsteady rhythm. He rocked on her, shifting from side to side.

'I like to keep my little woman under my control,' he said

with a small laugh. 'Under my control. Under my arse.' He looked down upon her. 'It's a wild night abroad, Angelica, wild and terrible things in the wind. Put bad thoughts into a poor man's head. Remember though, you must remember, I'm in charge here. I'm the one in charge.'

He hoisted himself a moment, kneeling over her still, then moved forward swiftly, laughing to himself, until his great bulk was right over her face. He sat again, abruptly, his full weight on her gasping face, smothering her. And she had almost given up hope of her life when he lifted again and moved back onto her breasts. One more time he sat down heavily on her and began to bounce on her, up and down, as if he were riding a donkey.

Finally he moved off her, squatting back down on her knees; he lifted the hem of her dress and she felt his hands fumbling with the elastic of her knickers. Roughly he drew down her linen and buried his face in her crotch, inhaling strongly. She felt his tongue then, licking the base of her stomach, moving down about her, entering her, probing. She closed her eyes and knew she was enjoying what she could of his probing.

He stopped suddenly and cursed. He moved off her. He lifted her off the floor and laid her, almost gently, onto her mattress.

'I'm sorry,' he said softly. 'I'm sorry, Angelica, I'm sorry.' He picked up the storm lantern and was gone, quickly. The blackness flooded the attic at once and she heard the heavy thudding of the bolts as he rammed them home. She heard him thumping down the stairway, the shed door closing. And then there was only the storm, the moaning of the wind, the splattering rain.

For a long time she lay, sobbing, half-excited, cold. 'One more time' he had said. She could still feel his great fist about her throat, his weight pressing down on her chest, her face, his tongue testing her. What did he mean? 'I'm sorry'. Those two words above all caused her more fear than she had known before.

She sat up and stared into the blackness. She could make out nothing. She groped her way across the floor to the gable wall. She knew she could no longer let herself be subject to his whims, his angers, his needs. She was hopeless before him, suspended on the thinnest possible thread that dangled from his life. Her fingers found the rope. Its strands were hard, cool to the touch, definite. A friend. She took it out and reached and dropped the end over a rafter; she tied it, her small fingers trembling, the darkness thwarting and worrying her. She swung on the rope a while to ensure that it would hold. She was growing excited now. More hurried. She remembered her good clothes hidden under the mattress. She heard the wind and the rain outside. She would leave the clothes where they were. She groped for the door in the gable wall. When she found it she loosened the twine that held it shut. Then she pushed hard at the door and it opened with a sudden whooshing sound of release. A rush of cold air and rain hit her and she shivered. She dropped the other end of the rope out into the darkness. She could see little beyond the opening; it was too black outside. She hesitated. But the sensation of his great, powerful hand about her throat remained strongly with her.

Our Father, who art in Heaven . . . She sounded the words in her emptiness. She scrambled up and lifted her left leg out over the threshold of the door. She held the rope tightly in both hands. She eased her right leg out into the void and allowed her body to drop a little. She was hanging out now, her back against the wall. She turned her body, cautiously, until her back was to the blackness and her elbows rested on the sill of the door. She took a great, heaving breath and eased one hand down the rope, then the other. She lowered her body and, as her hands on the rope took her weight, she was suddenly terrified, hanging in the darkness, the wind and rain challenging her. She held on, her eyes pressed tightly closed, breathing with difficulty.

Her panic eased and she began to lower herself further, her body scraping the wall, her knees and elbows suffering against the rough stone surface. But she was strong, she held herself against the wall, the rope was firm, she was determined.

Before she had time to suffer further she was on the ground, breathing heavily. She let go of the rope and stood, her back to the tangible world. She gazed into the storm. She could see almost nothing. But she was free. Wet, cold, and free. She knew where the fence was. Cautiously and soundlessly she made her way across the wet ground. Nettles and thistles touched her knees and calves but she did not fret over such petty things. Already she knew she was independent of the will of Big Bucko, she was in direct contact with the world, with her own will. She reached the rough bank of scraws and scutch grasses that formed the ditch. She could make out the form of the crooked stakes that held the barbed wire fence, loosely, crookedly, leaning and sagging like a drunken old fool. She moved to her left. There was a place...

She cut her knee slightly on the wire as she climbed, but then she was in the next field, out already from the mad acres of Big Bucko's ground. She paused again. The winds and rains came against her. She raised her face into the storm and relished its grip and power. She was empty now, suddenly empty of all demands, empty too of comfort and the security of a familiar place, empty too, she realised, of any knowledge of destination, or purpose or direction.

And then, not far away, she saw a faint glimmering light. It was like a soft call to her, shining, then disappearing as the storm harrassed the foliage between her and it. She moved forward, cautiously, the rain streaming down her face. She was soaked and glad of it, glad that the world might wash her clean of Big Bucko's life. She moved with care, all senses alert, as an animal would move. She reached the next ditch and climbed it and her feet touched the firm surface of the road. She crossed the road and heard the rustling and creaking of the leaves and branches of a wood. She climbed another fence and was in a grove. At once the storm was held back and she stood in a black cavern of shelter.

Now she could see that the light came from a window on the far side of the grove. It gave her some guidance; she kept her arms out in front of her, touching the comforting bark of trees, her feet shuffling a soft ancient shyness out of the deep carpet of pine needles. She reached a wall. Across a yard was a house, a great window, beyond the window a room. The curtains were not closed. She paused. She could see, to her right, the shape of outhouses vaguely outlined by the light. She moved along inside the wall, leaving the window to her left. Then she climbed the wall and dropped down onto the ground of a yard. The side of the grove, too, was sheltered from the storm. She stood awhile, allowing the shapes of the outhouses to grow clearer to her. She had never been afraid of darkness and silence; they offered her shelter.

Cautiously she explored the sheds; there was a carthouse, a stable, a workshop. She heard the shuffling of cattle. She opened the workshop door. It was dark inside, beautifully dry and still. She could distinguish nothing. She groped about in the darkness, her fingers touching a worktop, tools; she found a rough, wooden stool and sat, gratefully. She suddenly felt very cold, aware of how wet and lost and purposeless she was. But she was free – she would not be his slave ever again. She wept. Long and openly the tears flowed, full from her years of sorrow, her breath no more than great sobs and sighs of loss, her body heaving under the ineluctable pressures of her hurt. She cried, and let it happen. She let those years fall from her, to mingle with the raindrops that fell from her onto the workshop floor. She sat still. Exhausted. But she had found a temporary hiding place from his pursuit.

At last she left the workshed and moved softly along the gravelled yard, keeping the wall of the house to her right. With great care she approached the window. As she drew near she could see the walls of a room and then, to her astonishment, she found herself looking in on the most beautiful room she had ever seen. The walls were bright, there was a cut glass oil lamp on a small table, vases of flowers carefully placed about the room, paintings on the walls, a lovely golden eiderdown on the bed that stood against one wall.

She was startled but not frightened when she saw the eyes of the woman in the bed fixed on her. She looked beautiful, but pale; pale, thin and weak. Her lips were too red, her eyes too bright, too large for her face that, in spite of its suffering, was lovely. The young woman was lying back on pillows, her long delicate fingers folded over the eiderdown, her face turned towards the window, a warm smile of welcome on her face. Such a smile that Angelica responded at once, her face pressed in wonder against the glass. She could see the woman's lips moving, she could guess the words; come in, come in please, please, please. And Angelica wanted to; she wanted to enter that world of light and comfort and companionship. But she could not. She could not. She was a fugitive, she was impure, she was evil. She could not enter a world of such wondrous, though fragile, perfection.

She decided. She would go back to her own shed, just for tonight; she would prepare her clothes for the following night. She would prepare Wee Eddie for her departure; she would ask him for a little money to get her away, far, far away from here. She would go back, one final night, one final day. Now she knew she could escape. She could be free. She could be happy. She smiled once more towards the woman in the room and then moved swiftly into the darkness.

July 1997

Flight . . .

When Marty heard the name his mother whispered, Jeremiah, he did not know whom she was speaking of. And then she whispered it again, with shame, yet with a distant, affectionate tone. 'Jeremiah James Dwyer', she said, and again she said it, softly, 'Jerr Dwyer'.

'He came home that one time,' his mother said. 'He sort of slipped onto the island, because he did not want people to know he was there. He was very much hated, you know, and never forgiven for . . . Anyway, he wanted to see that his mother's grave was looked after. At least that's what he told me. And I believed him. He seemed changed. Gentle, repentant. Of course he went to see his brother, Wee Eddie that was, Eddie Dwyer, working in Mahon and Sons. And Eddie came and told me Jerr was on the island. At first I was scared but then Jerr actually came here, almost at once, before I could do anything. I tried, at first, not to let him in but he spoke so softly, he was so repentant, he seemed so kind . . . very changed. So I let him in and he spoke to me a long time, offering his regrets for all that he had done. And then he went away again. I felt sorry for him then, and I began to think back over the past, over all that had happened since he had left, since I . . . And I felt very, very sad indeed, knowing what had happened. And when he came to me again, the very next night, saying he was going to go away again, back to Scotland, to Stirling I think he said, and he would never come back again, and he was kind and gentle to me, and I forgave him everything and he fell down on the floor, on his knees, and thanked me, and a great flood of emotion came over me, some great wave of feeling, of loss, or shame, or love, oh I don't know what, some longing, too, and it was that night, just once, and it was good for me, and for him, and it was gentle, and loving, and I felt at peace after it. I felt at peace. And ever since then he has sent money sometimes, not a great deal, but enough to help us along a little . . .'

Marty sat in the darkness. They were quiet then, for a long, long time. And then Marty said the name into the darkness, while the winds continued to howl outside and the rain battered against the window, 'Jeremiah James Dwyer, Big Bucko. Jesus.' And that was all. He sat quietly for a while longer. Then at last he stood up, leaned over his mother and kissed her softly on the forehead.

'I'm sorry, Mum,' he said. 'I am deeply, deeply sorry for causing you pain today. You will not have to worry about me any more. I promise. Forgive me.'

She looked up at him and smiled and held his hand and squeezed it. He could scarcely make out her face but he could see she was crying quietly to herself. Marty left the room, softly, and moved into his own room.

Very early the next morning he rose. It was not yet bright, but the day was going to be still and calm. He could hear the ocean breaking softly against the rocks on the shore. He could hear seabirds in the distance, and close by a blackbird was already beginning to sing. He dressed quietly. He opened the window of his room and climbed out onto the grass outside. He shut the window very quietly behind him. Then he turned and began to walk swiftly away from the house.

December 1951

There and not there...

Florrie came awake with awful suddenness. Her eyes were open, bright with exceptional clarity. The house was silent, dawn light softening the curtains. She felt as if some noise had flung her out of sleep, a dull thud, like that of a nail being driven into timber. She grew aware of a not unpleasant tingling sensation on the right side of her body, the side that still knew some sensation. There was a distant slooshing sound somewhere inside her head, sporadic and ugly.

She knew, when the daylight grew a little stronger, that Edward was there, slouching at the doorway and smoking a cigarette, leaning against the wall, his legs crossed at the ankles. She would know by his features if he was pleased that she had done her duty by the children, and by Angelica. He would not speak. He might smile that shrewd and knowing smile that would tell her, see you soon, Florrie, see you soon, then he would go, fading slowly back into darkness.

She had things to see to. Urgent things. She heaved herself awkwardly, with her useless arm, her useless leg, until she was sitting on the edge of the bed. The room was cold. She was colder than she had ever felt in her life before. She heard her own laboured breathing in the silence of the room. She imagined she could see a small cloud from her own breathing. The light must be strengthening. She looked quickly towards the door. He was not there. Not yet.

She reached her good hand far in under the mattress. Her fingers touched the paper. She drew it out with a sigh of satisfaction. It was a brown envelope. She left it on her pillow. Then she allowed her body to slide down the side of the bed until she was sitting on the floor, her back against the eiderdown. She fell to her right and moved slowly, like a maimed crab, across to the old dressing table under the window. The effort left her exhausted. She leaned her head against the drawers, closed her eyes and rested. A small wave of nausea rose through her, then receded. Her breathing was harsh, the tingle in her right side more marked, the sound of stirring water in her head more persistent. She needed cleansing, she knew that, with blessed water and sacred oils before she began that awful, final journey. She pulled out the bottom drawer of the dressing table. Underneath her folded clothes there was something wrapped carefully in brown paper, tied in twine, untouched for years. Her right hand lifted it out and she let it drop to the floor beside her. She pushed the drawer shut. When she lifted her head she caught a glimpse of her hair in the lowest part of the mirror. She was not old, not really old, but her hair was a dirty grey and thin as the edge of a haystack after a day of storm. The light from the window was stronger. She tried to lift herself, to see herself more fully in the mirror, but she saw only her forehead, its sourdough crinkled skin, fleshy and livid, and her eyes, the sickly grey of long-dead ashes. Oh she could remember that hair, so black and shiny and full that Edward had called it his summer night of stars; those ashen eyes had burned him up then with their fire. Once upon a time. Long, long, long ago.

She turned and he was there, as she knew he would be. He was formally dressed as if for some ceremony, though as usual the tie was badly knotted; he had chosen the wrong shirt, the cuffs frayed, sweat stains on the collar, and, as usual, he had forgotten to shine his boots. She had scolded him so often over such footling things, scolded him because the world had darkened so quickly after the first glow of love. It darkened when they moved into this bleak house and they began to labour the bog before the house into a meadow and the bog behind the house into green fields. She had berated him because the world turns with such a niggardly kindliness that she had dreaded at once the passing of their love. She had berated him because the honey lost its savour so quickly and the wax it left behind in the mouth was hard and dull and tasteless. And he, being short of temper and stiff with the pride of his poverty, had taken a long, harsh revenge.

He was not smiling, just standing inside the door, his hands lazily in his pockets. Not watching her, just waiting. Incongruous. And not unwelcome. His presence comfirmed something to her, foolish as she was, slumped on the old linoleum of the floor, the frayed carpet disturbed where she had dragged herself across it. She picked up the brown paper package and worked her way back to the bed. She left the package on the bed and began to drag herself up onto the low, decrepit armchair. When she was seated there, weary and panting heavily, she reached and drew the heavy shawl about her shoulders and settled herself to wait.

Edward's eyes moved about the room. They passed over her as if they did not see her, as if they were seeing nothing. But passing over her like that they chilled her through. She shivered and wished he would leave. He was leaning into the room as if willing something to happen, leaning towards her out of his absence. She wondered for a moment if she could touch him, should she succeed in dragging herself across the room. She wondered if she would speak to him, but she was too tired, too weary. And there would be time for that. Time! She tried to laugh at the word but only a quick snort escaped from her nostrils. She laid her head back and started to remember, as if this was what she had yet to do, as if this was, once again, what he was telling her to do.

⋆

There was the girl, you see; that was where it all began, the terror, the destruction, the woe. She was a wild flower, and a lover of wild flowers. They called her Alison, one of the Connors family, Ted's daughter, Alison, sweet Alison. She was sixteen, little more, a child of the open spaces, of the road, of the seashore. Her home was a small canvas cloth drawn over a frame of smoke-strengthened yellow canes bent taut, a home that travelled with her when the others travelled on, in carts, in caravans, on foot. Their animals – donkeys, horses, dogs – trailed along before, beside and behind them. Because of the flowers, and the fine air of the night, and sometimes because of the comforting thrumming of rain on the stretched canvas above her, Alison loved her silent, shifting world. She knew the flowers, the wild ones; she could draw their names out in the sand or in the mud; she gathered and kept them – the scarlet pimpernel, the clovers, fumitory, vetch – she kept them in water in a corner of her cavern and cried when they withered away so quickly, when they became, in spite of her, small black threads of blackness. She knew their properties and their seasons – milkwort, heartsease, yarrow, the yellow flag, chickweed and shepherd's purse, groundsel, daisy, butterbur. But she could not speak their names because she was deaf from birth, Alison, sweet Alison, who spoke only with her eyes and with her hands.

Sometimes the smoke from the camp fires drifted into her canvas tent, noontime or late evening, the smoke that would bring tears to her eyes and call her out to sit with the others; the children drifting about the edges of the carts and caravans and tents, playing their stick games, fighting their fights; the dogs would lie, at caution, peering out from under the carts and the tarpaulins, or sniffing through the dumping-hole at the furthest rim of camp. Alison would sit in her own knot of silence and watch the branches on the fire spit and spark, how the green became black, then red, then white, and floated away into the sky at last in tiny grey specks to take their places with the birds and the stars. She would laugh her strange, barking laugh and her face would grow beautiful a moment, alight with a wisdom the others could not share. And the travellers would look at her and love her, their Alison, their sweet, silent Alison.

She sat and watched the tinsmiths at their work, the strong arms beating and the hammers rising and falling soundlessly, the metal gleaming in the fires from the camp, the small soldering irons glowing white with the intensity of their heat, weeping their small white-hot tears. She watched her own father work, absorbed, accurate, impressive. She saw the tin mugs, the buckets, the cans, all gleaming and fashioned and restored and she would laugh again when the sun caught them and sent a silver brightness to dazzle the eyes of the powerful, violent men. She would watch the women too, at their labours, some of them with their children returning from foraging among the poor houses of the villages round about, returning often with bread, sugar, tea, small gifts of coins, sometimes toys for the youngest, a bicycle frame, a chair to mend, a kettle.

There were fights, too, among the men, terrible, bone-shuddering fights, their faces caught up in anger the way cloth is crumpled between clenching fingers, their fists become murdering knobs of wood. Alison would hide in her Plato's cave when the fights began, watching only the shadows that moved against her canvas walls as the men, big and brown and anguished, broke each others' bones and drew each others' blood. She knew terror then, how a small wild flower like herself, like the daisy, the buttercup, the speedwell, could so quickly be crushed into dust by great iron boots. She avoided the camps when the men drank, scared of that male blundering anger.

The travellers would stay a month, two months, three, then they would move on, leaving behind them a trampled, blackened patch on the earth, and coloured rags like wild flowers scattered about on the thorns of the bushes. But never would they harm their pretty, unspeaking, unhearing girl who smiled and ran like a child, gathering her cowslips, bird's-foot trefoil, lady's finger, making her gay bouquets of silent words that she would sometimes offer to a warring man or a grieving woman, or that she would keep in the soft darkness of her own tent until she wept again to see how swiftly they drooped and languished. They admired how subtle she was too, how she sneaked out of her tent into the night as if her eyes, compensating for the loss of speech and hearing, could bring her flawlessly through the darkness, feline, watchful, sleek. Wishing to contribute, as well as she could, to the people among whom she lived, making her way about the houses and yards, silent as a cat or an old red fox, or a shadow.

In the morning, left outside the tent or tarpaulin cavern of another, there would be eggs, or vegetables with the clay still gripping them; or tools, a hammer, a chisel, a saw; sometimes there would be a hen or a goose, its neck twisted. And special things for her father and mother, and her brothers and sisters. Gifts from their sweet Alison.

Then she discovered the Dwyer place, that small cottage on the great acre field with its ramshackle, leaning shed, its cobbled, miscreant hen house, and the pickings she could be sure of almost every night. Sometimes she would find a hen roosting behind the shed and she would have it by the neck before it could open its beady eyes. Sometimes she opened the door of the makeshift coop where the hens roosted high on the handles of old brooms, and she would take the eggs, six, or seven, sometimes ten, brown and white and warm, and she would be gone again, as soundlessly as she had come, the eggs held safely in the small packet she could make of her dress.

Big Edward Dwyer quickly came to know there was something amiss about his field. He had his traps and he set them for the fox to have its leg shattered between their teeth. But in the morning the traps would be sprung, the teeth closed on air. He knew. But he was scared to go into the tinkers' camp a mile away across the fields, scared of their strength and strangeness, their sudden rages and rushes.

Until the night he came home late from Donie Halpern's pub, heavy with drink, his face bloated with anger, his bitterness in no way sweetened by the alcohol. He had set his traps, hoping now to catch a human foot. He came softly around the corner of his house and saw the wooden door of his shed ajar. He could hear the uneasy shifting of the donkey inside and he knew he had his tormentor. Edward stooped and picked up a great stone in his right fist. He moved stealthily towards the shed.

There was a bright moon that night and it lit up the ground where he walked. His shadow moved before him and it fell across the door of the shed. He shifted his body quickly against the jamb of the door and stood to listen. He could hear the breathing of the animals within, he could hear the shifting of something on the straw of the floor. He heard the slight creaking of the steps that led to the loft and he knew he had cornered his thief.

Swiftly then he moved, shoving the door open before him, letting the light of the moon stream in ahead of him. He saw her at once, high above him on the steps. She was young, he could see that, and pretty; he could see, too, that she was wearing nothing under the rough grey cloth of her dress. He grinned, hugely, and dropped the stone onto the cement floor of the shed.

The young woman looked down at him and there was a candour and innocence in her eyes that took him aback. Her right hand rested on the rail of the wooden steps.

'Get down outa that, you bitch you!' he hissed at her.

She looked at him and shook her head, gently. She lifted her left hand and drew it softly across her mouth. Then she smiled down at him and for a moment he was smitten by her beauty and delicacy. He moved forward and stood behind her, watching up the steps to where she stood and he could see the lovely flesh of her thighs and the swelling challenge of her buttocks. A great pain went surging through his stomach, his head, already fuddled with the drink, became almost crazed. He reached for her and dragged her down the steps and held her roughly against his big, heaving body. He was surprised she did not cry out, nor speak, he could see her lips clamped shut though there was terror in her eyes and she tried to draw away from him. He flung her down onto the straw where the cow was standing and as she fell her dress rose over her belly and the big man could not contain himself. He moaned loudly and fell on top of her, and though she struggled and fought against him, her small fists like tiny flower stems touching his unshaven face, she could do nothing against his force as he entered her, his penis, hard and large and moist, thrusting terribly against her, hurting her, breaking her, forcing itself deep inside her and her cries, inaudible outside the echoing cavern of her own mind, rushed and broke themselves against the harsh walls of her sorrow.

When he had finished with her he stood up, buttoning his trousers, saliva on his lips, sweat on his face, his eyes still wild, his whole body shuddering. He leaned down for her and she cringed from him, but he gathered her up with some gentleness. He led her out from the shed into the field where the moon shone steadily on a silver world; he held her by the hand a while and looked into her face, wondering at her silence, at her youth and beauty, wondering even more at his own brutality.

'If you tell,' he whispered at her, 'if you so much as breathe a word I will deny it all and I will come with the men of the island, all of them, all of us, and we will burn your camp to the ground and I will kill you, I swear it, I will kill you and all that belong to you.'

Of course she did not tell, she did not know how to, nor did she know for certain what it was had happened to her. She tried, once, to tell, when her belly had begun to swell and her mother tried to find out who had done this thing to her. But she could not tell, or would not tell. She smiled at them. She went on smiling.

Edward did not see her again, not during those months while the tinkers stayed in the old quarry beyond the hill, nor did she visit the house again, or the shed, or the hen house. She tried to blot out the memory of that night from her life. But the big man grew quiet in himself and cringed away from the awareness of the hurt that he had done. Florrie, bemused, removed and overwrought already by her own difficulties in the house, could not wring from him the cause of his moroseness, his sudden diffidence, his startled, guilty look when a knock came suddenly to the door. The tinkers left, taking with them all their tents and caravans and carts, leaving behind a great, trodden, black patch on the quarry floor, a multitude of coloured rags on the bushes, like blood.

But they were back in the winter, appearing on their old haunt like frost. Edward noticed them at once and his whole being chilled. He was left alone, it was as if his sin had been a windblown springtime seed that had been taken from him high and far and had disappeared. But he watched the camp, he watched the tinkers on their rounds, coming and going among the houses, begging. And he could not see her.

In the camp Alison was no longer alone in the smoke-filled dimness of her canvas cave. There was new life there, a strong, healthy life that gave her joy. And no, she did not, could not or would not, tell. They asked her the child's name and once, kneeling on the soft edge of the camp, she had drawn the name out with her finger on the soft clay. Angelica, she had drawn. Angelica. Then she had laughed her strange, barking laugh and had rubbed the name into a great clay smudge and had run back to be with her child, alone, in the tent.

And then one day Edward saw her, coming from the camp, wandering away, carrying her burden, carrying the child in her arms down towards the seashore. He followed at a cautious distance. The young woman sat awhile on the sand at the edge of the cliffs and Edward watched, his big frame hidden behind a hedge. She was giving suck. To his child. He believed it. And for a moment a surge of joy and pride rose within him. A surge quickly swallowed up by fear, shame and contrition. She sat alone and he did not know what to do. He watched. She laid the child down on a rag on the sand and she bent over it. He could see her laughing, he could see her joy in the child. He could see her hand moving on the sand, playing with it. Writing. Then she gathered up the infant and moved away, slowly, up the sand track along the side of the cliff, rising, back towards the village, moving among the rocks and the cliff edge, gathering her flowers, her wild sea-edge flowers, saxifrage, campion, thrift, spurrey, stonecrop, spurge...

When she had topped the rise Edward got up and went down to where she had sat and saw the name Angelica written out clearly on the sand. Angelica. He smiled. His whole being grew urgent with pride and contrition and he followed her, quickly, scaling the sand track, up and up until he too came out on the cliff top and followed the sheep path along the edge. The ground rose steeply over the rocks and sea. He had to pick his way carefully and he grew fearful for her, and for the child. His child.

He saw her moving slowly as if in a gentle waltz, carrying her burden, too near the edge of the cliff. He called out to her, but she did not turn. He hurried then to catch her up, determined to touch her one more time, to hold the child, to make some atonement for his sin. He hurried, and the cliff rose ever more steeply and the rocks and ocean below were ever more threatening.

She turned, at last, as if some breath of his urgency had touched her and she saw him coming frantically towards her, the big man, and the same terror and anguish she had known before caught her like a fist about her throat and she cried her small, high-pitched half-animal cry of terror. She began to run, the child in her arms swaying as she moved, she turned to see how his arms waved wildly at her, how his great red face seemed swollen with anger and determination.

And that is how they fell, both of them, Alison and Angelica, two small, frail creatures, that is how they fell over the sudden rim of Tinkers' Cove, a long, deep fault in the cliff face, the sides dark with the black face of the rock, the water below rushing and seething in from the great ocean beyond. Edward saw them fall, he saw the swiftness of their disappearance, how she had looked back towards him at the very worst moment, how she had turned away again, too late, and had stumbled and fallen and disappeared in the length of time it takes to raise a man's hand to his mouth in terror.

Big Edward Dwyer had never been in the sea in his life. He did not like the sea. He could not swim. He saw no reason why he should ever learn to swim. He was a small landholder, a sometimes migrant; he lived in the corner of a big field. Around the field were hedges and fences and beyond the field were other fields, other fences. Then more fields and fences and hedges. And then, admittedly, the sea. But it was far enough away for him to know that never would a wave of that sea wash into his fields.

When he came to the lip of Tinkers' Cove and looked down across the cliff into the black, swaying waters sixty feet below him, he was at a loss. He felt cold through and through. He could not see the girl. But the child was there, tossing about on the waves. The baby looked no bigger than a piece of flotsam from a broken barrel, washed in by the waves towards the rocky end wall, afloat for the moment among the debris, the shadows. He watched as another surge of water entered the cove and rose high, washing along the flanks of the cove, rushing in towards the rocks and the floating child. Before he realised he had made a decision he had thrown his jacket on the ground behind him. And then, fool that he was, he had leaped off the lip of the cliff and out onto the air over that awful chasm. He remembered screaming, he remembered flailing his arms about, he remembered his legs moving as if he were running on the air to keep his balance, to avoid the dreadful thud of his body against the walls of the cove. Then it was all darkness and confusion. His heavy boots took him down like a boulder, his mouth was open, his eyes too, but his breath was taken and he was filled with the terrifying taste of the salt ocean rushing to fill all the spaces of his head and throat and chest. A sudden silence, too, and he was living in the silence of nightmare.

His feet touched something, rock or weed or base, and he remembered thrusting with all his might, his knees bending to give him thrust, his head lifted to whatever memory of light, pale green and distant, hovered above him. Then he was up again, his head above water, his hands thrashing wildly towards the rocks, his mouth coughing out the salt death that had rushed, laughing, to bury itself within him. His fingers scrabbled at the rocks and held, he drew himself against the solid comfort of their bulk, shaking the blindness from his eyes.

The infant was a bundle of cloth, bobbing helplessly among the leavings of the waves' violence. He could reach his right hand, but as he did so the bundle was washed from him and he fell sideways back into the water, his arms skittering for hold on the water's back. Somehow, by dint of the violent thrashing of arms, legs and upper body, he remained long enough afloat to catch the burden to his chest while his left hand lifted towards the rocks. He gripped, and another wave hefted him, banging his knees hard against the cliff. His boots found purchase on something beneath him and he felt safe, safe for the space of a long intaken breath and its slow release. The child in his arms did not stir. The eyes were closed, the mouth open. Edward looked up; there was a wall of rock above him, water dripping over its clefts and crannies. Beyond the churned water of the cove he could see the Atlantic gather itself again to come rushing and carousing against him. To his left he could see a fault in the wall and he began to edge towards it, his right hand clutching the bundle of the child against him.

He realised, quite suddenly, that he was crying, that the salt taste now on his lips and tongue was a mixture of the ocean's water and his own tears. A lesser wave, coming high and silently along the wall of the cove, washed him up to the waist, gripping and tugging him as if it wanted him back down to its core of darkness. He was cold and terrified, even more so now for the small creature he was carrying. He began to work his way up along the cleft in the cove wall. His boots were firm enough to hold him, even on the slightest crack in the rock face. He paused often, moving his left hand slowly. Holding his body, like a lover's, in against the cove wall. He looked up. There was a great space of sky above, silver-blue and grey, the light beginning to fade, grey clouds dreaming lazily in their own easiness. He rose steadily, sobbing, the child lifeless and light under his arm. Soon he was able to lay the bundle on a shelf of rock and hoist himself out of the sea's reach. He stood on a ledge of rock assessing the safest way up.

Then at last he saw the girl. Her body floated some depth under the surface of the water, swaying like seaweed with the sway of the sea. She was a ghost moving in her own world, part of the sea, as silent as always, her dark blue dress waltzing with the waltz of the waves, her arms out at her sides, her face, just visible below the water, watching up towards that same space of sky. He watched her, numbed with grief. The body lifted and fell, sometimes a hand and arm seeming to reach up towards him out of the churning swell. But always, as he watched, she was drifting out towards the mouth of the cove, drifting slowly towards the embracing anonymity of the ocean.

He turned to the child. She was sickly white, small and helpless, the linen cloths about her body knotted shapeless by the sea. She did not stir. She did not appear to be breathing. Edward screamed in anger and frustration, against the sea, against the treacheries of his God, and above all against himself, his great and unforgiveable sin.

He held his hands out over her, like a priest about to perform a blessing. How could he possibly know what to do? Or if there was anything left on earth to do. She was so slight. Angelica. He whispered the name over her as if it were a baptism. Had she come from the unutterable cavity that was before life only to drown, before she had grown aware of who she was? His two big hands lifted her, turned her, gently. His right hand rubbed her back, as if he knew. Nothing happened. He turned her again. The face was blank, the mouth open. Stone still. His hand rubbed her chest. Then he lifted her and pressed her tiny body against his in a gesture of helplessness and the suddenness of the movement made her splutter and cough. Sea water and mucus ran from her mouth and her hands lifted quickly, as if she could do something about her life and living. She gasped, heaving breaths that seemed bigger than her own body, spasms shaking her, and he held her against his body and loved the heaving of that life.

More urgently than ever he began to climb again, rushing to get her to some dry and warm spot, to bring her – home. He knew then, as the first awareness touched him, that he could not bring her to Alison's people. What could he say? How could he explain? They would blame him, they would know at once, they would kill him. They would take the child into their own rough and wild existence, they might even resent her being alive while their own Alison had been drowned. He reached the top of the cove and sat for a moment, trembling with the cold that seemed to have touched his bones, and as he looked down into the cove he felt a sudden rush of gratitude that he had survived.

It was afternoon when he got home. Florrie sat in her kitchen. Outside the rains had begun again and there was a gloom over the island. The wind was rising and a chill had entered the room with the big man. Big Bucko was out somewhere, in the shed, in the hen house, somewhere. Florrie had lit the lamp already and had left the flame down low. The house was filled with shadows moving restlessly against the walls. When the door opened her husband had seemed to bring the treachery of the sea in with him. He stood in the dim light, drenched through and through, holding before him a small bundle. He stood, framed by the open door, holding the bundle out like a gift, or like a sacrifice.

'Angelica,' he whispered to her. 'Her name's Angelica.'

They found the body three days later. It lay high on a sheltered strand down near Blacksod Bay. It lay among the flotsam in a line of stranded jellyfish, wrack, starfish, a broken spar. Alison lay as if at peace, as if she had stretched out on the sand for a rest. Face down, as if examining some tiny thing. They did not find the baby. They searched the coast again, they entered coves and gullies and examined the high tide leavings. They did not find her. Some of them, the mothers, whispered it was just as well, it was just as well for both of them, in the end.

They buried their sweet Alison in a far corner of the graveyard, removed from the settled dead. She lay, a wooden cross marking her mound, her name carved deeply into the wood. Alison. The hedge above her was a fuchsia hedge and in summer the scarlet flowers would hang their exotic lamps in wonderful profusion over her. A pale dog rose trickled its way through the lower branches of the hedge; the wasps would be many, drugged and foolish after the summer; the ridiculous crane-flies, the harvesters, would cling to the leaves and, astonished, disintegrate into death. Alison. At rest, and forever silent.

They waited a while in the camp for the baby's sake. Then they gathered themselves together. They took Alison's canvas tent, its wooden frame, her pots and plates and cutlery, her clothes, her few books, the gifts that had been heaped on her for her Angelica; they took them all and bundled them into the caravan where she had been born. The caravan stood alone in the centre of the quarry field, its long shafts stretched out along the ground as if it had grown weary of the journeying and the shifting of the seasons; its once gaudy colours were faded, its tin chimney stood out crookedly over the canvas roof, its long, horseshoe shape looked old and weary, its four cartwheels chipped and often mended. One of the tinkers went back, carrying the last bouquet; there was chickweed, groundsel, daisies, foxgloves, cowslips and shy violets. He laid the bouquet on the top step of the caravan, before the painted door that was half-door, half-window. They had poured what oil they could spare. He lit a roll of newspaper, held it from him, turning it until it caught and flared, then pushed its torch in through the open window. The net curtains caught at once. There was a great sigh from the caravan and a sudden outbreathing of flames. The tinker turned and joined his companions at the edge of the field. They stood a long time in silence, watching, listening to the whispering of the flames. Then they turned and left the island, their caravans and carts and animals all moving wearily in a long thin line along the side of the road.

December, 1951

A good coffin . . .

But all of that was long ago, long, long ago. Now some slight noise in the kitchen brought Florrie back suddenly into her bedroom. The morning light had brightened the room. She was cold. Her feet were bare on the old rug. She looked towards the door. Edward was gone. She tried to call out but she was too weak. Her right side was burning and the sound in her head had settled into the softly flowing sound a small stream makes. She opened her mouth and only whispers came, like slight, grey-white moths.

Big Bucko opened the door.

'What'll you eat?' he called.

He stood, darkening the room. Big. Oh my God, she thought, still with a trace of original pride, isn't he a great big bucko after all? She beckoned, weakly; she pointed to her open mouth. She beckoned again. Reluctantly he came over. She tried to reach up to him but she could not raise her arm high enough to touch him. She whispered.

'I'm goin', Jerr, I'm goin'.'

He lowered his head towards her and she saw the great Adam's apple, the rough stubble on the big jaw, the stiff black hairs just visible inside his nostrils.

'There's things must be done,' she went on. 'Things to be seen to, and quickly, Jerr, my eternal soul depends on them.'

She pointed to the small envelope on the pillow.

'That's to bury me,' she whispered. 'A good coffin, son, a bit of a headstone, a small cross, no more, the cross painted white, my name on it, no more. Florrie Dwyer, that's all. And then write on it RIP, and under that write the full words, Rest, In, Peace. Promise me now, Jerr, that you'll do that, exactly that. Promise me. Rest in peace. Wrote out full.'

He was counting out the money, pound notes, ten-shilling notes, put by carefully over years. His mouth dropped open. He counted it out again. He was nodding distractedly. She tried to reach for him. Her right hand was too heavy, like lifting a sack of wet sand.

'Rest in peace,' she whispered. 'Promise me, promise a dyin' woman. Promise your mother. Promise.'

'I promise, Mother, yes, yes, yes, I promise.'

He put the money back neatly into the envelope. He tucked the envelope into his inside pocket. She held his jacket fiercely, trying to pull her near-dead body closer to him.

'The parcel,' she urged, 'the parcel!'

He picked the package off the bed, snapped the twine and tore away the brown paper. He unfolded a long white garment. There was a picture of the Mother of God on the front dressed in blue, above her head a rainbow of stars, she stood astride a globe and under her feet a snake writhed.

Florrie grinned proudly. 'My shroud,' she whispered. 'Let them bury me in that, Jerr. Get them to bury me in that. Do these things, Jerr, do them, an' I'll be happy.'

He promised. He dropped the shroud back onto the bed.

'Will you eat, Mother?'

She shook her head impatiently. 'No, no, just a sup of hot milk, like a good lad. And you must send for Father Crowe. You hear me? Send for Father Crowe. I must see Father Crowe today, first possible minute. Go yourself Jerr, now, there's a good lad. Go down to the priest's house and tell him to come to me today. Our Wee Eddie has made a good move there, he'll come to me now, I can tell. But you must go and ask him. Now, Jerr, now.'

When he left her she sighed deeply. She tried to reach for the shroud to fold it back properly but it was too great a task. She sank back in the chair, her head against the backrest, her mouth open. For a while she watched the light from the world move along the walls. She was weary, but at peace.

December, 1951

A serious man . . .

It was afternoon before Big Bucko left his muddy acres to walk to the priest's house. The day was grim, a cold wind blowing from the north, carrying with it the chill of vast areas of ice and snow. The sky was heavy with grey clouds and the island lay wet and shivering about him. Big Bucko's mind was a plaque of dullness as he walked, indifferent to chill as he could be to warmth.

He heard the sound of excited young voices from behind Jim Madden's cowshed. Big Bucko moved, as usual, with his clumsy, unhurried gait. He crossed the old planks over the drain into the yard. He came round the edge of the cowshed. Four boys were prancing and posturing about Wee Eddie. It was four against one. They lunged at him, throwing punches, feinting, shouting at him. He parried, hopping nimbly from foot to foot. Big Bucko saw the five poor schoolbags flung down against the cowshed wall. He roared in anger and moved forward, his huge fists bunched. The four boys turned and saw him and stood stock-still in terror.

'Fuck off, Jerr!' Wee Eddie shouted. 'This is my fight. I don't want you. Fuck off! Mind your own business!'

Big Bucko stopped. At once Wee Eddie had darted forward, his fists swinging and one of the boys was swept backwards against the wall of the shed, blood already beginning to trickle from his nose.

'Good lad, Eddie!' Big Bucko shouted. 'You'll bate the shite outa the lot a them!'

Wee Eddie looked at his brother, looming like the gable wall of a house. Wee Eddie laughed with pleasure and lunged once more at another boy. He gripped him by the lapel of his jacket and swung him out into the yard and then struck him, hard, in the chest, knocking him back onto the ground. Wee Eddie roared with sudden confidence. The boys hesitated, too conscious of the great power of the big man possibly turned against them.

'Good lad, good lad!' Big Bucko screeched. 'Take his innards out and stuff them into his ears, that's it, knock him arse to ground and lep on him, prance on him, lay him out like a fried egg!'

It was over. The four boys, stunned and startled by the new spirit and ferocity of Wee Eddie, suddenly muttered among themselves. Wee Eddie stood back, his fists poised. The world stood still a moment. Big Bucko's face was a red, grinning vegetable. But he was the excuse the four boys needed.

'OK, Eddie, OK, you're in, you're in.'

They turned quickly, picked up their schoolbags and were gone, disappearing round the corner of the cowshed, running with poorly contained dignity from the scene of the fight. Wee Eddie seemed to sag a little at their disappearance and the afternoon had moved suddenly towards darkness.

'Great lad, Eddie. You're able for the lot a them. No bother to you. Fair play to you. What was all that about?'

'Father Crowe was in school an' he said soon is a big Mass in the chapel an' the lads that are good at the catechism an' are goin' to be confirmed can come an' serve the Mass an' there's a party for them after. An' I answered all the questions, no bother, as I do know them all by heart. The lads were annoyed an' jealous too, I suppose. They told me they wouldn't let me join the gang of them that does the Mass serving as I was nothin' but a big swot.

An' I said I'd bate the guts outa them if they didn't let me. So now I'm to serve the Mass but I can't cos I haven't got the stuff.'

'What stuff?'

'The surplice, the soutane, an' them black slipper things you wear on the altar. I don't have nothin', Jerr, an' I can't serve the Mass.'

'We'll soon see about that, Eddie,' Big Bucko said with sudden enthusiasm. 'Where do you get that kind of stuff?'

'Mahon's.'

'Right. Let's go.'

'Now?'

'Now. Throw yer bag in behind the gate. Let's go.'

The wind was coming sharp as knives across the island. They walked the mile to Mahon's in silence, Wee Eddie hopping from the grass verge to the road and back again, flinging stones at the white, already chipped cups on the telegraph poles, bouncing stones along the road in from of them. Big Bucko plodded along. Grace Mahon was standing in the warm glow from the oil lamps. She looked Wee Eddie up and down, clucking with delight at the news that here was another young boy chosen for the service of the altar. She chatted happily to him as she bustled about, opening cardboard boxes, pointing out the lace edgings, the special buttons, the strong eyes on the slippers, the fine thongs to fasten them.

'He's a wonderful boy is young Eddie Dwyer,' she muttered several times to Big Bucko.

'Give him the best you've got, Grace,' Big Bucko said. 'The very best. He's a fine young latchicko. He beat them all at the catechism.'

Big Bucko stood beside the counter, glancing up at the office. He could see Alice Mahon busy with papers and fasteners. He shuffled uneasily. He was wearing his father's old coat and it hung too tightly on him, the sleeves were too short and a button was missing from the waist. He reached inside his jacket pocket and took out a brown envelope. Wee Eddie's eyes opened with astonishment as Big Bucko counted out the notes; pound notes green, ten-shilling notes orange-brown. Grace thanked him, rolled the notes and packed them into a small canister. She fitted the canister into a tin and pulled a chord; the canister sailed across the air, slowly, wobbling like a drunken dancer, and disappeared into Alice's office above them. Big Bucko watched with pride as Alice bent over the task of counting out the money and checking the piece of paper Grace had sent. Alice put the change into the canister and it came swinging back down the shop to Grace.

'That's a wonderful contraption, that!' Big Bucko praised.

Grace fumbled with the change and handed it over quickly, trying to avoid contact with Big Bucko's hands.

'Tell Alice,' he began awkwardly, sniffling, his hands shoved deep into his pockets. 'Would you tell Alice, I was – I was, well, askin' after her?'

Grace nodded, a small grin not well concealed on her plump face. She rubbed Wee Eddie's head affectionately.

'I'll be proud of you in those things up on the altar, young man,' she said. 'Wouldn't a woman be lucky now to have a little son like yourself, all good and holy, and able to do so many jobs around the house, too.'

She slipped a shilling into the young boy's hand. She gave Big Bucko the parcel all neatly wrapped in brown paper and tied with twine, then she ushered them out into the day.

There were small flurries of snowflakes mingled with hail-stones and little short arguments of rain as they headed home. Wee Eddie was stunned by what had just happened and Big Bucko was striding out as if he had solved all the world's riddles. He had opened his hand, he had dispensed serious money, not on his own behalf. He was beneficent, one of God's gifts, a serious man. He felt anxious to display his wealth.

Donie Halpern's pub was to the left. Big Bucko hesitated. It was cold, the winds and steady labouring of the darkness moving in had made the world feel somewhat unwholesome. He stopped. There was a long pause as he tried to shoulder all his responsibilities. There was a tiny, nail-white, laid-back moon, pale yet in the evening sky, reticent, pagan, determinative.

'Right!' he decided. 'It's a special evenin'. You're an achillite. I want to celebrate that. We'll wet the cassock you got. An' the sandals.'

He turned into the pub. Wee Eddie looked through dusk towards the village. He was hungry. He had had his lunch in school – his sandwich of bread and sugar and his mug of cocoa. But he would have to see the inside of the fabulous Donie Halpern's pub. He would have mythologies to narrate in the sacristy to his new companions.

Big Bucko drank that evening with steady determination. There was nobody else drinking when they went in. Eddie had lemonade. Big Bucko stood at the bar, Donie behind the counter as usual, bemused and taciturn. Wee Eddie sat on the form against the wall, his precious brown package on the bench beside him. It was, truly, a special day.

Two men came in at about seven o'clock.

'Jerr!'

'Tom! Johnnie!'

'Cold, by God!'

'Surely.'

'Two whiskeys, there, Donie, please!'

'On me!' Big Bucko announced.

'That's big of you, Jerr, thanks.'

'Wettin' the young lad's success, Min. Celebratin' the intilligince of the wee lad yonder who bate farts outa them all at the catechism the day.'

Wee Eddie finished his lemonade and stood up to go.

'Sit!' Big Bucko insisted. 'We'll go in a minute. I have to finish my drink. I have to chat with my friends. Then we'll go.'

He bought another lemonade for Wee Eddie. He bought himself stout, and whiskey. He stood tall.

July 1997

Troubled waters . . .

Marty turned slowly up the long sandy lane to Bendy Finnegan's house. Daylight was only beginning to move in over the island. Here and there larks were rising from the earth and beginning to sing. An occasional blackbird's song touched him with the possibility of happiness but he shrugged it off. And always there were the cries of the gulls, swooping already over the sea.

The Finnegan house was long and low, nestling in a declivity at the end of a scutch grass field. There were net curtains on the windows that were grey with age and dust. The old green door had rotted underneath and there were long greenish strips of stain running down the once whitewashed walls. A rusted barrel at the corner of the house was brim-full of rainwater from the gutters. Bendy's van was parked on a small grassy knoll to the right of the house. Marty knew that Jackie's motorbike would have been wheeled round the back and into the kitchen.

Very softly and patiently he knocked on the window where he knew Jackie slept. There was no response for a while. He scraped and tapped with his nails on the glass and at last Jackie Finnegan's bleary, sleep-heavy face came to the window. He drew back the dirty curtains and lifted the window.

'What the fuck! Marty! Do you know what time it is?'

Urgently and softly Marty insisted. 'Are you going out to the Widow's Purse today? Fishing?'

'Yes, we're going out. Midday, most like. So what the fuck are you waking me up at this stinkin' hour for?'

'It's really important, Jackie. Please help me. Please. Will you tell me where the key is, the key to the engine of the punt? I have a job I need to do. Then I'll meet you at the mouth of the harbour – no, a few hundred yards from the harbour mouth, out in the waves, say at twelve o'clock? Or whenever you come out.'

Jackie grinned. 'Hah! I heard about you and herself. Caught in the nude, you awful eejit! Caught in the act. Caught in the storm. Caught –'

Marty urged him. 'Please, Jackie, it's very important. I promise you. Let me have the punt, tell your father later on, and that I'll bring it to the mouth of the harbour and meet you there. Then let him take me out fishing with ye, and it's the last time, I promise. And he won't have to pay me or anything. There's something I want to do when we get out to the Widow's Purse. OK?'

'Are you goin' to do the decent thing with Danni, then? Wha'? Gettin' married an' all. But I hear, my dad says, she's goin' back to Dublin first thing today. In great trouble with them oul' eejits from Luxembourg.'

Marty was getting agitated.

'OK, OK,' Jackie said. 'The key to the outboard on the punt is taped in under the seat at the stern of the *David*. You'll need to fill her up with juice though – the way you filled up the young wan from Dublin!' and he laughed quietly to himself.

Marty had already turned from the window and was beginning to run back up the sandy lane towards the road. Jackie watched him for a moment, then shut the window and drew the curtains.

Some time later Marty was out on the ocean in the small punt. The boat hopped and sank between the low waves with a pleasing rhythm. He sat in the stern, his right hand holding the tiller, his elbow on the gunwale, his legs stretched out in front of him. The sun was warm, the day would be exquisite. He kept close to the shore and he could see the people up in the village as they moved about their business or searched for their holiday pleasures. A cormorant flew close by him, he could see its black round eye, he could hear the flapping of its scrawny black wings as it flew over the water. And once, as he passed the mouth of a small bay, he saw the head of a seal bobbing inquisitively over the water. It was a day to expect contentment. It was a day, he thought, for being on the ocean with someone you loved. He held loneliness at a distance as he guided the little boat along through the waves.

When he reached Tinkers' Cove he cut the engine and took out the small paddles that helped him guide the boat safely in from the sea to the wall of the cove. He saw the rope he had tied to the mine stretched taut from one wall to the other side. He was pleased that everything was safe, in spite of the great storm of the day before. He drew the punt against the wall of the cove and released the rope on that side. Cautiously he rowed towards the mine where it bobbed idly, a glumly grey shape with its dangerous spikes reaching out of the sea and sinking again. He slipped the rope through the iron loop on the top of the mine, ensuring the other end was still fully attached. Then he rowed to the further wall and released the rope from there. The mine was drifting perilously close to the end wall by the time he had attached the full rope to the stern of the punt. Very cautiously he began to row out towards the open sea. The rope sagged in the water, then slowly rose as it tightened, drops of sea water sluicing from it. Then he was out on the sea, the mine, at the end of the rope, some thirty feet behind him, following.

At last boat and mine had cleared the walls of the cove. Marty breathed more easily. As he rowed the mine dipped just under the surface of the sea and all that was visible was the long rope from the stern of the punt, reaching out into the water. He was satisfied. He continued to row slowly and carefully, but turned away from the harbour and made for the cliffs at the other end of the island. Soon he was moving well out of sight of the land. The sea was getting choppier, the waves more threatening out here. He did not care. The gulls above him looked almost translucent against the perfect blue of the sky. He was at home on the sea. He had no fear. He had his purposes.

Soon he took the paddles out of the water and left them in the boat. He started the engine again and moved, always cautiously with that burden trailing along behind him, out towards the open ocean. It was a long voyage that he had in mind for such a small craft. He was heading for the Widow's Purse, for Bendy Finnegan's favoured fishing ground.

December 1951

After long labour . . .

It grew dark. Florrie was still sitting back in the old chair. Still waiting. For a short while her eyes had remained wide open, focused. She had time to notice how very, very cold her old body was. She could not move that body now except for her eyes. Her breathing was harsher than ever, her inhaled breath giving her little relief. She was anxious about the darkness. She had thought it could be little after noon.

Although her body felt heavy and dulled she felt as if her senses were all vitally alert. The silence hummed about her. Her eyes, when she opened them, pierced the gloom and she could see all the objects about her clearly defined: basin, jug, Sacred Heart picture on the wall, the scrape marks along the timbers of the bed frame. But now, in the darkness, the whole world about her seemed to have disappeared. Or her sight had gone. She did not care about that. She waited.

At last she heard footsteps in the kitchen outside her room. Soft stepping. Hesitant. She knew a wonderful relief. Softly, slowly, she heard the latch lift on her door. She was saved. She whispered the words, 'Thank God. Thank God.'

She heard the door close gently behind the visitor. 'Father Crowe,' she whispered, 'I'm so glad you've come.'

She laid her head back against the chair. She tried to gather her whole life into this moment of salvation. She began: 'Bless me, Father, for I have sinned. Father, it's years – decades – since my last confession. Too long, Father, too long.'

A hand, warm and kindly, was laid for a brief moment on her forehead, reassuring, touching her brow, touching her wisp of hair. She heard her visitor sit on the bed close to her. She hurried. She spoke to God through Father Crowe, begging forgiveness for her sins, for the bitterness she had directed on the girl through no fault of the poor child's, she told the story, her story and Big Eddie's story and the child's story, she begged forgiveness for her betrayal of God, of all she had been taught to believe so many years ago.

'My sins, Father, my many sins. I deserve Hell, for I have hurt the little child, perhaps beyond repair. Forgive me Father, forgive me. And save my soul from the fires. I'm heartily sorry for all my sins . . .'

She was exhausted, all her breath leaving her in the whispered words. But she had spoken to her God and she knew that He was a great and a good God. She waited. Her eyes were too heavy for her to open. She felt the gentle touch of a hand on her shoulder, a soft, kind touch, and a small smile warmed her face. She felt the caress of fingertips gently touching her on the lips; she tried to kiss the fingertips but she had no strength. She heard, she was certain of it, the words she had longed for so many years to hear: 'I forgive you, I forgive you, I forgive you . . .'

The fingertips touched her once more on the brow and her whole being flooded with joy and peace. She let go then, she let go the tiny hold she still had on the world and her fall was an easy one, like the grateful easy decline into well-deserved sleep after long labour.

Big Bucko and Wee Eddie found the door of their house open when they came back. Big Bucko was mumbling to himself, weaving his way through the darkness as if there were obstacles other than air to hurl himself against. Wee Eddie tried to guide him. He had his package carefully wedged under his arm.

Big Bucko lurched against the jamb of the door. Wee Eddie darted past him and fumbled for the oil lamp on the table. Big Bucko stumbled in and went straight to the chair beside the dead fire. He sat down heavily. The door of their mother's room stood ajar. Wee Eddie held up the lighted lamp and a small army of shadows rushed about the room. He came to the door, his mother was in the armchair at the side of the bed. Her head had fallen forward, her hands lay still by her side. Her eyes were open as if she was staring with extraordinary intensity upon the floor. Wee Eddie called to her softly, 'Mammy,' he called, a tingle of fear already running across his body. Big Bucko kept mumbling in the corner of the kitchen. Wee Eddie stopped halfway across the bedroom. He knew. The silence was intense in the semi-darkness. He stood, chilled by fright and sorrow. And by fear.

'Eddie!' Big Bucko called. 'Bring that fuckin' light in here!'

Wee Eddie decided. Moving slowly he left his mother's room, closing the door quietly behind him. Big Bucko was slumped forward on his chair, elbows on his knees, head in his hands.

'Light,' he mumbled. 'Light, I need light.'

Wee Eddie left the lamp on the table. He picked up the storm lantern from its place on the windowsill. He lit it carefully. Then he moved to the door and out into the yard. The light, sickly and yellow, fell on the soft mud before him.

'You'd better go in to Mother,' he said to Big Bucko from the door. 'Soon, though. You'd better steady yourself up a bit first. Then go and talk to her.'

Big Bucko did not look up. 'Mother?'

'Go in and see her after a few minutes. When you're steadier.'

Wee Eddie went out, closing the door of the house behind him. Holding the lantern carefully he moved as quickly as he could across the rough slippery earth towards the shed. The night was still and very cold. There were stars. He pushed open the door of the shed. There was a heavy wooden bolt; he pushed it home. The cattle shifted uneasily. He looked about the shed. On a rough shelf fixed to the wall he found the hammer and a box of nails. He took them. He began to climb the stairs, calling her name gently. The lantern's light threw the boards of the trapdoor and the loft floor into the clearest detail. The iron bolt was not pushed home and he wondered. The light filled the loft with a glow that reflected warmly off the piled-up hay. She was standing ready, dressed in all the clothes she had. She smiled at him and nodded.

'Mammy's dead,' he said in a loud whisper. She nodded again. 'Jerr is going in to find her. He'll go mad. He'll take it out on you. He's drunk. You'll have to go. And I'll have to come with you. I'll have to hide till he calms down.'

She kept nodding assent.

'Quick,' he said to her, 'the chair.'

He took the old wooden chair from the corner. He lifted it and smashed it against the wall. It shattered easily. Urgently then he pulled the legs off the seat and laid it over the trapdoor and nailed it down, half on the floor, half on the trapdoor, three six-inch nails on either side. 'That'll slow him down a bit,' he said.

He pulled the hay from the small door in the wall. He untied the door from the nail but did not open it. He drew the rope from the rafter and tested it was securely tied. There was a sudden crash as the door of the house was flung open. They heard a confused shouting sound from Big Bucko.

'I'll have to leave the lamp,' Wee Eddie whispered. 'He'll have seen the light.'

He put the lamp down and pushed open the door onto the night. They heard a great pounding on the door of the shed downstairs. They heard him fling himself against the door of the shed. Wee Eddie motioned to her to take the rope. She kissed him then, suddenly, on the lips. It was a quick word of praise, or gratitude. It was a prayer. Then she was moving swiftly and nimbly out through the high door. At that moment they heard the old wooden bolt of the shed door shattering. They heard him begin to climb up the steps. Wee Eddie climbed out quickly after Angelica. Then they were both moving swiftly towards the fence. The kindly loveliness of the night threw a clarity over everything. They moved rapidly, Angelica knowing her path. The noise of Big Bucko's pounding on the trapdoor sounded across the night. They heard the sound of shattering wood. They looked back as they crossed the fence onto the road. He was standing at the high door in the gable wall, the storm lantern in his hand. They saw him turn, they heard a crash as he smashed the lantern to the floor. Almost at once they saw the flames as the hay caught fire. They stood together, stunned, as the fire seemed to become an instant inferno.

Wee Eddie made a move to go back to the shed. Angelica held him firmly by the arm.

'Stop!' she said. 'You must not go back!'

He was astonished. He looked at her and his face was a pale shape of amazement, his mouth hanging open in wonder.

'You can talk?'

'Look!' She gestured towards the shed. Big Bucko was at the small door again, a black shape outlined against the lurid light of the flames. He was holding the rope, lowering himself. They watched. She took Wee Eddie's hand for companionship, for comfort.

'He'll let the cows out first,' Wee Eddie whispered. 'And the ass. He'll do that first. Then he'll come after us.' He turned and stared at her again. 'You can talk!' he breathed.

'Yes,' she said. 'I can talk. I didn't want you to know. I didn't want him to know. That I could tell. What he was doing to me. I went today to tell your mother. You were out. With him. I came down the rope. I went into the room. She was very sick. Very sick. She was praying, I think. The poor old woman. It wasn't her fault . . . None of it was her fault.'

The fire behind them was a conflagration, lighting up the poor acre. They heard the roars of the terrified animals.

'Come!' she said, drawing him across the road, drawing him towards the gate of McTiernan's house.

July 1997

At sea . . .

Under the clear sky of early afternoon Bendy Finnegan held the *Saint David* close to the mouth of the harbour, waiting. Jackie, his tall hayfork of a son, scanned the bay and the coastline. There was no sign of Marty and the punt. They circled awhile, Bendy growing angry and impatient. Then he turned the boat again, shouting a curse to his son, calling to his boat to 'Giddy-up now you lovely bitch!' and heading at once for the open sea.

Behind them a small flock of gulls kept up their sharp and scraping screeches, diving for what they could find in the wake of the trawler. The waves were gentle here, the ocean resting after the great shock of the day before. Jackie sat in the stern, anxious and angry at the failure of Marty to show up. His father would give him what's what, that was sure.

Some time later, as they approached the fishing grounds, the day had begun to darken a little and the swell had risen. Bendy and Jackie both grew a little anxious, remembering the storm of the day before. They began to lower the great net into the sea. Almost at once Jackie spotted it: the great Spanish trawler, coming towards them from the grey horizon to the west. Without saying a word he pointed out the ship to his father.

'Fuck them to hell!' Bendy spat. 'They'll not scare us out of here, that's for sure. We'll stick it out this time. Keep going with that net.'

Anxiously Jackie watched as the shape on the horizon grew larger. Slowly the great net slipped down into the darkness of the water. Suddenly Jackie shouted out in surprise. He pointed again, a little to the south-west. There was a small boat, a very small boat, appearing and disappearing between the waves and at once Jackie knew it was their punt, and he knew it was Marty, out so far and in great danger.

'Well fuck him for a hammerheaded bollix!' was Bendy's comment. 'What in the name of Christ does he think he's doing? He must want to get himself drowned. That's what he wants. You sure pick a strange lot of hammerheads for your friends, Jackie.'

'We'll have to get to him, won't we?' Jackie asked, cautiously.

'Fuck him!' was the response. But Bendy had already fastened the trawl to the boat and was moving towards the wheelhouse. He moved the *Saint David* slowly towards the punt which was lolling in the swell some half mile away. The great trawl was dragged through the sea as they made very slight progress. And all the while Jackie was watching the Spanish trawler moving at great speed towards them. He stood high on the bow of the *Saint David* and began to wave to the small figure in the punt, hoping to point out the dangers to Marty. He thought he got a quick wave of Marty's hand in response.

For several long minutes the three craft approached one another; the *Saint David* seeming to make little progress, the punt now almost directly ahead, the huge trawler bearing down on them. The day, apart from the grumbling of the half-decker's engine, seemed to have fallen silent, as if in anticipation. There were no birds visible. The sea had turned a black-blue colour and the swell was growing perceptibly. Bendy stood in the wheelhouse, his hand grasping the wheel, his teeth clenched. Jackie stood on the bows, holding on grimly, watching. For a while trawler, punt and half-decker formed a straight line and Jackie began to fear that the Spaniards might not have seen the tiny boat; they were bearing down on top of it. Again he waved wildly, pointing, gesticulating, shouting into the gathering wind. The punt moved slowly. Marty was visible, hunched low into the tiny boat, holding the tiller tightly.

Then the moment of danger passed. The punt had gone through the line of the trawler and was now to the right of the approaching *Saint David.* Half-decker and Spanish giant were heading directly towards one another, less than half a mile between them. Bendy hesitated. He was cursing loudly. He slowed the half-decker a little more, undecided whether to head straight for the trawler or turn towards the punt. They were scarcely a quarter of a mile from the Spaniards when they could see that Marty had turned the punt back towards the great trawler and was making directly for it. Bendy cut the engine dead. There was a huge silence. Jackie watched in terror as the Spanish giant bore down on top of the tiny punt. Trawler and boat almost collided, there was a terrible explosion and both vessels vanished in a volcano of spray. Both men on the *Saint David* watched, stunned, as the noise of the explosion echoed across the ocean. It seemed to them as if the sea had lifted itself high up and around both the trawler and the punt and was now pouring down on them with its terrible anger. The half-decker drifted, Jackie clinging hard to the bow rail, Bendy moving in a half-trance out from the wheelhouse.

It took some time for the scene to grow clear again. It seemed to the astonished watchers like a great pall of smoke clearing away from a burning shed, or like a thick mist blowing slowly away in a light breeze. Gradually the stricken trawler emerged from the spray and smoke. A great silence had descended over the ocean, as if the ocean itself were stunned and shocked into placidity. The whole turning of the earth paused. There was a huge, jagged gash in the prow of the trawler, at the waterline. The ship was already leaning forward, like a stricken bull slowly bending its foreknees. Around the ship the sea seethed and seemed to boil. There was no sign from where the *Saint David* drifted of the small punt.

'Look!' Jackie shouted. 'Starboard side. They're bailing out!'

Bendy watched as the sailors began to lower two large craft over the side of the smitten trawler. There was feverish activity as the ship leaned further and further forward in a gesture of surrender. The ocean settled a little, the day seemed to pick up its impetus. Bendy and Jackie could hear the frantic calls of the sailors on board the ship. Bendy moved suddenly. He went back into the wheelhouse, muttering about Marty, the punt . . . The half-decker began to move forward again, cautiously, the huge trawl still holding it back, weighing it down.

'Drag in that net, Jackie,' Bendy shouted back to his son. 'It'll only keep us stuck here longer than we want. Haul it in man. Quick.'

Jackie bent to the winch and began heaving the net back into the half-decker. Slowly the *Saint David* began to close with the stricken giant. Bendy let the boat shift slowly forward and came back to help draw in the net. At that moment the whole ocean seemed to be alive: there was the noise of engines, the gentle but strong purring of the *Saint David*, the still loud and powerful sound of the large ship's engines, the cries of men, the washing of the waves. The two islandmen worked feverishly, Bendy muttering all the time the name of Marty, Marty, Marty. Soon the net was bundled on the deck and Bendy was back in the wheelhouse.

'Keep an eye out for the lad!' he called to his son and Jackie climbed back up on the bows, holding to the rail, watching ahead.

Bendy put the half-decker to the full of its power and it began to move quickly towards the trawler. The big ship was sinking fast, the front half of it already under the water, the stern rising always higher into the air, the fittings on the deck clearly visible, some of them shifting forward with a screeching noise. Bendy steamed quickly round to the right-hand side of the stricken vessel, moving in a circle as close to the ship as he dared. There was nothing visible in the water. They came around the stern of the ship and they could still see its two massive screws feverishly active in the air, whirling uselessly. The large stern of the ship stood high over them, its roundness perfect, its shape from here wonderfully lovely. Then they saw the two dinghies. The sailors were rowing feverishly away from the stricken ship. Jackie counted.

'There's eight of them!' he called back to his father. 'They're getting the hell out of it. They must all be safe. I can't see Marty.'

The half-decker moved around to the other side of the trawler. By now the two dinghies were well away. The men had stopped rowing and were watching back towards their giant. Bendy slowed the half-decker and moved along at a safe distance from the sinking ship. All at once the engines of the trawler stopped and only the soft sound of the *Saint David* could be heard. Bendy cut the engine to idle and a low and gently mournful sound came from its engine as it drifted along by the sinking ship.

There was another pause in the turning of the world. The trawler now seemed to be fully upright in the water, rising still high as a building over the sea, its lower half lost already in the water. Then it plunged rapidly, as if it had made a decision. It appeared to dive directly downwards, willingly, almost with a whoop of delight. It disappeared. There was silence, water swirling quietly around where the ship had gone down. Then there came a great surge of water, the sea rising in a final gasp as the ship was swallowed into the depths. The ocean seethed and swirled wildly for a while and the small yellow punt, ripped and torn, appeared bobbing like a child's toy over it. The punt was empty, the engine had been ripped off, the small stern destroyed. Then all was silent. A few small pieces of timber floated to the surface. A piece of cloth. A slick of oil. Then nothing. Nothing.

Bendy moved the *Saint David* towards the yellow punt, guiding it carefully, Jackie reaching out over the gunwale, trying to grasp it. Jackie spotted the blue rope leading from the ring on the prow and vanishing into the water. He reached for the gaff and as the half-decker passed the punt again Jackie reached and caught the rope, hoisting it out of the water. There was a scorch-mark at the end of the rope where it was ripped and torn. He hauled the punt on board. Neither of the men spoke. The ocean round them was empty now, the two dinghies already moving slowly towards the east and the island.

'Might be with some of them fuckers in the dinghies,' Bendy said. He turned the half-decker and made towards the sailors. They stopped rowing and watched, in silence, as the *Saint David* approached, then circled them. In silence they gazed at one another as Bendy took the boat slowly past them. There was no sign of Marty.

'Fuck you!' Jackie shouted at them.

Bendy turned the half-decker again and headed back out towards the detritus on the surface of the ocean. For a long time the *Saint David* circled, slowly, the circle widening every time. Then, as the evening light began to fade, Bendy turned the boat towards home.

December 1951

Out of the darkness . . .

Ruth McTiernan lay awake and restless. Sometimes now she moaned with the pain, sometimes she would take tiny sips of water. Eoin sat by her bedside and saw how her hand was thin as a branch of hawthorn, fragile as porcelain. Then she seemed to come wide awake; her eyes opened and Eoin was happy to see a clarity in them, the light of awareness on her face.

'Eoin,' she said, and her voice was firm, though weak. 'You're here!'

He raised her gently in the bed and arranged the pillows behind her. She smiled and spoke of her hunger. She sipped at the water. She asked for tea. She took some fingers of lightly buttered toast. She turned often to look out the window towards the trees.

'I have had such strange dreams,' she told him. 'Strange, and yet very real.' He tried to calm her and she smiled faintly, and leaned back into the pillows. For a long time she was silent, breathing gently. He held her hand. There was peace. The darkness had come quickly but there was a small lamp lighting in a corner of the room.

'It's a good time,' she whispered to him. 'It's a good time of the year to die. Christmas coming. The child . . .'

He soothed her and she seemed to sleep another while, though at times her fingers pressed his hand. When she gripped him suddenly and sat up in the dim light of the room, her left hand pointing to the window, he was startled and knew a quick chill of fear.

'The angel,' she whispered, her eyes wide open. 'I can hear her coming.'

He could see nothing in the glass but the faint reflection of the room.

'Listen!' she urged him. 'I heard her coming before, it's like the rustling of leaves, or like running water.'

He got up quickly and moved to the window. He stood to one side and listened. He knew at once there was somebody out there, someone stepping cautiously over the shingles of the yard. He waited, moving in behind the curtain. He watched Ruth's face reflected in the glass; she was watching eagerly and then he saw her face soften with a kind of relief, she smiled, her fingers beckoned. Cautiously Eoin peered round the curtain. Then he saw her; a girl's face, the hair unkempt, the face unclean but pretty, the eyes clear and intelligent looking, the lips smiling. Rapidly he flung wide one of the shutters and stepped out into the yard, taking the girl firmly by the wrist. She cried out and at once another figure jumped forward from the darkness and began to punch and kick at him until he released the girl and caught the boy by the arms. He could see that this child was younger, thin and tall and angry. The girl stood close to them, her hands up to her face, shaking with the fright she had got.

'Please,' she said then. 'Please let him go. We don't mean any harm. Please.'

By now Mr McTiernan had come out into the yard from around the side of the house. He was carrying a lamp. Mrs McTiernan followed him, cautiously holding her dressing gown tight to her neck.

'It's Wee Eddie Dwyer!' Sissy McTiernan exclaimed. 'Who brings the eggs.'

Sissy peered hard at the girl who was cowering, trying to find shadows where she might hide. Eoin pulled and pushed the boy towards the door of the house and the girl followed.

'It's alright,' Eoin was saying. 'You mustn't be afraid. Come on in. Ruth would like to see you. She's seen you before, through the window. She wants to see you, to talk to you.'

Gently then he released the boy. They stood, the two intruders, alert, stiff as hares poised to run, but Eoin could see how the girl still hesitated. She seemed to gather herself then, plucking courage out of the air, out of the steady hold of her shoulders.

'Is she sick? The pretty woman?' she asked Eoin.

'Very sick.'

'She's beautiful, she looks like she's made of glass,' the strange girl said and there was sadness and ready sympathy in her voice.

'Come on in and talk with her, let ye.' Sissy McTiernan was effusive now, her warmth and kindliness eventually persuading them. As they came around the front of the house they could see the shed in the Dwyer field; it was a great paroxysm of flames. The fire lit up the area about the house, the fences, the ditches, the sombre outline of the old house. They could see a big man in the otherworldly glow ushering animals away into a corner of the field. They turned then, Wee Eddie and Angelica, and went into the McTiernan house.

December 1951

By name and nature . . .

There was quiet throughout Mahon's General Stores. It was two days before Christmas. Alice moved in a desultory way about the shelves, a notebook in her hand. Taking stock. She was checking things through all over again, without much heart. Grace was sitting on a high stool behind a counter. She was crying softly. In a far corner of the stores Aenghus Fahey was measuring floorboards with an uneasy sense that there was something more amiss with the sisters than Ruth McTiernan's death a few days before might warrant. It seemed the beginning of a day that did not appear as if it would ever end.

'Poor Ruth!' Grace said out loud to the store.

'Yes, yes. But it was inevitable,' Alice responded testily.

'And there's those two children, God help them, what's going to happen to them at all at all?' Grace rubbed her eyes and face with a small white handkerchief.

'You're a sight, Grace!' Alice offered. 'What'll he think if a traveller comes in now?'

'Oh to hell with the traveller!' Grace said sharply. Alice was taken aback. Grace stared at her and sniffled. Her face was blotched and ugly from the tears. Ugly, thought Aenghus, glancing over at her. 'Put a man off!' He got down on the floor again, measuring.

'I feel, Alice,' Grace went on more quietly, 'you know, I feel that there's something gone out of our lives. Something pure, with poor Ruth, like, and with those awful goings-on in the shed. Oh God. Something soft and kind has left us. I feel as if the world has taken us over somehow. As if – as if all we have come to care about, Alice, is money. Profits. Sales. I'm not saying there's anything wrong with that. But what else is there in our lives? I mean . . .'

'Pish to that, Grace! Aren't we doing very well? Aren't we comfortable? Well off? Our future secure?'

'That's just it, Alice. But where's . . . oh I don't know, hope, maybe, where's hope? I wish I could use words better, Alice. Alice, are we . . . happy?'

'I don't know what you're talking about, Grace. What else do you want?'

'That's just it, Alice, we have everything. And I'm grateful. But I'm not peaceful. I'm not content. When I saw that poor girl Angelica, when I heard her story, that terrible, terrible story, and when I saw Ruth there before she died, so beautiful, so young, all wasted, wasted, wasted . . . I begin to wonder what truth is at all, at all, and what's real any more?'

Grace was crying again, her face buried in her hands. Alice stood still, looking at her, but there were tears gathering in the corners of her eyes, too. Aenghus Fahey knelt on the ground, listening, unsure.

'We've lost – spirit, Alice,' Grace tried again. 'That's the word. Spirit. We've been making money and nothing else. And we're worried about money. Always money money money. We've lost the balance there used to be between ourselves and the world. As if we were living two lives. Neither of them real.'

The door opened suddenly and Big Bucko came in. He wore a long brown overcoat, a black diamond stitched roughly onto the sleeve. He closed the door behind him. Grace and Alice stiffened when he came down between the counters. Aenghus lowered himself behind the counter until he lay almost prone along the planks he was supposed to be measuring.

Big Bucko advanced uncertainly. He sensed the hostility ahead of him. He stood, his hands hanging foolishly at his sides. He breathed deeply, drew himself up, and spoke.

'I've come about a coffin!' he said quietly. 'I'll be wantin' the best ye have. For my mother. An' I want candles, an' things, to give her a wake. Please.'

'I'm sorry for your trouble, Mr Dwyer,' Alice managed.

He stood in the shop, head bowed. 'Mr Dwyer'. It felt strange, as if he had acquired a new dignity. As if Florrie's death had dressed him in a fine, rare cloth. Grace looked at him and could not speak.

'We'll go out to the workshop, so,' Alice said, and she moved to the door. Big Bucko glanced cautiously at Grace and followed, slowly. When the door closed behind them Aenghus stood up suddenly out of the gloom.

'That's a quare class of a fella, surely, Grace,' he said.

She had forgotten his presence. 'My goodness!' she gasped. 'You frightened me. I didn't know you were there.'

'I'd best go out, Grace, and explain what I have.'

She stood up. 'I'll come, too, Anus. The McTiernans will be down soon and they'll be after a coffin, too, God help us all. And there's things we'll have to discuss. Things.' He was surprised and grew ill at ease at the firm tone of her voice. A new Grace, he thought, and the thought did not make him happy.

The shed was bright; what light there was came in through the high windows, the smell of sawdust pervasive and pleasant. There were four coffins finished and standing together on wooden frames in the centre of the workspace. Aenghus stood proudly to one side as Big Bucko moved awkwardly to the coffins. Grace, too, went to inspect them.

'God rest her,' Grace said, 'but poor Ruth won't be taking up much space.'

She stood near Big Bucko, scarcely conscious of his presence.

'This one,' Big Bucko announced, pointing.

Aenghus came up slowly. He stood a short distance away.

'Jerr,' he began. 'I'm very sorry for yer trouble an' all to that, but do you mind me askin' now, who'll be payin' for this here coffin?'

Grace and Alice were taken aback.

'Oh Anus,' Grace said, 'not now, man, not now.'

Big Bucko took some notes out of his pocket. He held them out, sheepishly, towards Aenghus. Aenghus shook his head, slowly.

'That'll buy you the bottom of a coffin an' a few nails,' he said, snorting contemptuously.

'Anus!' Alice reprimanded him.

'No Alice, now, no,' Aenghus said. 'This man here has a fondness for tellin' me off an' for callin' me all sorts of things. Now he wants my services an' I have a right to know if he'll be able to honour his debts. That's all.'

Big Bucko seemed to collapse within himself. He stood holding the money, his hand dropping slowly back by his side. He looked towards Alice and Grace. There was a long silence. Somewhere, in the living world outside the workshop, a dog barked, distantly. Big Bucko had reached another wall. And he could not see his way around or over or even through it. He shuffled, put his hands, with the money, into his pockets. He closed his eyes, took a deep breath, and decided.

'After I put my poor mother in her grave,' he said, 'there's a choice for me. I know that. A choice. This is it.'

He squared his shoulders. He opened his eyes. He looked towards Alice.

'I have a fine house, now. An' 'tis mine. An' I have cows and an ass. Chickens. Eggs. Two acres. An' turbary rights to keep me in turf all my days. First. So.' He looked down at the ground. Concentrating. 'I'll offer you a cow for one of your coffins.'

Aenghus was shocked. Then he grinned, barking out a short, ugly laugh.

'What would I do with a cow?'

Big Bucko looked up, a retort seething on his lips, but he held himself back. He inhaled deeply.

'You could sell it at the fair, first Tuesday.'

'I could then,' Aenghus agreed, reluctantly.

'So,' Big Bucko carried on, 'that's that bit settled.' He turned towards Alice again. 'I'll see my mother safe to her rest, then. After that, I'll have to leave the island 'cos I know there's no place left for me here. Folks is hard. Livin' is hard. An' folks won't understand our troubles. They'll not understand what I had to put up with. They'll not forget. An' they'll not forgive. What happened with my father, that wasn't my doin'. When we was bein' robbed of our livin'. By them tinkers. But they won't believe, nor care about us. 'Cos we're not respectable. I don't care for myself, but I care for Wee Eddie. An' I don't want him to suffer for what I've been. I'll emigrate. To Glasgow. I've an uncle... an' I'll take Wee Eddie with me.'

He was speaking quietly and firmly. Now he paused.

'That'll be no good for Eddie,' Grace said loudly.

He looked at her. 'That's the way things'll have to fall then, Grace Mahon. What's for him here at his age if I'm forced to go? It's one half of the choice. Only half.'

Slowly Big Bucko turned back towards Alice again. 'So. Alice Mahon. I've always had a soft spot for yourself. Now. If you'll have me, you'll have the house too and it's yours, an' I'll be good to you for always. An' we'll have Wee Eddie, too. An' all. That's the other half. That's it. So.'

There was a stunned silence. In one corner of the workshed a small fly buzzed in the soft grasping arms of a cobweb. Big Bucko backed away slowly as if he expected an attack on his person; he looked at Alice. She was breathing heavily.

'Am I to understand that's a proposal of marriage?' she said.

'Yes, ma'am. You are indeed.'

'Hold on there now,' Aenghus intervened angrily. 'Hold your horses there now for a wee minute. Whoa up there now. You've no right to ask Alice Mahon for anythin' after the way you've carried on, from what's bein' said around here. You're lucky you're not taken up by the police and sent to jail for the rest of your sorry days.'

'I'll ask you, Anus Fahey,' Big Bucko said without looking at him, 'kindly to hold your tongue and stay out of this. This is no business of yours.'

'I'm bloody sure it's my business!' Aenghus shouted. 'I'll not have you comin' into my workshop, expectin' my hard work for charity, then insultin' a woman I'm goin' to ask here an' now myself to become my very own wife!'

Everybody looked at him. Aenghus stood, bulked and aggressive, his fists bunched at his sides, his face red with anger and determination, his eyes fixed on Big Bucko. It was Grace who broke the silence.

'Alice,' she asked softly, 'are you going to marry Anus Fahey?'

'I'm not then!' Alice replied angrily. 'I'm not goin' to marry anybody. And nobody has asked me to marry them. And never did. And never will. And I'll not marry anybody, ever. That's the truth of it. So there!'

Aenghus looked at her. 'But,' he said. 'Alice Mahon, you must have known I was leadin' up to it?'

'You're a fool, Anus Fahey,' Alice replied. 'You're a fool. I told you I was not the marryin' kind. And I thought... Grace, she... until she began to see what kind of a man you really are!'

Alice looked at her sister who was standing, leaning against a workbench, her left hand raised to her mouth.

Aenghus stood numb, gazing at Alice. Big Bucko looked angrily from one to the other. Grace gave a great sigh. Her eyes met Alice's. There was a rare brightness in Grace's eyes. She seemed to shiver slightly, as if she had cast off all hesitation from her person, like clothes. She began to laugh, softly.

'Enough,' she whispered, in a voice barely audible in the large space of the workshed. 'We've had enough. But there never does seem to be enough. Does there?'

Alice came and held her gently by the arm. Sisters. Alice 'n' Grace. Grace 'n' Alice.

'So!' Big Bucko said testily. 'I'm to be ignored, is that it?'

Aenghus roared suddenly and came rushing at Big Bucko, his fists raised. The force and suddenness of the onslaught knocked

Big Bucko back against the wall of the shed. Aenghus swung his right fist at his head but Big Bucko parried it easily with his left hand and pushed Aenghus back from him. Big Bucko grinned foolishly, though there was a light of hatred and anger and frustration in his eyes. With surprising speed and agility he threw his coat on the floor beside him. He raised his fists. Alice screamed at them. Grace backed slowly away from the bench.

It was a terrible, crunching fight. Both men were alert with rage. They crashed into the benches. One of the coffins fell and knocked to the floor with a searing, splintering sound. They fought hard. Aenghus was knocked backwards and fell heavily over the timbers of the broken coffin. He rose, shouting, and rushed at Big Bucko. Aenghus cursed loudly as he fought. Big Bucko was silent, concentrating on his fighting, pushing forward with determined gravity. They fought on, ignorant of the world about them, careless and indifferent to anything but their own angers and rages and frustrations. They knocked over the tools. They smashed another of the carefully wrought coffins. They thudded against the walls. They fell, screaming and rose, red-faced, hating, determined.

The women moved away slowly, calling out all the time, first with annoyance and then with fear. Then they left. Alice stood awhile, watching in through one of the windows, wincing as blow followed blow. Then she put her head down between her hands, blocking the noises out. She closed her eyes and shook her head, helpless as a frightened child. Grace turned from the workshed door and went back quickly into the stores. She passed rapidly between the counters and down the narrow passage into the house.

The fight continued with growing urgency. Aenghus grunted loudly when he struck or was stricken. Big Bucko maintained his concentrated gathered silence. Just as they both fell together against a workbench, bringing it down and all its tools and pieces of timber, its boxes of brass screws and crucifixes, Grace Mahon walked back into the workshop. She held a shotgun in her hands. Calmly she levelled it, aimed it at the wall over the wrestling pair, and fired.

The explosion was deafening in the confines of the workshed. The shot knocked plaster off the wall and it fell, skittering like a heavy shower of hailstones, over the two men. They went still, astonishment blanching their faces. Slowly Grace lowered the shotgun and levelled it towards the two men. They began to gather themselves awkwardly off the floor, brushing their faces with the backs of their hands. Grace stood steadily, her hands unshaking, her body firm, the double-barrel of the gun aiming directly at them. Alice came to the door and stepped inside, both hands to her face, her mouth wide in astonishment.

'This is the way it is,' Grace announced calmly. 'Alice and me are reclaiming our ground. Right now. And forever. Both of you will leave this place at once and never darken the doors of Mahon's stores ever again. Never again!'

Aenghus, his nose bleeding, his lip already swollen and ugly, cuts over both eyes, made a move towards her, his right arm raised.

'Now, Grace . . .' he began.

Calmly Grace turned the gun directly at him, raised it to her shoulder, closing one eye. Her right hand cocked the second hammer, 'I've one shot left, Anus,' she said softly, the words filling the space with menace. 'It would give me the greatest pleasure to burst your lying, cheating chest wide open.'

He stopped. Big Bucko stood with his back against the wall. His face, too, was bloodied, he held his right wrist in his left hand, as if it were broken. He was shaking his head, slowly, slowly.

'You're sacked, Anus!' Grace said, quietly.

Aenghus looked towards Alice. She took her hands away from her face. She laughed a short, contented laugh. 'You're sacked, Anus Fahey,' she said. 'Get out of our shed. Get out of our sight. Go back to Coventry, or Dagenham, to your post office, to your lies. Go back to where you came from. Go. GO!'

'This is the way it is,' Grace repeated, the shotgun still aimed at Aenghus Fahey. 'Mr Dwyer can have his coffin. He can bury his poor mother – God rest her soul. Then he can take himself away. To Glasgow. To New York or Timbuctoo. But Wee Eddie Dwyer stays here. Angelica too. Wee Eddie can turn this place into a proper workshop. No more coffins. No more of that. Angelica can work about the shop. They'll both be paid. And cared for. The both of them. They'll be like our very own children, mine and Alice's. They'll be Mahons, that's what they'll be. And Wee Eddie can have the house, Angelica too, and the cows, and the bogs. Jerr Dwyer will sign them over. That's the way it'll be. Exactly so. And at once. The stores will be back to the way they were, peaceful and purposeful and true, no grabbers and thieves and liars lurking amongst the timbers. So. That's the way it's to be. As from right this very minute.'

Alice moved slowly and stood by her sister, her hands joined before her, and she smiled.

'That's the way it's going to be,' she added. 'Thank God for it. Thank God.'

Aenghus was about to speak again but Grace took a small menacing step towards him. He spread his hands in a gesture of submission.

'Two good coffins left,' Grace went on. 'Mr Dwyer, you can have one of them. The other is for poor Ruth McTiernan. That'll be the end of that. Wee Eddie will soon have this place back in shape. We'll make furniture. Tables. Chairs. Cupboards. And we'll be able to live in our own place again without the hammering of death always in our ears.'

Big Bucko moved slowly towards the door. He stooped and gathered up his coat. He dusted it absent-mindedly. He nodded. 'Thank you ma'am,' he said. 'That's fair and reasonable. That's generous of you. And I'll make sure Wee Eddie –'

'You'll not go near Wee Eddie!' Alice interrupted. Grace shifted the shotgun in Big Bucko's direction. He backed towards the door, his hands half raised before his chest. 'Wee Eddie is from now in our care,' Alice went on. 'We'll look after him, Grace and me. And we'll look after the other poor child, too, that poor, poor child, Angelica. They'll be our own. Like

Mahons! Strong and proud!'

When the two men had left the workshed Grace collapsed onto the floor, falling as if her legs had disappeared from under her. She sat amidst the woodshavings, the smashed timbers, the brass screws, the crucifixes. The shotgun slipped slowly out of her grasp onto the floor. Alice knelt down beside her. They looked at each other for a while, silently.

'Thank God, Grace, thank God,' Alice whispered, and they embraced one another, rocking slowly together on the floor of their workshed. Alice 'n' Grace. Grace 'n' Alice. Mahons.

August 1997

There and not there . . .

The high season of holiday-makers was in full swing. The island seemed densely populated with caravans, foreign cars, campers. The weather promised to be fair, the seas calm. The days were to be bright and warm.

Angie was in her bedroom searching for the words of a prayer. She knelt a long while, settling her body back into that once familiar shape of pleading and waiting. She closed her eyes. There was only darkness and an overwhelming surge of loss and sorrow. She got up quickly.

She opened the curtains and looked out at the caravans in the quarry field. The morning sun made the chrome and windows gleam. Suddenly she knew she had found the answer to the prayer she had not been able to formulate. She left the house and went down slowly to the field.

All the clothes had been taken in off the clotheslines. There was a quiet bustle about the caravans. Angie had sensed this some days before. They were leaving the island again. They would be gone now for a long, long time. Nora Connors came out from her caravan and watched Angie approach. The children were gathering up bits and pieces of debris from around the field and piling it all into a pyre near the ocean edge of the field. They paused and watched, silently, as Nora came forward and embraced Angie tightly.

'Nora,' Angie said. 'Are ye leaving?'

Nora drew back from her and looked away.

'Aye, honey,' she said. 'In a few hours now we'll be gone. There's nothing left but sorrow and misery in this place.'

There was a long pause. Nora fiddled with her apron strings.

'I'm coming with you!' Angie announced, suddenly.

Nora turned back to her, a smile of joy on her face.

'Jesus, Angie darling, that'd be wonderful. Wonderful entirely.' She paused. 'Just hold your hold for a minute now an' I'll go and find Ted.'

She turned excitedly away. Then she turned back. 'Angie, honey, now, it's a hard livin' mind, pushin' an' grindin' an' worryin' about next week's bit a mutton. 'Tis only shiftin' the burden off the one hump on our back onto another hump.' She hesitated, hoping she had not said too much. 'But of course, duckling, you were born to it, though you didn't know it, you were born to it, an' it'll come aisy to you. I'll go an' find Jim and Jack, an' I know for a dead certainty that Ted'll give you a hero's welcome.'

Nora turned away, then faced Angie again. She was laughing with pleasure and the two of them hugged each other fiercely.

By early afternoon Angie had collected from the house what she needed. She locked the door behind her and hurried down towards the quarry field, without once looking back.

'I'll drop in to Wee Eddie Dwyer in Mahon's on the way out, if that's alright with you, Nora,' she said. 'He can have the key. He can use the place if he likes. But he'll keep it safe and clean just incase.'

The jeeps and vans were already linked up to the caravans. Jack Connors's van was at the gate of the quarry field, ready to go out onto the island roads. Ted Connors sat in his car, his own caravan cleaned and ready for the trip. Two of his grandchildren sat with him. Angie went with Jim Connors and Nora in their jeep and the other children followed with Nan Maughan in the oldest car.

For a while Angie sat quietly, her face pressed to the side window of the jeep. The ground in the quarry field was trampled flat though over by the hedgerow the wild flowers still grew strong: chickweed, groundsel, daisies, foxgloves, cowslips and shy violets. She turned down the window and listened a while to the waves breaking on the rocks beyond the field. She closed her eyes, drinking in the sound. Then Jim Connors started the engine of the jeep.

January 1952

There and not there . . .

They called him Anus, Anus by name and Anus by nature. They called the other one Big Bucko. Aenghus Fahey and Jeremiah James Dwyer. A new year dawning. Together they took the morning bus off the island. They sat silently, both of them still half asleep as the bus urged itself along the wet roads, the darkness almost palpable about them. They took the train in Westport, got into the same carriage, hefted their old suitcases up onto the rack, sat and stretched their legs out on the seats opposite. A few other travellers glanced in, moved on, deciding to search for other carriages. The train moved out from the station, great clouds of steam puffing from it, hanging over the western edges of the town.

Aenghus laughed. 'Look, Jerr,' he said, and he produced a bottle of whiskey from his coat pocket. 'We've a bit of a journey ahead of us. Might as well have a little sup to keep the spirits high. Wha'?'

'Fuckin' rain!' Big Bucko replied. But he smiled and sat up. He reached into his coat pocket and produced another bottle of whiskey. He held it high. They both laughed. They drank from the bottles. The train chugged its way slowly between fields that were wet and cow-churned. Here and there, on hedges, in back gardens, in unheeded meadow corners, tiny green clumps of daffodils were beginning to push up through the dark soil. There was a dim light on in the carriage even though the morning was already beginning to brighten. Both men looked out of the grime-smudged, rattling window. They watched their own faces peering back at them. Then the light went out.

'I have an old uncle in Glasgow,' Big Bucko muttered. 'Works in some class of a builder's yard. I'll get work with him.'

'Glasgow, it's not all that bad a place,' Aenghus offered, 'once you get used to the natives an' their strange way of talkin'.'

They drank.

The train stopped in Castlebar. Once again the men stretched their legs across the carriage onto the seat opposite. The door remained closed. They heard the high, sharp whistle of the guard. The train moved on again.

'There's mighty fine women in Glasgow, Jerr, we'll have us a right time tryin' to get round them all. Wha'?'

'Women!' Big Bucko grunted. 'Fuck them all!'

'That's the idea, man. That's for sure, Jerr, that's for sure.'

The train gathered speed, heading east, into the future. The two men lapsed into silence. They drank slowly and methodically, sucking from the mouth of the bottles like slobbering, innocent babies. They were leaving behind them the dark island, the original landscape of innocence, the silences and the great, high skies. They carried the future with them, big men both, survivors, experts, peers.

Aenghus Fahey lounged back on his seat. Big Bucko sat across from him, leaning forward, watching his feet. Together they seemed to fill the carriage.

'Women, Jerr,' Aenghus began again. 'Sure you can't trust them. Not an inch. They'll lead you up the garden path and then they'll turn on you and scrape your eyes out with their cat's claws. That's what they'll do. God spare me from women. That's what I say. God spare me from women!'

Big Bucko lifted his head and took another great slug out of his bottle. 'Fuck them all!' he muttered. 'An' fuck the island, too.

You'll not see me back in that godforsaken spot. Fuck them all. Fuck them all!'

'That's the spirit, Jerr, that's the idea. Fuck them all. By God but when we get to England we'll set about it rightly. You an' me, man, you an' me. On the buildin's. An' there'll be loads of work for us, fine strong men both. An' the women, tons of them eager for us, slaverin' for us, Jerr. An' we'll enjoy the pickin's man, enjoy the fruits without havin' to cultivate them. Wha'? We'll be the right playboys over there. What do you say? Sure the whole damn country will have to be straightened out. An' you can be sure of one other thing, Jerr, damn sure.'

'What's that, Anus?'

'I'm never settin' foot in this bloody black hole of a country either, never, ever again. There! That's the whole of it for you now, the whole fuckin' truth of it.'

They both drank, long deep draughts.

Strong men. Big buckos, both.